Doorway to Murder

A Blackwell & Watson
Time-Travel Mystery

CAROL POULIOT

First published by Level Best Books 2019

Second edition

ISBN: 978-1-947915-14-5

Cover art by Sean Eike

Interior Design: SRS

Level Best Books

www.LevelBestBooks.com

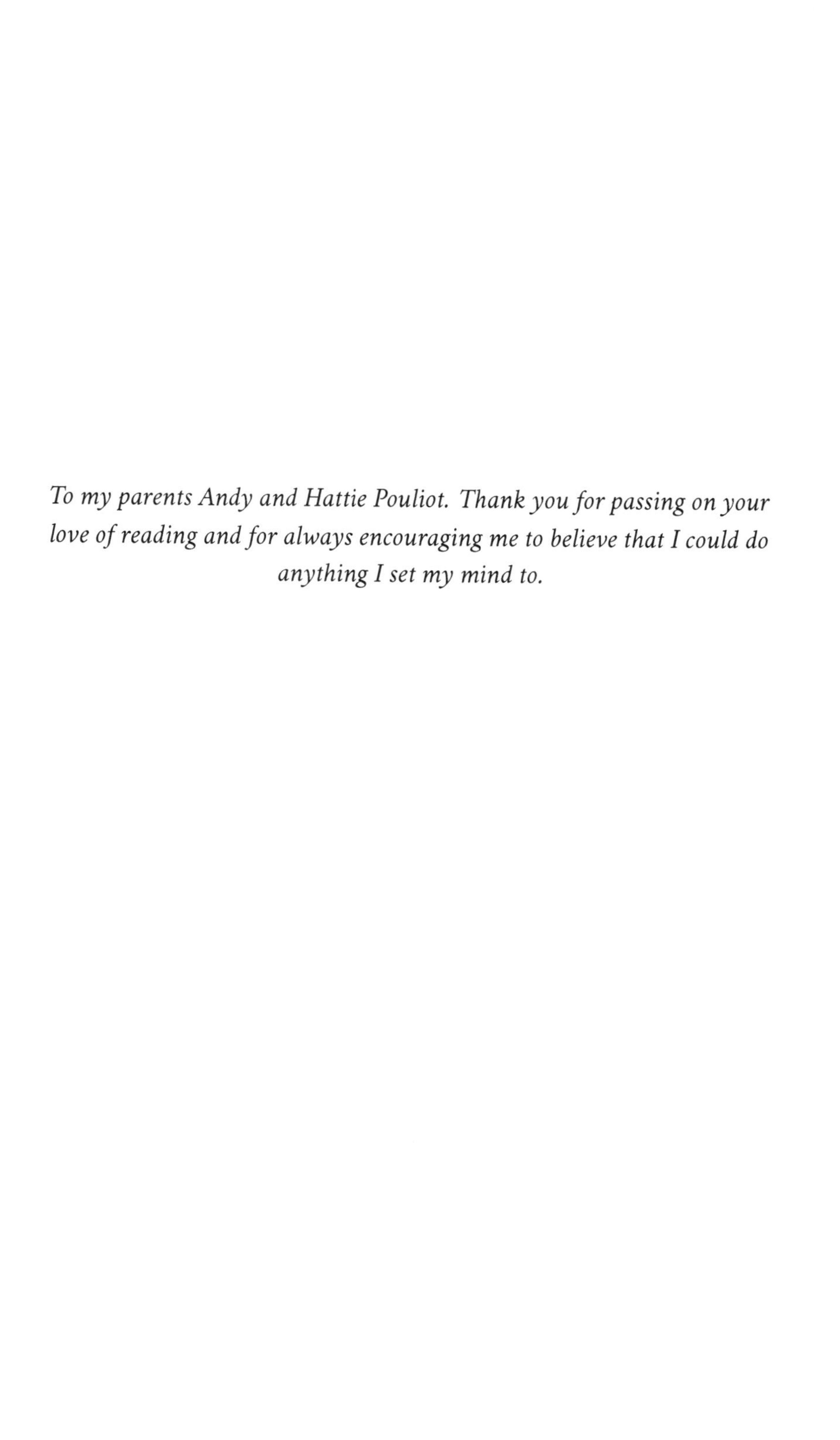

To my parents Andy and Hattie Pouliot. Thank you for passing on your love of reading and for always encouraging me to believe that I could do anything I set my mind to.

"The past isn't dead. It isn't even past."

- William Faulkner

"How often have I said to you that when you have eliminated the impossible, whatever remains, *however improbable*, must be the truth?"

- Sherlock Holmes in *The Sign of Four* by Arthur Conan Doyle

Praise for Doorway to Murder

With its fresh premise covering two eras that crackle off the page, Carol Pouliot introduces compelling characters to lead her series forward. Add a sharply written mystery with clever plot twists, and you have all the elements that make *DOORWAY TO MURDER* an accomplished debut. - Marni Graff, award-winning author of The Nora Tierney English Mysteries and The Trudy Genova Manhattan Mysteries

Mystery. Romance. Time-travel adventure. *DOORWAY TO MURDER* is the total package. Carol Pouliot interweaves the past and present as easily as I turned the pages. I highly recommend this fun read. - Betsy Bitner, award-winning humor columnist, *Times Union* (Albany, NY)

There's nothing I like more than a time-travel tale, but how much better to get a crisp, fair-play police procedural, too. The atmosphere grabbed me. The ending surprised me. I'm already looking forward to Steven and Olivia's next adventure. - Catriona McPherson, multi-award-winning author of the Dandy Gilver detective stories

Steven and Olivia make a great couple of crime busters in this era-jumping romance and hard-boiled police procedural. Join them. You'll be glad you did! - Steve Axelrod, author of the Henry Kennis Nantucket mysteries

I really like this unique time traveling twist. I . . .couldn't guess who did it and what would come next. I want to read more. - Secret Pearls Reviews

The Blackwell & Watson

Time-Travel Mysteries

by Carol Pouliot

Doorway to Murder (#1)

Threshold of Deceit (#2)

LAST FRIDAY NIGHT – PRESENT DAY

Chapter 1

Unaware of the blizzard raging all around her, Olivia Watson slept peacefully and dream-free, snuggled under a pile of blankets and thick comforter. A nightlight glowed at the end of the hall and the carriage clock on the mantle downstairs ticked away time. Like a lump of coal, Mr. Moto was curled up at the foot of her bed, tail twitching every now and then, little body rising in deep kitten breathing.

Hissssss shattered the silence. A current of air caressed her face and Olivia's eyes flew open. Her heart was hammering against her chest, blood pounded in her ears. All her senses rocketed to high alert.

Someone was in the house.

She cautiously moved her head to look toward the bedroom door. She gasped as her breath caught in her throat. A man stood inches beyond the threshold, backlit by the light in the long tunnel of hallway.

Olivia wanted to scream, to reach out to the bedside table and grab the phone. To slam down the buttons for 911. To run. To *do something.*

She couldn't speak. She couldn't move. Her arms and legs felt like wood. She lay trapped in a cocoon of covers.

She became aware of the ticking clock. *Oh, God. How long have I got? Please, help me. I swear I'll go back to church. Please, just this once. Help me!*

The man had not yet moved. His left side faced her—his features were in profile, his back to the extra bedroom as if he'd just come out. He seemed to have heard the kitten. He slowly turned to peer into the dark room. Olivia remained frozen. Her eyes widened. Her heart seized and she stopped breathing as he craned his neck and squinted at her. In the shadows she saw a puzzled look come over his face. He straightened and shook his head as if to clear his vision. He turned back and walked through the wall.

Olivia cried out, exhaling forcefully as she sprang up. Her body shook out of control. She fumbled for the lamp and light flooded the room. The kitten flew over the covers and nestled in the crook of her arm. Olivia hugged him close, stroking his silky fur, rocking back and forth, whispering words of comfort, as much for herself as for him.

It took a long time before she was able to go back to sleep that first night.

FRIDAY NIGHT – 1934

Chapter 2

The man bent forward Sisyphus-like, struggling to plow through snowdrifts already up to his knees. He was a big bear of a man bundled up in a heavy brown overcoat and woolen hat, with a long scarf wrapped around his neck and face. Thick flakes stuck to his lashes. He could barely see where he was going; but he knew if he stopped, the blizzard would bury him. He pressed on, stumbled, nearly fell into the street—it was impossible to tell where the sidewalk ended and the road began. Not that it mattered. Nothing was moving.

The clock in the tower struck two. Its knell echoed through the streets mingling with the howling wind.

How much farther? I could still turn back.

But he didn't.

As he fought his way down what he hoped was the Margate Road, a moonbeam reached around a cloud, striping the path before him, illuminating the way. He was on the right track. After what seemed like hours, he reached his destination and paused to catch his breath. Listening and looking around to make sure he was still alone, he turned into the alley behind the First National Bank and Trust Company.

The man took a key from the depths of his pocket and fit it into the opening. He closed the door behind him but left it unlocked. He moved to the side and quickly turned off the alarm. In near darkness, he made his way from memory to the large, walk-in vault. He flipped the switch on his lantern. Shadows leaped up on the walls and snaked across the ceiling.

In the dim light he squinted at the numbers. He pulled off his dripping hat and shoved it in his pocket, then wiped the melting snow out of his eyes. He spun the dial ten to the left, eighteen to the right, back to the left four marks. Click. He heaved the door open and entered. He unsnapped the lock on his satchel and began stuffing in bills.

As he attempted to close the over-filled bag, he heard a scraping in the hall. He froze, cocked his head to listen, but, before he could react, someone flew at him. With lightning speed, the attacker hit him hard. The man dropped like a stone, dead before his head hit the floor.

The assailant filled his own bag, took his weapon and, leaving his victim crumpled on the smooth cold floor, closed the vault. He spun the dial and moments later walked out through the bank's rear exit, pulling the door tightly shut.

As the killer crept up the alley, the wind and snow were already erasing his footprints.

SATURDAY – 1934

Chapter 3

Officer Jimmy Bourgogne threw open the heavy glass door as he ran into the long, crowded diner. He looked around wildly, spied the two detectives in the back, and hurried through a haze of sizzling bacon and percolating coffee.

"Steven, Harry, you gotta come quick! The chief got a call. Leo Castleman's been murdered."

"What?"

"They found his body in the bank vault. Come on!" Jimmy was practically jumping up and down. "Doc and the photographer are already on their way. Hurry! We gotta make tracks."

Detective Sergeant Steven Blackwell threw some coins on the table as he and his partner, Detective Harry Beckman, grabbed their hats and coats, rushed past the red-topped counter stools, and fled the warmth of Bailey's Diner.

The First National Bank and Trust Company was housed in a fifty-year-old, brick building on the corner of Victoria Avenue and Tulip

Street, only steps from the diner. It took the men no time to reach the scene. They edged around a black Ford sedan parked in front of the main entrance, climbed over a snowbank, and sprinted up the wide staircase.

Bank guard Eddie Littleman waved them inside. "The chief's downstairs with Mr. Harrison, the assistant bank manager." Littleman almost saluted. "Jimmy, he wants you to wait for Doc by the alley door."

Steven turned the corner at the bottom of the stairs and saw the silhouettes of Chief Andy Thompson and John Harrison talking at the far end of the long dark hallway. In the dimly lit basement, Thompson's middle-aged physique presented a sharp contrast to Harrison's tall slim frame. As he approached, a nearby light revealed details in the banker's elegance and the chief's slightly rough appearance. *A classic case of appearances being misleading,* Steven thought. He'd pick Thompson to work with any day over the self-involved, obnoxious Harrison. The chief was a brilliant policeman and Steven considered it an honor to work with him.

Though the banker, in his late thirties, was only a few years older than Steven, they'd never really known each other. Steven's family had moved to town when he was eleven. He tried to make friends but for some reason John Harrison was never interested.

"Beckman, here," called the chief, pointing to some wooden stands attached with rope. "Secure the scene before you dust."

Harry Beckman placed a wooden stand on one corner, stretched out the rope across the hallway, and set a second stand on the opposite corner so that the device blocked the empty hall to the left of the vault. He repeated the action to bar the hallway next to the safe-deposit box room located on the right.

Steven entered the vault and saw vice-president and branch manager Leo Castleman sprawled on the floor near a wooden table. He lay face down, his head turned toward the left. Blood had pooled under and around the right side of his head, soaking into his coat collar and scarf. A knitted hat stuck out of a coat pocket. A lantern flickered next to an empty leather bag beside him.

Two large money bags with *Brinks Company* stamped in black letters on the canvas occupied the table. One bag was flat; the other was bunched up and partly open, revealing rolled coins and a few bundles of banknotes. Several ten- and twenty-dollar bills littered the floor.

Steven looked for footprints. He didn't see any clear marks, so he lay down, clicked on his flashlight, and looked from several angles. Nothing useful. He examined a three-tiered, rolling cart tucked away in the right corner. Each shelf held a teller's drawer full of cash and coins.

He pulled out a notebook, did a quick sketch then joined his partner at the back door.

"Find anything, Becks?"

"Nothing we can use. Lots of partials and smudges. Whoever it was probably had gloves on. Damn! It was freezing out last night. Anybody would've been wearing gloves." Beckman shook his head. "Nothing left behind either. No threads, no bits of cloth."

"Maybe we'll get something in the vault."

"We live in hope."

Steven stuck his head outside and told a shivering Jimmy Bourgogne, "Doc Elliott and Gray ought to be here pretty soon, Jimmy. Keep it clear, okay?"

"Will do!"

"Detective Sergeant Blackwell," Chief Thompson called. "Do you know John Harrison?"

"Yes, we were in school at the same time. Morning, John. Sad business, huh?"

Harrison, impeccably dressed in a pinstriped suit, crisp white shirt, and dark tie, nodded at Steven. "Blackwell."

Steven observed Harrison's cold eyes and pinched mouth. Clearly, he wasn't pleased to see him.

"Mr. Harrison, tell Detective Sergeant Blackwell what happened."

"I got here about nine and used my key to the front door. I noticed the alarm was off. I assumed Mr. Castleman changed his mind and came in. We take turns on the weekend, you see. I checked his office but he wasn't there. I called out. No one answered. I thought maybe he was opening the vault for the head teller, so I came downstairs."

As John Harrison described his movements, Steven pictured the scene. He saw Harrison descending the marble steps in the near dark and finding an empty hallway. He would have been confused. It was early on a Saturday morning. None of the employees was there. Why was the alarm off? Who shut down the system? And when? Was that person still there, hiding, ready to strike?

Although Knightsbridge was a small town, safe and peaceful most of the time, a bank is always susceptible to robbery. Harrison would hesitate to look around the corner or into an unlocked room. The cellar would be filled with shadows. Steven imagined he'd be afraid.

"Did you turn on the lights, John?"

The banker frowned. "When I got down here."

Over the years Steven had learned that John Harrison was preoccupied with social status almost to the point of obsession. He likely considered his elevated position as bank manager above Steven's job as a policeman. Steven was sure that Harrison expected him to address him formally with the respect due his office.

"No one was here, Detective. I checked the back door. It was locked."

"Is that door used?"

"Only for emergencies. Since I was here, I decided to open the vault for Connor MacIntyre. I knew he'd be in in a few minutes. He's responsible for getting the tellers' drawers ready today."

Detective Beckman sauntered over but stood aside quietly. Harrison paused and everyone seemed to shift. The chief cleared his throat and removed his hat. Orangey-red hair sprang out everywhere. The chief was, indeed, in need of a haircut. Beckman hit a pack of Lucky Strikes against his palm, extracted a cigarette, lit it, and pocketed the dead match. He inhaled deeply, then blew the smoke toward the ceiling. John Harrison clenched his jaw, shifted his weight, and looked from one policeman to another.

After several long seconds, Steven said, "John, you were about to open the vault?"

"Yes. Well, it was very shocking." He looked down his patrician nose at the officers.

Steven idly wondered if the man truly was this arrogant or if it was put on for the occasion.

"Mr. Castleman was just lying there. And there was all that blood. I couldn't believe it. I wasn't sure what to do. I wanted to see if he was alive."

"That's all right, Mr. Harrison. Take your time. Tell us what happened," Thompson soothed.

The banker nodded. "I was going to shake him to see if he'd groan or make a sound. My hand accidentally touched his face. It was cold. *He* was cold. I came upstairs and called the police. That's it. I waited until you got here, Chief Thompson."

"Thank you, sir. Don't worry. We'll get whoever did this."

Steven turned to his partner. "Detective Beckman, why don't you take Mr. Harrison upstairs and have him write down his statement while everything's fresh in his mind?"

Beckman pinched out his cigarette, slipped the dead end into a pocket, and nodded. "I'll set up the meeting room, too. And I'll get a list of the employees."

"Good. I'll be up in a minute."

"What about the bank, Chief Thompson?" asked Harrison. "Should we open today?"

"I don't see why not. We'll be here or in the meeting room. We'll interview your employees one at a time. Your customers won't even realize anything's wrong."

When Beckman and John Harrison had left, the chief eyed Steven and growled, "Right, Blackwell. I don't have to tell you that this is gonna be a *big* case." He let out a torrent. "What the hell was Leo Castleman doing in the bank? In the middle of the night. In the middle of a lousy snowstorm. And how did he manage to get himself killed in the damn vault?!"

Steven knew when not to interrupt his boss. He stayed silent.

Thompson closed his eyes, paused to catch his breath then glared at Steven. "No mistakes, Blackwell. Dot your 'i's and cross your 't's. By the book! This one goes a hundred percent by the book." He smacked a fist into his hand to punctuate his final three words. "All right, get to work." The chief looked down at the murdered man, shook his head, and whispered, "I hate this case already."

Chapter 4

Patricia Castleman was having her favorite kind of morning—long and lazy. She'd banished yesterday's miserable snowstorm and the interminable train trip from her mind.

When she had arrived at her sister's house last night, she was tired and short-tempered. The housekeeper took her suitcase upstairs and unpacked toiletries, a satin nightgown, matching pink robe, and velvet mules. Shortly after, her sister brought up a light supper and a bottle of wine. Patricia drank two large glasses of Chardonnay and looked through the March issue of *Vogue,* picturing herself modeling the latest evening wear—long, sleek, slip-like gowns that hugged her body—and chic, two-piece, daytime outfits with spectator pumps designed for city shopping or museum visits. She day-dreamed through the evening, then turned out the light.

Today was much improved. The sun shone and snowy Syracuse, New York, glittered like Tiffany's windows. Patricia was rested and ready to enjoy the day. She and her older sister sat in Louise's elegant cream-and-blue dining room at one end of the mahogany table, a second cup of rich coffee and the remains of buttered toast and jam on china plates in front of them.

Though Patricia tolerated her sister's company, she had no real affection for her. Patricia's feelings for people always related to her—how they could be of use to her, how they could help her get what she wanted. She trusted no one, never shared confidences. She presented an image to the world and made no exceptions.

Louise sighed, "I'm glad you came for the weekend, Patsy. I hate it when Tom's gone. The house feels so empty."

"I like it when Leo's away. I can do whatever I want."

"It seems like you do that anyway. Doesn't Leo mind all your visits here? Or the trips you took last year to Saratoga to see that friend of yours? What's her name?"

"Hazel. No, he doesn't even notice." She pushed around a few crumbs. "You said Tom's up for a promotion," she said, covering her crossed legs with the robe that had opened and cascaded down her thigh.

As Louise droned on about her husband's job prospects, Patricia tuned her out and thought back to the promotion that Leo had received—the one that had changed her life.

They met in Syracuse after her high school graduation. Patricia had applied for a typing position at the First National Bank and Trust Company and was hired for the secretarial pool. She worked hard and was transferred upstairs to the executive offices. Shortly after, Leo requested her as his personal secretary.

Patricia could tell Leo was attracted to her. He was good looking, charming, and ten years her senior. He was smart and moving up fast in the echelons of bank management. Love never entered into it. He was the way out of her dreary life and her way up in society.

It had been so easy to reel him in.

They married within a year and Patricia Castleman, née Patsy Osborne, quit her job at the bank and began her rise as society wife, determined never to return to her childhood poverty. She had her hair dyed blonde, went to a salon for the right manicure, bought the latest fashions, learned proper etiquette, and hired the decorator du jour to "do" their dining room and parlor. After several years Leo got his big break—a promotion to vice-president and manager of the Knightsbridge branch of the bank in Upstate New York.

Patricia set down her cup and pushed back from the table, interrupting her sister's litany. "Let's have lunch out. What do you think? I know it's only ten thirty but I want to do some shopping. We don't have any of the big stores like you've got here. I want to pick up a few things at Dey Brothers, maybe stop in Chappell's, and, naturally, get some chocolates at Schrafft's. We could eat at Schrafft's. What do you say?"

"Sure, Patsy, that's fine with me. I'll order a taxi for us."

Forty-five minutes later, primped, powdered, and poised to improve the local economy, Patricia descended the staircase. Mrs. Leo Castleman always dressed for effect. She had replaced last year's passé cloche hat with a more fashionable one shaped like a plate, which she wore tilted to the side in what she considered a rakish and alluring pose. Her new wool coat was fire-engine red, accented her small waist, and was hemmed to show off her shapely calves. The butter-soft, gray leather gloves caressed her hands and matched the handbag she carried on her arm.

Patricia was ready to leave when the telephone trilled. Louise, in the middle of pinning on her hat, hurried to the foyer to answer it.

"Yes, this is Louise Haydock...that's my sister...one moment." Puzzled, Louise handed the black Bakelite receiver to her sister. "It's the police."

Patricia frowned, unclipped her left earring, and took the phone, turning away from her sister. "Hello...oh, Chief Thompson, how are you?...Yes...no...what's going on?"

Louise couldn't make out what was being said.

"No!" Patricia dropped the instrument and fell back onto a wooden deacon's bench, her head in her hands.

Louise grabbed the telephone. "Chief, what happened? What did you tell my sister?"

Chapter 5

Shortly after Chief Thompson left the bank, Steven heard a booming voice in the alley. "Cock-a-doodle-doo, Jimmy Bou."

The county medical examiner, William Elliott, MD, had arrived. Gray hair, ashen face, steely stubble covering his cheeks and chin, Doc Elliott resembled the dead he came to examine. He was a husky man going to fat who had chain-smoked for decades. He was in lousy shape. Any day now, Steven expected the coroner would be the corpse that needed examining. But somehow Doc Elliott kept on going. In recent years, he arrived at the crime scene in his own black Ford sedan, which, like its owner, huffed and puffed on the slightest incline and smallest hill.

"Hey, Doc, you sound chipper this morning," Steven said as the ME and photographer paused at the door, stomping their feet to knock off the snow.

"Well, the sun's shining. Gotta be grateful for that."

Doc Elliott pulled off his knitted hat and stuck it in a coat pocket, then removed his gloves, stuffing them in the other pocket. "Leo Castleman. Who would've imagined he'd end up like this?"

Gray Wilson slid off soft leather gloves, pulling one finger at a time. He neatly folded them into a pocket of his dark blue Chesterfield. He unbuttoned the overcoat but left his fedora on. Tall, slender, and dressed to the nines, the photographer looked like he belonged on Fifth Avenue. Hell, he looked like he *owned* Fifth Avenue. Wilson did swell work for the police but nurtured a dream of being a fashion photographer on Madison Avenue.

"Morning, Gray, how're you doing?" Steven extended his hand; they'd been friends for years.

"I'm okay, but the doc is cut up about this one," he whispered. "I think he's putting on an act."

"Yeah, I know."

The photographer set down his bag and unpacked his Graflex Speed Graphic Press camera. He checked the light exposure, adjusted the shutter speed and aperture, and began his task. He efficiently shot the dead man from all angles and made sure he got every part of the vault.

"I'll have these for you Monday morning, Steven. He's all yours, Doc." He stepped to the side out of the way.

Doc Elliott struggled to his knees and greeted the victim with a familiar melody, "What's your story, morning glory?" The ME was famous for singing while he worked. He broke into the popular tune "Heat Wave."

Steven looked over at Gray and grinned. "Gotta love him. I wonder if it ever gets any easier."

The medical man looked up. "It doesn't." After a moment, he pronounced, "Cause of death looks like a couple blows to the head. I'll know for sure when I get him up on the table. For now I'd say somebody snuck up from behind and hit him with something hard."

"Time of death?" asked Steven.

"That's going to be a little tricky. It's chilly down here. That can affect the stiffening of the body. Although he *is* still in his heavy coat, so maybe not so much." Elliott rubbed his chin. "His upper body is already rigid, but look." Doc lifted Castleman's leg. "See how the foot is still limp? Based on what I've seen over the years, I'd say sometime after midnight and probably not much later than five this morning. The stiffening starts in the face around three or four hours after death then works its way through the rest of the body. Maybe I can narrow it down. I'll do my best."

"Thank you, sir. You always do."

Doc Elliott turned to the mortuary attendants who had been waiting quietly by the door. "You can take him now, boys. Let's go out the back like you came in so we don't disturb the customers upstairs. Nice and easy now. That's it." He grabbed his medical bag. "I'll try to have results for you tomorrow, Steven."

"I appreciate it, Doc. Hope you can enjoy the rest of your weekend."

As Gray followed the medical examiner out he said, "Steven, let's get together and catch up. It's been a while."

"It has been that. Maybe supper and a couple of beers next week at The Three Lords?"

"Sounds good." He sighed. "I'd hate to be in your shoes. Leo Castleman, of all people."

"It's the job, Gray. Doesn't matter who the victim is, you know that. We treat 'em all the same."

"I know. Well, see you." He buttoned his coat and turned the collar up against the cold.

As Gray went out the back, Beckman came down the stairs.

"Becks, what took you so long?"

"I was talking with Ruth Hanover. Boy, she *sure* is a looker!"

Steven raised one eyebrow.

Beckman looked astonished. "Don't tell me you never noticed the gams on that dolly. She steppin' out with anybody?"

"Concentrate, partner. We've got a job to do. Don't you ever think of anything else?"

Confusion slid over Beckman's movie-star face. "Like what?"

Steven shook his head. He knew that his partner enjoyed his Valentino reputation and fed it every chance he got, but he also knew Becks was a darn good cop.

Beckman sat down on a step, stretched out his long legs, crossing his ankles, and flipped through his notebook. "Okay, slave-driver. I got Harrison's statement. And I interviewed him while I had him there.

"Said he was home last night. Lives alone, so no alibi. Has no idea what his boss was doing in the vault. Said it was unlike Castleman, that he wasn't the type of fella who'd steal from his own bank. But, get a load of this...," Beckman cocked his head and smirked. "He said since we found him in the vault with a bag next to all the money, he must have *misjudged* Castleman. Said he must not have known him as well as he thought he did. Made a big show of being reluctant to admit it." Beckman made a face. "Jerk."

Steven wasn't surprised—this was classic Harrison. All through school, he had witnessed Harrison put down other people in an attempt to make himself look better. The boy had not changed.

"No love lost there." Beckman went on, "He said Castleman did an acceptable job as bank manager. That's his word, *acceptable*. Wanted me to believe he does a better job. I think he already sees himself in the top position.

"I asked if he knew of any enemies Castleman might've had. Or if there was bad blood between him and an employee. He said no to both questions. He was polite but didn't really offer much." Beckman got up and brushed an imaginary spot on his trousers. "I thanked him, told him we'd have more questions later. He seemed anxious to get to work."

"Good. That's done for now. Who else is upstairs?"

"Connor MacIntyre and Ruth. Oh! And the guard Eddie. He's still there, too."

"Let's split up a while, Becks. How about you stay here and do the interviews? I'll send Will Taylor over to go through Castleman's office. He's good at details. If there's something pointing to why Leo was in the vault last night, he'll find it."

"Sure, that sounds good."

"Castleman's brother works at the mill, he'll be there today. I'd like to notify him personally, and as soon as possible, so he hears it from us before the gossip starts going 'round. I'll take Jimmy with me if you don't mind."

"Yeah, that's fine. Jimmy should grab every chance he can to sit in on an interview. Part of his training." Beckman put his notebook and pencil in a jacket pocket. "You go ahead. I'll take care of things here and meet you later."

The Mohawk River Sawmill stretched out along the southwestern edge of town. It was a large, two-story, rectangular building constructed of roughly hewn logs whose natural coloring had darkened over many years. It had been added onto several times and resembled an over-grown log cabin with a paddle wheel attached to one side. The sawmill had always been one of the biggest employers in the area and, thanks to President Roosevelt's Civil Works Administration building projects, the mill still buzzed with activity.

As Steven down-shifted and turned into the parking lot, the sight before them took his breath away. The natural beauty of the region where he lived thrilled him; he never tired of gazing at the landscape. Behind the mill and beyond the river, the Adirondack Mountains rose tall and proud, giving shelter to deer, moose, black bear, fox, and myriad other animals. On most winter days, it was hard to tell where the mountains left off and the sky began, the snow-capped peaks blended so smoothly into the cloudy skies. But today the sun shone brightly on an ice-blue backdrop and it was easy to make out the pine trees—spruce, northern white cedar, and fragrant balsam fir—that marched up and down the slopes.

"Eh, Steven," Jimmy cleared his throat. "Are we going in?"

"Oh, sorry. Woolgathering."

The mill was crowded and noisy. Everywhere they looked, men were carrying, lifting, dragging, or cutting logs into lumber. The huge room resonated with the shrill sounds of chain, band, and circular saws. The air was thick with sawdust, and sawdust covered every visible surface. *It's a good smell,* Steven thought, *a fresh, productive smell, like someone is accomplishing something.*

When Steven asked where they could find Lawrence Castleman, a workman pointed up.

Through a picture window in the mezzanine-level office, he saw a large man speaking on the telephone. They climbed the stairway to an open door. Steven knocked on the doorframe.

Lawrence Castleman waved them in and indicated two wooden chairs in front of his desk. Steven had time to observe Leo's brother while he finished his conversation.

This Castleman, he thought, *looks built to suit his profession.*

The man filled out his buffalo-plaid shirt and sported a tattered lumberman's cap which covered most of his light chestnut hair. The hand grasping the telephone receiver was more like a paw, big and thick, with large knuckles.

This same husky build somehow hadn't seemed such a comfortable fit on his brother, who'd spent his days in a posh office, midst the elegant surroundings of the bank. Much as Steven was loath to acknowledge it, John Harrison was better suited to that atmosphere than Leo had been.

Castleman hung up the phone and dropped into his wooden swivel chair, which sprang back under his weight. He grabbed a half-cigar from the ashtray, scraped a match across the bottom of his sizeable boot, and puffed until the end glowed.

"What can I do for you gentlemen?"

Steven introduced himself and Jimmy and showed his badge and ID. "I'm sorry we have bad news, sir. Your brother Leo was found dead this morning."

Castleman choked as an abrupt intake of air mixed with cigar smoke. He shot forward, coughing. "What? There's some kind of mistake. Not Leo." His face crumbled and his eyes filled up. "Oh, God, no." He slumped back.

"I'm very sorry, Mr. Castleman."

"Larry. Everybody just calls me Larry," he said automatically. "What happened? Where was he? How?"

Steven explained the circumstances then asked, "Can you think of anyone who may have wanted to harm your brother?"

"No, I can't." Larry Castleman shut his eyes and swallowed hard. Steven was surprised to see a slight tremor in the hand holding the cigar. "As far as I know, things were good at the bank. I've run into people he works...," he bowed his head, "*worked* with from time to time. You know, in the pub or Pinky's. Everybody I ever talked to seemed happy there."

He shoved a fist into his eye and rubbed. "Leo was a good boss. I think his customers were satisfied with the service they got. I never heard of any complaining or grumbling about getting a raw deal. You know, a loan that was refused or something."

Jimmy took notes while they listened.

The lumberman continued, "This doesn't make any sense at all. Was Leo working late? Did he get snowed in because of the storm?"

"We don't think so."

Steven signaled Jimmy to take the next question.

"Mr. Castleman, do you know of any financial trouble your brother might have had?"

Larry Castleman gaped at the young officer. "Wait a minute. You're not suggesting...no! Absolutely not! My brother would *never* take money from his bank. There *has* to be another explanation."

He stared at the wall, sinking further into his chair. Half a minute passed. "Has Patricia been told? Does she know?"

Steven explained that Chief Thompson was contacting Leo's wife. "Mr. Castleman, where were you between midnight last night and five this morning?"

"What? You don't think...?" He pursed his lips and snorted in disgust.

"We have to ask everyone, sir. It's routine."

"Home. I was home asleep." He stood and pushed his chair out of the way. "I need to call my wife, Detective Blackwell. Is that all?"

"That's it for now. We'll be in touch."

On the way out of the parking lot, Steven asked, "So, Jimmy, what do you think about Lawrence Castleman?"

Jimmy didn't miss a beat. "His reaction was genuine. He didn't know. And I think he loved his brother."

"I agree. Good observation. But will we check his alibi anyway?"

"Yes, we will," declared Jimmy. "Because that is what we do," he added for emphasis.

Steven couldn't help grinning.

"Listen, I'm starving," he said. "Let's grab something to bring back for lunch."

He pulled the car alongside the curb in front of Joe's—"the best sandwiches in town"—and left the engine running. They bought thick roast beef sandwiches and strong coffee to fortify themselves for the afternoon ahead.

Chapter 6

Steven needed to get organized. He wanted to sort out his notes and think about the impressions he'd formed so far. Years ago, he'd discovered that during an investigation, two things helped him the most. One was the simple act of spending some quiet time away from all the talking, analyzing, and never-ending discussions. That way he could arrange things in his mind and create order out of the facts, gossip, and observations that he had.

The other was setting up and working on the murder board. The visual organization gave him the ability to separate the significant from the inconsequential, see patterns, and notice connections. Many times while Steven sat and stared at the board, the solution simply came to him. This was also one of the many reasons why he liked working with Beckman. Becks understood and appreciated Steven's methods and gave him the silence and the space he needed to think.

He ate at his desk, mulling over the morning's events. The roast beef tasted swell and the horseradish sure cleared his head.

Steven hadn't been getting enough sleep lately. His mother's heart attack a month ago had shaken his world. He was still trying to come to terms with the devastating loss of his closest friend and confidante. Evangeline Blackwell had been in her studio, at her easel working on a new painting, morning sunlight flooding the room, when she dropped to the floor. A long, difficult murder case had followed right on the heels of the funeral. And now he was plagued by these troubling visions.

Every night for the past week, when he passed his mother's bedroom, Steven thought he saw a woman. Of course, that couldn't possibly be. Any sane man knew that. He was annoyed with himself for what was obviously a kind of weakness. Blackwell men were made of stronger stuff than that! Maybe if he caught up on his sleep, his mind would stop playing tricks and those disturbing hallucinations would go away.

Beckman came in as Steven was rolling the large, framed blackboard into the center of the room. They spread their notes out on a work table. Steven took a piece of chalk and at the top, in the middle of the board, wrote VICTIM—LEO CASTLEMAN. He left room for several photographs then added the information they had so far. *Vice-Pres., Mngr. First Nat'l Bank/Trust Co. Married to Patricia. No children. Killed in bank vault. COD—blows to head. TOD—Fri. PM-Sat. AM, time?? Pos. larceny?*

He moved to the left side of the blackboard and wrote SUSPECTS. Underneath he listed: *John Harrison-asst. mngr, Connor MacIntyre-teller, Ruth Hanover-teller, Eddie Littleman-guard.* He added Lawrence Castleman's name, but wrote *doubtful* next to it. It was too soon to eliminate anyone, but Steven's gut told him that Just-Call-Me-Larry had not killed his brother. Plenty of time to cross him off after they had dug some more and verified his alibi.

"All right," said Steven. "Let's start with Eddie Littleman. I don't know much about him, do you?"

"Nope. Seems like a happy fella. Whenever I go to the bank, he's friendly. He didn't have much to say. Said he was home asleep. I'll check. And we can have the patrolmen ask around."

"Okay, what about your girl, Ruth?" asked Steven. He'd heard her this morning long before he saw her, those high-heeled shoes tapping a staccato beat as she crossed the lobby.

Ruth Hanover was a tall, angular woman. From her high cheekbones to her pointed chin and beak-like nose, to the eyebrows plucked to within an inch of their life, she jutted out everywhere. Her hair was a mass of dark brown layers that looked like the beautician had been reading a book while she cut it. *She could've fallen on the victim,* Steven thought. *That would have done it, a dozen puncture wounds from all the angles on that woman.*

"Hard to say. Maybe if she was angry or desperate."

"Does she have the strength, Becks? Those were powerful blows."

"She might be stronger than she looks. But I can't see her battling the storm, sneaking in, and bashing him on the head. And I can't see *why* she would have wanted to kill Castleman. She seemed grateful he took a chance and hired a girl teller."

"Right, but let's say she did it. Why?"

"Maybe Castleman tried puttin' his paws on her and she didn't like it."

"Possible, although killing him seems a bit drastic for that." Steven wrote *Means? Motive?* next to Ruth Hanover's name.

"I'll check her alibi Monday," Beckman continued. "If she was home like she said, her mother might've heard her go out during the night."

They moved on to the other teller.

"I'd hate it to be MacIntyre," said Beckman. "His family's had more than their share of bad luck. The two youngest kids nearly died from that fever at Christmas. They were all quarantined for several weeks and he couldn't work, but *jeez* I hope it's not him. And," he hastily added, "I have to say I believed him when he said he was home sleeping. It rang true."

"Yeah, that's a sad story, Becks, but look at the facts. *Could* he have done it? Yes, he's strong enough."

"Okay, Steven, but what about this? How did he know Castleman would be there?"

"He could have overheard his boss talking about coming back then hid in the alley and followed him inside. It doesn't matter that MacIntyre doesn't have the combination because Castleman was already in the vault when he was coshed on the head. They could have been partners and MacIntyre betrayed him."

Steven wrote *Means? Yes.* "I'll tackle him. You take the wife and neighbors."

"Okay."

"As for Harrison, I want another go at him."

"Maybe he set this whole thing up to get Castleman's job," Beckman suggested.

"People have killed for less."

"Exactly."

"There's one thing I do know about John Harrison," Steven continued. "He's ambitious. I don't think he'd be happy as second-in-command for long. Remove Castleman. Create some suspicious circumstances. Harrison is poised to step into the top spot. What do you think?"

"Yeah, I can picture that."

They worked for the rest of the afternoon, discussing information, raising questions, taking turns playing devil's advocate, whittling it down to bare facts.

It grew dark and Steven's stomach was growling when, at last, he put down the chalk and stepped away. They'd done a good day's work. The board clearly showed what they had so far.

Steven and Becks agreed that both Harrison and MacIntyre had the means to commit the crime, were of sufficient strength, and could have been in cahoots with Castleman to steal the money, then betrayed him. Either could have overheard a conversation and learned that Leo would be in the vault. Neither man had an alibi. Harrison lived alone and Mac's wife would likely back him up. As for reasons other than money, it was too soon to know anything for sure. They would look into other motives in the next few days.

As for the other interviewees of the day, they agreed that Ruth Hanover was an unlikely suspect and predicted that she would be eliminated quickly.

Becks trusted Steven's judgment of Lawrence Castleman. He added that whenever he had seen the brothers together, at a restaurant or pub, or at an event like the Fourth of July fireworks or the Labor Day picnic, they'd seemed close. Becks wrote Lawrence Castleman's name in his notebook for a follow-up interview.

They returned to their desks to prepare their reports. Beckman sat forward on the edge of his chair, tight up against the wooden desk, hunched over the paper. His dark blond hair fell onto his forehead, his concentration fully on the task at hand. He wrote rapidly, unaware of his surroundings. His reports were always meticulously crafted, his facts accurate, his impressions thoughtful and incisive, his opinions clear and to-the-point.

Steven's approach was slower and more introspective. He got another cup of coffee, then sat and thought. He considered every action, every moment, everything that everyone said during the entire day, from the moment he had entered the vault until five minutes ago, when he and Becks had finished their discussion.

He became aware that the sun had set and street lights glowed beyond the window near his work area. He could tell the temperature outside had plummeted because it felt cold inside. He'd been conscious of his fellow officers leaving—he'd heard the scraping of chairs, the rustle of coats and jackets, the thump of boots being dropped as men struggled to pull them on, the sounds of "good night" and "see you tomorrow."

When he had everything in order in his mind, he picked up a pen and began to write. He was on the third page when Becks cleared his desk for the night, donned his gear, and said goodbye.

Steven looked up briefly. "See you tomorrow." He finished at six thirty, tired and hungry but satisfied with the day's efforts. He gathered his things, turned out the desk lamp, and stuck his head in Thompson's office.

"Here's my report, Chief. I'm going home. I don't think there's anybody left. Are you almost ready to leave?"

"Yeah," sighed Thompson, looking exhausted, every one of his fifty years showing on his face. Dark circles rimmed his hazel eyes and his shoulders sagged. "In a few minutes. I'll read your report then go. The missus'll be annoyed with me for being late for supper." Another sigh. "Again."

When Steven got home, the only things he could think about were food and sleep. He wolfed down a couple of peanut butter and jelly sandwiches and drank two large glasses of creamy whole milk, then stretched out on the sofa where he promptly fell asleep for the second night in a row.

A noise outside woke him a few hours later. He dragged himself up off the couch, groaning, trying not to wake up completely. With one eye open, he turned off the lights and slowly climbed the stairs. As he was going into the bathroom to brush his teeth, he glanced into his mother's bedroom.

There she was again.

SATURDAY – PRESENT DAY

Chapter 7

By seven thirty, the snow had stopped falling, the wind had died down, and the plows were out. By eight, the snowbanks along the main thoroughfares in town reached over six feet high, but most of the streets were passable. Children were bundled up in colorful snowsuits, knitted hats, and mittens, jumping into the mountains of snow, throwing snowballs, making forts, and digging tunnels. Echoes of gleeful screams and laughter filled the neighborhood.

Olivia awoke slowly and stretched. She kept her eyes closed for a moment and burrowed deep under the toasty covers, happy that it was Saturday and she didn't have to get up. She was looking forward to meeting her two best friends, Liz and Sophie, later for dinner, but until then, she had the whole day to herself.

She felt a little hop, a slight fall, another hop, and the impression of something or some*one* who didn't quite have his sea legs yet. Mr. Moto, finished with his own elaborate stretching and yawning, was working his way from the bottom of the bed over all the hills and mounds of the covers.

"Hey, you. That was a long trip, huh?" The kitten mewed. "I know, you want your breakfast. Okay, let me get into the shower."

Olivia threw the covers aside and jumped out of the warm bed, hurried across the cold wooden floor, and got into a steaming shower. She wrapped a bath towel around her and stood in front of the mirror as she dried her hair. A slender woman in her early thirties with rich brown hair and gold-flecked hazel eyes looked back at her. Olivia liked the new bob that her hairdresser had given her last week. It was easy to take care of and showed off her auburn highlights. She padded back into the bedroom, pulled on a heavy knit sweater, a pair of leggings, and thick socks, then went downstairs.

Mr. Moto was sitting in the cheery red-and-white kitchen on the floor by his bowls, complaining loudly. Olivia filled his dishes first, then made her coffee and a bowl of oatmeal. She set her breakfast on the dining room table and sat so she could watch the growing activity in the neighborhood while she ate.

Outside was a winter wonderland; the sun shone and reflected off the snow. Little by little, adults were coming out of their houses to join the already cold, wet children. An elderly couple, walking past Olivia's house with their brown-and-white cocker spaniel, noticed her in the window and waved, mouthing a *Brrrrr*. Olivia smiled and waved back.

After a second cup of coffee and a quick glance at the online news, she spent a few minutes playing with the kitten, throwing his gray felt mouse across the room as he sped to catch it. He always tried to stop as soon as he reached his mouse, but the old oak floors were slippery. Invariably, he slid right past. After the mouse exercise, Olivia dangled a piece of bright blue yarn tied with a puffball of colored bits at the end. Mr. Moto reared up on his hind legs and swatted it. Ten minutes of this exhausting workout and the kitten was done. He scrambled up on the cushion in the bay window and promptly fell asleep in the sun.

Olivia answered her e-mail and Facebook messages, then checked her Twitter account and tweeted a couple of comments on the up-coming Syracuse University basketball game and last night's storm—#Areyoukiddingme?! She cleaned the kitchen and bathroom, and put a fresh set of flannel sheets on her bed. She spent a half hour practicing her kickboxing exercises. Just before noon, Liz texted, wanting to go for a run. Olivia answered *yes,* bundled up against the freezing temperatures, and headed out. As she jogged down the street, her mind drifted to the man in the doorway.

For a week now she'd been seeing visions of a strange man at her bedroom door. The first night's terror had hit her like a physical blow and left her gasping for breath. The second night's shock made her question her sanity. Was she imagining this? His appearance on the third, fourth, and fifth nights had left her intrigued.

Olivia had lived alone for over a decade and had toughened up both mentally and physically. Her kickboxing training during the past two years had boosted her confidence—she knew she could take care of herself. Although she was adventurous and sometimes took risks, notably when she was traveling, the risks were always calculated. She felt comfortable and secure whether she was in the States or overseas. She had never imagined she could feel vulnerable in her own home.

Olivia's mysterious nocturnal visitor appeared at her bedroom door for six straight nights. He never spoke, never came any closer. He loomed over the threshold, looked in at her, and disappeared. By the second night, she was no longer frightened. She had figured out that he wasn't real—walking through the wall had been a good clue. But what was he? A ghost? A dream—though she'd swear she was awake? Olivia was actually getting annoyed. *Who the hell is this guy? And what's going on?* She wanted to know. She was determined to find out.

Olivia met Liz at the corner and they headed to the Riverwalk, a popular three-mile path that ran along the Mohawk River and was well-maintained in all seasons. They ran the length of the trail and back, then slowed down and walked a couple of blocks into the center of town.

"Ooh! That felt good," said Liz, panting.

"Yeah, but the cold air kills your throat," said Olivia between breaths.

"Worth it, though."

"I blame you for this," Olivia kidded. "You and your obsession to run every day no matter what the weather is."

"Ha! You love it and you know it," Liz chortled.

"Yeah, you're right. Listen, I'm going to swing by the library. A book that I need came in."

"Okay, see you tonight."

Olivia rounded the corner, passed Deb's Beauty Salon—waving as she walked by the window—said *hi* to a neighbor coming out of the hardware store with a new shovel, then turned into the library where she headed to the adult services desk.

"Hey, Sue, I got your e-mail."

"Olivia! Yes, we finally located your book at the Library of Congress."

"Awesome. I thought this job would be easy but it's been a challenge."

"Yes, a real quest!" The librarian's face glowed with the thrill of the chase.

"When I started my agency, I didn't realize how exciting it was going to be researching so many different topics. It's like being on a treasure hunt."

Sue laughed. "You and Indiana Jones!"

Olivia pictured her business cards with Indiana Jones's fedora as her logo instead of the Sherlock Holmes-style magnifying glass. *Not.*

Olivia owned The Watson Agency, a small, one-woman enterprise that did research for college professors and writers. The reality of owning her own business resulted from conversations she'd had with her parents after her father's heart attack. Olivia's baby-boomer parents had enjoyed their work, but had often talked about chucking it all and going to California. When she was growing up, they'd shared memories of listening to the Beach Boys and The Mamas and the Papas when they were teenagers. Sometimes they sang "California Dreamin'" as they sat on the front porch drinking wine.

During the post-heart attack discussions of the meaning of life and the universe in general, always with a bit of Jim Morrison and Jack Kerouac thrown in for good measure, Paige and Henry made a point of telling their daughter that life was short. She should do what she was passionate about.

Olivia had never thought of her work as a reporter as *just a job*, but all those conversations seeped in and settled in the nooks and crannies of her mind. After her parents had finally packed up and headed west, Olivia took a leap of faith and filed the DBA forms with the county, indicating she was doing business as *The Watson Agency*. She'd use her investigative skills, self-discipline, and sense of curiosity to help people find out what they needed to know. She got lucky with her first client, a professor at Hamilton College who needed background research for a book he was compiling. Olivia did the job. He was pleased and referred her to a colleague at Cornell University. Her business took off and now, five years later, Olivia worked for people all over the Northeast—from writers in New York City to professors at Boston College.

"Sue, I better be going. I've still got things to do and I'm meeting the girls for dinner later."

"It's wonderful the three of you are still so close. I know you must have relied on them this past year."

Olivia's face glazed over as she said dully, "It was a long time ago."

As she descended the steps, Olivia felt the familiar ache in her gut and lump in her throat. *Blindsided again, damn it.* She wished she would stop reacting like this. *It's been almost a year. I'm over it. I don't want to think about it.* She slammed the persistent feelings into her emotional closet and threw the door shut. *No more tears for you, you son of a bitch!*

When Olivia got home she saw the kids next door playing in the yard.

"Oliviaaaaaaa!!!"

Seven-year-old Andrew ran toward her as fast as his bulky snowsuit would allow. In his brown jacket and pants, he looked like a bat waving his arms and dancing from side to side as he tried to gain purchase on the slippery surface. His five-year-old sister Abbey, in her puffy pink snowsuit, struggled to keep up with him but kept falling on the slick, packed snow. Olivia braced herself as both children barreled into her and grabbed onto her legs.

"Hey, guys! What do you think of all this snow?"

"Cool!" Andrew answered.

"I *like* it," said Abbey. The pom-pom on her knit hat bounced as she jumped up and down.

Olivia reached over to set her backpack on the porch as the kids held on for dear life and Andrew loudly related all the things they had done in the snow that afternoon. "Have you made snow angels yet?" Olivia wanted to know.

"What's that?" Abbey squeaked.

"Look, I'll show you. Stand here and watch." She peeled their mittened hands off her pants, made sure they weren't going to fall over, and went to the edge of her sidewalk. She faced them with her back to the unbroken expanse of snow. "Ready?"

The children waited eagerly. Abbey's eyes were big with anticipation.

"Okay, here I go." Olivia fell straight back onto the snow. To gasps of delight, she began to move her arms and legs up and down, in and out, making the wings and skirt of an angel.

Both children squealed, "Me, too! Me, too! I wanna do it!"

Olivia got up and helped position them in a safe spot. Andrew and Abbey both made beautiful angels and were excited to get their parents to come see their handiwork. Olivia helped them up and brushed them off. As she mounted the front steps, Andrew stopped in mid-run home. "Hey, I saw your friend last night."

"What? What friend?"

"The man who came to your house in the funny car."

"Andrew, nobody came to my house last night."

"Yes," he insisted. "I *saw* him. I got up to go to the bathroom and looked out the window. He got out of a big green car and went in your house. Bye. See ya." And he ran off.

"Oh, my God," she whispered.

Chapter 8

It was already four o'clock. Olivia poured a glass of seltzer and spent a few minutes checking her e-mail. Only one required an immediate answer; the professor for whom she'd done research on *time* the previous autumn was requesting some additional material. She accepted and told him she'd send it to his office later in the week. She made sure Mr. Moto was set for the night and went upstairs to get ready.

Giovanni's Italian Bistro occupied an old stone building on the Margate Road. The sign hanging outside the door attested to the fact that the family-owned bistro had been in operation since 1934. The Firenzi family had emigrated from Tuscany. From their first taste of the blended flavors of garlic, oregano, olive oil, and fresh cheese in the antipasto to the richness of the *Vitello al Marsala,* the citizens of Knightsbridge were hooked. The restaurant survived the Great Depression, then flourished over the decades and was *the* place to go when looking for a mouth-watering meal. When the weather was good, Olivia and her friends ate under the Cinzano umbrellas on the cobblestone patio; but tonight they were toasty warm at a table draped with a red-and-white checkered cloth, their faces glowing from the light of a blazing fire.

"I love this place," said Olivia. "Every time I come here, I feel like I died and went to heaven."

"Me, too!" agreed Liz. "Heaven is either a restaurant like this or a *pâtisserie* like yours, Sophie."

"Merci," said the resident pastry chef and business owner. "Let's order. I'm hungry."

Olivia, Liz, and Sophie had been best friends since childhood, and over the years they had grown even closer. Except for her parents, there was no one in the world that Olivia trusted more. Each had supported the others in times of crisis or loss and had happily shared moments of joy and success. Liz and Sophie had been there for Olivia when her world fell apart. She and Sophie had cradled Liz as she wept over her miscarriage. And when Sophie had decided to open up the *pâtisserie*, Olivia and Liz painted for days.

Olivia was eager to discuss the past week and get her friends' take on things, although she'd already guessed how they would react. Sophie would immediately be afraid for Olivia. Liz would take it in stride. Olivia forced herself to wait until they'd ordered and been served their wine. They raised their glasses and clinked.

The ritual completed, Olivia began. "I need to talk to you guys about something."

Sophie looked at her with interest. Liz, who had heard the tension in Olivia's voice, quickly said, "What is it?"

Olivia took a deep breath and launched into her tale.

The expressions on her friends' faces told Olivia that they rode the same roller coaster she'd been on all week. Horror turned to shock, then confusion, finally settling on curiosity.

"Why does this stuff always happen to you?" whispered Sophie. Her brows furrowed and her face blanched, making her fair complexion appear even paler.

"What do you mean?" asked Olivia.

"Well, I don't know anyone else who nearly got kidnapped in South America."

"And what about that guy who followed you around all day through the bazaar in Cairo?" said Liz. "You're like a magnet for adventures. Although, I have to say, this is a new one."

"Well, I could have done without this one. I've hardly had a good night's sleep all week."

"I'll ask the obvious question to get it out of the way," said Liz, topaz eyes sparkling in the flickering candlelight. "You're *sure* you weren't dreaming?"

"To be honest, for a minute I *did* think maybe I was reliving that awful night at S.U."

When Olivia had been a student at Syracuse University, a man had forced his way into her dorm room in the middle of the night. She'd awakened when she'd heard him fumbling with his key in the lock, thought it was her drunken roommate, and opened the door. Luckily he had been stoned and she had been able to back him out into the hallway and lock the door. Nevertheless it had scared the hell out of her.

"But no, Liz, I don't think so. I felt wide awake. And if you had seen Mr. Moto…*he* knew someone was there. He flew over the covers. Normally, he can barely make it over the blankets, he's so small."

"So, this has been going on all week and you're still ok. I'm going to focus on that right now," said Sophie, taking a swallow of Zinfandel.

"Let's look at this logically," said Liz, probing further. "You were awake. The house was locked up, right?"

Olivia sighed with relief and gave Liz a grateful smile. Liz always accepted things calmly and met them head on rationally. "Of course. I check all the doors and windows before I go upstairs every night.

And I set the alarm. There's no way someone could have gotten in without setting off the alarm."

"All right. We can also forget the idea that you're going crazy or there's something wrong with your brain. We know you're fine."

"We're running out of options here," observed Sophie.

"Something else happened that was strange," said Olivia, remembering.

"Like there haven't been enough weird things so far," said Liz sarcastically.

Olivia told them what Andrew said about seeing her friend last night.

"Wow," said Sophie and Liz in unison.

Olivia let out the breath she hadn't realized she was holding. "Oh! I feel so much better telling you guys. I was getting scared that something *was* wrong with me. But now that I think about Mr. Moto's reactions, it's *got* to be real. If it were all in my head, he *couldn't possibly* have sensed anything."

"And who did Andrew see?" said Liz rhetorically.

"Exactly! There was no one at my house last night. Whoever this guy is, somehow he exists, right?"

"Maybe he's a ghost," said Sophie, reaching to dip a hunk of Italian bread into the dish of seasoned oil. "Maybe you just found out you're a medium and you can see dead people."

"You watch too much TV, Sophie," snorted Liz. "Tell us some more what it felt like, Liv. Go back to the first night. Maybe there's a clue that we missed."

"Well, the first night, obviously I was terrified. I kept thinking, *What do I do? How am I gonna get out of here?* Then the other nights, when he was peering into my room..."

"Ohmygod!" Sophie always made it sound like one long word. "This is giving me the creeps," she cried and drank a big gulp of her wine.

"Sorry, Sophie, but at first it *was* creepy. Then when he straightened up and shook his head and I could make out a little of the expression on his face…I don't know…I didn't feel threatened any more. He acted confused." She took a drink of her Cabernet Sauvignon. "Then he walked through the wall, for heaven's sake. That's our big clue. Obviously he can't be real."

"But he's something," said Sophie.

"Olivia, remember the research you did on *time*? Didn't you tell us about a theory where time *folds over* on itself?" asked Liz, leaning back as the waiter served their salads. "Wasn't there something about Einstein believing in time travel?"

"Now we're talking about time travel," Sophie said excitedly. "I believe in that."

"You're right, Liz," Olivia said. "Einstein thought that time could fold over or twist around itself. He said that what we call the past, present, and future is only an illusion. He believed it was possible for two objects to occupy the same space but at different times. If you subscribe to his theory, which I do, why couldn't time fold over at the moment when two *people* are in the same place? They could see each other. Maybe even communicate."

"Ohmygod!" exclaimed Sophie again, her voice rising to a near squeak, her red curls bouncing as she shot forward in her chair. "Do you think that's what happened to you? The guy was in your house at a different *time*?"

"I have no idea. But wouldn't it be awesome to talk with someone living in another time?"

"Remember when we were kids and we used to have sleepovers at your house on Friday nights?" asked Liz.

"Sure, of course. And…?" Olivia raised her eyebrows.

"All those movie marathons and big bowls of popcorn. I'll never forget how crazy your mom was about *Somewhere in Time* with

Christopher Reeve and Jane Seymour. We must have watched that movie a half dozen times."

"I loved that movie!" said Sophie. "So romantic."

"Well, we were at that impressionable age, starting to like boys." Liz rolled her eyes. "But my point is that in the beginning, the characters were in the same place but at different times."

"Mackinac Island. The Grand Hotel," said Sophie dreamily.

"Right," Liz paused then stared at Olivia. "So...about your mysterious stranger...what are you going to do?"

Olivia changed into a pair of plaid pajama bottoms and a fitted T-shirt, turned on a reading light, and got into bed. She propped the new David Baldacci against her bent legs and settled in. As she turned a page, a rush of air caressed her cheek. If she'd been able to actually see it, the air would have looked like the swell of an immense wave, only vertical. She peeked over her book.

There he was, standing as he had every night before, in the middle of the hall, peering in. This time, though, there was enough light to see clearly. The Roman nose suited his handsome face. He had strong features, dark eyes, dark eyebrows, and a five-o'clock shadow. He stared at her.

"Hello," she managed to whisper. It sounded almost like a question.

"Hello," a low, husky voice replied in astonishment. He stared. "Are you *real?*"

"Of course, I'm real. Who *are* you? What are you doing in my house?" She slowly set her book aside and slid the covers down to free her legs in case she needed to move fast.

"This is *my* house. Why are you in my mother's room? Are you a ghost?"

That's a good one, Olivia thought. *He thinks I'm the ghost.* "I live here. This is *my* room."

"No, *I* live here."

"Maybe I should call the cops."

"I *am* the cops," he said sardonically.

"How did you get in? What's your name?" she insisted.

"Fine," he rolled his eyes. "It's Steven. Steven Blackwell," he replied, shaking his head. "This is ridiculous. I must be losing my mind." He sunk down on the floor facing her from the other side of the doorway. "What's going on here?"

"Steven, what's the date today?"

"The date? February 24th. Why?"

"What year is it?"

"It's 1934. As I'm sure you well know."

"Oh…my…God! No, for me it's *not* 1934. It's 2014."

His eyebrows shot up and his mouth dropped open. "2000…," he croaked. "2014? Is this some kind of weird joke? Did Becks put you up to this? 'Cause I gotta tell you, I'm really too tired for this."

"I have no idea who Becks is. And no, it's not a joke. I'll tell you what I think is happening."

He raised both hands and shrugged. "Sure."

Olivia explained Einstein's theory of time folding over.

"Holy mackerel! It sounds like something out of a book!"

"Yeah, if you read science fiction."

"I do. Okay," he said reluctantly, "let's say your idea's right and it *is* Einstein. I want some concrete evidence. Something that *proves* it."

They both sat quietly.

After a minute he ventured, "I've got a thought. Do you have any change?"

"Change, like coins, you mean?"

"Yeah, a penny, a nickel."

"Sure, over there on the dresser."

"Go get a coin." He dug into his pocket and pulled out some change.

"I have a penny. We'll each roll our coin over to the other person. We'll be able to see the date stamped on it."

"I don't know what's going on, but it's interesting." She made a face. "Whatever it is."

"This sure isn't the way I thought *my* day would end."

"Yeah, no kidding." She allowed herself a small smile.

Olivia slowly got out of bed and sidestepped to her dresser, not wanting to turn her back on him. She took a quarter from her wallet and cautiously approached the door. She stopped a couple of feet from the threshold and waited.

He crossed his legs and looked up at her. "By the way, you haven't told me *your* name."

"Olivia. It's Olivia Watson."

He nodded and gave a small bow. "I think we should go one at a time, Olivia. Ladies first."

Olivia tossed the quarter through the opening. It disappeared.

"Hey! Where'd it go?"

"Wait. I'll get another one." She returned with more coins. "Why don't I try handing it to you?"

Somewhere in the back of her mind, it registered that the hallway looked different. Then she noticed his clothes and his slicked-back hair. He looked like he had walked out of an old black-and-white movie. She bent toward him and extended her hand into the center of the doorway. Steven reached out. She felt his hand touch hers. Her eyes widened. His face registered shock. She handed him the quarter.

He turned the coin over and read out loud, "2013! Unbelievable!" He whistled and shook his head. For a moment he just stared at the quarter, his mouth agape. Then he reached over the threshold and handed her a shiny copper penny.

Olivia held it in the palm of her hand. "1933. And it's brand new!" She gave in and sat down, then looked at him in wonder. "Now what?"

They eyed each other without speaking.

Steven broke the silence. "This can't be happening. Where did you hear about this theory of Einstein's?"

Olivia explained the work she did at her research agency. "I just did that job on *time* a few months ago. It's still fresh my mind. Besides, there's been speculation about time travel for years," she said. "Einstein's not the only one who thought it was possible."

"So in 2014, is it common? Have you done this before?"

"No! Of course not. This is as crazy for me as it is for you."

"Listen, I'm a cop. Every day it's my job to find evidence that proves the things people tell me are true. I need something else. This is just too far-fetched."

"Do you have another explanation?"

"No, but I want more proof. You seem to be accepting this a lot more easily than I am."

She wanted to say *Look at the way you're dressed! And that hair. Who does that anymore?* Instead she rose and walked to her bedside table. She picked up her laptop, returned to the doorway, and sat back down. She lifted the cover and tried to decide on something that would be convincing. She asked, "What's the last movie you saw?"

"What's that you've got?"

"It's called a computer and it's going to give you all the proof you need. So, movie?"

"I saw *The Big Shakedown* last month. Bette Davis is real swell."

Olivia typed it in, hit a couple of keys, and raised the volume. She turned the screen so Steven could see it. His eyes popped out and he stared. She let him watch for a minute.

"What's playing in town right now?"

"A new Clark Gable picture called *It Happened One Night.*"

She worked her magic and showed him the screen again.

"How are you doing that?"

She ignored his question. "What's your favorite song?"

"I don't know. I like Bing Crosby. Maybe 'Shadow Waltz.'"

Olivia went to YouTube and typed in the title. The crooner's smooth voice oozed out of her laptop.

She waited until he'd sung a few bars then said, "Steven, my point is this: you can tell me absolutely anything and I can type it in. You can watch it, read it, listen to it, learn it. It's technology of the twenty-first century that no one in 1934 is even dreaming of yet."

Steven pursed his lips, wrinkled his brow, and sat without speaking.

Olivia sighed. "Okay then. Franklin Roosevelt is president of the United States in 1934. He's going to be elected two more times. He'll die in office and Harry Truman will become the president. The Depression is going to last several more years."

"Wait! Stop! I don't want to know...the future." He unfolded his legs, stood up, and paced up and down the hallway.

Bing was still singing in the background.

After some minutes, Steven returned to the doorway, sat down again, and silently listened as the song ended. The laptop went quiet.

"So, Einstein was right."

SUNDAY – 1934

Chapter 9

Sunday morning, Steven did something he rarely did—he stayed in bed awhile after waking. Stretched out, covers up to his chin, nose cold, he struggled to take in, to accept the incredible events of last night. Although the idea seemed impossible, he couldn't help believing. He was especially relieved that he hadn't been hallucinating or conjuring up a ghost.

The woman, Olivia, seemed genuine enough. She had appeared as confused as he was. The strange machine that she had was something he never could have imagined. He'd been stunned to see Bette Davis and Charles Farrell cavorting on the small screen. Then she somehow got Clark Gable and Claudette Colbert to appear as well. That film had only started showing a couple of days ago! How had she done it?

And there was something different about her. She didn't act like any of the women he knew or had ever known. She wore strange clothes like nothing he'd ever seen. Certainly these were clues to consider.

Then there was the quarter. It was definitely a genuine American coin. He recognized the U.S. Mint's work.

Well, well, well. Nineteen thirty-four was turning out to be a very interesting year.

Steven got out of bed, walked to the bathroom, and eased into the tub. In the hot water, he washed his hair and scrubbed with a cake of Ivory soap. He let it float in the bath. He remembered when he was a kid, pushing down the bar of Ivory trying to make it stay under the water. It had never worked. The soap popped back up every time. As his mother used to say, *C'est la vie.* Thinking of her, Steven winced, as though he'd rubbed something rough over an open wound.

Steven toweled himself dry and dressed in his Sunday suit, a gray, double-breasted jacket and straight-legged trousers, white shirt, and dark tie. Before going downstairs, he looked into his mother's room and let his eyes linger on every piece of furniture, every knickknack. There was no sign of anything out of the ordinary.

In the kitchen, he put water on to boil then filled a bowl with Wheaties, added sugar and fresh whole milk. The kettle whistled and Steven made his tea. He sat at the table lost in thought as he ate.

What would tonight be like? Would she be there?

He had so many questions to ask. What did Knightsbridge look like in 2014? Did people still eat at Bailey's and shop at the A&P Market? Did the Yankees still play baseball? Was flying only for aviators like Charles Lindbergh and Amelia Earhart or could ordinary folks go up in the sky and look down? Did the police solve crimes like he did? Steven thought of Olivia's amazing machine and wondered how the police might use something like that. After all, she had said she could find out anything with that apparatus. Maybe there was a way to use it to look inside the mind of a suspect and find the truth.

The clock on the living room mantle struck the half hour. He washed his dishes, set them on the draining board, and packed his lunch. He thought longingly of the meal his aunt was going to serve today and wished he didn't have to work.

When Steven arrived at the First Methodist Church, he saw that this morning's service promised to be as well-attended as usual. He parked his Chevy alongside the curb and joined the congregants, everyone dressed in their Sunday best, walking up the flagstone path. The white clapboard church, with its steeple reaching skyward and bright red door, welcomed Steven and gave him a feeling of comfort. He enjoyed the ritual of the familiar prayers, readings, and hymns. Sometimes at the end of a difficult work day, Steven would stop to spend a few minutes alone in the silence and peace, sitting in a pew, trying to empty his mind of the images that had gathered there or to make sense of the terrible things people did to each other.

After the service, Steven relished seeing his friends and neighbors in the community room. This was often the only social time he had all week. It was hard to keep up with family and friends when everyone worked six days a week—and his days seemed longer than most. Here, however, Steven could relax and enjoy what he thought of as "normal conversation." He liked catching up on neighborhood news and village gossip and often had the chance to reminisce with an old friend—though these days, Steven missed the donuts and coffee they'd shared before the crash of '29.

Arthur and Helen Sinclair and their fourteen-year-old daughter Annie approached. Steven stuck out his hand and he and Artie shook. He hugged Helen and winked at Annie, as he gave her plait the ritual tug. She grinned.

Steven and Artie had known each other for years. Artie was the first boy who'd befriended him when he was the new kid in school. Because of his father's Navy career, Steven's family moved often during his childhood. When he was eleven, his father received orders to ship out. Robert Blackwell told his wife Eve—he rarely called her Evangeline—to take the boy to his home town. Three years later, the Great War broke out. When the fighting ended, a distinguished Captain Blackwell was awarded command of a ship. Because he would be out at sea for long stretches of time and because Steven was settled in high school, his mother decided to stay in Knightsbridge rather than live on a naval base.

Over the years, Evangeline Blackwell put down deep, lasting roots and, even when Admiral Blackwell was assigned to the Department of the Navy in Washington, D.C., she stayed in Knightsbridge. They managed to see each other as often as possible. Somehow the unusual arrangement worked for them.

"Artie, it's great to see you and the family."

"Steven, I heard about Leo Castleman. How awful. Was he really stealing money from his own bank?"

"You know I can't comment. It's early days. Still a lot of work to be done."

"His brother Larry manages the sawmill, you know. He's my boss."

"I had the unpleasant task of breaking the news to him. Were they close?"

"Must've been. They saw each other every week for poker night."

They chatted a few more minutes before Steven left for the station.

The Knightsbridge Police Station was located at the corner of Margate and Hickory, next to the firehouse and one block down from the main thoroughfare in town. It was a good central location and in the nice weather Steven often walked to work. Today, however, he arrived in his 1929, dark green, four-door Chevrolet sedan.

Steven was thrilled when he'd finally saved enough to buy his first automobile. He took a long time selecting the make and model. He knew if he needed to use it in the line of duty, the Chevy would perform beautifully. The six-cylinder engine was powerful and fast and the weight of the chassis was evenly distributed, making it very stable. Although he was rarely involved in high-speed chases, careening around corners like Jimmy Cagney, the motor car could handle anything he threw at it.

When Steven entered headquarters, he saw Officer Frank O'Laughlin slouched at the front desk, clearly unhappy that he had pulled duty on a Sunday. Steven prided himself on getting along with almost everyone he'd ever met; but, in spite of all his best efforts, he had a hard time with Frank. Lazy, insolent, and mocking, the man did a sloppy job and didn't care. Steven's strong work ethic bristled at Frank's attitude. The officer had hindered more than one investigation because of the way he did—or, rather, didn't do—his job. Chief Thompson had reprimanded him any number of times. But for the good of the department, Steven made an effort to be pleasant whenever he was around O'Laughlin, hoping that eventually Frank would change his ways.

"Morning, Frank. How are you?"

"Sick of winter, Blackwell. Sick of the snow. Sick of the cold. Sick of slipping on the ice."

In the summer, it was "Sick of the heat, sick of my uniform sticking to me, sick of sweating." Frank complained about everything. Steven had never heard one good thing come out of his mouth.

"Any word from Doc Elliott yet?"

"No."

Never anything extra from Frank, not even words.

Steven continued down the hall to the CID room. *Criminal Investigation Division* was a grand-sounding name for such a small police station, but it was an important and necessary department nonetheless. The CID room was where the detectives had their desks and where the murder board was set up. It was the hub of every investigation. The men working the case came and went freely. They would stand at the murder board checking developments and discussing the investigation. Significant gains were often made in this unassuming room with the lofty name.

After stowing his gear and greeting his partner, Steven dialed the medical examiner's telephone number.

"Morning, Doc. Sorry to bother you at home but I wondered if you had any news on the Castleman autopsy?"

At his desk across from Steven, Beckman stopped reviewing his notes and listened to the one-sided conversation.

"Yep, that's what we thought…Two, huh? Making sure, I suppose…Right, well, I didn't really expect too much…Oh! That's a surprise! Any idea what it's from?…Right…Uh huh…What about time? Were you able to narrow it down any?…I see…Yeah, that's fine, Doc. Thanks very much. I especially appreciate it on a Sunday."

"What'd he say?"

"A blow to the head with a blunt object. Two in all," Steven told him.

"Making sure he was really dead," said Becks.

"Doc found a sliver of wood in the wound. You're not going to believe what it was."

"What?"

"Ebony."

"Ebony! That sounds exotic. What the heck do they make out of ebony?"

"Well, besides piano keys, which I doubt is the case here," Steven smirked, momentarily losing his focus and picturing the killer wildly flinging piano keys at the victim, "the only thing I know is golf clubs."

"I don't think there was enough room in the vault to get a good swing at him with a golf club."

"It could be something else. A walking stick or just a piece of wood.

We'll check the mill. See if they've got any."

"Okay, so we got a piece of ebony. Hey, *The Maltese Falcon*!" exclaimed Becks.

"What?"

"*The Maltese Falcon*. It's a new book I read a while ago. Dashiell Hammett's the writer. You heard of it?"

"No. What's it got to do with the case?"

"In the story, some people were looking for a statue. They kept calling it *the black bird*. I don't remember if it was actually made from ebony, but it gave me the idea. The weapon could be some kind of statue."

"All right. So we've got a piece of ebony. Maybe it's a hunk of wood. Or a golf club, a walking stick, or a statue."

"Whatever it turns out to be, I think our killer's pretty strong. Even if it's a medium-sized piece, you've really gotta whack him hard to kill him."

"I agree." Steven recalled the rest of the ME's information. "As for time of death, Doc said most likely closer to midnight than to six. So say twelve to three. Let's work with that."

Steven grabbed a piece of chalk and added the new data to the murder board then turned to his partner. "It's almost noon, Becks. People should be home from church but not starting their dinner yet. Last night, the chief told me Mrs. Castleman would be back today. Let's go see the widow."

Chapter 10

Leo and Patricia Castleman lived on Swan Lane in the exclusive part of town. Their two-story home was classic Georgian architecture, built of a beautiful red brick with white trim. Its elaborate front entry boasted paned windows and rounded columns on either side; curved stone steps led to the front door. Steven used the brass knocker to announce their arrival, then showed his badge and ID to the thin, aging Negro woman who answered the door.

"Police, ma'am. Is Mrs. Castleman in?"

The maid led them into a large foyer. As they skirted a polished table displaying a vase of fresh flowers, Steven caught his reflection in a gold-framed mirror hanging on the wall above a carved credenza. His new fedora looked swell. He snapped the brim and smiled.

Patricia Castleman made an entrance. There were no other words for it. She slowly descended the wide curving steps, one hand lightly resting on the banister. Her nails were long, carefully shaped, and lacquered. She held her head high in a regal fashion. For a brief moment, Steven wondered if he was going to have to kiss her ring. And speaking of rings, the rock on her left hand must have set

Castleman back a pretty penny.

"Good afternoon, Mrs. Castleman. I'm Detective Sergeant Blackwell. This is Detective Beckman."

Both men politely took off their hats.

"Gentlemen," she inclined her head slightly. "We can sit in the parlor." She led them into a room where a blaze in the fireplace warmed the apricot walls and cream-colored, floor-to-ceiling drapes.

Patricia Castleman sat on one of two sofas, upholstered in a shade slightly darker than the walls. She leaned back against the deep cushions, her navy silk crêpe de chine dress rustling as she arranged the flowing skirt around her. She crossed her legs and her silk stockings echoed the sound. She said nothing, but looked expectantly at Steven, who sat with Beckman on the couch facing her. Becks took out his notebook and a pencil.

"Mrs. Castleman, I'm sorry for your loss. I understand you were in Syracuse at your sister's house when you got the news of your husband's death?"

"Yes, I came home immediately."

"How often do you visit your sister?"

"We don't have a regular schedule. Maybe once a month. Sometimes once in six weeks. It depends."

"Do you have your driving license?"

"Yes. I bought a new Silver Arrow last year but I don't take it that far in the winter. I travel by train when the weather's bad."

"Can you tell me why your husband would be in the bank vault in the middle of the night?"

"No, I can't. It sounds ridiculous." She lightly ran her hand over the already smooth skirt of her dress.

"But he *was* there, ma'am."

"Well, I don't know why he would be, Detective. He spends enough hours at the bank during the day."

"Did your husband have any enemies?"

"Evidently."

Steven stood and walked around to the back of the sofa. He looked down at her for a long moment. *She's a cool one,* he thought.

"Pardon me, but you don't seem terribly upset."

"Leo and I led separate lives, Detective. He worked long hours. Sometimes six days a week. I found things to occupy myself. I don't even remember the last time we had a conversation."

"Is there anything you can tell us that might help in the investigation, Mrs. Castleman?"

"No, Detective. I'm sorry. There isn't."

As Steven and Becks followed the circular drive to the Chevy, Steven exclaimed, "Jeez! Have I got frostbite on my face? That is one cold cookie."

"Maybe she's in shock. Or sad. Death of her husband. And not by natural causes. People react in different ways."

"I know they do, Becks. But there was nothing behind her eyes. They were like deep black pits. Well, we'll see. We'll check their finances..."

"A Pierce Silver Arrow must have set them back!" Becks interrupted. "That baby's loaded!"

"I wonder if they really could afford it. A lot of people were wiped out in the crash."

"Maybe she's been spending too much and it caught up to them."

Steven nodded. "I'll bet you dollars to donuts they had money troubles and he decided to help himself to a few thousand down in the vault. Then someone helped *him*self to what Castleman was taking. The question is, who knew he'd be there? Did he have a partner who turned on him? Did someone overhear Castleman say he'd be there? Maybe it was somebody who actually saw him go into the bank that night. Let's see if we can scare up a witness, Becks."

Earlier Steven had sketched a map of the buildings in the general vicinity of the bank, especially noting those that looked onto Bank Alley. Only one business was open on Sunday.

"I want to start at *The Gazette*," he said. "The newspaper offices are directly behind the bank. Reporters work 'round the clock. And there are plenty of staff late at night running the press and getting the papers ready to deliver in the morning. If anybody noticed something Friday night, you'd think it'd be a newspaperman."

"Good idea."

Steven parked in the alley and the two policemen entered the building. The smiling receptionist in the lobby directed them upstairs to the noisy newsroom where a thick cloud of smoke hugged the high ceiling. The room sizzled with action. Reporters hustled. Typewriters clacked. Telephones rang. Receivers banged down.

Steven asked a scrawny youth with greasy hair and acne if the managing editor was around. The copy boy spun around in mid-run, nodded toward an office in the back corner, and raced away.

Sam Silverstone was a balding, middle-aged man. Blood-shot eyes and dark circles behind wire-rimmed glasses attested to his lack of sleep. Like any newsman worth his salt, he was skeptical of everyone and everything. Steven had always liked him. He was a nice guy.

"Hi, Sam."

"Afternoon, Steven, Harry."

They shook hands and the editor waved them to a couple of wobbly chairs in front of his paper-laden desk. Silverstone sat down on a creaky, swivel chair, leaned back, and took a swig from the bright pink Pepto-Bismol bottle that he kept on his desk. "Heartburn," he grimaced. "Again." He took a second swig. He eyed them over stacks of file folders and old newspapers.

"Bad business, boys. Bad business. You here to give us a scoop? I was gonna send a reporter 'round to see you later. Looks like you saved me the trouble."

Steven laughed. "Not quite, Sam. We need to talk with everyone who was working Friday night."

"Yeah, I heard he caught it in the vault, huh? So the perp went in the back door, did he?" the newspaperman asked shrewdly.

"That's what we think right now. I'm hoping one of your guys saw or maybe heard something."

"We had a skeleton crew that night because of the storm. Two of the fellas couldn't make it in. You want to talk to Roy Renard. He's in charge of the night desk so he's not here now. Probably home sleeping. Like the other guys. Ernie Coaltree and Herb Steadman. They run the press so they work nights, too." He scribbled on a piece of paper. "Here're their addresses. They all live in town."

Back in the lobby, Steven gazed out *The Gazette*'s side door. "Let's see. Across the alley we've got the Shell Gas Station."

"That closes up early. No chance anyone would've been there."

"Right. Next door we've got the A&P, so nobody there in the middle of the night either."

They stepped out into the cold and shivered up to the corner.

"Look, Becks. Across the street we've got four houses, maybe five, close enough so somebody could have seen something if they were awake and looked out a window at the right time. Maybe we'll get lucky."

Steven looked at the paper Silverstone had given him. "Herb Steadman's on Maple across from the baseball park. Ernie Coaltree's down on Second Street."

"Coaltree's not too far from the station. We can catch him on the way back."

"Right. Roy Renard's down the street here, across from the high school. Why don't you go over there? After you're done, check 318 at that end. They're probably too far over to have seen anything, but you never know. I'll start with the Fordhams at 310 and we'll meet in the middle."

Beckman loped down the street toward Roy Renard's house. The newspaperman answered the door himself, glanced at Beckman's shield and ID, and invited him inside. Renard had squinty pale eyes and a face that came to a point at the end of his nose. Beckman's first thought was of a mole, burrowing through dark underground tunnels.

"I'm Detective Harry Beckman, Mr. Renard."

"Call me Roy."

"I imagine you've heard about the murder of Leo Castleman?"

"Oh yeah, people been talkin' 'bout nothin' else." His cigarette was burning down dangerously close to his fingers. He seemed not to notice.

"Did you see anything Friday night that might help us? Notice anyone going in or out of Bank Alley? Or the back door of the bank?"

"Naw. Sorry, Detective. Two of my guys never showed up and I had to cover for 'em. Ran myself ragged all night long tryin' to pick up the slack. Didn't even take my usual breaks *and* I had to rush through my supper."

"Okay. Give us a call if you remember anything."

"Will do."

Beckman made his way along Victoria to number 318. A middle-aged man answered the door. Unfortunately for the policeman's inquiries, the man had slept through the night and saw nothing. Beckman had no better luck at number 316. No one answered the door. He made a note to return Monday.

Steven knocked loudly on the door to number 310, hoping that Catherine and Ray Fordham had been up with the new baby during the night. But when Catherine answered the door his spirits fell. The young mother had awoken from a much-needed afternoon nap and was obviously dismayed. Her pale eyes were tired, the fine brown hair seemed fly-away, her housedress had stains on the shoulder, and her apron needed washing.

"I know why you're here, Steven. Leo Castleman, right?"

Steven nodded.

"I didn't see anything. The baby fussed half the night and I spent most of it trying to rock her to sleep. The bedroom's in the back so even if I had looked out the window...," she shrugged. "And Ray snored all night long. So I know he didn't see anything."

"Thanks, Catherine. Sorry I woke you up. If you think of anything, call me."

"Okay. Bye." She shut the door quickly.

Steven moved on to number 312, his cousin Jim Blackwell's home. Martha answered the door and called out to her husband, "Jimmy, Steven's here. Come on back to the kitchen. Would you like a cup of coffee?"

"I'd love one but I can't take the time, Martha. I'm meeting Beckman in a few minutes and I don't want to keep him waiting. Thanks, though."

"Sure. Another time. Oh, here he is."

"Hey, Stevie. I can't believe it about Leo Castleman! I assume that's why you're here?"

"Yeah, I'm hoping one of you saw something Friday night? Or maybe you heard something? Say between midnight and three."

"Jeez, I'm sorry but I slept right through the night. What about you, honey? Did you get up to go to the bathroom?"

His wife giggled. "We celebrated our anniversary Friday. Jimmy made us a couple of cocktails before we turned in. I was a little looped. Slept like a baby. I'm sorry, Steven. Maybe Mrs. Coffin, next door..."

"Sure, I know Mrs. Coffin. The piano teacher, right?"

"Yes, she's elderly now. She's always up during the night. Poor thing doesn't sleep very well."

"That's a good idea, honey. But you'll have to wait until Tuesday, Steven. She's gone to visit her daughter in Utica. She said she wouldn't be back until late Monday."

As he descended the front steps, Steven tried not to feel disappointed. He'd been doing this job long enough to know these things took time. Nevertheless he hoped this case wouldn't drag on like the last one.

Becks arrived and his face told Steven everything he needed to know.

"No luck for you either, huh?"

"Zip!" his partner said disgustedly. "Renard was too busy working to notice anything. The fella at 318 never woke up all night. And nobody was home at 316."

"Let's take a break, Becks."

"Good idea."

"We'll go back to the station, warm up, have some lunch. We can write up what we've got so far. Then, depending on the time, we can go over to Ernie Coaltree's and Herb Steadman's later or even tomorrow. What do you say?"

"I'm with you, partner."

They could see their breath as they sat in the icy motor car waiting for the engine to warm up.

"How can it be colder in here than it is out there?" Beckman moaned.

Several minutes later they entered the warm, but mostly deserted, police station. Beckman headed straight for the noisy radiator at the back wall in the detectives' room. He carefully put his gloved hands on the hissing metal unit.

"Aah," he sighed. "I'd like to sit on this thing for about two hours. I'm ready for spring."

It gets dark early in winter. By the time Steven and Becks finished talking with Ernie Coaltree, the *Gazette* employee—who sadly had seen nothing, heard nothing, and knew nothing—night had fallen. The small town of Knightsbridge glowed, as lights in house after house flickered on.

"Time to call it a day, Becks. I'll drop you off on my way home. We can leave Herb Steadman until tomorrow."

"Now, *that's* a plan. I'm ready to put my feet up. I think I'll open up a nice cold Genny and do nothing all night long."

Steven let the automobile idle in front of the two-story clapboard home and waited as his friend climbed the steps. When Becks stepped onto the porch, he turned and waved. Steven shifted into first, released the clutch, and pulled away from the curb.

As he drove up the street, the investigation was already fading from his mind, replaced with thoughts of Olivia. Only a few more hours and he'd see her.

SUNDAY – PRESENT DAY

Chapter 11

The ringing phone woke Olivia. Face smashed into her pillow, her hair spread out in disarray, she reached out an arm and blindly groped on the top of her nightstand for her cell. She opened one eye and saw on the caller ID that it was Sophie. She answered groggily, "Morning, Sophie."

"Olivia, did I wake you?"

"It's okay."

"Did he show up?"

"Yes!" Olivia twisted round in the covers then sat up, fully awake now. "Let's get together at your place. I can't wait to tell you guys all about it."

"Ohmygod! I can't believe it. You talked to him?"

"Yeah, but I want to tell both of you together."

"Sure, okay. How about eleven in our corner? I'll put a sign on the table to save it."

"Perfect. I'll text Liz."

"See you in a bit."

Sophie's *Pâtisserie-Café* was a popular hangout on Embankment Road, near the Riverwalk. Comfortable chairs and tables were scattered under shady trees in the back and in good weather the lawn was always crowded. Patrons relaxed, chatted, read newspapers, and tossed bits of croissant to the hungry ducks that waddled up from the water.

Sophie had inherited the century-old house from her grandparents several years ago. She lived upstairs and ran her business on the main level. Her dad and brother Marco were carpenters and had renovated both floors to her specifications. Inside was tribute to Sophie's passion—anything and everything French. She had decorated it as a literary café, in black and cream, with portraits of French writers hanging on the walls and famous quotations beautifully scripted under glass on the tabletops. Voltaire, Balzac, and Baudelaire, as well as Simone de Beauvoir, Camus, and Sartre kept the pâtisserie customers company.

Olivia and Liz met at the counter, where the white-aproned staff was serving customers.

Sunday was the busiest day of the week. Earlier, the glass-fronted cases had been full of mouth-watering, calorie-laden, waistband-tightening, to-die-for French pastries. There were many-layered napoleons and *mille-feuilles,* delicate *madeleines,* glazed *tartes, éclairs* oozing with cream, croissants, and *pains au chocolat,* which were chocolate-filled croissants. Throughout the morning, however, the cases steadily emptied as customers made purchases to eat in and ordered bakery boxes to go.

Olivia and Liz made their selections and took coffee and pastries to the Descartes table—*Je pense donc je suis.*—where they joined Sophie, who was taking a well-deserved break and drinking a large Americano. They air-kissed and settled on the caned Parisian chairs.

"Good timing. Things are slowing down a bit," Sophie said.

Liz turned to Olivia and jumped right in, "So, what happened?"

Olivia took a deep breath. "I think he's real. He said he lives in 1934."

"You're kidding!" Liz's jaw dropped.

"Oh. My. God!" said Sophie, dragging it out for the first time in her life.

"I know," Olivia said, breathless. "I think it really *is* Einstein." She told them about the coin experiment. "It was strange though. When I slid my quarter through the doorway it disappeared. Neither one of us could see it. It was like time actually had folded over. Then when we handed each other the coin, it worked. Right in the middle of the doorway. Maybe that's the magic spot."

"Ohmygod." Sophie was back to normal. "I can't believe this."

"It's hard to wrap your head around. So what did you do next?" Liz asked.

"Once we did the coin thing and I *really* looked at him, it made sense. It's the only explanation—crazy, I know—but I believe it. I think this is really happening."

"What do you mean when you *looked* at him?"

"There's no way this guy lives now. The clothes he had on belong in the museum, Liz. And his hair was slicked back. So old fashioned!" She wrinkled her nose.

Liz's eyes widened. In love with all things vintage, Liz was the curator of the local history museum. "Ooh! Think of the stuff you could get for my exhibits, Olivia." Then she added in mock seriousness, "If you figure out how to time travel, I might have to go with you."

They all laughed.

Olivia went on. "Even after the coins, he wasn't convinced though so I got out my laptop. I asked him about some movies and songs that he liked then I played parts of them so he could see and listen. I actually liked the Bing Crosby song."

"Oh brother, here we go," said Sophie. "It's not enough that you watch all those old black-and-white films; now you're going to start listening to what's-his-name."

"Hey, don't knock my Charlie Chan movies."

"Well, if this guy is real, the two of you ought to get along just fine." Sophie rolled her eyes. "You'll have a lot of stuff to talk about."

"Did you find out anything about him?" said Liz, ever practical.

"His name's Steven. He's a cop."

"That's it?"

Olivia nodded. "Yeah, but I'll learn more tonight. We agreed to meet again."

"What if it doesn't work?" Sophie sounded worried. "What if you just sit there in your room and nothing happens?"

"It's going to work. I *know* it is."

"You'll have to text us after...," Liz stopped mid-sentence. "I was going to say *after he leaves* but it's his house, too. How did you get rid of him last night so you could go back to bed?"

"We said good night and he went into what I assumed was his room. He closed the door and that was it."

"If he does show up, I'll get to hear it in person tomorrow morning." Liz looked over at Sophie and explained, "Olivia's helping at the museum. We've got that big delivery coming."

"Oh, that's right. My volunteer work. It's gonna be fun!"

"What delivery are you talking about?"

"Miss Sinclair's house. Remember when she died last month, she left all that stuff to the museum? Well, it's been boxed up and it's arriving tomorrow. I'm so excited, I can't wait. This is an enormous coup for the Historical Association."

Miss Annabel Sinclair had been one of Knightsbridge's oldest residents when she passed away in January. Passionate about history and dedicated to the community, Miss Sinclair had donated both time and money to the local history museum.

Liz looked at her watch. "Hey, it's almost twelve thirty. I've gotta go. Joe's off today and we promised each other we'd spend the day together. Olivia, nine o'clock, okay?"

"I'll be there. What are you doing this afternoon, Sophie? Want to go to a movie?"

"Sure. Perfect thing to do on a snowy day."

Olivia returned home after an enjoyable afternoon at the movies—you could always count on Chris Hemsworth. She made dinner and ate while watching another episode of *House of Cards.* She poured a second glass of wine and brought it upstairs with her. That morning, she'd left without picking up or making her bed, so she took care of those chores now. She didn't want Steven to see the mess.

Olivia was still thrilled with the renovations she'd made to her bedroom. The large room had enough space for her queen-sized bed and the flat-screen TV on the wall opposite. In the bay window she'd arranged a loveseat, small table, and reading lamps. This was her haven, her refuge from the world. Olivia was old school. Although she liked the ease of traveling with her Kindle, at home she preferred curling up with stacks of books and magazines, and of course her favorite movies from the thirties and forties—Charlie Chan, Mr. Moto, and *The Thin Man*. Somehow, those times seemed more relaxed. She realized there was nothing stress-free about the Depression or a world war. But in the movies, at least, everything was slower paced and seemed easier.

She opened her book and settled on the small sofa to read. She got lost in the novel and was actually surprised a while later when she heard his voice.

"Hello, Olivia." Steven stood in the hallway smiling. Tonight he wore soft gray corduroy trousers, a white dress shirt–collar unbuttoned and open–and a wool cardigan with two front pockets.

"Hi!" She rose and went to the door. "What's that you've got?" she asked, noticing a newspaper in his hand.

"It's today's paper. I thought you might be interested, what with the research you do and all."

"Cool! Thank you, Steven. That's really thoughtful. Actually, I was a journalist before I started my business. I'd *love* to read today's paper."

She reached out into the doorway and he handed her a fresh clean copy of *The Gazette* dated Sunday, February 25, 1934. *One more piece of proof,* she thought. *Go, Einstein!*

The headline shouted:

MURDER AT THE BANK

On Saturday morning, February 24, the bludgeoned body of Leo Castleman was found in the vault of the First National Bank and Trust Company. The 44-year old bank manager was discovered lying on the floor, still wearing his heavy overcoat. Assistant manager John Harrison came across the victim when he opened the vault to prepare for the morning's business.

Knightsbridge Police Chief Andy Thompson stated that there appears to be a substantial sum of money missing from the vault. The police found two partly empty Brinks delivery bags near the body. Thompson told this reporter that it is too early to speculate on anything. He added that the case is in the capable hands of Detective Sergeant Steven Blackwell, who has been with the department for a number of years. Blackwell is being assisted by Detective Harry Beckman.

Castleman's widow, Mrs. Patricia Castleman, was unavailable for comment.

Olivia's eyes grew large. "You're working on a murder case?"

He shook his head sadly. "It's terrible. Mr. Castleman was a nice man. An important man, too."

Olivia decided to sit down. Hopefully they'd be there a while. She had a lot of questions. "So you're a detective. Do you like it?"

Steven sat on his side of the doorway and his face lit up when he replied, "Yes, I do. This is the *best* time to be a cop!"

"Why do you say that?"

"We have what they call the Bureau of Investigation. It's in Washington, D.C. The man in charge—his name is Hoover..."

"Oh, I know him. J. Edgar Hoover?"

He gave her a surprised look. "You still know the name, huh?"

"Sure, he's sort of a legend."

"Mr. Hoover thinks police work should be a science. He set up a federal crime lab in Washington, D.C. a couple of years ago. All the police stations around the country can send evidence to be analyzed. We do our bit to help, too. We mail in statistics on the different kinds of crime we deal with. I don't know what they're doing with that information but..." He shrugged. "And you know what else? They're putting together a file of fingerprints from all across the country. It's exciting. It's going to change police work forever."

"Cool! I guess it *is* a good time to be a cop."

"So, Olivia, how come I only see *you* in my house? Where's your family?"

"I live here by myself."

His mouth fell open. "All alone? In this big house?"

"Yes, it's not unusual. A lot of women live alone. I'm single. I make decent money."

"You bought the house?"

"Sort of. I grew up here. My parents moved to California a few years ago and I moved back to town. We have an arrangement so that eventually I'll own it."

"I see." He was quiet a moment. "What day is it where you are?"

"Sunday, February 23rd."

"It's Sunday here, too. Only the 25th." He looked away a moment and gave an embarrassed laugh. "I guess you can see that," he said, pointing to the paper.

"We must be moving in a sort of parallel direction. Have you told anyone?"

"Are you kidding? Artie would think I'm nuts and Becks would probably lock me up in one of the cells. Don't tell me you have?"

She nodded. "My two best friends."

"Why?"

"I needed to make sure I wasn't going crazy. I always talk things out with them."

"What'd they say? I see you're not locked up yet."

She laughed. "Right! At first they were scared for me—you know, a strange guy in the house in the middle of the night—but I think I convinced them." She waved the newspaper at him. "And this will go a long way in proving what's happening." She set the paper aside. "So, what do you do when you're not working? Do you play sports?"

"Not in the winter. I read a lot. But when the weather's nice, I like to go for a drive on a Sunday afternoon. I have a Chevy," he stated with pride. "She's beautiful. Dark green sedan. And she handles like a dream."

"Awesome. I like exploring. Sometimes when I'm out driving I take a turn just to see where it goes."

"You have an automobile? Is that common in 2014? For women, I mean."

"Oh, yeah," she nodded. "What else do you enjoy doing?"

"I like baseball. The New York Yankees! That's my team. And I play, too. The fellas at the station put together a team every year. We play all spring and summer." He sighed. "What about you? What do women do in the twenty-first century?" His jaw dropped. "I can't believe I said that. It feels like I'm in a Jules Verne novel."

She laughed and hummed the theme to *The Twilight Zone*. "Oh, sorry. It's the song to a science-fiction-y kind of show. To answer your question, things have changed a lot in eighty years. According to my mom, it all started back in the sixties. She said that she never even owned a pair of jeans until she was in college."

"Jeans?"

"Oh, um, denim pants?"

"You mean like what farmers wear?"

"Yes but no. The same material but they're like…fashion…you know, stylish."

It was clear by the look on his face that he did not understand a word she was saying. Olivia jumped up and grabbed her laptop. She googled images of jeans and turned the screen so he could see. His eyebrows flew up and his eyes popped. "That's not at all like farmer's dungarees. They're quite…eh…tight."

"Yeah, well there are all kinds of styles. Everyone wears them. Men, women, kids." She closed the cover but left the computer in her lap. "So basically, I guess women had had enough of having to stay home and wash and cook and clean. They sort of revolted."

"A women's revolution?" He laughed. "You're kidding, right?"

"Not like a war revolution. More like a protest. Like when women wanted to vote, weren't there demonstrations and stuff?"

"Oh, I see."

"Most women work now. We don't live with our parents after college. We take off and travel whenever we want to. We're freer. We have the same choices that men have. It's more equal."

"My mother would have loved 2014. She was very free-spirited. So, Olivia, what do *you* like to do when you're not working?"

"I practice a sport called kickboxing. It's great exercise. And I can use it for self-defense, too, if I ever need to."

"I don't think I've ever heard of it."

"I'll show you some time. Let's see...what else? I've always loved books. I read a lot. Actually I'm doing something different tomorrow. I'm going to volunteer at the history museum. My friend Liz works there. A local woman, a Miss Sinclair, died last month and she left all of her belongings to the Historical Association. I'm going to help Liz catalog stuff for the exhibit. I'm psyched."

"Did you say Sinclair? That's funny. I have a friend named Artie Sinclair. That's a coincidence."

"Wow, it is! Maybe she was related to your friend. She was ninety-four. Let's see." She did the math. "If she was ninety-four when she passed away, in 1934 she would have been around fourteen. Her name was Annabel Sinclair."

"Annie! That's Artie's daughter."

They stared at each other.

"Steven, this feels *strange*. This woman's a direct connection between us. She's *real*. A real person who lived long enough to span the gap between your time and mine." Olivia let out a breath. "I can't take this in."

"*You* can't take it in? I saw Annie at church this morning. She's a normal fourteen-year-old kid with freckles. And she's crazy about movie stars." Steven laughed. "She keeps this scrapbook with all the newspaper and magazine clippings that she can get her hands on. She's got pictures of Jean Harlow and Greta Garbo, Clark Gable and Robert Barrat. All of her heroes' pictures are pasted in that scrapbook. She's quite a kid. Lately she's been talking about becoming a teacher."

"Miss Sinclair was a history teacher. Oh my goodness! Steven, I think it's the same person. Should I find out?"

He looked troubled then whispered, "It never occurred to me that you'd tell me something about someone I know." He considered his answer. "Yes, I guess now that it's come up, I do want to know. But only about Annie. I don't want to know anything else. I suppose it's comforting to know she'll have a long, happy life. *Was* she happy?"

"I think so. She was one of the most popular teachers we ever had—kind of a local legend. She made learning fun. The kids loved her. Yes, I think she was very happy." Olivia saw mixed emotions run over his face. "I'm sorry if you're upset about Annie, Steven."

"It was a shock, that's all. This just became very real."

MONDAY – 1934

Chapter 12

Steven could see nothing but his own image staring back when he turned his head to look out the window. Thick, whirling snow filled the air and heavy clouds covered the dark sky. In the quiet, near-empty police station, he leaned back in his chair mentally preparing for the morning meeting. Whenever he was working a case, Steven looked forward to getting his men together each day to update them on the progress being made and give everyone an opportunity to share case-related, as well as what he called *unofficial,* information.

The problem was people lied during an investigation. Some lies were, of course, made up by the guilty parties to save themselves from being arrested for crimes they had actually committed. But many were about things not connected to the case. They were stories and exaggerations about insignificant or imagined events. People told lies to cover up embarrassing actions. They created distorted impressions of a potential suspect not because he or she was guilty, but because of a long-standing feud or a past offense. A person might lie to protect a loved one or because he simply didn't want to get involved. So many people lied to the police, and for so many reasons.

Steven believed that an effective way to counteract all this deceit was to know the community as well as possible. This was where the cop on the beat played a crucial role. He saw people every day, spoke with the shopkeepers and businessmen. He provided valuable insights and background information on the cast of characters that made up an investigation. Steven eagerly anticipated the briefings, always wondering what the patrolmen on his team would have to tell him.

The policemen came in one by one and in small groups, removing their heavy winter jackets, stowing their lunch pails, laughing, and talking.

"That was some blizzard!"

"Still haven't finished shoveling."

"That Amos and Andy really get me."

At eight o'clock, the men gathered in the crowded patrol room, which already smelled of smoke, coffee, and wet socks. They sat on the few available chairs, perched on the corners of desks, and stood against the walls. Most wore their dark blue uniform and held a cup in one hand and a cigarette in the other.

Steven finished reporting what they'd accomplished over the weekend and was now summing up. "We don't have a lot to go on yet. No footprints. No usable fingerprints. The few we got all belong to bank employees who are authorized to be where the prints were found." He paused and took a drink of his coffee. "Now, the fragment of ebony that Doc Elliott recovered from the wound will be significant when we find the murder weapon. That's something we all need to be on the lookout for in the next couple of days."

"Ebony's not very common," said a burly patrolman.

"I don't know if I've ever even seen anything made out of that. It's black, right?" asked a young officer holding up the back wall.

"That's right. We've got to be aware of anything made out of black wood," Steven answered. "As always, I want everyone to pay attention to the conversations that you have, the conversations you overhear, and the impressions you get from what someone is *not* saying. You're all out and around town every day. You fellas on the beat, stop and pass the time of day with folks. Get people talking. Who's been complaining more than usual about money? Is somebody in the middle of a financial crisis?"

Laughter at this. A couple of hoots and "Yeah, me." Steven smiled and nodded. The Depression had hit hard. People were struggling.

He continued, "Information like that will go a long way to building a motive for the robbery aspect of this case. However, having said that, I believe there has to be more than money involved here. You know what I always say: love and money. Two of the most powerful motives for murder.

"What do we know about the Castlemans' marriage? When Becks and I were at the house yesterday, the widow didn't seem to be grieving very much. Is she having an affair? Has she been seen with another man?

"Also, why was Leo Castleman in the vault in the middle of the night? In a blizzard no less. Who knew he'd be there? Think about those things as you go about your day. And for the next several days. Let's start putting together a picture of the people involved here.

"Now, for today..." He gave out Monday's assignments.

The meeting broke up. Chairs scraped across the floor as the men got to their feet and prepared to work. The room buzzed with speculation. Everyone was excited at the beginning of a case. There was the thrill of the chase. Each man had his own ideas of how to ferret out information. They'd ask their friends, their brothers, their uncles, and cousins.

Will Taylor was especially pleased with his assignment. Steven put a lot of trust in his ability to read people. He'd enjoy spending time with folks today, listening to what they had to say about the robbery and murder, delving into the histories, connections, and relationships they'd had with the victim.

Jimmy Bou grabbed his partner for the day and asked him to map out a route to the businesses they had to visit while he made some telephone inquiries.

"I'll be at the bank for a good part of the day," Steven said to Becks. "If we miss each other, I'll see you here later. We can go over what we've got and update the board."

"Sounds good."

Becks shrugged into his coat, adjusted the angle of his hat, and headed out the door.

Steven drove to the crime scene, parked against a snow pile, and climbed the front steps. The lock clicked as Eddie Littleman let him enter. Inside, the tellers were getting ready for business. Steven heard the ruffling of bills and an occasional *thunk* as someone struck a roll of coins on a hard edge to break the paper wrapper, then the sound of quarters, nickels, pennies, and dimes spilling into the compartments of the drawers.

Steven went up to John Harrison's office and stood a couple of steps inside the room. The banker was reading some papers, head bent low over his desk. He had dressed impeccably again today in a navy double-breasted wool suit, fresh white shirt, and crimson silk tie. Every hair was in place due to a liberal amount of Hair Slik. Steven watched as he pretended to be absorbed in his work. After what seemed like a long time Harrison looked up, squinting slightly, lips pursed, jaw tight.

"Yes, Officer?"

Steven let the intended insult slide. "I'll be using the meeting room to conduct interviews this morning, John. I'll need to talk with you later in the day."

The banker acknowledged this with a curt nod and returned to his paperwork.

Steven crossed the marble-floored lobby, skirting the brass-legged, glass-topped tables with their pigeon holes full of deposit and withdrawal slips. He found Henry August in one of the tellers' cages, verifying his drawer count.

"I need a few minutes of your time, Mr. August. Come with me, please."

Henry August was a white-haired man with faded green eyes. It was not yet ten o'clock on a Monday morning and already he looked tired. Steven was soon to discover that *tired* was the perfect description of August.

Indeed, the old man was exhausted—tired of the monotony of decades on the job, of scrimping and saving to make ends meet, tired of the Depression and life in general. The poor man fairly sagged in his chair. Before he even began his questions, Steven doubted that this man had the energy to fight a storm in the middle of the night, to say nothing of having the strength to wield a piece of wood forcefully enough to kill someone.

"I understand you've worked at the bank since you were nineteen, Mr. August. That's quite an accomplishment."

"Yep, right out of high school," he said, looking Steven in the eye. "Wet behind the ears I was. But I stuck with it and learned the job," he added proudly. He slumped back in his seat and grumbled, "By all rights, I should be head teller now. But Mr. Castleman gave Marty Carpenter that job two, three years ago. And him not even fifty."

Steven shook his head in camaraderie.

"Never did understand that, myself. Wasn't right. I've been here more 'n forty-eight years. Loyalty and experience should count for something. A man gives his life to a company. They should notice that."

"I agree. Are you having money problems?"

"Not if I keep workin'. We're managin' okay but it's real hard these days. The wife is good with her budget but we lost almost everything in the crash."

For a minute Steven thought August was going to cry. The old man rubbed his large-knuckled fist into rheumy eyes and went on. "They'll be takin' me out of this place, feet first. You mark my words. I'll never get to rest. That's what I need more'n anything right now. Some rest."

Steven took the teller through the usual questions. Do you know of anyone who hated Leo Castleman? Can you tell me anything about the relationship between the victim and his wife? Are you aware of any financial problems that Castleman had?

Henry August couldn't shed a light on anything. He never listened to gossip. He had rarely interacted with the bank manager. He did his job and went home. He could add nothing to what Steven already knew.

As the meeting room door closed behind him, Steven considered the man further. There was a good deal of resentment toward Leo Castleman over the loss of the promotion. And resentment builds up over time. What had he said? Two or three years ago? Henry August goes into work every day, every week, for years and sees somebody else in the position he feels should be his, getting the extra pay he thinks he deserves. That's a lot of bitterness and anger as well. Though August had seemed in fair control of the anger, Steven admitted to himself. Strong emotion can give a man strength. But would it be enough to battle that storm and wield the fatal blow? Maybe. Steven revised his earlier opinion and kept Henry August on the list of suspects.

He called Carl Dickson next. Steven introduced himself, showing his badge and ID.

"Detective, I'm sorry to meet you under these circumstances. I've heard good things about your work. I'll be happy to help any way I can."

Sitting across from the accountant, Steven marveled at the fact that, in a town the size of Knightsbridge, he had never run into this man before today. He certainly would have noticed him if their paths had crossed. Well, unless the man was wearing a hat.

Carl Dickson was of average height though slightly stooped, probably from leaning over ledger books for twenty years. He had long fingers and strong-looking hands. What was noticeable and, Steven thought, almost laughable was his hair. The man looked like a skunk. He was aging in the most unfortunate way possible. His thick, black hair was separated right down the middle by a strip of pure white. Poor fella.

"I understand you and Marty are responsible for the deliveries."

"Yes, with the two of us it creates a system of checks and balances."

"Take me through the procedure you follow when you're expecting a delivery."

"Sure. When the Brinks truck arrives with the money we've ordered, one of the guards gives Marty or me the invoice. That's a list of every cent that's delivered. There's a record of the denominations and the serial numbers of the bills. For rolls of coins, the amount is noted and the way it's divided up. So we know exactly what we have." He looked expectantly at Steven then continued. "We both count everything to make sure the order's complete, then we cross-check with the figures on the invoice."

"When was the last delivery?"

"Friday morning. There were two bags totaling just under $50,000.

It was mostly ones and fives, with some ten- and twenty-dollar bills. It's payday this week for most of the businesses. Plus we've got that big bridge project down on Route 5. That makes for a lot of cash."

"We'll need to know exactly how much was taken and what denominations. And I'll need the serial numbers from all the missing bills."

"Sure, we figured you'd want that. Marty and I are planning on spending the next few hours going through everything. We'll have all the information later today. Is that okay?"

"Perfect. Give the station a call and we'll send someone over to get it." Steven shifted in his chair, took a beat pretending to consult his notebook then said, "Now, Carl, where were you Friday night?"

Dickson looked taken aback. His brown eyes widened. The bookkeeper had clearly thought the interview was over.

"Friday. Oh...eh...of course. Home. I was home all night."

"Can anyone confirm that?"

"Oh, sure," he appeared to relax and leaned back in his chair. "My roommate. I live with my cousin. He'll tell you I was home."

Steven raised his eyebrows. "And where can I find your cousin today?"

Steven wrote down the man's name and place of employment then rose from the table instructing Dickson to send in Martin Carpenter.

Business at the bank had been brisk all morning. The line in front of Henry August seemed to never end. Naturally his customers were curious. Everyone wanted to talk about the murder, on this of all days, when he was so close. The interview with the police had shaken the teller badly. His hands still trembled, he dropped coins and grabbed bills that all seemed to stick together. He was distracted and had to count everything two or three times to be sure that he got the amounts right.

Why had he done it? And the timing! He squeezed his eyes shut and groaned inwardly. My God, the timing couldn't be worse. Had Leo found out? Had he told anyone? August wished he were dead.

Chapter 13

As Carl Dickson passed through the lobby after his interview with Detective Sergeant Blackwell, he noticed that Henry August looked paler than usual. The teller seemed flustered as he counted out a stack of one-dollar bills and piled them in front of a customer. Dickson absently wondered why the farmer's wife would need to withdraw so much money at one time. That was more than most men made in a week. Well, none of his business. He had other things on his mind today.

Funny how the interview had made him nervous. As soon as Detective Blackwell began questioning him, he'd felt the urge to lie. What the hell. The police didn't need to know everything, did they? Forget it. Blackwell had a reputation for being sharp. He'd figure it out. Best to let the police get on with it. Besides, he had more pressing things to do this morning.

Dickson had put one foot on the staircase to the mezzanine when he heard her voice. He turned and watched as she stopped at one of the brass tables. The accountant slowly reversed direction and casually approached her.

"Good morning," he said then leaned in and whispered, "The police are here asking questions about Friday night. We need to talk."

"Of course, they are." She continued to write out the deposit slip, refusing to look up at him.

"Can I see you tonight?"

"I don't think that's such a good idea." She finished her chore and left the pen hanging by its chain. It swung back and forth under the edge of the glass surface.

"But..."

"I'll call you when things die down. Do not contact me." She glared at him. "You're going to ruin everything."

Head teller Marty Carpenter ambled into the meeting room, leaned over to shake hands, and sat down. Steven had known him since childhood. He'd been friends with Marty's younger brother.

"Steven, good morning. This is such a thing to happen. I can't imagine what Leo was thinking! How could he do something like this? Then, of course, to be killed like that. It's unbelievable."

Carpenter was a smallish, rawboned man with bowed legs. Steven had always thought he looked like he belonged on a dude ranch, had pictured him riding horses and roping cows, wearing a cowboy hat over his balding head. But the thick glasses didn't suit the cowpoke image. Steven quickly curtailed his imagination and began the interview.

Marty confirmed the delivery procedure.

"What can you tell me about Leo Castleman's relationship with the employees?"

"Good, Steven, real good. Leo was a square guy. He treated everybody fair. He listened if you had a gripe or if there was a problem." Carpenter looked away a moment.

Steven knew the look. He made it a policy to give people time to make the right decision and tell him whatever it was they knew. He remained silent.

"I'll be honest, Steven. I've had some money problems. After Mom and Dad left me the house, I met with Leo to fix a schedule of mortgage payments I could manage. I still owe some. Not a lot, but the way things are these days, anything seems like a lot." He leaned forward, his eyes boring into Steven. "That house means everything to me. My parents worked all their lives to be able to afford a house of their own. I can't lose it."

"I understand, Marty. And I've seen what you've done to your place. You do beautiful work."

"Thanks. Well, a couple of times in the past few years, Leo gave me an extension on my monthly payment when I ran into trouble. He was real understanding. Always helped people." He scowled. "Now, Harrison. That's another story. I hope he doesn't get Leo's job. Although I don't know who else would." He brightened as he thought of an alternative solution. "Maybe they'll send somebody from the main office to take over. Boy, I hope so."

"Why do you say that?"

"Come on, Steven. You know John Harrison. He hasn't changed one bit from the snot that he was in school. Only cares about himself. He won't understand people's problems like Leo did." Carpenter considered a future with Harrison. "Jeez, I hope they send somebody from Syracuse. Otherwise, this place'll never be the same."

"Marty, I've got to ask…where were you Friday night?"

"You're kidding, right?"

"No, I'm not. You know we have to ask everybody these questions."

"No, that's not what I meant. I understand that. I mean the blizzard. Who in their right mind would've been out Friday night? I was home, Steven. All night. Didn't even walk the dog, it was so bad out."

"Okay, that's it for now." Steven stood. "Thanks for being straight. I appreciate it."

"Hey, we go back a long way. Anything I can do to help you with this." He paused with one hand on the doorknob. "Steven, there's gotta be some explanation. Leo was a good man. He sure didn't deserve what he got."

Steven decided to speak with Castleman's private secretary next. He climbed to the mezzanine where the executive offices were located. As soon as he reached the top step and turned, he wished that he'd worn sunglasses.

Ginny Fitzgerald sat poised at her typewriter looking like the burning bush—red wool coat sweater with a wide, shawl collar; red wool, pleated skirt; fiery copper, shoulder-length hair blazing like it was only a matter of time before the entire office went up in flames. The one thing that broke up this wall of fire was a delicate porcelain complexion.

Stunning. It should be overwhelming, this total effect of red, *but it isn't.*

At that moment Steven thought she was one of the most beautiful women he had ever seen. He'd seen her around town, of course, and he knew her well enough to say hello and pass the time of day. He'd always thought she was pretty but somehow sitting here straight-backed and regal, reminding him of those alabaster statues of Egyptian cats, she looked magnificent. He idly wondered if she was stepping out with anyone. How had he never noticed her?

"Excuse me, Miss Fitzgerald?"

Ginny stopped typing and her eyes filled with tears. *Aha,* Steven thought, *someone else who cared for the man.*

"Would you come to the meeting room so we can talk privately?"

She sniffed, dabbed her eyes with a hankie, and nodded.

When they'd settled, Steven said, "You were fond of Mr. Castleman?"

"He...he was my godfather. He was such a good man. I don't believe what they're all whispering."

"What are they whispering?"

"That Uncle Leo was stealing money from the vault when…when…it happened."

"You called him *Uncle* Leo?"

"Yes, he wasn't really. He was my father's best friend. I've known him my whole life."

"Miss Fitzgerald, Ginny, you can be a big help. Tell me about your godfather. What was he like?"

"He was kind and understanding. Always trying to help people. Like after the stock market crash, sometimes customers came in for a loan or an extension on their mortgage. He tried to help even if the banking guidelines said he shouldn't. He would bend the rules a little if it would help people get back on their feet or stay in their house."

Bend the rules. The words caused Steven to consider the possibility that Castleman had intended to take the money to help a desperate client. That was an angle he hadn't thought of.

"I thought that was wonderful. And you know, not one person defaulted? Everyone kept up their payments. I know because I keep track of the paperwork." She dried her eyes and blew her nose. "The only person I can think of who asked for an extension and didn't get it was Marty Carpenter. Uncle Leo said no because he'd already given Marty a couple." Ginny was regaining her composure.

Steven made a couple of notes then said gently, "This next question is a bit delicate. Understand, Ginny, that we have to know everything about the people involved in a crime. Whether they're the victim or a suspect."

"Okay."

"How would you describe your Uncle Leo's marriage? Were they close, your godfather and Mrs. Castleman?"

"I don't know. They didn't really act like a married couple. And I didn't see them together very often. My mom thinks Patricia was just using Uncle Leo. She says Patricia never loved him."

"What do you think, Ginny?"

"Maybe. I never saw her hold his hand or look at him in that way, you know?"

Steven nodded. "Yes, I know what you mean. What about your godfather's feelings for Patricia?" he asked.

"He was crazy about her. Anything Patricia wanted, she got. He was always buying her clothes and jewelry. Even now when some people can hardly pay their mortgage. Uncle Leo would do anything for Patricia. All she had to do was ask."

"Did they ever socialize with your family? Come over for a meal or an evening?"

"My mother used to invite them for dinner but Patricia always gave an excuse why they couldn't come. I know they went to public functions, like dinners and banquets, but they never came to our house."

"What about Patricia's friends?"

"I don't think she has any."

"What does she do with her time?"

"She spends most of it on herself. She has her hair done and her nails. And she shops. She shops *a lot.* She goes to see her sister sometimes. Oh, wait, I'm lying! She visits a friend in Saratoga. But I don't know who it is."

"I see. Coming back to the whispers you spoke of. Do you know why your Uncle Leo might need a lot of money?"

"No. There has to be an explanation. He would *never* take money from the bank."

Steven told Ginny he'd be in touch and cautioned her not to discuss what they had talked about.

As the door closed behind her, Steven looked at his watch. Already twelve o'clock. He decided to go back to the station. He'd return later to re-question Connor MacIntyre and tackle Harrison.

Chapter 14

Beckman was enjoying a profitable morning. He'd started at number 316 Victoria Avenue where John Franklin opened the door slowly then, seeing the badge and ID, swung it wide open.

"Come in. Come in, Officer."

"Thank you, Mr. Franklin. I'm Detective Harry Beckman."

"Oh, sure. I know who you are. Seen you around town with Steven Blackwell. You're here about the murder. Come on back to the kitchen. I was about to have my second cup of coffee. Have some and set a spell."

Beckman followed the older man through the dusty living room and cobweb-filled hallway into a kitchen in need of a good scrubbing. Franklin quickly said, "I'm not much of a housekeeper. My good wife Eleanor, God rest her soul, always did a bang-up job keeping the house clean. Could eat off her floors, you could. She's probably turning over in her grave knowing the mess this place is in."

Beckman tried to protest but Franklin talked right over him.

"My niece comes once a month to help me out and give the place a real good goin' over. She'll be here tomorrow as a matter of fact." He grimaced. "And not a day too soon, huh? Well, you get used to things. Not much else you can do." He poured a cup of coffee and set it on the kitchen table, pushed over the sugar bowl and milk bottle.

When they'd both taken a drink, Beckman asked if Franklin had seen anyone going in or out of the bank Friday night.

"Well, no. I am very sorry to say that for once I actually slept through the night. Of all nights, don't'cha know. Normally I'm up at least once or twice."

Beckman's hopes fell and he was annoyed at himself for sitting down before finding out the man had nothing to tell him.

"But, I have two things to say about this business. Number one is I've known Leo Castleman for years and I don't believe he would steal money from his own bank. If you're telling me that's what happened, then all I have to say is he must've had a powerful reason why. Leo's one of the most honest men I've ever had the pleasure of knowing. If he did do this, he must've thought he had no other choice. Musta' been something like life and death. So, that's that," he pronounced.

"And the second thing is…," he took a drink of his coffee, "…lucky for Mrs. Castleman that John is such a good friend of the family. She'll need some support now."

"John? John who?"

"Harrison. Leo's assistant manager."

"How do you know this, Mr. Franklin?"

"Well, one time last year. Lemme see. It must'a been late March or early April, I saw 'em havin' lunch together. My Eleanor was in the hospital the last few weeks before she passed. One day she was having tests, so I decided to get some fresh air. You know what hospital air is like." He settled back and stretched out his legs. "So I took a walk down to that little restaurant. You know the one? It's out-of-the-way, over on Warwick, down the road from the hospital. Mrs. Callahan runs it."

Beckman thought the man would never get to the point. "Yes?" he said encouragingly.

"Mother's Kitchen, that's the name. Anyways, I went in to get a bite to eat and there they were. Mrs. Castleman and John Harrison. The place was empty. Don't know how she stays in business. Anyhow, I said hello and she introduced him as a family friend. That's it really."

"Did you ever say anything to Mr. Castleman about having seen them?"

"No, I doubt it. Probably not. Didn't give it a thought. She says he's a friend o' the family, so he's a friend o' the family. Didn't mean nothin' to me. My wife was dying, Detective. I had a lot on my mind."

"Was that the only time you saw them together?"

"Yeah, I think so. Why? Are you suggesting something irregular?"

"No, not at all. We have to be thorough." Beckman put away his notebook. "You've been a great help. Thank you for your time. And for the coffee. If you think of anything else, please call the station. You never know when even the smallest bit of information can turn out to be important."

"Of course I will, son. Of course. I'll see you out."

So far, so good, thought Beckman, as he made his way along Victoria.

The day was still cloudy, but the snow had stopped and the air smelled clean. He was glad to be out of the station for the morning, able to walk around town. Several times along the way people stopped him. Some were friends, some he didn't know. They all had a question or a comment about the murder and the rumor that Leo Castleman had been stealing money from the bank. Beckman skillfully sidestepped the questions and made mental notes of the comments. He arrived at Herb Steadman's modest home shortly before ten thirty, waded through piles of snow on the front walk, and climbed the icy steps.

Steadman answered the door and invited the policeman inside. Beckman kicked the snow off his boots and followed him into the living room. The newspaperman was in his late forties. He was tall and robust and had a full head of chestnut-brown hair. Intelligent, blue eyes looked like they didn't miss a trick.

"I imagine you want to know what I saw at the bank Friday night. Is that right, Detective?"

"You saw something?"

"Yes, I did. I was surprised when nobody came over yesterday. I left a message at the station."

"I'm sorry, sir. What was the message?"

"I called Sunday morning after I heard everyone talking about what happened. I spoke with Officer O'Laughlin. Told him I'd seen a man go into the bank in the middle of the night. He said he'd pass the information to the officer in charge of the case."

Beckman seethed inside. *Damn that Frank! Again! How many times is he going to screw up before the chief fires him?*

"I see. I'm sorry but I didn't get the message, Mr. Steadman. Would you mind telling me what you saw?"

"Sure. I took my supper break at two in the morning like I always do. The table in our break room is under a window that looks out on the back entrance to the bank. I was having my dinner and I noticed a man go in the alley door. He was big and husky. Bundled up in a heavy overcoat, hat, and scarf of course, because of the weather. Couldn't see his face, though, because his back was to me."

"How could you see with all the snow flying around?"

"The bank's not far away because the alley's pretty narrow. And every now and then a gust of wind would clear the snow out of the way so it was easy to see what he looked like. I mean his shape, you know."

Becks nodded and made a note.

Steadman thought some more. "He was carrying a small case. 'Bout a foot high, maybe two feet wide. Bigger than a briefcase. He had something else in his hand but I couldn't tell what it was. He took what I suppose was a key out of his pocket. He opened the door and went in."

"Then what happened, Mr. Steadman?"

"Nothing. That was the odd thing. Nothing happened. The alarm didn't go off. At the time, I figured it *was* Mr. Castleman because of his size and he seemed to have a key. I thought maybe there was some kind of emergency he had to take care of. I don't really know what that would be but…"

"Sure, I can see how you'd think that."

"It was about then that one of the fellas came into the break room and we got talking. I didn't give it another thought. I forgot about it until I heard what happened. First thing I did was call the station. When nobody came over, I figured my information wasn't important."

"I apologize for the mix-up, sir. Did you see anyone else go into the bank?"

"No, I finished my dinner and went back to work."

Beckman asked about the lighting conditions in the alley and how Steadman had been able to see in the middle of the night. Herb explained that there was a fixture which lit up the area around the door.

"And before you ask me, no, I don't need glasses," added the newspaperman astutely.

Beckman grinned. "Thanks, Mr. Steadman. Again, I'm sorry I didn't get your message. Can you come over later to make a formal statement? We need to get it in writing and have you sign it."

"Sure. When do you want me to go? I'm off today. I can go anytime."

Beckman remembered that Frank was working.

"Whenever it's convenient for you. But, when you get there, ask to speak with Chief Thompson. Tell the officer at the front desk that I told you to ask for the chief. I'll call ahead and let him know you're coming. He'll put you in touch with someone who can take your statement."

"Sure thing. I'll go over in a bit."

Beckman stood and extended his hand. "Thank you again, sir. I appreciate you taking the time with this."

"Of course, Detective. Why wouldn't I? It's what anyone would do."

Beckman strode down Maple Avenue toward the Texaco station on the corner. A sign on the edge of the property announced that a gallon cost ten cents. He saw his neighbor pumping gas and shouted a greeting. The man waved and continued to fill the tank of a spectacular Packard Twin Six. For a moment Beckman felt weak in the knees. *What I wouldn't do for an automobile like that.* The luxury motor car was a pristine white with trim the color of an expensive bottle of burgundy wine. It was a Phaeton and had whitewall tires and a fifth wheel that rode along the driver's side above the running board. He could see himself driving smartly along the streets of Knightsbridge, a good lookin' doll in the seat next to him. Beckman wondered momentarily who the owner was. Must be some rich guy passing through. If it was someone who lived here, he certainly would have noticed that baby.

He shook off the fantasy and focused on his reason for heading to the gas station. In front of the building near the tall, red Coca-Cola machine was a public telephone booth. He went in, closed the folding door, inserted a nickel into the slot, and dialed. When Frank O'Laughlin answered, he asked to be put through to Chief Thompson.

"Chief, I've got good news and bad news."

"Get to the point, Beckman, I'm busy."

"We've got a witness. One of the *Gazette* employees saw a man enter the bank in the middle of the night. I've got the description. And the fella was carrying a small case."

"Why are we finding out about this now?"

"Mr. Steadman—that's the newsman..."

"Yeah, I know Herb."

"Well, he called the station Sunday morning and told Frank." Beckman paused to let it sink in. "O'Laughlin never told anybody."

Beckman moved the receiver away from his ear as his boss exploded in anger. He gave it a couple of seconds then continued.

"Steadman's coming over to make a statement later today. I told him to ask for you."

"I'll handle it," the chief grumbled, then slammed down the receiver, making Beckman wish he had kept the telephone away from his ear until the very end of the call.

It was coming up on noon. Beckman checked his notebook and decided to swing by Ruth Hanover's house. After speaking with her mother, he'd return to the station for his lunch break. He'd go out again later to interview Mrs. MacIntyre and their neighbors. Beckman was saving Patricia Castleman for late in the afternoon.

The Hanovers lived in a two-story house on Second Street. Becks immediately saw that the woman who answered the door was Ruth's mother. She had the same magnificent aquamarine eyes and high cheekbones.

"Good morning, Mrs. Hanover. I'm Detective Harry Beckman with the Knightsbridge Police Department. Do you mind if I come in for a minute? I'd like to ask you some questions about Friday night."

"Of course, but I don't see how I can help." She led him along a runner of newspapers spread out over the carpet into a small cramped parlor. "Please, sit down. Is this about Mr. Castleman? Ruth was very upset when we heard the news."

Beckman ignored her comment. "I need to know if your daughter was home Friday night."

"Ruthie? Yes, of course she was. You're not suggesting she had something to do with that business?"

"No, ma'am. We have to know where everyone was when it happened. Was Ruth here all night long?"

"Yes, absolutely."

"How can you be sure? You would have been sleeping, wouldn't you?"

"Normally I would, yes. But Friday I must have eaten something for supper that didn't agree with me and...," she reddened. "I was in the bathroom all night long. If Ruth had gone out, I would've heard her. *And* seen her, for that matter."

"I see."

"For heaven sakes, Detective, who in their right mind would have been out during that blizzard? It was terrible. I heard the wind blowing so fierce I thought a tree was going to fall on the house." She paused to catch her breath then rushed on before Beckman could get a question out. "And another thing, why would our Ruthie hurt Mr. Castleman? Of all people! He's the one who gave her a job. And a teller's position at that! All the other tellers are men," she added proudly. "Mr. Castleman helped our family a great deal when he gave my daughter that job. We're doing okay but every little bit helps. No, Detective, you look somewhere else for the person who did this. Not at my Ruthie."

Earlier he and Steven had believed it unlikely that Ruth Hanover was strong enough to wield those fatal blows. Now her mother seemed to be taking away a motive. Beckman sensed she was telling the truth. He'd check some more but imagined her name fading from the list.

The police station walls were vibrating when Steven returned. Anger bounced off ceiling and floors. Shouts echoed in the corridors. Chief

Thompson was screaming at Officer Frank O'Laughlin. It mattered not one bit that he had closed his office door. Everyone in the station could hear. The hall and doorways were crowded with officers peeking out, avidly listening to the dressing-down. They all knew Frank was on borrowed time. They'd been talking about it for months. Everyone had been affected by the lousy job he did.

Suddenly it got quiet. All heads turned to Chief Thompson's office. Frank wrenched open the door, smashing it into the wall, threw his badge and ID on the floor, and stormed out to begin his six-week suspension.

Chapter 15

Patricia Castleman felt wonderful. The police were releasing her husband's body, so she could plan the funeral and get it out of the way before the weekend. She'd telephoned the funeral parlor and arranged an appointment with Maurice Gettman as soon as she got the news. Now she was putting the finishing touches on her carefully chosen outfit.

She'd selected a dark green tweed suit—black was simply too depressing on such a glorious day. As the fitted, calf-length skirt slid over her hips, the rich fabric of the lining whispered across her silk stockings. She tucked a paisley scarf in the neckline of the short, molded jacket, fastened pearl earrings, and slipped a gold bracelet on her wrist. She took last year's coat and cloche hat from the closet, chose a pair of soft leather gloves and matching envelope-style bag, into which she tucked a handkerchief, and made a mental note to be sure and use it when seated across from the funeral director. It would not do to neglect a show of emotion and distress on this sad occasion.

The peal of door chimes announced her taxi. Patricia took a final look in the full-length mirror and was satisfied.

"I am so very sorry for your loss, Mrs. Castleman," oozed Maurice Gettman, as he attempted to guide her to a chair. Patricia was disgusted by this man and moved to the side so that she did not have to touch him. He was everything she loathed in a man. He was stooped, thin, and had combed a few sparse strands of oily hair over a bald pate. *Ick. Let me get this done and get the hell out of this place before I'm sick.*

An hour later, the arrangements were made. Patricia insisted that the customary three-day wake followed by the funeral was too much. A wake on the day before the funeral was enough. After all, everyone already knew Leo was dead. The newspaper notice would inform them of the service times. Let people take the responsibility to rearrange their schedules if they wanted to pay their respects.

Patricia shocked the funeral director when she chose, not the top of the line as befitting Mr. Castleman's status in the community, but a casket in the middle price range. *Why waste all that money when you were only going to put the damn thing in the ground,* she thought.

The director was pleased, however, when she asked him to conduct the funeral on the premises. Leo had never been a religious man, she explained, had not attended church regularly. She did not think it appropriate to pretend otherwise. They discussed what Gettman would say and the music. Patricia remembered to feign a sniffle and dab her dry eyes with the handkerchief. She requested that he take care of the flowers and *any other details that I simply can't think of right now.*

What Patricia really wanted to do next was stop in The Three Lords for a nice big gin and tonic, but she forced herself to go straight home. She'd make one herself.

As soon as she'd kicked off her pumps and downed half of her cocktail, she called her sister.

"Patsy, how are you? Are you holding up all right?"

"You know me, I'm fine." She took a swig of her drink, the ice rattled. “I just got back from making the arrangements. Calling hours are Thursday afternoon and evening. The funeral’s Friday at two. We can’t go to the cemetery because the ground’s too hard to dig the grave. I guess when somebody dies in the winter they keep ‘em until spring. I don’t know. Never thought of this stuff before.”

“Don’t think of it now either. It’ll all be over soon and you can start putting your life back together. Do you have everything you need? What about money? We never had a chance to talk Saturday before you left. Will you be all right alone in the house?”

“Yeah, thanks. I’ve got enough money. And I’m used to being here by myself. Don’t worry.” She took another drink.

“Tom and I will do whatever you want. We can come Wednesday morning and stay through the weekend. Or he and the kids can come home without me. I could stay longer if you’d like that.”

“No, I have to get used to it sometime. Might as well be now. Come Wednesday night for dinner. You can plan on going home after the service Friday. That way it won’t ruin your weekend.”

“Patsy! How can you say that? Ruin my weekend?” She sighed. “Sometimes I don’t know how you think.”

Chapter 16

When all the hoo-ha had calmed down, Steven asked, "What was that all about, Becks?"

"Frank screwed up again."

"I figured that out by myself, partner."

Looking like the cat that got the cream, Beckman said, "We have a witness."

Steven's face lit up, his eyes popped, his jaw dropped. "Whoa! Who? What? Where?"

Becks laughed. "It was Herb Steadman. He saw a man the alley between the *Gazette* offices and the bank at two o'clock Friday night..."

"How is he so sure of the time?"

"That's when he always has his supper break."

Steven nodded.

"Anyway...he saw the man take something from his pocket and open the back door."

"He had a key," Steven concluded.

"I'd say so. Steadman also made a point of telling me that the bank alarm didn't go off."

"Knew how to shut down the system."

"Right. The description sounds like Leo Castleman—tall, husky. Steadman didn't see his face, though."

"How could he see at all?" Steve looked perplexed. "Between the pitch black night and the blizzard, I'm surprised he could see across the alley to say nothing of this kind of detail."

"I asked him about that. Said the light over the back door is bright and shines down on the entrance area. And he said the wind kept blowing snow away, so he had no trouble seeing."

"Finally, Becks! We finally caught a break in this case."

"Amen, brother. Oh, one other thing."

"There's more?" Clearly the heavens were smiling down on them today.

"Mr. Steadman said the fella was carrying a small case, maybe one by two." Becks illustrated the dimensions.

"That's not very big. Why would he have gone through all that trouble to take such a small amount of money?"

"Maybe he planned to take some and hide the rest. It'd be easy to stash some of it in his desk or a file cabinet. He'd think his office would be safe, wouldn't he?"

"Sure, if he hadn't been killed, we wouldn't have looked there right away."

Steven got up from his seat and strode to the murder board, eager to see their progress written in black and white.

"So how'd you do this morning?" Beckman asked.

"I talked with some of the bank tellers and Castleman's secretary, Ginny Fitzgerald. Possible motive for Henry August, he resents Marty Carpenter for being promoted over him. Possible motive for Marty as well, he's got money troubles."

"Don't we all," sighed Becks.

"Yes, but Marty is in danger of losing his house. And you know how much he loves that place. After he inherited the house from his parents, he realized he couldn't afford to keep paying the mortgage. Evidently he talked with Castleman who gave him a couple extensions but he *refused* Marty's latest request."

Steven wrote while he updated Becks.

M. Carpenter promoted over H. August. Motive AUGUST?

Carpenter's request mortgage help refused. Motive CARPENTER?

Conducting an investigation in a small town was tricky. You had to interview friends, neighbors, and relatives. For Steven there was never a question of where his loyalties laid: with the victim, always with the victim. He felt responsible for uncovering the truth, in this there was no room for sentiment. It was a shame Marty hadn't told him about Leo's refusal. Now Steven would have to re-question him. This time he wouldn't be so nice.

"I also questioned Carl Dickson, the accountant. I don't see anything there. We can talk to him again if something comes up. And Ginny Fitzgerald—she's Leo Castleman's goddaughter, did you know that?"

"She's a looker. Wonder if she's steppin' out with anybody."

Steven shook his head. "She's the one who told me about Marty's mortgage extension being rejected. She said that Castleman was a swell fella, everybody liked him... ."

"Everybody but one," Becks cocked his head, raised his eyebrows, and gave Steven a look.

Steven nodded in agreement. "I asked her about the Castlemans' marriage. Figured she'd have some insight. Her mother doesn't think Mrs. Castleman loved her husband. But, Leo was crazy about his wife, would do anything for her according to Ginny. She also said Patricia spends a lot of time and money on herself..."

"Like her Silver Arrow! That must've set Castleman back a pretty penny."

"What do you think about Harrison, Becks? What's his relationship with the widow?"

"Just because Mr. Franklin saw them together that one time doesn't necessarily make a relationship, Steven."

"It does if the lunch is in an out-of-the-way place. And if she introduced him as a family friend rather than someone her husband worked with. There's deceit there."

Murder cases created familiar patterns. Human beings seemed to forever be repeating themselves. Time after time, the motive was jealousy, revenge, or greed. There were variations but at the end of the day, not much changed. Once again, it looked like love and money were the reasons behind the crime.

"Let me see what I can get out of her this afternoon," Beckman said.

"Yeah, maybe I was too abrupt. You could try a softer approach. Women seem to tell you things."

"It's my charm and good looks!"

"Right, keep that Valentino reputation alive."

"Did you see this stuff here on your desk?" asked Beckman. "Someone came over from Doc Elliott's office and Gray Wilson stopped by."

Steven returned to his desk where he discovered the autopsy report and a stack of eight-by-ten, black-and-white photographs. He read through the ME's findings, selected the best shots of the crime scene, and taped them to the board. He continued to update their progress. Based on Beckman's assessment, he crossed off Ruth Hanover's name. Based on his own, he eliminated Ginny Fitzgerald.

"What do we know about Leo Castleman's character? By all accounts he was an honest, upright man. What pushes someone like that to steal? What would cause him to betray his principles *and* the trust the bank put in him? Jeez, Becks! It's got to be a powerful motive."

"We've gotta look into his finances. Maybe he was carrying a lot of debt. What if he was gonna lose his house?"

"But a bank manager must be able to falsify records. There has to be a way he could change information on paper to make it look like his affairs were in order, even if they weren't. Wouldn't that be easier than battling a blizzard in the middle of the night? Let's check the main office in Syracuse. Maybe they've got information the local branch doesn't."

"It sure would be harder to doctor the books fifty miles away."

"Damn! Look at the time. We'd better get cracking before the day's gone. While you're winning over the widow, Becks, I'll be at the bank."

Bright sunlight blinded him and Steven quickly shielded his eyes. The cold bit his face but the blue skies lifted his mood. He walked to his car with a jauntier step. He thought of Olivia. *I wonder what kind of day she's having. She'll be at the museum now, unpacking boxes, discovering all kinds of things.* He hoped that nothing would keep them from meeting tonight.

As John Harrison crossed the mezzanine to his office, he caught a glimpse of Steven entering the bank. He groaned silently. *Steven Blackwell. It had to be him on this case.*

The banker despised Steven, had done since they were kids. Until the Blackwells moved in, life hadn't been too bad for a child growing up in small-town Knightsbridge. Most of the kids were pretty much in the same boat. No one had a lot, but the majority had enough.

The Harrisons had less than most. They lived near the edge of town not far from the railroad tracks. Their house always looked like it needed a fresh coat of paint. John wore the same two pairs of pants and shirts to school every other week—wear one, wash one, his mother used to say. John was embarrassed by his father's menial job. Although he never thought about why he felt this way, deep down inside John always knew he deserved better.

Then one day Steven Blackwell and his fancy French mother and big deal Navy father came back to Mr. Blackwell's home town to live for good. They all knew she was some la-dee-dah artist from Paris but she was so nice that everyone liked her. The kids figured that The Admiral made buckets of money, but the family never showed off. Steven had lived all over the world and had met interesting and amazing people, but he was friendly with all the kids and never bragged about his experiences.

For reasons the young John Harrison could not understand, everything changed for him because of the Blackwells. Somehow the delicate balance of things had been disturbed. Jealousy and hatred began to grow. And they knew no bounds. The nicer Steven Blackwell tried to be to John Harrison, the more John loathed him. It became the singular focus of his life to make a lot of money, become someone important, and show them all.

Now, nearly twenty years later, the hatred was still alive and glowed like a burning coal in the pit of his stomach. Despite the fact that John had forged a successful career as a banker and had reached the level of assistant manager, what rankled more than anything was that Steven Blackwell still had power to make him feel *less.*

Harrison was working at his desk when Steven knocked on the frame of the open door and entered without permission. Steven had decided that if he was enough of an irritant to the man, Harrison might get frustrated and give something away. Steven was sure he knew more than he was saying. He'd see what this strategy would yield.

"Again, Officer? Can't you see I have work to do? With Leo gone, I have his job and my own." The banker heaved a sigh. "What is it now?"

"I'd like to know where you were Friday night, Mr. Harrison."

"In bed, asleep. Where else would I be?"

"I'm sure I don't know. Can someone verify that?"

"How dare you! You can't question my private life like that."

"In fact, I can, John. This is a murder investigation. We question everyone. About everything. Including you."

"No, Officer..."

"Actually, it's *Detective.* Detective Sergeant Blackwell." He studied Harrison's reaction. Good, he was starting to get under the man's skin.

"Well, *Detective,* no. No one can corroborate. I was alone."

"What is your relationship with Patricia Castleman?"

"I don't have a relationship with Mrs. Castleman. She is, or rather was, my boss's wife."

"But you know her."

"Of course, I know her. To say hello. She comes in to see Leo, or she did. I've had polite conversations with her. That's all."

"So you've never had lunch with her? In a restaurant? Say Mother's Kitchen?"

"No! Look, *Detective.* I have work to do. I didn't have anything to do with this. And I don't know anything about it. I've given you my time and answered your questions as a courtesy, but that's enough. I know my rights. I don't have to talk to you. Let me get back to my work."

"Sure, John. You can get back to work." Steven leaned over the massive desk, glared into the hard eyes, then smiled as if he had a secret. "I'll come back another time." He left the assistant manager boiling in his office.

Steven ran into his next interview on the stairs. "Mr. MacIntyre, I'd like another word, please. Let's go down to the meeting room."

He got right to the point, "You left something out of your earlier statement to Detective Beckman." Steven watched resignation crawl across the man's face.

"I suppose you'll be checking my alibi with Sarah?"

Steven nodded.

"She won't be able to verify it."

"Why is that?"

"Around one in the morning, I went downstairs to the kitchen. I couldn't sleep. I knew the police would be checking everybody's finances. I may as well tell you, Detective Blackwell, we're broke. A while back, two of my boys had scarlet fever. My youngest caught it first, then my seven-year-old." His eyes flooded, his voice broke. "We almost lost them."

As Steven listened, he thought, *this man didn't do it. He'd never take the chance of getting caught and being sent to prison. This is the kind of man who'd work day and night, give the last slice of bread to his children, and go hungry himself. He would not steal and kill.*

"While we were quarantined, there wasn't any money coming in. Last week, Mr. Castleman arranged a special loan for my family. I was so relieved, I can't tell you. It's not a lot but it's going to make all the difference for us. When Detective Beckman asked me about Friday night, I didn't know what to say. I don't have any proof, but I was sitting at the kitchen table trying to figure things out."

"What happens to the loan now?"

"Thank heavens, the paperwork's done! Ginny typed it up and I signed the agreement Friday morning. I don't see how that could change. I'm going to bring it up to Mr. Harrison tomorrow."

As MacIntyre returned to work, Steven thought, *fathers and sons. Was there any greater bond?*

Although Steven's father had been away for a good part of his childhood and teen years, he'd never felt that his dad had neglected him in any way. Even now, at thirty-three, Steven still kept the shoebox stuffed full of letters that his father had faithfully sent home.

These letters, lovingly hand-written, had created and nurtured a deep feeling of warmth and affection between father and son. They'd comforted the boy and contributed in a very real sense to his education. Steven's father told him about all the places where his job took him, managing to slip in lessons for a productive life without seeming to lecture. As his mother instilled in him her free-spirited nature, her open-mindedness, and her childlike sense of wonder, his dad had given him an understanding of rules and law and order. He had passed on to his only son an appreciation of the profound comfort one could get out of establishing daily routines, as well as the satisfaction that a certain amount of regimentation could bring to his life.

Steven adored his parents and would be forever grateful for the gifts they had given him. He was especially aware of the well-balanced blend of qualities he had inherited when he was working on a case. His mother had contributed to his ability to understand what made human beings tick and his dad had provided the tools to carry out the job.

Steven spent the rest of the afternoon writing his report and preparing paperwork to get a court order for Castleman's financial information. Night had fallen when Will Taylor and Jimmy Bourgogne checked in. He listened to the highlights and suggested they write their reports in the morning. By six thirty, Beckman still hadn't reappeared. Steven hoped that meant he'd broken the widow's silence and would have a lot to tell him. He tidied his desk, donned his outer gear, and turned off the lights.

A thrill went through Steven as he sat, waiting for the engine to warm up. Tonight. He was going to see her again tonight. He stomped on the clutch, threw the automobile into first, and headed home.

Across town a man sat in the dark. He had turned on no overhead light, no lamp, upon his return home. He'd loosened his tie and thrown his jacket on an overstuffed chair in the corner of the living room. Bile green in some awful nubby fabric. He'd always hated that chair. At least with the lights out he didn't have to look at it. He sprawled on one end of the sofa, feet, with his shoes still on, propped up on a long, low table. He was on his third Gibson; the cocktail onions sat on the table near his feet, having made him sick to the stomach. His face was blank. He sat and drank.

The sudden shrill ringing of the telephone shattered the silence in the house. He struggled to his feet, bumping the onions to the floor, where they rolled under the couch. He crossed the room and picked up the receiver, nearly knocking the square black base off the stand.

"Hello," he answered with a raspy voice.

"Hi. It's me."

"You're not supposed to call here. We agreed."

"I know. I just wanted to know…"

"Stick to the plan. We said no contact until things die down."

"But…"

"No," he hissed. "We made a plan. Stick to the damn plan. You're going to ruin it. We'll meet when we said we would. Don't call again."

He slammed the phone down and stumbled to the drinks cart, where he made another cocktail. He sat in the dark drinking until the glass fell from his hand and he passed out in the early morning hours.

MONDAY – PRESENT DAY

Chapter 17

Olivia jaywalked across Victoria toward Hickory, breathing in the clean winter air. It was a beautiful day—sunlight streamed through breaks in the clouds and the temperature had already warmed up to thirty-four. She slid on her sunglasses as she hopped onto the sidewalk. Passing under a canopy of branches, Olivia hoped they wouldn't break and dump a bushel of snow on her head. As she strolled past century-old houses, Olivia realized this was the same neighborhood Steven saw every day. She rounded the curve near the snow-filled baseball park and imagined him playing on a bright summer day. She saw him swing the bat and heard the crack resonate over the field as it connected with the baseball. She pictured him running, maybe sliding, dust and dirt flying, into second base to the cheers and hoots of his teammates. She could almost smell the grilled hot dogs.

Olivia had been up since six. She'd eaten her yogurt and a slice of peanut butter toast while skimming *The Washington Post* on her laptop.

Off and on throughout the day, she'd check *The Huffington Post* and *CNN*. She pushed her laptop out of the way and settled in with the print copies of *The New York Times* and the local *Gazette* and her daily mug of espresso. Although the online news stories were up-to-the-minute, she couldn't let go of her *New York Times* subscription, which was delivered to her door every morning. There was something about holding those big sheets of newsprint.

Olivia was a news junkie. It was one of the things that had made her a good reporter when she worked at *The Syracuse Post-Standard*. She needed to understand what went on in the world like she needed food, water, and air to breathe. She kept up with all aspects of the news. She read newspapers and Twitter feeds. She listened to NPR as well as a few podcasts.

Olivia reached the corner where an authentic English pub sat in all its historic glory. The Three Lords oozed with atmosphere and had long been a favorite haunt. Olivia navigated a narrow trail past snow-covered mailboxes peeking out of drifts and finally arrived at the Knightsbridge History Museum, a plain brick box, originally built as an elementary school in 1928.

Liz stood in her office studying a large display board on an easel, coffee mug in hand.

"Morning."

Liz spun around and Olivia watched as her dark blonde hair settled back in perfect razor-cut layers. For a brief moment, she thought of Helena Bonham Carter disapparating in one of the Harry Potter movies.

"Oh, hey, Liv! Look at my new floor plan. What do you think?"

Olivia read the labels on the themed rooms—Toys and Games, The Kitchen, and Communications.

"Makes sense. Wow, you did a lot of work."

"It's been so much fun. I can't wait to get everything unpacked."

"What have you got for me? Do I get to play with some of the toys?" She grinned.

"I've got something better for you. Newspapers! Miss Sinclair saved boxes full of the most famous headlines from the past century."

"Awesome! Thanks."

"I figured you'd like that. Right up your alley."

They joined volunteers and staff in a workroom crammed with cartons, crates, and rolling carts of every kind. Liz gave out assignments.

Olivia was paired with her friend and neighbor Isabel, a retired teacher who became somewhat of a surrogate grandmother when Olivia's own beloved grandmother developed Alzheimer's disease. Caught in the cruel snare of the debilitating disease, Gram had drifted further and further away, eventually not recognizing five-year-old Olivia. When Gram passed away the summer before Olivia started first grade, it was nothing short of miraculous that Olivia found herself in Isabel's first grade class. It was in Isabel's warm and nurturing class that Olivia had first met the two little girls who would become her lifelong best friends.

With Olivia pulling and Isabel pushing, they managed to get their cart into the elevator and up to their second-floor room. They were out of breath but eager to start. Liz had given them one of the museum's laptops and they agreed to take turns logging in information.

Isabel removed the tape from the first box and grabbed a yellowed copy of *The Knightsbridge Gazette*.

"The end of World War II! JAPAN SURRENDERS. END OF WAR!"

Olivia typed the title of the newspaper, the date, and quoted the headline. They set it aside. Next was the November 23, 1963, issue of *The New York Times*: "KENNEDY IS KILLED BY SNIPER AS HE RIDES IN CAR IN DALLAS; JOHNSON SWORN IN ON PLANE."

"Evidently, they're not in any order."

Olivia and Isabel discovered the bombing of Pearl Harbor, the arrival of the Allies in Europe for the "Great Invasion," the famously inaccurate "Dewey Beats Truman" in 1948, the humiliating denials and eventual resignation of President Nixon, and the impressively over-sized headline in *The New York Times* in the summer of 1969, "MEN WALK ON MOON." They had to force themselves to stay on task and not get into conversations about the thrilling history the papers represented.

The piles of newspapers grew.

"I don't believe it!" Isabel held up the first paper from the next box. The *Gazette* headline shouted "MURDER AT THE BANK." The date read *Sunday, February 25, 1934.*

Olivia swallowed hard. It was the same paper that Steven had given her last night, only this copy showed every one of its eighty years. The pages were yellow and brittle edges had torn off. "Oh my goodness!"

Isabel nodded. "*Oh my goodness* is right. Knightsbridge's very own scandal. And people think nothing ever happens in a small town."

"Isabel, that's your birthday," said Olivia as the realization of the date sunk in.

"It is and I heard about this practically every year on my birthday."

"What do you mean?"

"You know how it goes. Everybody remembers where they were and what they were doing when the kids were born. In my case, it was all about the murder. By the way, did you know I was born in the pub?"

"What?" Olivia gaped.

"Yes, my mother had moved in with her cousin–he was the owner–about a month before I was born. Long story. Anyway she remembered the customers gossiping about this. It was big deal."

"It'd be a big deal now, too. It's not every day you find someone murdered in a bank vault." *Should I ask the next question? Why not?*

"Who did it? Do you know?"

"I'm not sure I ever heard. But evidently the killer was someone everybody knew and never suspected." Isabel reached the end of the article. "Oh look, they mention my father-in-law. Blah, blah...'assisted by Detective Harry Beckman.' I didn't realize this was one of his cases."

Olivia was eager to see what was going to come up next, maybe there were more articles about Steven's case. But Isabel pulled out a copy of *The New York Times* reporting the legendary Woodstock Music Festival in August 1969. She felt let down.

"Hey, speaking of your birthday, are you all set for tomorrow night?"

"Yes, but, Olivia, you know you girls don't have to do this again. We could just go out for a drink."

"We want to. If it wasn't for you, who knows how long it would have been before we met."

Isabel had assigned Olivia, Liz, and Sophie to be learning partners that autumn during first grade. She'd pushed their desks together and said they'd be working as a group for the year. They clicked immediately and soon became inseparable.

Recently they had begun taking turns hosting a birthday dinner for their much-loved former teacher. Isabel's daughter Jennifer had moved out of the area a few years ago and often couldn't get home when her mother's birthday fell on a weekday.

Isabel reached over and patted her hand. "You're sweet. Well, all right. You know I'd love to come. But promise you won't go to a lot of trouble."

"Promise." She crossed her fingers under the table and gave Isabel her best Cheshire-cat grin.

They worked through the morning, took a sandwich break around noon, then walked up and down the hallway a couple of times to stretch their legs. Isabel couldn't resist looking in her old classroom as they passed.

"I spent a lot of happy years in this room. I was Miss Covington back then."

"Right, your maiden name."

They unpacked two more boxes that afternoon. Olivia found only one additional newspaper chronicling Steven's murder investigation. The banner on the *Gazette*'s front page announced that this was the Monday morning edition. Olivia marveled that a small town like Knightsbridge had its own newspaper, but did they actually publish a morning *and* evening edition back in 1934? Surely the population back then was much less than the current 50,000. Maybe the evening edition was made up of short updates of the day's news and a lot of advertisements. She set the paper aside to read after Isabel left.

At three o'clock, Liz stopped to tell them the other volunteers were leaving. Isabel straightened up, groaning a bit, and announced she could hear a nice hot bubble bath and a glass of Chardonnay calling. They laughed.

"Come on, I'll walk you down," offered Liz.

LEO CASTLEMAN MURDERED
BANK MANAGER FOUND DEAD IN VAULT

Olivia read the first two paragraphs quickly. It was typical small-town coverage and recapped some of Sunday's information. When the article focused on Steven, she slowed down and read carefully.

Chief Andy Thompson stated that Detective Sergeant Steven Blackwell is in charge of the case. Blackwell is a veteran on the force and has a stellar record of arrests leading to convictions. He is being assisted by Detective Harry Beckman, who has been with the department for five years. Thompson added, "Every available officer is working on this case."

Mrs. Castleman was out of town when her husband's body

was discovered yesterday morning. She rushed home late Saturday night.

"Hey, what's so interesting?" Liz had returned and quietly come up behind her. She was now peeking over Olivia's shoulder.

"Look! Steven's picture. We found the paper with the murder he's working on right now!"

"Holy cow!" Liz reached for the newspaper. "Are you kidding me?" She read a bit. "Why would she save this one? I get all the national and world events. But a local murder? Weird." She studied the photograph. "So, this is your guy? Looks exactly like you described him. Nice."

"You know what I'm thinking."

"Do I want to hear this?"

"I wonder if there are other papers from this week. Maybe she saved the whole coverage. Nothing was packed in order. There might be more in another box."

"What are you talking about? Even if they *are* all here, you can't say anything."

"What if he gets stuck? He told me they hardly have any clues so far. What if the week goes by and he can't find any evidence? I could maybe...point him in the right direction?"

"But this has already happened! You can't interfere with what's already taken place."

"I wouldn't be changing anything. If it was reported in the paper, it happened."

"Don't fool around with this, Olivia. These are real people's lives. You've gotta put it out of your mind." She glanced at the article again. "Here, look what it says: 'Veteran police officer. Stellar record of arrests and convictions.' He knows what he's doing. The man is good at his job. Leave it alone."

"I suppose you're right. Besides, we don't even know if there are any more."

Olivia added the paper to the 1930s pile, checked that the information was saved on the flash drive, and set everything aside for the following day. She and Liz walked out of the museum together.

The temperature had plummeted, so Olivia didn't dally. She made it home in less than fifteen minutes.

Olivia didn't know why, but she felt upset. Was it the *Gazette* articles? Or seeing his picture in the paper? Was it Liz's admonition not to get involved?

No, a little voice whispered. It's because you *are* involved. You already feel *connected* to him.

No, her brain said. That's ridiculous. Besides, he's not even real.

Yes, said the voice. He is.

Olivia settled at the kitchen table with her laptop to finish writing the article on Budapest that was coming due. In addition to her hunger for learning, Olivia's other passion was travel. For as long as she could remember, she had dreamed of packing a suitcase and taking off to explore exotic places. She travelled as much as she could. She got credit cards that offered free airline miles and hotel rooms. She'd inherited a small sum from her grandmother. When she turned eighteen, she transferred it to a separate bank account dedicated to her precious trips.

A couple of years after setting up her agency, Olivia took a second leap of faith and wrote an article on a trip she had taken to Devon and Cornwall, England's West Country. She sent it to *National Geographic Traveler* and was thrilled when it was accepted and published. Her freelance career was launched.

Now, her latest article was: *Budapest: City of Spas*. The Hungarian capital had been a revelation, boasting 118 private and public spas where visitors could soak in thermal baths ranging from pleasantly warm to near-boiling water. She carefully read through the file, making sure she had noted the large central market, the ubiquitous violin players who serenaded diners in many of the restaurants, the amazing variety of architecture, and the recently opened underground hospital from World War II. She saved it again and made a mental note to check it one final time before sending it to *Travel + Leisure* in the morning.

Her stomach growled. *Six o'clock already?* Olivia put on a pair of yoga pants and long-sleeved T-shirt. Then, because the house felt chilly, she added her fleece bathrobe. The extra layer usually did the trick. She fixed a quick dinner and ate in front of the TV. The news anchor segued from a report on the Middle East to the problems a wacked-out celebrity was having. *Why is this guy news?* Disgusted, she switched over to *House of Cards*—she'd been binging Season 2 for several days.

The camera zoomed in on Kevin Spacey and the episode ended. Suddenly Olivia felt tired. She decided to spend the evening snuggled in bed with the new issues of *Time* and *National Geographic*. Maybe that would help dispel the gloomy mood that still hung over her. And she knew she'd feel better when she saw Steven and they'd had a chance to talk. She was eager to tell him about her day. She'd decide later whether to say anything about the newspaper article.

Hours later, Steven stood quietly at Olivia's bedroom door. She was sound asleep, propped up against two pillows, magazines spilling from her lap, lights still burning. He felt an acute sense of disappointment at not being able to sit and talk with her again tonight. He hadn't realized he was looking forward to it so much.

TUESDAY - 1934

Chapter 18

Steven awoke feeling sluggish and out of sorts. He rolled over and stretched to turn off the alarm. He hadn't slept well and already his head felt like it was full of scratchy cobwebs. He needed to be sharp today, to concentrate on the case. Maybe some extra coffee would help.

The first person he saw when he arrived at the station was Jimmy Bourgogne. Jimmy Bou was turning into an excellent cop. Steven thought he'd make a good detective someday. He needed a bit more seasoning. Then, if Chief Thompson agreed, he'd officially take him under his wing, like he had Beckman, and train him to be their next detective.

The young officer followed Steven down the hall to the CID room. They chatted while Steven stowed his lunch box and settled in. Steven noticed Jimmy's uniform. The pants were too short and bony wrists stuck out of his shirt sleeves. He made a mental note to say something to the chief. Maybe the department could scrape together enough money to get him something that fit.

The lanky policeman jumped right in. "I've got good stuff for you, Steven. From my investigation yesterday." He bounced from foot to foot.

"I can use some good news. What've you got?"

"I went over to the railroad station." He consulted his notes. "The DL&W has a train that leaves for Syracuse at five p.m. Monday through Saturday. I talked with the ticket agent. He remembers Mrs. Castleman buying a ticket for that time."

"That's swell, Jimmy."

The patrolman's eyes shone. "Then I got lucky. A train was pulling in and I found the conductor that was actually on the one last Friday. He said Mrs. Castleman did a lot of complaining. She was annoyed the trip was taking so long. Like the storm was his fault, you know?"

"Okay, good. Did you get a hold of her sister Louise?"

"Yup! She confirmed that Mrs. Castleman arrived around seven thirty. Said she stayed home all night. She was positive."

"So we verified the wife's alibi."

"I found out something else."

"What's that?"

"I asked what they usually do when Mrs. Castleman visits. She told me that Patsy...she calls her sister Patsy...kind of funny, huh?" Jimmy tilted his head and made a face. "Anyway, she said her sister has friends in Syracuse. She doesn't know who they are. Mrs. Castleman goes out with these people and doesn't get in until late."

"Hmm. That's interesting."

"Well, it made me think, you know? Yesterday morning at the meeting, you asked us to try and find out if anybody's seen Mrs. Castleman with another man. After I came back, I read the updates on the murder board. Someone saw her with Mr. Harrison."

Steven knew where this was going, he had already thought of it, but he let Jimmy explain.

"What if they're having an affair but they meet in Syracuse? Knightsbridge is a *really* small town. Everyone knows everybody else's business. It would be pretty hard to keep an affair secret, wouldn't it?"

"That's good thinking, Jimmy. And I agree. There's something about Mrs. Castleman that bothers me. We'll definitely run down your ideas."

Jimmy beamed at the compliment.

"What about checking the businesses near the bank?" Steven asked. "How much were you able to get done?"

"We got to all of 'em. Nobody was open late Friday night. Even The Three Lords and Pinky's shut down early 'cause of the blizzard. We went to the hospital and talked to some people there. But we couldn't find anybody who was out or even looked out a window. Sorry."

"No, no. You did a great job. I didn't actually expect any of the businesses would be able to tell us much. But we've gotta check."

Steven went to update the murder board. As he was writing, he heard morning greetings and snatches of conversation echo through the building. The station was coming alive. The men shook off their wet coats and hats and hung them on hooks in a small back room. They put away lunch boxes. Someone got a pot of coffee going. Several officers came into the CID room to read what was new on the board.

Will Taylor arrived without his usual quiet confidence. His broad shoulders slumped a bit and his mouth was drawn. "I'm afraid I don't have much to tell you, Steven. I did what you asked yesterday and spent time at Bailey's, Joe's, and the Y. The talk was all about Castleman stealing the money. Everyone kept saying how he was an honest man. Nobody could imagine what would make him take money from his own bank. Believe it or not, they all seemed more shocked at that than at the murder."

"That's what Becks and I found out, too."

Steven returned to his seat and Jimmy Bou perched on the edge of Beckman's desk. Will pulled over an extra wooden chair, spun it around, and straddled it, resting his brawny arms on the back.

"I think that's the key to this whole thing," said Will, reaching to push dark hair off his high forehead.

Steven saw the well-developed muscles rippling across his chest and down his arms beneath the material of the snug uniform and absently wondered if Taylor lifted weights.

"People *should* be talking about the murder but the buzz has been about the theft. I say Patricia Castleman wanted money and somehow she convinced her husband to rob the bank." Will pointed as if to punctuate the end of his statement.

"Some guys are a sucker for a dame. They'll do anything for love," Jimmy Bou chimed in. "Some women can wrap a fella right around their little finger."

"Speaking from experience, are you, Jimmy?" Beckman had arrived and caught the end of the conversation.

Jimmy Bou blushed and quickly slid off the desk. "Well, you know."

Beckman joined in. "Speaking of Mrs. Castleman, I didn't have any luck, Steven. I tried every trick in the book but she isn't talking. I've got a feeling she knows something but I couldn't get it out of her. Sorry. Looks like my charm failed, she wouldn't budge."

"Then let's approach it another way." Steven stood and paced back and forth. "I agree with Will. Money is the key to this case. *But* I think she's the key to the money. The wife is the one person with enough influence over a man to convince him to go against his principles. And all we keep hearing about is Castleman's principles! I believe that Patricia Castleman hounded her husband until he agreed to steal the money. Leo Castleman's goddaughter Ginny told me that Leo would do anything for Patricia."

"She would've had to work on him a long time. It's a big thing to go against what you believe in," observed Will.

"It sure is," Steven said. "I think she planned it very carefully. Told her lover that Castleman would be there. Then that person killed him and took the money. We need to prove she was having, and probably still is having, an affair. And obviously we've got to find out who he is."

"That makes sense to me. It's like I can see the whole thing clearly," said Jimmy Bou.

Steven hid a small smile. "Right, I want the two of you," he indicated Will and Beckman, "to go to Syracuse today. Jimmy's got a good point. If she's having an affair, she's not doing it here. She'd be a fool to meet someone close to home. Visiting her sister would be the perfect excuse."

Steven gave Will and Becks photographs of Patricia Castleman and John Harrison.

"Now, people having an affair have to go somewhere. Canvas all the hotels that you can. Becks, you're from Syracuse. You must know the kind of place a guy would take his mistress."

"I am *offended* that you would say that, Detective Blackwell!" Harry Beckman said in mock outrage.

They all laughed. Everyone knew Beckman's reputation.

Steven raised his eyebrows and smirked. "As I was saying, Patricia Castleman isn't some dolly you find on a street corner. She thinks she's something special. She'd insist on a nice hotel that cost money. Skip the cheap places. Start with the best and work your way down the list."

Steven's excitement was catching.

"And restaurants," Will jumped in. "He'd take her out for a meal."

"That's right. Check the top restaurants as well as out-of-the-way neighborhood ones, too. Maybe they have cozy lunches in a little spot where the locals go. They might have a favorite place near their hotel or down some side street."

"I know where we can go," said Becks.

"Good. I already talked with the chief. He called ahead to the Syracuse Police Department to let them know you're coming. They've offered extra help if you want it. It's your call.

"Chief Thompson's authorized a vehicle and money for gas and meals. But he did ask if you could stay overnight at your parents' house, Becks. You know money's tight. It would save the department if you didn't have to stay in a hotel."

Steven knew that Syracuse was a sizeable town and wasn't sure how long their investigation would take. He also guessed the weather was going to slow them down.

"I'm sure we can. I'll give my mother a call before we leave and let you know. She'll probably be thrilled. She's always saying I don't go home enough. They'd like it if I visited every weekend." Beckman laughed. "Parents, huh?"

A flash of anger at Beckman's casual attitude toward his parents flew through Steven. What he wouldn't give for one more day with his mother. Then without warning, it happened again. A lump choked his throat and his eyes filled up. Every time that he thought he was handling the pain, it rushed back to assault him. He quickly swiped a hand over his eyes and forced the still raw grief back down inside, where it landed like a stone at the bottom of his stomach.

Becks and Will left after the briefing. As predicted, Beckman's mother was delighted at the prospect of seeing her son and meeting one of his colleagues. She excitedly told him she'd make up his old bedroom and the spare room right away. She also said, her voice full of happiness, that she'd make his favorite supper.

Steven wanted to see Molly Coffin as soon as possible and departed right after Becks and Will Taylor. He hoped that his cousin's elderly neighbor had indeed been up during the night and had seen something helpful.

Freezing rain drenched him in an icy bath and seeped inside his collar as he ran for his automobile. Glancing up, Steven felt the weight of the sky like a leaden shroud pressing down on everything in sight. He drove up Hickory, windshield wipers working furiously, and took a right on Victoria. He overshot Mrs. Coffin's house, turned around, and parked directly in front. He was in no mood to get any wetter or colder than he already was. Steven grabbed the brim of his hat, pulling it down over his face, and shrunk into his collar turtle-like. He made a mad dash for the porch.

A short, plump, woman with white hair and sharp blue eyes answered the bell. She had a pixie face and remarkably smooth skin for someone her age.

"Good morning, Steven." She threw the door open wide. "Come in, come in. Get out of this horrible cold and damp."

Steven gratefully entered the toasty house.

"I've been expecting you. Your cousin told me you'd be over. Come on back to the kitchen. No, leave your boots on. Wipe them off on the mat. It's only water after all. Here, give me your things." She draped the dark brown, double-breasted overcoat over a chair near a heater and hung his camel-colored fedora on a hook by the door.

"Mmm, smells good in here."

"I've baked so the kitchen's nice and warm. We'll have tea." She beamed. "You'll be very glad you came. I did see something Friday night!"

Steven followed Molly Coffin through the hall to the back of the house. He sat on a colorful homemade cushion at the table next to a foggy window, where rivulets of water snaked down the glass. She busied herself gathering teapot, creamer, sugar bowl, cups, spoons, napkins, the butter dish and a knife, and a plate of muffins that made his mouth water. All this was set on the kitchen table with some ceremony.

He waited patiently. At last, eyes glittering, Molly Coffin sat down and whispered excitedly, "So, I think I have a clue for you."

"Tell me what you saw, Mrs. Coffin."

"I got up in the middle of the night to go to the bathroom, as usual." She made a face. "I looked at the clock on my bedside table. It was about two thirty. When I came back into the bedroom, the wind was howling something fierce and I thought I'd take a peek outside. I opened the curtains. I saw a man right across the street! I was so surprised anybody would be out in that blizzard that I looked really hard to see what he was doing."

"Can you describe him?"

"He was tall and, I think, slender. I couldn't say for sure because he was wearing a bulky coat. But I had the impression that when he took his coat off, he would be slim. I couldn't see his face because he had a hat on and a scarf wrapped all around. He was coming out of Bank Alley and heading toward my house. I'm guessing that he was either going up School Hill Road or maybe Chiltington."

"Why do you say that?"

"If he was going to walk up Victoria, he would have simply turned right or left. And he didn't, he was getting ready to cross the street."

Very observant, Steven thought as he polished off his first banana muffin. "That makes sense. Go on."

"I've since wondered why he paused at the curb. I think it was the wind. He was bent over like he was fighting it."

"Could you tell if he was carrying anything?"

"Yes, I was getting to that. Every now and then, a gust of wind swept away the snow and I could see quite clearly." Molly sipped her tea. "He had something like a walking stick in his right hand. Wait. Let me think. Let's see, he was facing me and the stick was on the left. Yes, that's right. It would have been his right hand. Mirror image, you see. Well, whatever it was, he was trying to use it to walk, but the snow was too deep. Looked like it was more of a hindrance than a help. And he had something in his other hand, too."

Steven sat up straighter and asked eagerly, "Could you see what it was?"

"It was a bag. It's funny because at first I thought it was Dr. Kranken making a house call. And I remember thinking, 'Oh, poor man. Having to go out on a night like this.' But then I realized it wasn't him. Dr. Kranken is shorter than this man was. And fatter too."

"Why did you think it might be him?"

"It was the bag. It looked like a doctor's medical bag. About this big." She held out her hands to illustrate.

"Coming back to the walking stick, Mrs. Coffin. Can you tell me anything more about it? Any description, any detail would help."

She closed her eyes for several seconds. "It was very dark, maybe even black, but honestly, Steven," she said shrewdly, "against all that white snow, I think anything would have looked black."

Steven nodded in appreciation. "Could you estimate how tall it was?"

"No, but it came to about here on him." She indicated a spot mid-thigh. "And it wasn't fat or thick. The man had his hand wrapped around the top with no trouble."

"This is amazing, Mrs. Coffin. You have a wonderful memory."

She beamed. "I hope it helps. Leo was a nice man. This is a horrible thing to happen."

Steven inquired about the lighting conditions in the street that night, whether or not she ever wore glasses, and how hard it was snowing when she saw the man. He sat with her until he was satisfied that her impressions were accurate and there was nothing else she could tell him. He was suddenly impatient to leave so he could analyze this new information.

Detective Sergeant Blackwell now knew where the money was.

Chapter 19

Steven returned to the station to talk it over with Jimmy Bourgogne. Jimmy Bou had good instincts and rarely censored his thoughts when he talked. As soon as ideas came into his head, he blurted them out. Steven found value in this. A number of times in the past, Jimmy had unknowingly stumbled on the key to a case simply by letting his thoughts run wild.

He was hanging up the telephone when Steven entered the patrol room.

"Jimmy! Come back with me for a minute. I'd like to discuss something with you."

Full of pride at being asked to consult on such a high-profile case, Jimmy strode confidently to Steven's desk. "Sure! You got it! Do we have new information?"

"As a matter of fact we do." Steven peered into the trash can. It was full of crumpled up paper. Perfect. "Jimmy, go get a broom."

"A broom?"

"Yes, and see if you can find another trash can full of papers. Oh, and get your lunch pail."

Jimmy left with a puzzled look on his face. He returned with the requested items and looked expectantly at Steven. "I don't get it. What are we doing?"

Steven directed his attention to the photographs on the murder board. "Tell me what you see here in this one." He indicated the picture of the Brinks bags.

Jimmy Bou leaned over, carefully considering the black-and-white enlargement, then said, "A big empty bag and a bag that's about half empty."

"Okay," said Steven, reaching into a trash can and removing an armful of paper wadded up in balls. Someone had been shooting baskets. He set the pile on a table near the wall. "This represents the money that was in the empty bag, okay?"

Jimmy nodded.

Steven reached into the second trash can and did the same with a smaller but substantial pile. Next he laid the broom down on the floor. "This is Leo Castleman."

He set Jimmy's lunch pail next to the broom. "This is the bag Leo brought with him. It was empty when we found it."

He grabbed his own lunch box, held it up, and, looking Jimmy straight in the eye, said, "According to an eye witness I talked to this morning, the man leaving the bank was carrying something that looked like a medical bag."

"So, where's all the stolen money?" Jimmy exclaimed, immediately cutting through everything as usual.

Steven smiled at him and slowly said, "Exactly."

Jimmy closed his eyes, picturing the bank vault and surrounding area. "Son of a bitch!" His eyes flew open and he stared. "The thief's got a safe-deposit box."

"That's what I think, too. The room with the safe-deposit boxes is right next to the vault. The question is *Has he had a chance to get the money out yet?* That's a lot of cash to sneak out of the building without being noticed. Our thief took nearly $50,000, mostly in ones and fives. That's a lot of cash."

"So, what's our next move?" Jimmy glowed with excitement.

"You clean up this stuff while I try to save some time. I'm going to ask the chief if he'll get us the warrant. In the meantime, you and I can go to the bank. I'll find out the procedure for getting a box. And you can start dusting for prints." Steven stood and grabbed his notes. Jimmy followed him out into the hall. "All the boxes are hidden behind locked doors in built-in cubicles. There's a spot on each door that someone would have to touch while they're sliding their box out of the compartment. To be sure, I want you to dust the entire front."

Twenty minutes later, Detective Sergeant Steven Blackwell and Officer Jimmy Bourgogne, thrilled to be riding shotgun in Steven's swell automobile, pulled up in front of the bank's main entrance. They hurried up the front steps.

Steven went directly to Martin Carpenter for the key to the safe-deposit box room. He handed it to Jimmy.

"Be sure you make a careful list of which box number goes with which print."

"Will do."

Steven led Marty to the meeting room again.

"Marty, I need you to tell me all about the safe-deposit boxes and how they work."

"Okay. When someone rents a box, the first thing they do is fill out an index card with certain information."

"Who do they talk to? Can anyone take care of it?"

"Basically, yes. Any of the tellers can but they're usually busy. What normally happens is they send the customer to either John Harrison or Leo Castleman. Before, I mean."

"I know what you mean. Can I see one of the cards, please?"

"Sure. I'll be right back."

Marty returned and handed Steven a three-by-five-inch index card printed on one side. There were spaces for the customer to write his name, address, and telephone number, if he had one, and a choice of three sizes—a small, medium, or large box. Steven thought the thief would have needed one, or possibly two, of the large ones. Near the bottom of the card was a line to record the number of the box assigned to the customer and one additional space for the customer's signature.

"Where are these cards kept, Marty?"

"There's a pile of blanks on the counter behind the tellers, and each of the executives keeps a small pack in a desk drawer. Carl Dickson is probably the only person who wouldn't ever deal with this. The ones that are filled out are in a cabinet by Ginny's desk."

Steven mentally listed the number of people who would have handled the card before it got to the customer.

"What happens next?"

"The customer signs the card. The employee gives him a key then takes him down to the safe-deposit box room."

"Tell me how the keys work. I've heard you need two keys to open a box."

"Yes, for security. The bank keeps a key. When the customer needs to access his box, someone goes with him. We have to unlock the room first, of course. Then, we unlock one part of the compartment door and turn it over to the customer. They use their key for the second lock. We leave the room before they actually take the box out of the cubicle and open it, so they have privacy. But we wait in the hall. When they're finished, we reverse the process then make sure the room is locked again."

"What if a customer loses his key?"

"We have an extra one for each box. Sometimes we need it in an emergency, like after somebody dies. A lot of times the family knows they have a safe-deposit box but can't find the key."

"Today is one of those emergencies, Marty. One of the fellas is bringing over a warrant. It's for the missing cash and any evidence connected to the theft."

"Oh! John Harrison isn't here. He should help you with this."

"Where is he?"

"He had to go to the main office. Won't be back 'til tomorrow."

"How often does he go to Syracuse?"

"Every now and then."

"Is there a calendar where the appointments are written?"

"Yes, Ginny has it. You want me to get it?"

"Not yet. I'll need a warrant for that, too. Right now I need the cards that show who has which number box. Bring those and all the keys and meet me downstairs."

When Jimmy heard Steven enter the room, he said, "I only did the medium and large, Steven. Do you want the little ones, too?"

"No, I don't think so. Not yet anyway."

Steven studied the three walls of safe-deposit boxes. There were several dozen small sizes on the back wall, three rows of five large boxes to the left, and about thirty medium-sized cubicles on the right. The compartments holding the boxes were built-in, and a small hinged door sealed each one.

Marty Carpenter returned with a patrolman.

"Detective Blackwell, here's your warrant."

"Thanks." Steven skimmed through the paperwork. "Now, I need you to go and ask the chief to get me another one." He told the officer about the appointment calendar. "When the judge signs it, come on back and collect the calendar from Ginny Fitzgerald.

"Marty, would you like to read this first, before we start?"

"No, I'm ready when you are."

"Let's see those cards, then," Steven said, slipping on a pair of lightweight gloves.

The index cards were in numerical order. The highest numbers represented the largest safe-deposit boxes. Steven deftly moved through the pack until he reached the three hundreds. Six or seven were registered to bank customers.

"All right, this is how I'd like us to do this."

He explained and they wasted no time getting started.

"Number 303," Steven read from the card, "the Reynolds family."

Marty Carpenter unlocked the door. Steven extracted the box, waited for Jimmy to dust the lid and sides then set it on a table. Inside he found what he'd imagined would occupy most of the boxes—the deed to the family home and the last will and testament for Mr. and Mrs. Reynolds. The three men were surprised to also see a baby's christening gown, carefully wrapped in delicate, white tissue paper, tiny white shoes, a rattle, and a much-loved stuffed rabbit.

"It was the influenza epidemic back in '18 that got her. Poor little thing. Only four months old," said Marty.

They moved on to number 305, which belonged to The Three Lords Pub. Once again they found a deed, this one to the bar and restaurant, and family wills.

The King family also kept wills in their safe-deposit box, number 306, as well as the paperwork for their mortgage, the title to an automobile, and a number of music books. Steven knew that Mrs. King was an accomplished flutist who also wrote music. He guessed that these were the original copies of her work.

Box 309 held the most unusual contents. It was registered to Giovanni's Italian restaurant. Steven, Jimmy, and Marty were amazed to find the box stuffed with recipes written in old-fashioned, spidery handwriting; some were in English, some in Italian. Steven could tell that the writer had used a fountain pen, or perhaps an inkwell. Some of the pages lay loose in the box. Some were bundled up and tied with satin ribbon.

"Ah," exclaimed Jimmy Bou. "The family treasures. Yum!"

They all laughed.

The index cards for box numbers 312 and 313 were clipped together.

"Dorinda MacDonald," Steven read aloud. "Widow of Matthew MacDonald. I don't know them."

"I don't think I've heard the name either," Carpenter offered.

The box felt light. Steven slid the lid out of the narrow channel, drawing it toward him. It was empty. He glanced at Jimmy and raised his eyebrows.

"That's odd," said the head teller, craning his neck to look into the box. "Nothing. Maybe they moved everything to 313. It could be that since her husband died, Mrs. MacDonald only needs the one. And she hasn't had a chance to cancel number 312 yet."

Steven and Jimmy repeated the procedure. Safe-deposit box number 313 was also completely empty.

Steven bent down and peered into the compartments where the boxes had been. Deep in the back of number 313, he noticed something.

"There's something back there." He faced the other men. "Both of you are witnesses to this, understood? Just in case."

Jimmy nodded eagerly. Marty looked worried. Steven reached in and pulled out a small wad of scraps of green paper. They were the torn, right-hand corners from the bottom of several ten-dollar bills. The denomination was easily identified by the numeral "10" on both sides. Steven's heart skipped a beat when he saw that the last three digits of the serial number were visible on the first torn banknote.

"These must've ripped off when Mrs. MacDonald slid the lid back on. Maybe the box was full and they got caught and tore," Marty guessed. "Then they fell to the back."

"Marty, I need to speak with Jimmy for a minute. Would you mind waiting outside?"

"Actually, I should check on things upstairs. Would that be all right?"

"That's fine. Give us a few minutes."

The door closed behind Carpenter. Steven took the list of stolen bills from his jacket pocket, found the ten-dollar denominations, and scanned the serial numbers. He checked then double-checked the last digits in the series. They had a match.

"Here it is. We got 'em!" He looked over at Jimmy, standing wide-eyed, holding his breath. "Breathe, Jimmy, breathe. I don't want you fainting on me in here. It's only one clue."

Jimmy Bou let out a deep breath. "Yeah, but it's a big one. This is exciting."

"In on the kill, huh?" Steven chuckled. "All right, let's check the numbers on the other pieces." He compared three additional torn corners with the list. They all matched.

"What next?" asked Jimmy. "This Mrs. MacDonald must be in cahoots with somebody who works at the bank, right? 'Cause the killer-thief put the money in here that night when the bank was closed."

"That's a possibility. Or it could be a false identity for Patricia Castleman."

"You really think it's her, huh?"

"I keep coming back to her."

"Why don't we bring her in and sweat her?"

Steven laughed. "You've been watching too many movies. We know where she is, we can bring her in any time." He slid box 313 back in the cubicle and closed the door. "Like I said before, his wife is the most logical person who'd be able to convince Leo to go into the vault. Who else would have that kind of emotional influence over a man as principled as he was?"

"His brother? What about Lawrence Castleman? Maybe he's a really good actor and has us fooled. Maybe he was in on it with Leo and betrayed his own brother. Cain and Abel?" Jimmy raised his eyebrows.

"Maybe. Yeah, we need to rule him out soon." Steven leaned against the table and thought for a moment, imagining the killer's plan.

"No. No, Jimmy, my gut says she's in this up to her neck. I know I'm repeating myself. But I'm telling you there's a *love* angle here."

"Well, maybe she's having an affair with her brother-in-law? It happens." Jimmy scratched his head and ran his fingers through his caramel-colored hair. Then he shuddered, "Ugh! Have you met *my* sister-in-law? I don't know how my brother lives with her. She's a real nag. That woman yells at him and tells him what to do all the time." He made a face which made him look like he'd just sucked a lemon.

Steven laughed. "No, I don't know her. But that's a thought, Jimmy. Maybe you've got something there. Make a note. In the next twenty-four hours, I want to either eliminate Lawrence Castleman or find some real evidence that keeps him on the board."

Steven paced back and forth considering this new theory. "Yeah, that's good. Patricia and her brother-in-law *Just-Call-Me-Larry*. Or Patricia and John Harrison, her husband's second-in-command. I can see both of them as possibilities but only, *only* if Lawrence Castleman is a good actor, as you said."

"Steven, when I looked at the suspect list this morning, there were still some bank employees on it. I think you crossed out the two women, Eddie Littleman, and Connor MacIntyre."

"Right."

"So the people still on the list are John Harrison, obviously. But also Henry August, Carl Dickson, and Martin Carpenter."

"Yes, but I honestly don't think those three had anything to do with it. Remember, Patricia Castleman is the key. Henry August couldn't be involved with her, he's too old. And although we haven't checked on Marty's alibi yet, or Carl Dickson's for that matter, neither of them is her type. Can you really see her with Dickson? With that hair of his?"

Jimmy snorted. "No kidding. She wouldn't be caught dead with a guy who looks like a skunk."

"Exactly. And I can't see Marty for this. He's too down-to-earth, he'd never go for a dame like her."

"So, we've narrowed down our suspects to John Harrison or the brother Lawrence, haven't we?" Jimmy asked.

"It looks that way. But, let's not jump to conclusions. We'll investigate until we're positive they're not involved. Now, we have to bag up this evidence. We need to make sure none of these other boxes contains any trace of evidence."

It took Steven and Jimmy an hour to verify there was nothing left to be found.

"We'll get a statement from Marty later, saying he witnessed finding the torn corners," Steven said. "Right now I want to get over to Route 5 and find the MacDonalds' address. The house numbers on that road start low close to town. This is a high number, so it's probably a few miles out. I'll bet it's a farm."

Privately Steven had his suspicions on what they would or wouldn't find, but he kept his thoughts to himself.

"We'll swing by the lab on the way and drop off your print evidence. I'm going to ask them to put a rush on it. We need a positive ID on the fingerprints we found on those two safe-deposit boxes *and* on the registration card."

"Even though we know whose they are, right?" Jimmy was nodding and looking at Steven as though they had a big secret between them. For a wild moment, Steven thought that they should be giving each other the "secret handshake" and climbing up into a "BOYS ONLY: NO

GIRLS ALLOWED" tree house. He enjoyed working with Jimmy. The kid was a character. And you certainly couldn't fault his enthusiasm.

"We *think* we know. *Think* won't stand up in court, Jimmy."

"Oh, yeah! Right! Sorry. Guess I let my excitement get the best of me, you know?"

"Not to worry. It's nice to work with someone who enjoys the job." He looked over at the younger officer. "Just don't let our suspects hear you talk like that." He grinned.

"No, sir! I'm okay now. You can depend on me," Jimmy said with such a serious face that Steven laughed out loud.

By one thirty, Detective Sergeant Blackwell and Officer Bourgogne were motoring out of town beneath a pale sun that was trying to break through heavy clouds but failing miserably. As they followed the slick road along the river, even the air inside the car seemed to blanket them with cold and damp. Jimmy shot a look at the water.

"Boy! Look at those chunks of ice. The current's moving fast. The river is dangerous this time of year."

"It sure is. But the lake's frozen solid. I was out last week checking my tip-ups."

"Yeah, my dad and I went last weekend to see if we caught anything. We got two yellow perch and a good-sized walleye."

"Swell!"

"You should taste the way my mom makes them. Dips 'em in batter and fries 'em up on the stove. Mmm! My mouth is watering thinking about it."

"We never had any lunch."

"Well, I am hungry. I could eat anything right now. Do you think we have time to stop some place real quick? I mean, only if we can take the time. I'm not putting lunch before the case, you know."

"Not to worry, Jimmy. I'm hungry, too. There's a lunch wagon up the road. Let's stop there. I'll treat you to a hamburger. Then we'll solve the mystery of Mrs. MacDonald."

Chapter 20

While Steven and Jimmy were warm and dry inside, Detective Harry Beckman and Officer Will Taylor were pulling into Syracuse. The weather hadn't relented one minute during the three-hour trip. Sheets of icy rain sluiced over the car. At times the wind carried the rain sideways. Black ice lurked everywhere. Twice they skidded on the treacherous road and almost ran off the pavement.

"What a miserable trip!" Becks exclaimed. "I know we've been in the car, but I swear I feel like a drowned rat."

"You said it! Harry, I know it's getting late, but do you think we could stop for lunch and some hot coffee? I'd really like to warm up before we have to go outside in this mess."

"Me, too. And I need to clear my head. The wipers are making me dizzy. I wish there was a way to make 'em pause every now and then. Yeah, we could use a hot lunch before we tackle the job. I know a place we can go."

Beckman parallel-parked the long, black police vehicle near Hanover Square and they entered a small, smoky lunchroom. The warmth of the eatery and mouth-watering smells drifting from the kitchen were heaven. A saucy waitress looked them both up and down as if she were having a hard time deciding which one she'd choose. As she led them to a table toward the back, Beckman silently raised his eyebrows at Will. The men ordered coffee and a cooked meal. The waitress turned to leave, then seemed to change her mind. She turned back, smiled, and leaned over the table in front of Will. She reached for the sugar bowl and placed it in the center of the table. She winked at Will and said, "Not that you need it."

Will Taylor smirked across the table and said, "I win."

"Evidently she goes for the strong, brooding type," said Beckman wryly.

The food arrived quickly and both officers dug in. As they wolfed down their roast turkey sandwiches and heaps of mashed potatoes with gravy, the rich aromas circled their heads and Beckman thought he'd swoon with sheer joy. "Mmm!"

Will asked, "Do we have a plan on how you want to do this? Should we stick together or split up?"

"Together, I think. At least to start. And I picked this place for a reason. There are several nice hotels and restaurants on Warren Street. The kind a fella would take a dame if he wanted to impress her. We can start at this end and work our way down."

When Beckman and Will left the diner, although the sky was still leaden, the rain had stopped. They were eager to get started.

Will Taylor was an outdoor man who preferred camping and fishing. Although he had been to Ottawa to visit relatives, he did not frequent fancy hotels. When he and Beckman arrived at The Yates Hotel, Will quietly gasped, "This place is huge."

The dark red Yates soared six stories high and took up an entire city block. They entered the elegant lobby, where well-to-do guests sat in deep leather club chairs, their feet softly cushioned by thick Oriental carpets. The police officers skirted several enormous potted palms on their way to the reception desk. Beckman introduced himself to the clerk, showed his badge and identification, and explained why they were there.

"Have you ever seen these two people?" He showed the photographs of Patricia Castleman and John Harrison. "Have they stayed in this hotel?"

The clerk shook his head. "No, sir. They don't look familiar."

They went into the saloon and Will was amazed at the bar. The gleaming wooden surface stretched out in front of them for what seemed like miles.

"I've never seen anything like this!"

Becks laughed. "They say this is the longest bar in Onondaga County. And I believe 'em. Just look at this thing!"

Beckman repeated his questions but neither bartender had seen the man or woman in the photographs. They exited a side door. A loud roar filled the air and Beckman grabbed Taylor by the arm, pulling him back.

"Will, look out!"

An enormous steam locomotive pulling a dozen cars thundered down Railroad Street.

"Where did *that* come from?"

Becks sighed and shook his head. "The trains are a real problem here. They need to build the tracks up high so automobiles and pedestrians are safe. Look at this, right in the middle of town. What were they thinking?" he added, brushing off the dust the thundering train had thrown on his immaculately clean and pressed trousers.

The two policemen continued along Warren Street, stopping at The Vanderbilt Hotel and the Hotel Manhattan, where they encountered the same disappointing results. Neither Patricia Castleman nor John Harrison looked familiar to any of the front desk clerks or bartenders.

No one remembered seeing either of them.

The officers trudged further down the street. Two blocks later on the corner of Jefferson, they looked up in admiration. The Hotel Onondaga was twice as tall as The Yates, its twelve stories towering over the nearby buildings.

They repeated their questions to the silver-haired manager at the reception desk and the half-dozen employees in the Dickens Room, the Tudor Room, and the Travel Room. After receiving the same negative answer from everyone, Will's enthusiasm waned.

"*Where* are these people meeting? How many hotels are there in Syracuse?"

"We've got one more to check. But I want to go upstairs before we leave here."

His first sight of the incredible floor-to-ceiling paned window in the Roof Garden Restaurant restored Will Taylor's mood as he gazed out at the view. "Look at that! I'm going to bring my girl here for her birthday next summer. Is that Onondaga Lake?"

"Yes, and there's a swell park alongside it. You could plan the whole day. Bring her here for lunch then drive over to the lake. There's an amusement park that has a carousel with carved horses all painted in different designs, like costumes. There's usually music in one of the bandstands, too. It'd be a great day."

"Thanks, Harry. That's a swell idea."

"Harry! Long time no see." The good-looking, tuxedoed maître d' extended his hand to Beckman.

"Marlon! How are you?"

"Aces! What brings you here? Business?"

"Yeah, we're working on a murder case that might have some ties here." Beckman introduced the two men, then took out the photographs. "Have you ever seen these people together?"

He studied the pictures. "Nope. Sorry to say I haven't." He caught several waiters passing by. No one recognized the two faces.

Back out on the sidewalk, Will said, "This was a wasted trip. We've got nothing."

"Don't give up yet, Taylor. There's one more hotel and we haven't even started the restaurants. Here, I've got an idea. There're a couple of places on the other side of the street. Why don't we save time and split up this last block? You check the restaurants and I'll take the Hotel Syracuse. I'll meet you at the revolving door."

"Sounds good."

"When we're done, we might as well call it a day and go over to my parents'. It's getting late anyway."

A short while later, Beckman, from his perch on the hotel steps, saw Will Taylor at the curb across the street. The afternoon's glum look had been replaced by a smile. Will gave Becks the thumbs up and mouthed *I've got something*.

After Steven's treat of fried hamburger steaks and onions, he and Jimmy got back on the road. They drove through a bleak landscape. Thick clouds hovered oppressively low and heavy snow blanketed miles of frozen fields where rows of corn stalks stood like broken soldiers. They passed white wooden farmhouses that blended in and bright red clapboard barns that made the only cheerful note in this grim environment. They checked the numbers on every rural mailbox. Steven explored uneven, rutted, frozen dirt driveways. The two officers bounced up and down and were thrown from side to side. Despite the plush, tufted upholstery of Steven's car, it soon became uncomfortable.

"I hope your car doesn't fall apart, Steven."

"It'll take more than this to hurt a Chevy! She's solid."

The policemen inquired at every house within ten miles in each direction from where the MacDonalds' home should have been.

Nothing matched the address on the bank index card. No one had ever heard of a family named MacDonald living anywhere in the area.

Finally Steven looked over at the young officer in the passenger seat and said, "Well, Jimmy, that confirms what I suspected."

"There is no MacDonald family, is there?" said Jimmy solemnly. "Somebody made it up. That has to be somebody who works at the bank. Lawrence Castleman wouldn't have been able to forge the information on the safe-deposit box card. Would he?"

Steven shook his head. "That's what I think. Let's go back to the station. We won't have the lab results for a couple of days. But we do have all of the bank employees' prints on file. We can do a preliminary match."

He pulled on the headlights. The road was suddenly bright with illuminated details.

"I believe we're going to find just one set." Steven glanced at Jimmy Bou, sitting upright and alert a foot away on the bench seat. "And that's going to be the prints of our killer and thief."

"And we know who that is, don't we, Steven?"

"Yes, Jimmy. We do."

TUESDAY - PRESENT DAY

Chapter 21

Olivia was enjoying her solitary walk to the museum this morning. Isabel had gone over earlier. As she listened to the flute-like trilling of a few intrepid birds who refused to go south for the winter, she had a sudden, vivid flashback. Transported by the morning air which somehow smelled the same—fresh and full of the day's promise—her mind flew back to her ten-year-old self traipsing over snow-covered sidewalks with Liz and Sophie on their way to school. The memory was brief but crystalline—she pictured her backpack stuffed with homework papers and books, she smelled the hot chocolate and tomato soup her mom had packed for her lunch. She smiled, relishing the wonderful memory.

The clock in the tower on the village green chimed nine as she was climbing the museum steps. When she entered the workroom, Olivia saw Isabel bending over a newspaper, her smooth, white helmet of hair falling forward like wings on each side of her face.

"Morning. Beautiful day isn't it?"

"Oh yes! Sunshine twice in one week. I'm not sure if I can stand the excitement."

"I see somebody already brought us some more boxes. And you got a head start."

"Look what I found!" Isabel held up a front page with the August 1959 headline "HAWAII BECOMES THE 50TH STATE." Isabel smiled. "J.R. and I went there for our honeymoon *and* for our twenty-fifth anniversary."

"I envy you. That's what I thought I was going to have," Olivia said quietly then quickly added, "Hey! I can't believe I've never even asked. What does J.R. stand for?"

"Junior. Harry Beckman, Junior. Born September 14, 1936." Isabel sighed. "I miss him."

The two women unpacked, sorted, and catalogued the contents of three more boxes. Olivia enjoyed reading the famous headlines but kept her eyes peeled. Sadly, there were no more papers recounting Steven's murder investigation. *Looks like the decision's been taken out of my hands. I suppose that's good. I would've been tempted.*

Isabel set aside a *New York Times* to copy an article for her daughter Jennifer, a geneticist who was working on a breast cancer vaccine at Johns Hopkins Hospital in Baltimore. The banner read, "SALK VACCINE WORKS."

Jennifer had always been interested in science. During several summer vacations when she'd been Olivia's constant babysitter, she had encouraged Olivia's curiosity about the world around her. Each week, Jennifer organized what she called "science field trips." They'd traipsed through the woods looking at mushrooms, leaves, and mossy logs, collected fireflies in glass jars, and made a photo file of butterflies on Jennifer's computer. Jennifer held a special place in Olivia's childhood memories.

Olivia and Isabel finished the final carton shortly before noon. Two long tables held towering stacks of newspapers—they guessed over 300 of them.

Isabel exclaimed, "That's a good job done!"

Olivia laughed. "You said it! We can celebrate that *and* your birthday tonight."

"I'm looking forward to seeing the girls. It's been since Christmas."

Olivia squinted up at the still-shining sun and readily donned her sunglasses. She increased her pace as she made her way home. She had a lot to accomplish this afternoon—additional research for Dr. Vanguard, fixing dinner, and decorating for the birthday party. *What a great day!* Her friends were coming for the evening and later on she hoped to see Steven. She'd been disappointed when she'd awoken in the middle of last night and realized that she'd missed him.

Olivia made a quick sandwich—thick crunchy peanut butter and rich blackberry jam—and washed it down with a glass of milk. She put a large pot of chicken chili on the stove to simmer and set the timer. She made sure the beer and Isabel's favorite Chardonnay were chilling in the fridge. She set the bottles of red on the counter, then went upstairs to her office.

On Saturday, Olivia had received an e-mail from the LeMoyne College professor for whom she had done research on *time*. If she'd only known then what she knew now! Dr. Vanguard had decided to inject what he called "a fun note" into the book he was writing. He wanted Olivia to compile a list of books on time travel: those considered popular fiction as well as classic stories in literature, from the 1800s through the present day. He also requested a listing of films. The physics professor planned to add an appendix so his readers could enjoy some less-serious reading or a time-travel movie.

Olivia's goal for the next couple of hours was to find the most well-known titles. She decided to arrange the books in chronological order using their publication dates. She smiled as she typed the first title on her list, knowing it would surprise people. She had chosen *A Christmas Carol,* by Charles Dickens, published in 1843. Everyone was so familiar with this perennial holiday favorite that Olivia bet very few ever thought of Ebenezer Scrooge's visits with the Ghosts of Christmas Past, Present, and Future as time travel. But in her opinion, they qualified.

Second was an American classic, Mark Twain's 1889 *A Connecticut Yankee in King Arthur's Court.* Although time travel was not the central theme in the book, Olivia included it because, according to the online summary, the main character does travel into the past. Due to a blow on the head, he journeys from the 1800s to fifth-century England, the time of King Arthur and Camelot. Sounds interesting, she thought. Maybe I'll get it out of the library next time I'm there.

Olivia thought that her third listing was the most obvious one, *The Time Machine,* published in 1895 by H. G. Wells. It tells the tale of an inventor known simply as The Time Traveler who meets people called the Eloi hundreds of thousands of years in the future. Steven had mentioned that he read science fiction. Olivia wondered if he had read this classic.

She was rolling right along now. Olivia skipped three-quarters of a century and jumped to 1969 and Kurt Vonnegut's *Slaughterhouse Five.* As she typed the title, she made a mental note to include it and the three previous ones on her list of movies as well. She ended the preliminary list with Michael Crichton's *Timeline* and Diana Gabaldon's *Outlander* series.

Olivia went to the stuffed and overflowing bookcases lining the walls of her spare room, dubbed *the library,* and grabbed some of the novels her mother hadn't wanted to take to California. She added to the growing list: Daphne du Maurier's *The House on the Strand, The*

Mirror by Marlys Millhiser, *Summersea* by Eileen Lottman, and finally her own favorite, *The Time Traveler's Wife* by Audrey Niffenegger.

She glanced at the time in the corner of the screen. *Yikes! Why was it always later than you thought?* She still had to hang the Happy Birthday banner and set the table, plus freshen up and change. They would be arriving soon. She quickly created the framework for the catalog of film titles and googled "time-travel movies." There were so many it was overwhelming. She decided to include everything that came up and check each one later. The list began: *Déjà Vu, Midnight in Paris, Back to the Future, The Lake House, Frequency, Peggy Sue Got Married,* and the classic *Somewhere in Time* that they'd talked about the other day. She typed in *Dr. Who, Time Bandits, The Butterfly Effect,* and even *Hot Tub Time Machine* and *Bill and Ted's Excellent Adventure.* At the last minute, she added a movie she'd watched with her mom and liked—*For All Time* with Mark Harmon and Mary McDonnell, filmed years before the two actors had starring roles in *NCIS* and *Major Crimes.* That was a good start. She'd work some more tomorrow then send the completed lists to Professor Vanguard by the end of the week.

The doorbell rang at six o'clock and Olivia ran downstairs still buttoning up her sweater. Her two best friends bustled in—Sophie carrying the cake, Liz with a brightly wrapped gift and beautiful bouquet of flowers. They were kicking off their boots when the bell rang again. Olivia opened the door for Isabel. They chorused "Happy Birthday" as she came in. Everyone hugged everyone else, then Olivia's guests hung their coats in the hall closet and they all padded into the kitchen.

"Mmm. That smells great!" enthused Liz.

"Chili is one of Isabel's favorites," said Olivia.

"Oh, Olivia, everything looks so beautiful," cried Isabel. "You girls spoil me."

Liz got a beer out of the refrigerator and Sophie opened the wine as Olivia dished out the chili. They sat cozily around the kitchen table and ate. After Isabel blew out the candles, they sang a rousing "Happy Birthday" and Isabel opened her gifts—a certificate for a manicure, a novel she'd been wanting to read, and a box of chocolates, along with the flowers that had graced the table.

Isabel stood up, went around the table, and gave each of them a big hug. "I don't know what to say," she said, her eyes glistening. "You're all just wonderful."

Olivia served coffee and dessert and Sophie began to reminisce about a game that the three friends had invented when they were in middle school.

"I remember," exclaimed Olivia. "It was when we started reading the Nancy Drew books. We all wanted to be detectives."

"I loved that game!" said Liz.

"What's this? I don't think I ever heard about this one," inquired Isabel.

"Our mystery game. Oooooo." Liz made an attempt at ghostly sounds.

Several evenings a week one summer, the three girls got together on Sophie's back porch and made out a "list of suspects." This consisted of descriptions of eight to ten completely imaginary people. They put both men and women on their list, as well as blonds, brunettes, redheads, bald and gray-haired people. There were short, fat people and tall, skinny ones. They used every combination they could think of. Their suspects were dressed in all kinds of different-colored clothing and drove a wide variety of cars. Some were on foot. Some wore hats or glasses. Some of the men sported a beard or mustache.

When the list was completed—they actually wrote it down in a notebook—they left the house and went for a walk around town. As they found people who matched the descriptions on their list, they would whoop and holler, thrilled that they could check off another suspect. It never failed to amaze them that they actually saw people they had described on the list.

"You know, I still can't believe it," said Olivia. "I don't remember one single night that we came home without finding most of those people we made up. And I think a few times we found all of them."

"I know, right? And our descriptions were really detailed," said Sophie.

"That sounds like a very creative game," said Isabel.

"Yeah, we were such prodigies," Liz sniggered.

Everyone laughed.

Steven was in the pantry putting a loaf of bread back in the metal bread box when suddenly he heard laughter. Wondering if he'd accidentally left the radio on, he turned and saw Olivia and three women sitting at the kitchen table. Steven was so surprised that he froze. Caught in mid-step, he carefully put his foot down so as not to make a sound. He had no idea if they'd be able to see or hear him, but he didn't want to take any chances. He quietly let his breath out and softly closed the pantry door until there was only a thin crack, through which he could see the kitchen and hear the conversation.

What was going on? They'd never been able to see each other in another part of the house. He peered through the narrow opening, careful to keep in the shadows in case Olivia or one of the women turned in his direction. I wonder who they are, he thought. The elderly lady must be her grandmother. Were the two girls cousins? Sisters? Friends? He realized that the only thing he knew about her family was that her parents had moved to California.

So, this is her kitchen, he thought. *Very cheerful.* The walls and cupboards were painted a creamy white and there were lots of bright red things all around. He noticed a red tea kettle on a streamlined stove and a pot of food that smelled delicious. He saw a stack of dishes on the counter, and coffee cups and small plates sitting on the red-and-blue plaid tablecloth. There were gift wrappings—beautiful paper and ribbons—littering the table. They must have had some kind of party.

Steven continued looking. A couple of electrical appliances whose function he could not imagine sat on the counter. Red-and-white polka dot curtains framed the windows and several green plants grew in small pots on the sill. His eye settled on an enormous steel box that must be the refrigerator. Steven could not believe the size of the thing. Why would anybody need such a huge icebox?

The elderly woman stood and said, "It's late. I'd better be getting home to bed. And you girls have to work tomorrow."

The women left the kitchen, chatting noisily.

Steven was overwhelmed with emotion. He was shocked to see Olivia downstairs in a completely different part of his house. He'd been sure there was something special, something magical, about the bedroom doorway. He assumed they would never be able to see each other in any other place. The fact that he could clearly see and hear, not only her but other people as well, was totally unexpected.

Just *think* of the possibilities! For the first time he could picture the two of them sharing a meal at his or her kitchen table. Did food taste the same in the twenty-first century? He imagined them sitting comfortably in the living room listening to the radio. They could discuss President Roosevelt's "Fireside Chats," laugh over George Burns and Gracie Allen, or follow the adventures of The Shadow. He wondered what her favorite shows were. She probably listened to the radio on that snazzy machine of hers. Would he eventually be able to go into *her* living room? What would *that* be like? Would he ever be able to go outside?

Steven's brain was buzzing. So many questions, thoughts, and possibilities were swirling around inside his head that he never noticed Olivia turn out the lights and go upstairs for the night. He exited the pantry. As he stepped over the threshold, his 1934 kitchen came back into focus. No more cheerful red-and-white polka dots. No enormous icebox. His kitchen looked empty and sadly disappointing—a free-standing, white enamel cupboard unit with built-in sections labeled for coffee, tea, and spices; a bin for flour; and the porcelain worktop that his mother had been so proud of. *Approved by the Good Housekeeping Institute!* He saw the tiny sink and small combination stove-kitchen heater. All very white. All very boring.

Steven sat at the table, *cloth-less*, thinking it through in the dark.

Chapter 22

Olivia set her glass of wine on the side table, clicked on the TV, and settled on the loveseat to wait. She saw and heard Steven at the same time. Her breath caught.

"Hi, Olivia."

He stood casually on the other side of the doorway.

"Steven!" She got up and went to meet him.

"Did you get a good sleep last night? You must have been tired."

"You came? You saw me?"

"Yes. Um, Olivia, I have something to tell you."

"About your case? Did you solve it?"

"No, not that. It's about...eh...what we're doing here."

"What do you mean?"

"We have some new developments...I saw you in the kitchen before."

"What? Oh, my God! You saw me?"

"Yes, I was in the pantry. All of a sudden I heard people laughing. I turned around and I saw you and three women at the table. I didn't know what to do. I didn't know what would happen if I tried to leave the pantry or if you'd hear me if I said something. I didn't want to take a chance that they'd see me or hear me—I didn't know who they were. I thought maybe two of them might be the friends you told me about, but I had no idea who the older woman was." He blew out his cheeks.

Olivia exhaled, "Wow! Well, first of all yes, the two younger ones were Liz and Sophie, my best friends. They know. The older lady was my neighbor Isabel. Today's her birthday and we gave her a little party. She does not know."

"I see. Well, I thought I'd better not do anything. I figured it was safer to wait and talk with you."

"Steven, this is exciting! It opens up all kinds of possibilities."

"I wonder why this is happening to us, Olivia. I mean to *you and me* in particular."

She shrugged. "Maybe because we're open to it."

"We did accept it pretty quickly."

"Or maybe our paths happened to cross at the right moment and…" She shrugged again then grinned and leaned forward. "I've got an idea. Are you game?" She sparkled with anticipation.

Steven had no idea what she was going to suggest, but he took a deep breath and said, "Sure. What do you want to do?"

"I want to come into 1934."

"What! How? What makes you think we could go into each other's time? Seeing you from the pantry is one thing, but one of us actually crossing the time barrier, or whatever it is, is a whole different ball game. How would you get back? What if you got stuck here?"

"It's the next logical step, isn't it? We've made the connection between your time and mine. But we both *belong* in our own time. I don't think I'd be in any danger of getting trapped in the wrong year."

"Hmm, we belong in our own time. That makes sense." He nodded.

"And I have an idea we can try before I actually do it."

"What's your idea?"

"I'll hand you something that *absolutely* belongs in 2014. I'll let go and step back. You reach into the doorway and set it on the floor of *my* bedroom. You should be able to put it back because it belongs in my time."

"All right, let's see if it works."

Olivia handed him her cell phone, backed into her room, and sat on the edge of the bed. Mr. Moto scrambled up onto her lap.

"What's this?"

"It's my phone."

"This is a telephone? Where's the cord? And the receiver? For that matter, how do you dial? Weird." Steven reached across the threshold and set the cell phone on the floor. "I can see it, but how can we be sure it's back in your time? I can turn around and see everything in 1934 and I can look into your room and see 2014."

At that moment, Olivia's phone rang. "Well, there's our answer! If it was in your time, it couldn't ring because you don't have the technology to make it work yet."

"Wow, we did it! Aren't you going to answer it?"

"No, that's okay."

"Olivia, I think we should try one more thing before you leap into 1934."

"What's that?"

"Your kitten."

"Mr. Moto? What about him?"

"Mr. Moto, that's a funny name for a cat."

"I'll tell you later. Now, what about my cat? Oh, wait. I know what you're thinking."

Steven saw her reluctance. "You'll risk yourself but you won't risk a kitten? Come on. Either you believe this is going to work or you don't."

She went to the door and handed the now squirming Mr. Moto to

Steven. The black cat howled loudly, scratched Steven's hand, jumped out of his arms, and ran back into the bedroom, where he escaped underneath the bed. Two angry green eyes glared at them from behind the dust ruffle.

"Well," said Olivia, "I guess that tells us everything we need to know."

"Okay then, are you ready?" He stretched out his arm and took her hand. He stepped back.

Heart pounding, Olivia crossed the threshold into the past.

Neither moved. They gaped at each other, hardly able to believe what they'd done.

"Welcome to 1934."

"Wow!" Olivia spun around in the hallway. "Are you kidding me? I don't believe it. We did it!" She caught her breath. "Is it okay if I look around? Do you mind?"

"No, of course not. I mean, yes, please, look anywhere you want to. It's your house, too. Sort of."

Olivia peeked in the doorway on the left. Now she understood. The night she'd seen Steven "walk through the wall" he'd actually been going into the bathroom. She looked into what appeared to be his room. It was very neat and organized. The bed was made, everything was picked up. One door was closed. She did not intrude.

Steven followed as she went from room to room. When they reached the end of the hall, he gave a mock bow. "Miss Watson from 2014, would you care to join me for tea?" he grinned. They were both silly with success.

She answered with a pretend curtsey, "Why thank you, Detective Blackwell. I would be pleased to have tea with you." She shot him a demure smile.

He held out his arm. They descended the stairs, made a U-turn at the front door, and strolled down a narrow hallway past the living and dining rooms. They stepped into the kitchen.

"Oh, you can really see the difference here. Appliances have sure changed a lot!"

"Yeah, I noticed that when I was in the pantry." He filled the kettle and set it on the stove. "I couldn't help noticing your party was all girls." He moved about the kitchen getting out cups and saucers and the rest of the paraphernalia for tea.

"Oh. Well, Isabel's husband died a couple of years ago. Liz's husband Joe is a doctor and he's on call at the hospital tonight. Sophie just started seeing Luc so..."

"What about you? Are you stepping out with someone?"

"Stepping out?"

"Spending time with someone special. You know, a beau."

Olivia coughed to disguise a small laugh that had escaped. *Beau? Good grief. Who am I, Scarlett O'Hara?*

"No, there's no one right now." She had been wandering around the kitchen examining the odd appliances—so clunky, nothing streamlined like she was used to. She stopped and leaned against a strange white enamel cupboard sort of thing. "I was engaged last year but it didn't work out."

"I'm sorry to hear that."

"Thanks. It was pretty bad. He cheated on me. At least I found out before it was too late." She hesitated. "I'm over it, but I don't like talking about it."

The kettle whistled and Steven focused on the tea-making. He got a bottle of milk out of the refrigerator—it reminded her of something she'd seen at a friend's camp years ago, all rounded corners and small—and set it next to the sugar bowl.

"Here," he said, "come sit down." He opened a bin in the strange cupboard and took out a package of cookies, which he placed in the center of the table.

"Oh my goodness, Fig Newtons! I love those!" She took one and ate a bite. "Hmm, tastes the same. So what about you, Steven? A special lady friend?"

"No."

With an unspoken agreement, they changed the subject.

"What was it like growing up in the…when *did* you grow up?" Olivia realized she had no idea how old he was.

Steven laughed. "I was born in '01. I turned thirty-three a couple of weeks ago."

Olivia closed her eyes and digested what he'd said. *'01, as in* nineteen-*oh-one.*

"Are you all right?"

"Yeah, it just hit me again. I'm sitting here with you eighty years ago—like fifty-some years before I was born!"

They were both quiet.

Olivia laughed. "And you have Fig Newtons! It's surreal." She took another cookie. "I read a Sherlock Holmes story a while ago…he said something like, 'When you have eliminated the impossible, what's left must be the truth.'" She paused. "As impossible as this seems, Steven, I do believe I just time traveled!" And she shouted, "Woo hoo!"

"I'm speechless," he said, grinning.

They drank their tea and munched cookies.

After a couple of minutes, she raised her tea cup in a toast. He mirrored her and they drank to the *possible.*

"So tell me about your childhood," she said.

Steven was a wonderful storyteller. He told her about weekends with his Aunt Jenny and Uncle Mike at their camp on Indian Lake. As he spoke, Olivia smelled the sharp musty scent of the forest floor, imagined him as a boy walking barefoot on a thick bed of pine needles, bending over to examine feathery ferns, squat toadstools, and soft, spongy moss. She saw the sun reflecting off ripples on the lake as his uncle pulled long flapping trout or huge squirming bass from the water while Steven and his cousin sat in the boat with raptured looks on their young faces. She heard the carefree, summertime joy. Steven kept refilling their cups and they polished off a dozen cookies.

"Oh my goodness, it's almost midnight!" Olivia exclaimed. "I need to get some sleep."

"Me, too. I have a big day tomorrow. I need to find some physical evidence. Even though I think I know what happened and why, what I *think* won't stand up in court."

"Who do you think did it?"

"The widow and her boyfriend, the assistant bank manager."

"Oh, classic! Love and money."

He shot her an astonished look. "How do you know about motives?"

"I read a lot of mysteries."

Steven turned off the downstairs light. They climbed the stairs together.

At her bedroom door, Olivia turned and looked up at him. "This was great, Steven. Maybe tomorrow you can come into my time, what do you think?"

"Now *that* is something I'll look forward to! Let's meet earlier."

"I'll be here."

"Swell. Good night, Olivia."

"Good luck with your evidence tomorrow. I hope you get 'em!"

Steven laughed. "It's only a matter of time. Criminals always make mistakes. I'll find them."

Impulsively, Olivia reached over and gave Steven a hug. Then she turned and walked back into the future.

WEDNESDAY - 1934

Chapter 23

"Morning, Chief." Steven knocked on the partially open door and entered the messy, smoke-filled office. He plopped down on a chair and waited for his boss to finish what he was writing. The chief's disheveled carrot-colored hair stuck out all over, and Steven noticed that his shirt strained to cover an ever-expanding belly. On one side of the paper-strewn desk sat his usual morning treat–two rich, iced pastries on a small plate–along with a large cup of the strong black coffee Thompson inhaled throughout the day. Steven was sure that somewhere in a drawer there would be a collection of teaspoons that had been eaten away by the "mud" the chief called coffee.

Andy Thompson grunted and set his pen down. "Tell me you got somethin' for me, Blackwell. It's been four days. We need something on this damn case."

"We're working on it, Chief. But we're playing it by the book."

"I got the mayor on my back, the president of the city council called twice, and Sam Silverstone keeps sending over that annoying reporter from *The Gazette*."

"You know it takes time."

"Yeah, *I* do, but do *they*? I can't keep stallin' everybody."

"Sure you can. It's what you do."

"Castleman was important in this town. Pretty soon they're gonna be out for my blood." He leaned far back in his chair, cigarette in one hand, pastry in the other. "So, whaddya got?"

"The stolen money was definitely in the safe-deposit box. The numbers match."

"Okay, I can spin that."

"The only fingerprints on the registration card and the two boxes were John Harrison's. We don't have official results from the lab yet, but I did a preliminary check. It's a match."

"This just gets worse."

"We *should* have found prints from the woman who's registered as the owner of those boxes . . ."

"I get it. I get it."

". . . a Mrs. Dorinda MacDonald . . ."

"Never heard of her."

". . . but there are no other prints at all. Only Harrison's."

"Maybe she had gloves on the day she signed the card. Or she hurt her hand and he signed for her. Maybe she wore gloves every time she went in and out of the boxes. Believe me, Blackwell, he'll have a plausible explanation all ready."

"Sure, Chief, I expect no less. I'm sure he's got his stories all lined up, ready to parade in front of us when we ask the right questions or make insinuations. But listen to this."

"Tell me it's good."

"Jimmy and I tried to find Mrs. MacDonald's house yesterday and we got nothing. I mean absolutely nothing. We covered a good ten-mile stretch of Route 5 in both directions from where the address should've been. We stopped..."

"Maybe she moved."

". . . and questioned all the people who live there. Nobody's ever heard of her. And there's no house, no farm, nothing. It looks like this woman doesn't even exist."

Thompson glared, then spat, "Okay, point one. Maybe. What else ya got?"

"I'm convinced that Harrison's involved with Patricia Castleman and she tipped him off to her husband being in the vault Friday night."

The chief rolled his eyes and groaned. "God, give me strength. I swear this case is gonna be the death of me." He did an impression of screwing up his face and pretending to cry. Steven thought it was very good. His boss actually looked like he might burst out in frustrated sobs at any moment. "Where's your proof? So far I haven't seen a shred of evidence."

"I realize that, sir. But, listen. How else would the killer have known that Castleman would be in the vault in the middle of the night? We've gone over all the other possibilities and eliminated everything else."

"What about a partner who betrayed him?"

"We thought of that. The partner would have to work at the bank because of the safe-deposit boxes. We checked every employee and no one fits the bill. Either they don't have a motive or their alibi is solid."

"All right, so what now?"

"I'm sending Jimmy over there this morning to shake up three employees who I know are hiding something. Once we've got them worried, Becks and I, or maybe Taylor, will go back and find out what they're lying about. If Jimmy doesn't do it first."

"That's a good idea. Bourgogne is very unassuming. People let their guard down in front of him. They underestimate him."

"Exactly. He's had success in the past because of that. Assuming nothing else comes to light, the only person left is Harrison. Like we said yesterday, there's the fact that he's been *seen* with Patricia Castleman. We have a witness who saw them having lunch together. Harrison denied it. But if there was nothing going on, why would he lie about it?

"Also," Steven pressed on, "Becks called last night with some good news. Taylor found a waiter who recognized the photographs of Mrs. Castleman and Harrison. He was sure he remembered them having dinner together in his restaurant not too long ago."

"That doesn't mean a damn thing, Blackwell. Patricia Castleman's from Syracuse. It makes sense she'd go home every now and then. Harrison has a responsible position at the bank. Whose main office, I hasten to add, is located in *Syracuse*." The chief pointed his finger to emphasize the name and Steven thought he heard an unspoken *ta-dah!* somewhere in the background. "I'm sure Harrison goes there for meetings or conferences or whatever. They could've easily run into each other and agreed to have a meal. Her husband's his boss. Obviously they'd know each other." The chief shook his head. "It could all be completely innocent."

"What about this? A clerk in the Hotel Syracuse definitely remembered Patricia Castleman. He identified her picture right away. He said the fella she was with looked a bit like Harrison."

"It's not there, Blackwell. You don't have it."

"Wait." Steven shifted on the hard wooden seat. "I'm sure about this, Chief. Give me one more day. Let me find somebody who can put the two of them together in a hotel."

Andy Thompson knew that police work was driven by evidence, but a lot of the time you got that evidence by following your gut.

"I want to send Becks to Saratoga tomorrow," Steven said.

"Why, what's in Saratoga? We're not made of money here."

"I know. But I wouldn't ask if I didn't think it was important. According to Ginny Fitzgerald, Mrs. Castleman goes there to visit a friend. That could be a cover story and what she really does is meet Harrison.

"Saratoga's farther away than Syracuse. They might think it would be harder for anybody to check or that no one would consider checking that far away. They'd probably feel safer there and not be so careful about being seen together.

"I want Beckman to show their photographs around the hotels and restaurants. That's not something we can do on the telephone."

"I suppose if I want results, I've gotta give you some leeway." The chief lit another Camel. "All right, he can have one day. That's it. And I'm not authorizing any fancy hotel. He can find a cheap place to stay overnight. When's Valentino gettin' back from Syracuse anyway?"

"Late morning."

"All right, what else? Anything on the murder weapon yet?" He took a drag on the cigarette. "Jeez, Blackwell, we need more than circumstantial evidence on this case."

"I agree. That's one of the things I'm going to concentrate on today."

Steven announced to the patrol room that the morning briefing would take place in five minutes. He stopped Ralph Hiller as the burly patrolman was walking past and explained what he needed. Steven grinned inwardly. Ask Ralph to do anything and you'd get two for the price of one. You never saw Ralph without his sidekick Pete McGrath, the station's joker.

After his team had assembled, Steven brought them up to date. Several officers asked a question or made a comment and a lively discussion broke out. Steven instructed Jimmy to go to the bank to re-question Henry August, Carl Dickson, and Marty Carpenter. He reminded him to reread the case notes of earlier interviews and to be particularly attentive of what was being said when the notes indicated the men had become nervous or uncomfortable.

"Jimmy, I want you to find out what each man was hiding. But, you'll have to be careful. And clever. Once some people start lying, they don't know when or how to stop."

"You can depend on me, Steven. I know what to do."

Steven went on addressing the group. "As I said earlier, our priority today is finding a piece of *concrete* evidence that definitively ties someone to the crime. Ralph's going to coordinate a thorough search of the town and as much of the outlying area as possible. We're looking for the murder weapon. I realize we've already had a go at it, but now that we've got a witness, we know more about what we're looking for.

"Molly Coffin said it looked like a walking stick. It's made of ebony. That means it's black. From her description, we're looking for something close to three feet long. She also said the man's hand was wrapped around the end. Look at your hand."

Everybody stuck out a hand.

"Imagine a piece of wood sturdy enough that you could lean on but small enough around so you can fit it in your hand. A tiny splinter was found in one of the wounds. Look carefully because the piece was very small. If we're lucky there may be some blood left on the weapon. That'll give those boys at our new crime lab something to work on!"

Steven handed Ralph a folder. "Pair 'em up any way you want, Officer. Most of the team's going out except Tommy." He looked toward the doorway where front desk officer Tommy Forester leaned in listening. "Sorry, Tommy, I need you to stay to cover the station. The chief will be here if you need anything."

"That's okay, Detective Blackwell. I don't mind. Maybe somebody will find it thrown into their back yard and bring it in. HA!"

"You never know. All right then, I want everyone else involved in the search. See Ralph for your assignments. Be sure to use your gloves. Turn over everything you see. Look under piles of stuff. Check down by the river. Good luck, everyone."

Ralph stepped forward, his line-backer frame hiding the men behind him. "I have maps with each team's part of town outlined. Detective Sergeant Blackwell wants everyone out on the street no later than nine. I'll call out each team. One of you, come and get your assignment." He called out two names. "You fellas cover the north side." He shouted two more. "Tackle the center of town. Coordinate with the others exactly where you set your perimeters so you don't cover the same streets." Ralph continued calling out pairs of names until he'd covered all points of the compass but one. "Pete and I'll take the south side."

One by one the policemen picked up their maps then moved out of the way to study their assignments.

Steven listened to the men planning and strategizing. This was a lengthy search and would occupy the entire day. Everyone was determined to cover their area before going home. In some cases, that meant the team would skip lunch and stay outside until dark. Steven knew these dedicated professionals would give their very best. If the murder weapon was out there, someone was going to find it before the sun went down.

Thanks to yesterday's warrant, Steven now had the calendar listing John Harrison's appointments at the main office of the bank. He began to compile a list of the days and dates when the banker had gone to Syracuse. He started in the spring of the previous year and saw that the visits were spaced about three weeks apart. Every one was on a Monday or a Friday.

Hmm, he thought, *perfect if your girlfriend visits her sister on the weekend.* Harrison goes up on a Friday and conducts his business. Afterwards he meets her at the station. They spend time together. She can pretend to her sister that she arrived later that night or the next day. Or, she tells her sister she's going out with friends and simply meets Harrison someplace in town. Same goes for Monday, simply reverse the plan.

Steven put through a call to Patricia Castleman's sister.

"Good morning, Mrs. Haydock. This is Detective Sergeant Steven Blackwell with the Knightsbridge Police Department. How are you today?"

"Fine, thank you. How can I help you, Detective?"

"I was wondering if you keep an appointment diary. I need to know the dates your sister visited you in the past few months."

"Why on earth would you possibly have to know that?"

"We like to be thorough, ma'am. Do you keep a calendar?"

"Yes, of course, I do. But, I'm not sure what you are implying with this request."

"I'm not implying anything. It's simply something I need to check. How about if I give you a while to find last year's diary and get this year's, too? I'll call back this afternoon."

Louise Haydock reluctantly agreed and they hung up.

The phone rang again immediately. It was Marty Carpenter. Steven thought he sounded out of breath.

"Steven, I just saw this morning's paper. I think I've got some information for you...about the murder weapon. But I don't want to get anyone in trouble."

"You won't, Marty. If the person you're going to tell me about didn't do anything wrong, they can't get in trouble, can they?"

"All right, I see that. It was when we were kids. November of my senior year in school. Right after the Great War ended. One of our teachers told us to bring in things our dads brought home to share with the class. I remember the walking stick John Harrison brought in. His father got it overseas. Harrison bragged that his father killed an enemy soldier with it. I think it's the stick you're looking for. I read the description in the paper. It sounds the same."

Steven wanted to shout out loud, but he kept his voice even and controlled. "Thanks, Marty. Telling me was the right thing to do. I'll follow up on it. But please don't say anything to anyone. Especially don't let Harrison know what you've told me."

"No problem, Steven. I avoid the man as much as possible."

Steven sat and considered how he wanted to proceed. Marty's information could be the key to finally solving this case. First thing in the morning, he'd get a warrant and search John Harrison's house for the murder weapon. *I've almost got you now.* He got up from his desk and walked over to the murder board. As Steven stared at the board, he tried to picture everything as it might have unfolded over the past several months or maybe longer. He attempted to get into the minds of Patricia Castleman and John Harrison, to think about it, and plan as they might have. He imagined the conversations between them.

She tells him she's unhappy, her husband ignores her, or doesn't understand her. She makes up stories, invents things that never happened. She gets Harrison to believe her. She plays on his vanity. This is his boss's wife. What a triumph it would be for him to take her away from Castleman.

One thing Steven had learned over the years was that John Harrison had a sense of entitlement as well as an enormous ego. It would have been more than a mere feather in his cap to get his boss's wife into bed. How Harrison would have silently gloated each and every time he saw Castleman at the bank. How ripe he must have been for the picking.

For a moment, Steven had to give Patricia Castleman her due. For incisive planning, it didn't get any better than this. This dame knew what she was doing.

How long would it take, he wondered, to convince someone not only that you loved him and he could trust you, but to persuade him to kill for you? In setting up her husband to be in the vault that night, Patricia Castleman had already betrayed *his* trust. How could you put your trust in someone like that? Why would you think she wouldn't betray *you* as well?

Unless you had something on her.

Now there's a thought.

Steven amended his theory. Maybe John Harrison doesn't love her. Maybe he played her as well. Perhaps he did it for the money. Or for the promotion to the top job. Or both. People have killed for a lot less. If he has something on her, he knows she won't betray him. He gets rid of the unwanted husband. They split a lot of money.

Jeez, what a pair! I think I'll pay a little surprise visit to Patricia Castleman before Becks gets back.

Chapter 24

Steven stopped by the front desk, told Tommy Forester where he'd be, and asked him to update Beckman and Will when they returned from Syracuse. "Tell them to hang around if I'm not back, Tommy. They can write their reports while they're waiting. There's something I need them to do today."

"Sure thing, Detective Blackwell."

As he drove up the street, Steven's thoughts drifted to last night. *Holy mackerel! This whole thing is incredible. If I can go into 2014 tonight, I'll believe anything from now on.*

Thinking about it, Steven felt like a character in the science-fiction novels he enjoyed reading so much. Although he wasn't going twenty thousand leagues under the sea like Professor Aronnax, traveling from the Earth to the moon like Michel Ardan, or journeying to the center of the Earth like the famed Professor Von Hardwigg, this would be just as exciting. *Just!* What was he thinking? They were only books, fiction. He would be *living* it!

What would he see in his time machine of a house? What would things look like in the twenty-first century? He already had a brief glimpse when he'd peered out into Olivia's kitchen last night. What else would he be able to see? Would he be able to leave the house? Could she take him outside so he could see the Knightsbridge of the future?

Cars! That's what he wanted to see most of all. Cars! What would they look like in 2014? Would you have to steer or would they go on their own? Steven bet that they'd be long and sleek. He recalled seeing a picture of a 1919 Peugeot after the Indianapolis 500 that year. Like a lot of eighteen-year-olds, he'd been crazy about automobiles. He remembered that particular model because it had looked like a cigar to him. He couldn't *wait* for tonight!

Steven pulled into the driveway at 22 Swan Lane. He put the Chevy in neutral, pulled the parking brake, and shut off the engine. The same woman he'd seen Sunday answered the door. This time she made him wait outside, stamping his feet to keep the blood circulating, until she had announced his arrival and Mrs. Castleman cleared him to enter the house.

Patricia Castleman was more aloof and colder than before. Clearly annoyed by this visit, she allowed him to follow her into the parlor but did not invite him to sit down.

"I can't believe you would bother me on a day like today, Detective. I'm in the middle of planning a funeral. These preparations do take time, you realize."

She wore a dark charcoal gray silk dress which rustled as she moved about the room in tight, twitching movements.

"Yes, I'm sure they do. Although," Steven arranged a confused look on his face, "I thought I'd heard that everything was settled yesterday. Maybe I have it wrong."

"The more public arrangements have been made, Detective. There *are* personal preparations as well." She glared at him.

"Yes, Mrs. Castleman, of course. And I do apologize for intruding on your . . ." He paused to see if it would have any effect. ". . . grief." It didn't.

"What do you want?" She stopped at the mantle to adjust the ornaments, exchanging their already perfectly balanced positions for an awkward arrangement.

"I have some follow-up questions." He pretended to consult his notes. "When you visit your sister in Syracuse, what do you do? What activities?"

She spun around. "How can this *possibly* be relevant?"

"It's all in the details, ma'am. If you wouldn't mind?"

She huffed and closed her eyes in an exaggerated gesture of gathering patience around her. Then she pursed her lips and frowned. "We go shopping. We go out to lunch. Sometimes we see a movie. We go to the theater. I spend time with my niece and nephew. Why you are taking up my time with irrelevant matters such as this, I cannot imagine."

"Your sister mentioned that you also see some friends when you're there. Could you give me their names, please?"

"You have *got* to be kidding."

Steven said nothing.

"They're friends from school and when I was working."

Poised with his notebook and pencil at the ready, Steven raised his eyebrows.

"All right, let me see...there's Betty Tulane, Maggie Fletcher, Veronica Baker, Mary Lou McMurry, and Joan Patterson."

"And their addresses and telephone numbers?"

"I don't know off-hand. I'd have to look them up."

"That's fine. I'll wait while you get your address book. And while you're getting it, I'd also like to see your appointment diary for this year and last, please."

"My what? What could you possibly want with my appointment

diary? No. Enough is enough. This is an intrusion into my privacy and I won't have it. You should be out there looking for my husband's killer, not harassing me during my time of mourning."

"I don't believe I am harassing you. It's a simple request."

"I don't understand of what use my personal calendar could be to you."

Steven sauntered over to one of the sofas and slowly sat down. He leaned back and crossed his legs. "Well, I'll be more than happy to explain all about police procedure. We can sit and discuss it while one of my men brings over a court order. That is, if you don't want to give me the diaries now. Although it could take a while. But I don't have any pressing appointments today."

Frustrated, she spat, "Fine. Okay, fine. I'll get them. Wait here."

Steven smiled after she'd left the room. Yep, worked like a charm. Every time.

He stood when she returned a moment later. He wrote down the information as she read aloud the addresses and telephone numbers of her friends. He scribbled something on a separate page in his notebook, tore it out, and extended his hand.

"I'll give you a receipt for the appointment books, Mrs. Castleman."

"A receipt? What do you mean a receipt? You don't think you can take these, do you?" She was getting flustered.

Good, Steven thought, *she gets upset, she'll make a mistake.* "Actually I do. I can take them with me and study them for as long as our investigation requires." He paused and looked directly in her eyes. "Is there a reason why I shouldn't look into your appointment diaries, Mrs. Castleman?" Another brief pause as he stared her down. "By the way, tell me about your relationship with John Harrison."

Steven was gratified to see a flicker of fear in her eyes. *I knew I was right! I've got you now, lady.* "How often do you get together for lunch?"

She looked like she wanted to spit at him. Or maybe claw his eyes out. "John Harrison is my husband's assistant manager. I have no *relationship* with him. And I do not get together with him for lunch. I don't know where you could have possibly gotten that idea."

"You were seen. We have a witness who saw you together."

"Your witness is mistaken."

"I see. Well, here is that receipt, Mrs. Castleman." Steven held out his left hand as his right closed on the two appointment books. He gave an almost imperceptible tug.

Surprised, she let go of the diaries. "Take them. I don't care!" She abstractedly smoothed a hand over her hair then curtly dismissed him. "Mary will see you out, Officer."

Harrison had said that the other day. "Officer" instead of "Detective," and here it was again. Steven was pleased to hear her feeble attempt at regaining what she thought was her superiority. "I'll show myself out, thanks." He leaned over and whispered, "We'll talk again."

Let her chew that one over.

Steven couldn't wait to get back to the station and check Patricia Castleman's visits to Syracuse against the dates of Harrison's business trips. Let them match, he silently pleaded.

It was obvious from the first glance that his wish had been granted. Dozens of dates coincided. Steven wrote down every day and date from the spring of 1933 to the most recent trip in January of this year. There was a pattern.

Steven strode to the murder board and grabbed a piece of chalk. Time for another update. He created a new heading—SUSPECTS (UNLIKELY)—and moved *Marty Carpenter, Henry August, Carl Dickson,* and *Lawrence Castleman* to that column. Steven was eager to discover what Jimmy had been able to shake out this morning. He hoped new information would eliminate one or more of the bank employees. The victim's brother merited another visit today and, hopefully, his name would be gone tonight as well.

Steven made room for a circle in the middle of the board and wrote SUSPECTS. He listed only two names under the heading—*Patricia Castleman* and *John Harrison*. He reorganized then streamlined all the information they'd accumulated so far. He added some new items to the background material on Patricia and Leo Castleman and John Harrison. From the circle, he connected lines to the evidence and included the source of the data. He diagrammed the relationship among the three of them and listed the coinciding dates when Patricia and Harrison had both been in Syracuse. Finally he added a copy of the photographs that Beckman and Will Taylor had shown to the restaurant and hotel employees.

He stared at the new board. *We're getting there, but I still need something concrete. The murder weapon or something that proves Harrison was at the scene. Because I can't see either of them cracking and confessing. I need more.*

Steven feared that one day soon his two main suspects were going to disappear. If that happened, he'd never be able to find them or get them back for trial.

His stomach reminded him it was past noon. *Where'd the morning go?* He unpacked his sandwiches, pulled out the large, bottom desk drawer, and propped up his feet. As he was enjoying his lunch, he heard the booming voice of his friend and partner echo through the hallway. *Ah, good. Becks is back.*

Harry Beckman sauntered into the CID room, hung his hat and coat on a hook, poured himself a cup of coffee, and sat down across from Steven. "So, what'd we miss? Anything break?"

"I paid a visit to the widow. I think we're getting someplace."

Steven told Becks about the calendar of bank appointments, Mrs. Castleman's private diaries, and the overlapping schedule of their visits to Syracuse. Will wandered in and listened.

"Do you want me to join one of the teams, Steven? I can go out and help look for the murder weapon." Taylor munched on a meatloaf sandwich and drank from his thermos of milk.

"No, thanks, Will. I've got something else for you and Becks, as soon as you both catch your breath." Steven explained that he wanted the two officers to go to the sawmill and re-interview Lawrence Castleman.

"Both Jimmy and I had the impression that Castleman's brother was genuinely shocked when we gave him the news. But I'd like your opinions as well. Especially you, Will. I want you to use that special sense of yours."

Taylor nodded.

"Check his alibi for Friday night. He said he was home but no one's had the chance to verify it yet. We need to be sure it really *is* Harrison that Patricia Castleman is having the affair with. Maybe she's been fooling around with her brother-in-law. Find out what he thinks of her and of his brother's marriage. See what kind of marriage *he* has.

"We'll ask about his money situation, too," said Becks. "Maybe we've been wrong and there's no affair at all. Maybe Leo and his brother were in it together for the cash."

"Yeah, Jimmy mentioned Cain and Abel earlier. It's worth checking into."

Steven stowed his empty lunch box and thermos. "There is one other thing, Becks."

"Uh oh. Already, I don't like the sound of this."

"Tomorrow morning, early as you can, I want you to go to Saratoga."

"Saratoga! What for?"

Steven explained the plan and the arrangements that had been made. "The chief's given his blessing, Becks. You're approved to go. For one day only. And," he emphasized, "you have to keep your expenses down to a bare minimum. The chief was adamant on that."

"Okay. I get it. But *one* day? It's going to take me half a day to get there. Then time to get my bearings, find a place to stay, and probably another half a day to check all the likely places. That's if I'm lucky."

"You know you can get one of their patrolmen to help. Chief Thompson talked with Saratoga's chief, told him you were coming. Stop at the station and get some help. That'd save time."

"Maybe. We'll see. At least Saratoga's not very big. I guess if I hustle, I can split my interviews into tomorrow afternoon and Friday morning." He glanced at his overnight bag. "I'll have to shift a few clean things later tonight."

"Do your best. If the weather doesn't cooperate and you lose time on the road, you'll have to stay an extra night. Don't worry about that. I can always square it with the chief. The main thing is to get a positive ID on Patricia Castleman and Harrison *together*. If you can get a confirmation that they're having an affair, it'll be worth the trip."

Detective Harry Beckman and Sergeant Will Taylor took a detour to Lawrence Castleman's house on their way to the sawmill. After twenty-five minutes of questioning Just-Call-Me-Larry's wife, both officers were inclined to believe he'd been home on the night of his brother's murder.

"I think it's unlikely that Lawrence Castleman *and* his wife are such good liars that they fooled four trained police officers," said Will, as Becks directed the motor car back across town.

"Yeah, I agree. But, we'll talk to him one more time and, like Steven said, use that intuition of yours to suss out anything that doesn't sound quite right." Becks turned onto Oak Street and, shortly after, pulled into the gravel parking lot fronting the Mohawk River Sawmill.

As Steven had done several days ago, Beckman and Will climbed the rough staircase to Lawrence Castleman's mezzanine-level office.

Becks knocked on the doorframe.

"Mr. Castleman, I'm Detective Harry Beckman and this is Sergeant Will Taylor." Both officers flipped open a small leather case holding a badge and identification card. "We have some follow-up questions."

Castleman waved them into his office and onto a couple of visitors' chairs. "Is there any news? Do you know who did it?" He looked anxiously from one officer to the other.

"Not quite yet, sir, but we're getting there," Becks assured him.

"What can I do to help?"

"Do you own a safe-deposit box, Mr. Castleman?" asked Beckman.

"No, I'm comfortable but we don't have that much." He opened a desk drawer and pulled out a cigar then struck a match across the sole of his heavy work boot. He puffed a few times to get it going. "My wife and I have been lucky during this Depression. All the extra projects going on in the area have allowed me to keep the mill running."

"How long have you been married, sir?" inquired Will.

A gentle smile lit up Castleman's rough face. "Twenty years next week. I got me the best girl in the county." He gave an abrupt laugh. "Well, you can tell that, can't you? She puts up with me." And he laughed again.

"What did you think about your brother's marriage, Mr. Castleman?" Beckman asked.

"Wasn't what I'd call a marriage," Lawrence Castleman scowled. "If you want my opinion, she was just using him. For his money, I mean. Leo was a soft touch. I think Patricia saw him coming a mile away. I doubt she ever had any feelings for him."

"You sound angry, sir" commented Will.

"Of course, I'm angry. Leo deserved a hell of a lot better than what he got. Now, if Patricia was the one lying in the morgue, you'd be looking at suspect number one," Lawrence Castleman pronounced. "Is there anything else, fellas? No? Good. I've got work to do."

And with that, he ushered them out the door.

Chapter 25

It was dark by five o'clock and all across town, lights flickered on. The temperature was falling fast. The smell of snow was in the air. People trudged home from work, cold, tired, and hungry. In warm, cozy kitchens, in neighborhood after neighborhood, families sat together around the table, ate supper, shared their day, and exchanged gossip. There was still much talk about the recent murder and scandal at the bank.

After the evening meal, wives and mothers stood wearily at the kitchen sink, washed, and dried the dishes. Kids helped, played, or started their homework. Men kicked off their shoes, enjoyed a second cup of coffee and a cigarette, and opened the evening newspaper. Tonight's headline, "POLICE STILL BAFFLED," was not comforting.

In one neighborhood not far from the Mohawk River, as it looped around to the east side of town, a lone man finished cleaning his kitchen. He had no wife to cook and clean for him, no children to greet him when he returned home, no one with whom he could share the burdens of the day. The man turned off the kitchen light and was heading for the living room when the telephone rang. He picked up the receiver on the fourth ring.

"Hello."

"It's me."

"How are you?"

"I'm okay. Listen, it has to be tonight."

"I know. I realized that today, too."

"Are you ready? Do you have everything?"

"Yeah, don't worry. It's almost over."

"I can't wait to get out of this town."

"Only a few more days. Be patient."

"I'm trying."

"I'll see you soon."

"Yeah, well. Good night."

Shortly after ten thirty, John Harrison turned out the downstairs lights and was about to head up to bed when the door bell rang. *What the hell,* he thought angrily. He spun around and crossed the dark living room to the front door. He snapped on the porch light to see who had the nerve to call at this hour. He moved one of the drapery panels aside and saw the man standing there. That figures, he mumbled with disgust. He let the drape fall back and undid the lock. He jerked the door open.

"Do you realize what time it is?"

"Sorry. It won't take long. Can I come in for a minute?"

Scowling, Harrison stepped aside to let the man in. "So, what is it?"

"Don't you want to turn on a lamp? It's pretty dark in here." Harrison's guest turned, stretched out a gloved hand, and closed the door behind him.

"No, I don't," he snapped. "I want to go to bed. I'm tired." He reached over and turned on a small lamp anyway. "Now, what's so important that it couldn't wait until tomorrow?"

"This," said the visitor, as he took out a gun and shot Harrison straight through the heart.

As John Harrison lay dead and bleeding on the patterned Brussels rug, eyes wide open, his visitor hardened his heart and tried to avoid looking at the man he'd just killed. Making sure he didn't step in any of the pooling blood, he crossed to the front entry, extinguished the small lamp and the porch light then let himself out, shutting the door tightly. He did not look back.

The neighborhood was dark and quiet as he made his way down Mulberry Lane. It had to be done, he told himself. Don't think about it. He had only walked one block when he leaned over to the edge of the sidewalk and threw up. Doubled over, he retched and heaved for a full minute. Disgusted, he took out a handkerchief and cleaned off his mouth. He shuddered as he folded the cotton square, the clean side facing out, then put it back in his pocket. He managed to go another four houses when a fox ran in front of him.

The animal was low and sleek, and in the moonlight his russet coat shimmered. It was an exquisite creature. The fox stopped suddenly and the man noticed that it had something in its mouth. The animal dropped the thing it had been carrying, which fell to the ground with a muffled sound. The man could not help himself. As the fox ran away, he leaned closer to see what it was.

It was his neighbor's cat, Mittens. All chewed up and bleeding.

The man heaved again and vomited until there was nothing left in his stomach.

Just don't think about it.

WEDNESDAY - PRESENT DAY

Chapter 26

Olivia awoke feeling like a child on Christmas morning. She had *been* there. She had been in 1934. If she could only share this amazing news with Professor Vanguard, *that* would shake up his research! She imagined the two of them sitting in his tiny office surrounded by teetering stacks of books and papers, discussing what it all meant and how it worked. He'd want to turn her experiences with Steven into a book or at the very least a paper. He'd want to announce it to the world. *Whoa. Forget it,* she thought, *I'm not a lab rat. Vanguard will have to keep on wondering.*

Last night, as soon as she'd returned to the present—or was it the future?—Olivia grabbed her phone and texted Liz and Sophie. *U wont believe what happened! Cant w8t 2 tell u! Meet at pub 5.30 Wed? xo*

As expected, they'd sent enthusiastic replies. She couldn't wait to see the looks on their faces when she told them about last night. This was getting good.

Olivia was eager for the day to fly by and the evening to arrive.

Whatever spell had enchanted her and Steven, she hoped the magic wouldn't run out before tonight. It wouldn't be fair if she could travel to his time, but he couldn't come into 2014. She knew he'd be looking forward to it all day. To have the opportunity snatched away because of some cosmic burp would be awful.

She jumped out of bed and padded downstairs into the kitchen to make coffee and feed Mr. Moto, who was sitting in the bay window watching the goings-on in the neighborhood. His little head slowly turned from side to side. Nothing escaped that kitten.

Olivia had a nine-thirty kickboxing session so she ate a light breakfast—scrambled egg whites and a clementine—and went right to her computer. She finished the lists of time-travel-related books and movies and e-mailed them. The only other work she had left to tackle this week was organizing some final notes on *crime during the Depression*, ironically a project she had been working on for Dr. Madeline Littlefield at Oswego State. If she had only known three weeks ago that she was going to have a real live Depression-era cop to interview, she could have saved herself a lot of time and energy. *Oh well, it never would have worked anyway.* She had to create a bibliography for all her research. Exactly *how* would she cite him?

Winter weather had returned. As she made a mad dash from the parking lot, icy rain snuck inside her collar, trickled down her neck, and chilled her spine.

The YMCA was located in a decades-old building and, every time she was there, Olivia thought she could feel the energy of all the people who had exercised and played sports there over the years. Paint peeled off the walls in the lobby, the linoleum was cracked, and oil from thousands of sweaty hands had polished and darkened the handrail that led downstairs to the locker room. The Y wasn't the slick kind of gym that you saw in TV commercials. There were no frills, no juice bar, no fancy lounge area, no hot tub. But it felt right. It had its own atmosphere that suited her perfectly.

Olivia exchanged her boots for cross-trainers, stowed her belongings, and went out on the floor to join the warm-up session. They did a variety of stretching exercises and jumped rope. For the next half-hour she practiced a combination of kicks and punches, wishing that she had known all this back in that alley in Marseille, wondering if she'd ever need to use what she was learning to defend herself or someone else.

After a cool-down and more stretching, Olivia headed for the locker room, breathing hard but feeling relaxed and satisfied. She took a quick shower, changed into her street clothes, and left. The temperature had dropped. She had to scrape ice off all the car windows and peel it off the wipers.

Olivia moved happily through the rest of the day, endorphins still jumping from her workout, memories of last night with Steven running through her mind like a video on a loop. Before she knew it, it was time to get ready. She donned a pair of jeans, a black cashmere sweater, and short black boots. She applied some light make-up then did a quick swipe with a lipstick called Sugared Maple. Examining herself in the mirror, Olivia liked what she saw.

The cobblestone building that housed The Three Lords Pub was over two hundred years old. Heavy wooden beams crisscrossed smoke-damaged ceilings that were supported by dark columns. The columns had been real tree trunks, the nubs where the branches had once been still evident. Loyal customers sat eating and drinking in booths, and on low stools around tiny tables scattered throughout the dimly lit room. The mirror behind the polished bar showed its age—there were a number of places where the silver backing was peeling off—but it still reflected the beautifully crafted fixtures with their painted porcelain and brass features.

Olivia joined her friends in the back of the crowded pub.

"We ordered drinks. I got you your usual."

"Thanks, Liz."

The Three Lords boasted an impressive selection of bottled beer and beer on draught. There was Fuller's London Pride, Guinness Extra Stout, Boddingtons Bitter, Bass, Black Sheep Ale, Theakston's Old Peculier, Sam Smith Nut Brown, and Newcastle Brown. There were so many wonderful stouts, porters, lagers, ales, and bitters that it was hard to choose. The selections changed from time to time and the owners also offered a long list of "guest" beers, on a limited availability. Olivia's favorite was Young's Oatmeal Stout. She always said it tasted exactly the way a beer should taste. Liz usually ordered a black and tan, made with a pale ale like Bass that took up about two-thirds of the glass and was topped off with dark mahogany Guinness stout. Sophie hated the taste of beer and ordered wine no matter where they were.

"Come on," urged Sophie. "Don't make us wait anymore. What happened?"

"I went back into 1934 last night."

"What?!"

"Ohmygod!"

"I did. It was awesome!" Olivia explained how they'd managed it. "I couldn't believe how easy it was. He took my hand and I stepped over the threshold."

"Just like that," said Liz in amazement.

Olivia nodded. "It felt weird though."

"Did it hurt? Did you feel sick? Or dizzy?" asked Sophie, worry creeping into her voice.

"No, not at all. Nothing. I meant it was weird being in my house but it didn't *look* like my house. Everything was so different."

"What did it look like?" asked Liz. "I'd *kill* to go back in time and look around."

"As soon as I walked into the hallway, I noticed a door on the left. Remember when I told you I saw him walk through the wall? He must have been going into the bathroom. Evidently somebody walled it up since then and made my en suite with the door in the bedroom."

"Ah," they chorused.

"It was pretty basic—claw foot tub, pedestal sink, the toilet was in two pieces..."

"What do you mean two pieces?" said Sophie.

"Where you sit and the back part with the water in it weren't connected but it seemed functional. And everything was very clean."

"I wouldn't mind a claw foot tub. Where did you go next?" asked Liz.

"The upstairs hall was beautiful—navy wallpaper with big white hydrangeas. Felt like you were in an English garden. There was a brass and glass console table under a mirror on one wall with a big Chinese vase on the floor next to it."

"Who did all this decorating?" asked Sophie.

"I guess his mother. My house was their family home. Steven lives there alone because his father works in DC and his mother died a while ago."

"Did you go downstairs?" Liz asked.

Olivia nodded. "The living room was my favorite—all Art Deco. Gorgeous! His mother had good taste. The furniture was sleek." She illustrated with her hands. "There was a couch—very streamlined—and two chairs. All in tones of cream and beige. There were a couple of tables, not sure what kind of wood. And there was an original Erté print on one wall that I'd give my eyeteeth for!"

"They must have had money," commented Liz.

"It was a gift. Steven's mother knew him."

"Who's Erté?" asked Sophie.

"Famous artist in the twenties."

"Oh, what about the kitchen?" asked the pastry chef.

"You could never bake in that kitchen, Sophie. There wasn't any space to spread out. Not a single decent countertop. The refrigerator was so small you couldn't fit a gallon of milk. And you should have seen what passed as a freezer—tiny doesn't even begin to describe it! Let's just say if you put a half-gallon of ice cream in there, there wouldn't be room for anything else."

Sophie looked horrified.

"And don't even *think* about cooking Thanksgiving dinner or making Christmas cookies. I don't know how women managed it."

"Next time you're there, take pictures," said Liz.

"You're assuming there'll be a next time?"

"Of course, aren't you?"

Olivia considered for a moment. "Yeah, now that you mention it, I guess I am. I think I've actually started to take it for granted. So far, we haven't had any trouble meeting when we said we would."

"No! Don't jinx it!"

"We'll be fine, Sophie. Don't worry. Sure, Liz, I'll take pictures."

"Get some of Steven, too," said Sophie.

"So, what did you do? Did you stay there a while?" asked Liz.

"After I looked around, we sat in the kitchen. He made tea and we ate Fig Newtons."

"How funny. Fig Newtons. Something so ordinary," Sophie observed.

"I know, right? I thought the same thing. In the middle of this unbelievable experience, eating regular old cookies."

The waiter—looking like he'd stepped off a pin-up calendar, the kind with hunky, bare-chested firemen dressed in pants held up by red suspenders—came over with a second round of drinks. He had a chiseled face and warm brown eyes.

"Here you go, ladies."

"Thank you!"

He took their orders—steak and kidney pie for Liz, fish and chips for Sophie, shepherd's pie for Olivia.

"Yum! Who needs food with him around?" said Liz after he'd left.

The others nodded enthusiastically.

Liz brought the conversation back to Steven. "So what did you guys talk about, Olivia?"

"Are you ready for the other big news?" said Olivia mysteriously.

Liz and Sophie shot each other a confused look. "What?" they said together.

Olivia leaned forward and whispered, "He saw all of us last night in the kitchen."

"No way," said Liz.

"Come on, Liv. How can that be?"

"I don't know, but he referred to you," she nodded to Sophie, "as 'the redhead' and you," she looked at Liz, "as 'the blonde.' And he mentioned Isabel. He called her 'the older lady.'"

"So this is happening all over your house?" Sophie's eyes were like saucers, her mouth partly open.

"It's like your house is some kind of time machine," said Liz.

"I know it's a lot to take in. I don't get it, either."

They were quiet for several minutes. Olivia knew they were trying to process this new information. She wasn't worried. They were her friends. They'd stand beside her no matter what. *Let's lighten the mood here,* she thought. She took a drink of her oatmeal stout.

"Guess what we're doing tonight." She looked around the table. "We're going to see if he can come into our time."

"Ooh, can we meet him?" asked Sophie.

"Yeah! We can…you know…just drop by…maybe with a bottle of wine," teased Liz.

"Don't make fun of me. Don't you want to meet him, too?" Sophie asked.

"Sure, but picture it—'Hey Olivia, what are you doing tonight? Oh, sorry. We didn't know you had company,'" Liz vamped.

"Okay. I get the point."

"Someday, Sophie, I promise. As soon as we figure out how it all works," soothed Olivia.

The waiter returned with their meals and the conversation took other directions. Liz talked excitedly about some of the toys that had been unpacked that day at the museum. There was an old Parcheesi game, a Magic 8-Ball, and a Ouija Board.

"Maybe we should ask it about Steven," commented Liz.

"Very funny," said Olivia.

"And we've got jacks, a pogo stick, a badminton set, and an old wooden croquet set."

"I can't wait to see everything," said Sophie.

"Joe keeps asking when he can come in and play with all the old electronic things. He thinks because he's my husband he should have special privileges. I keep telling him, the stuff's not even unpacked yet!"

"Well, that's kind of a guy thing, isn't it?" commented Sophie as she popped a French fry into her mouth. "Electronics, I mean. Gadgets. They're all crazy about that kind of stuff. At least most of the guys I know have been."

"It does seem to be a pattern," agreed Liz.

"I think that's what Steven'll be interested in. The TV and technology. And cars. He's wild about cars."

It was late when they bundled up against the arctic cold, scraped more ice off their cars, and carefully drove home.

Olivia closed up the house for the night and went upstairs. Before she even opened her book, she heard his voice.

Chapter 27

"Hello there, Miss Time Traveler," Steven called from the hallway.

Olivia laughed. "Hey! How are you?"

"I'm fine. The question is how are *you*? Did you have any after-effects today from last night?"

"No, nothing. I felt normal."

"No headache? Muscle aches? Sick to your stomach?"

"No, I'm fine. Really."

"All right. That's good. I'm glad."

"Do you still want to come into 2014?"

His face lit up. "Of course! I've been thinking about it all day."

"Okay. Here we go."

Olivia slowly walked to the door.

"You're sure?"

He laughed. "Yes. Positive."

Olivia looked up into his warm brown eyes. She stretched out her arm. He took a deep breath and reached into the doorway. She felt the warmth of his hand as it closed over hers. She backed up, one small step at a time.

Steven walked into the future.

They stood there for a second–eyes wide and sparkling, mouths open–then together they shouted. "We did it!"

"Holy mackerel! Am I really here? I can't believe it."

"Believe it. You're here. Go ahead and look around. It's okay."

Steven walked into her master bath. "I've *never* seen anything like this!" He leaned over the edge of the tub. "What are all those holes near the bottom?"

Knowing a picture was worth a thousand words, Olivia turned on the water and the jets.

"Whoa! I bet that feels wonderful."

"It sure does, especially on a cold night. Or when you're tired and aching from doing a lot of physical work." She hesitated. *Oh what the hell,* she thought. *In for a penny...* "You can try it sometime if you'd like to." She grinned. "I promise I won't look."

"Hmmm." Steven grinned back. When he returned to the bedroom he caught sight of the television mounted on the wall. "What's that?"

"It's a TV."

"What's a TV?"

"You know, television."

"No."

"I'll show you. Come here."

Olivia sat on the end of the bed and felt the mattress give under his weight as Steven sat next to her. She pointed the remote at the flat screen and turned on the power. She hit the channel numbers for TCM—she watched a lot of her favorite classics on that network.

"Is this a motion picture?"

"Yes, a movie. But you can watch anything you want to. There are channels for sports, news, home decorating, history, all kinds of stuff."

Steven gaped at her. "It's hard to take all this in."

"Here," she said. "This is called a remote. It turns the TV off and on and changes channels. Channels are like the stations on the radio."

Steven nodded.

"I'll set it on three. See this arrow?" She explained how the remote worked. "The program will change. You can see for yourself what there is."

Steven tentatively pressed the channel-up button, a commercial for Ford trucks came on. "Oh, wow!" He watched then pressed the remote again. CBS was running *CSI*.

"You'd like that. It's a detective show. You can see how cops solve crimes now."

"Are they real cases?"

"No, but the way they work is real. At least I think so. You can see modern techniques and stuff you don't have yet."

He sighed. "I could sure use some *modern techniques* right about now. Five days and not a shred of proof. I *hate* to wrap up my cases with circumstantial evidence. You know what I mean?"

"I do."

"It's a matter of pride. Of doing the job right."

"Be patient. You'll find something."

"I sure hope so. We had a big storm Friday night—a lot of wind and several feet of snow. There aren't any clues left near the crime scene. And because of the blizzard, no one was out. The bars and the pub closed early."

"Do you still think it was the guy's wife and the assistant manager?"

"Yes, I'm even more sure today. This afternoon I compared her appointment diary with the bank calendar that has all the executives' meetings on it. Patricia—that's the widow—and John Harrison, the banker, were both in Syracuse on the same weekend more than a half a dozen times in the past year. I sent Becks—he's my partner, a swell guy—and another officer to Syracuse to try and find some physical evidence that proves they were there together."

"You'll get there, Steven. I know you will. Here," she said, taking the remote from his hand and keying in a channel. "I've got something that'll cheer you up."

"Baseball! You can watch baseball games?" His face lit up.

"Yeah, and it's not any old baseball. This channel is all Yankee games."

"Oh, I'm living in the wrong time! You're serious? You wouldn't kid me about something as important as this, would you, Olivia?" He pleaded in a mock tone, grinning in sheer bliss.

She burst out laughing. "You know something? For all the changes in technology and clothes and stuff, people haven't changed one bit. You sound exactly like my dad. He's a Yankees fan, too. Big time!" She laughed again. "And no, I'm not kidding. It really is all Yankees on this channel."

"Can we watch awhile? This is so...I can't even think of the words."

"Sure, would you like a beer while we're watching?"

"That'd be swell, thanks."

"Here, if we're going to watch, let's be comfortable." Olivia pulled the TV out from the wall and angled it toward the small sofa. "We can sit over there and still see the screen."

"Wait a minute. It's winter. How are they playing baseball?"

"Oh, it's not live. It's a game they already played and they show it again."

"I don't care *when* it was played. This is great!"

Boston was ahead when they started watching. Steven leaned forward and encouraged his Yankees. He yelled and whooped and hollered. He moaned and groaned and scolded the umpires. He completely lost himself in the game. When it finished—Yankees 9, Red Sox 6—he leaned back and took a long pull from his beer.

"That was swell! I can't imagine being able to do this all the time."

"Well, you know the good thing about that, don't you?"

"What's that?"

"You can."

"What?"

"Come upstairs and call me. You can come in and watch anytime you want."

Steven slowly shook his head, mumbling, "I can watch the Yankees. Any time I want." A huge grin spread across his face.

"Hey, I almost forgot. I promised the girls I'd take a picture of you. Do you mind?"

"Oh…uh…sure, I don't mind."

Olivia walked to her closet and reached up to the top shelf for her camera. "Cameras are different now. You don't need film anymore."

"Really? How does that work?"

"I have no idea. Okay, smile."

She snapped the picture. "Oh, that came out great. You look good. See?"

"That's the picture you took?" He shook his head in amazement. "I can't believe the amount of progress that's taken place." He added, "I'd like one of you, too, Olivia."

"Sure."

She showed Steven how to use the camera and they exchanged places. He clicked the button then they admired the results on the screen.

"This camera is aces!"

"I have an idea. Wait a minute."

She ran out of the room. When she returned she was carrying a tripod. She screwed the camera onto the small platform and set the apparatus a couple of feet from Steven.

"There's a timer. I can take a picture of both of us together." She looked into the viewfinder and fussed a bit. "That's good. Don't move now. I'm going to set the timer and sit next to you. We'll see a flashing light right before it takes the picture, so you'll know when to smile."

She slid onto the couch. They both smiled in anticipation. The flash went off.

"Let's see how it came out," he said excitedly.

Olivia showed him the digital image. There they were, sitting side by side smiling.

"Proof," he said simply. "When you get these developed, if I can take a copy back with me and the picture is still there—if it hasn't faded—this is proof that I've really crossed over in time."

For several remarkable moments they contemplated the enormity of what they had done.

Then Olivia said, "Developed? You don't have to wait. I'll be right back."

She went into her office and uploaded the images. She printed copies for both of them and returned to the bedroom where she thrust out her hand and said, "Here. These are our pictures."

"How did you do that? You developed them here? In the house?"

She nodded. "We don't have to take them anywhere. I transferred them to my computer and printed them out myself."

"It's like magic." He looked down at the photographs in his hand then shook his head. "I need some magic on this *case*," he groaned in an exasperated tone.

"No luck today?"

"No, I sent the whole team out searching for the weapon that killed Leo Castleman. We know it looks like a walking stick and it's made out of ebony. A witness gave us a good description and some approximate measurements." He stood up. "My men worked until it got dark and they had to stop. No one found anything."

"Maybe tomorrow," she said hopefully.

Olivia walked him to the doorway.

"Will I see you tomorrow night?" Steven asked.

"I'd like that."

"Me, too. Thank you for everything, Olivia. Tonight was...indescribable, I guess. I never could've imagined the things you showed me."

"I love our pictures."

"So do I. I hope they don't fade away."

She held up her hand. "Fingers crossed!"

Steven stepped over the threshold. Olivia saw the flowered wallpaper appear in the 1934 version of her hallway. He looked at the photographs and his face lit up.

"Look! I can still see us! The pictures are still there." He waved them around.

"Hooray!"

"I've been to the future!"

THURSDAY – 1934

Chapter 28

When Steven gazed out the bedroom window the next morning and saw the thick, swirling flakes, he was reminded of a snow globe his mother had once owned. It had been a favorite possession. *Whatever happened to that treasure?* He'd have to look in her studio and maybe rummage around the attic one of these days to see if he could find it.

As he dressed, Steven realized that he was smiling. Last night had been unbelievable. He still couldn't take it all in. The future was beyond anything he ever could have imagined. That enormous television, for starters. What a great invention that was going to be. He wondered how long he'd have to wait for it.

And the film-less camera! Before going to bed, Steven had set the photographs on his bureau next to the 2013 quarter. Now, he picked up the picture of Olivia by herself. She was beautiful.

Several minutes passed before he realized that he'd better get a move on or he'd be late for work. He groaned. *Work*. This case was going nowhere fast. That new phrase he'd heard the other day said it perfectly. *Going nowhere fast.* That described him to a "T" right now.

Steven was frustrated. He needed a break. Today was day six and he still had nothing. Oh, all right, he had his ideas and his theories. And they were good ones. His analysis had been careful and thorough. He was sure he knew what had happened but, in order to get this case to court and prosecuted successfully, he must provide the district attorney with indisputable physical proof.

All of a sudden he thought of Judge Randolph. Steven suspected that his father had spoken to his life-long friend about keeping an eye on him after Evangeline's death. The judge and his wife often invited Steven to their home for a meal. The Randolphs had no children and Steven sometimes wondered if he was the son they'd always wanted.

In the past, Judge Randolph had shown that he understood Steven's methods and valued his abilities. Occasionally, he'd been lenient in the requirements for a search warrant. If Steven explained everything clearly, perhaps he could get a warrant to search John Harrison's house for the murder weapon.

Buoyed by his plan, he hurried to the kitchen where he drank a hasty cup of tea, scalding his mouth in the process and swearing briefly, something he never did. He threw together a couple of sandwiches, wrapped them in waxed paper, and stowed them in his lunch box.

Steven brushed several inches of snow off his car and shoveled out the back end while the engine warmed up. He shifted into reverse and backed to the curb. He craned his neck to see around the ever-growing snowbanks and slowly edged into the unplowed, deserted street. The short journey took longer than usual but he arrived at the station without mishap. He grabbed the hand railing, glad that someone had already sanded the icy steps, and headed directly to the chief's office.

Chief Thompson wasn't in yet. Steven looked at the clock. What was the matter with him? It wasn't even seven yet. He'd better slow down and get a hold of himself or he'd start making mistakes.

He flicked on the light in the CID room and settled at his desk. He spread out the case files. He studied, checked, read, and reread. He turned in his chair and concentrated on the murder board. He took a deep breath, closed his eyes, and let his mind trace all the important points of the case.

Yes, it was the only solution that made sense.

Steven considered the early morning hour and decided it would be all right to telephone the judge at home. After all, they were practically family.

Mrs. Randolph answered on the second ring and was delighted to hear his voice. "Steven! How are you, dear? We haven't seen you in ages."

"I'm fine, Mrs. Randolph. Thank you. How are you and the judge?"

"Oh, we're the same as always. Do you want to speak with Hal? He's coming down the stairs."

Randolph took the proffered receiver from his wife.

After saying hello and politely inquiring into the judge's health, Steven said, "I was wondering if you had a few minutes before court this morning, Judge. I need another warrant but I have to explain some things to you. Could I stop by your office?"

"Have you had breakfast yet, son?" The judge's voice boomed cheerfully into Steven's ear.

"Eh, no, sir. I haven't."

"Why don't we skip the office visit and you come over here right now and join us. You can tell me all about it over buckwheat pancakes and maple syrup. We'll even throw some bacon in the frying pan. How's that for enticement, huh?"

Before Steven could answer, the judge continued, "Now I won't take no for an answer. We'll see you in a few minutes." And he hung up.

Steven put down the receiver grinning. He should have known. He pulled on his coat and hat, giving the brim of the fedora a snap. He made sure he had his notebook and returned to the front desk where Tommy Forester was rubbing his shirtsleeve across the surface in an efficient, if unorthodox, way of dusting.

"Good morning, Detective Blackwell. I didn't know you were here already."

"Yeah, that's me. Sneaky as a cat burglar." Steven returned the smile. "I'm on my way over to Judge Randolph's house in case anyone's looking for me in the next couple of hours. You have his home telephone number?"

Tommy consulted a list of phone numbers and addresses belonging to the town's most important citizens. "Yup. Do you want me to tell the chief anything when he gets in? Should be any minute now," he added, looking up at the clock on the wall.

"No, I'll fill him in when I get back. I don't imagine I'll be in time for the morning briefing. Have Jimmy tell the men about his interviews yesterday. And Will can let them know about his and Beckman's visit with Lawrence Castleman." Steven opened the door to leave then remembered. "Oh, and, Tommy, have them remind everybody to catch up on their paperwork and get their reports to me and the chief by noon today."

"Sure thing, Detective."

The Randolphs lived on a spacious lot at the corner of Swan Lane and Chiltington Road, several doors down from the house that Steven and Olivia shared. The gardener-cum-handyman, Earl, was sanding the steps when Steven pulled in.

Earl was an intelligent man who'd been forced to leave school at age twelve to help on his parents' farm. Earl liked knowing things, but he especially loved words. He read everything he could get his hands on and was self-taught in a wide range of subjects. The jack-of-all-trades and the policeman played word games every time they met.

Steven parked his car under the porte-cochere and used a newly cleaned path to walk the short distance to the front door.

"Good morning, Earl. How are you today?" He extended his hand to the scrawny, curly haired man.

"Fine, Detective Blackwell. And yourself?"

"No complaints. You still enjoy listening in on *Amos 'n' Andy*?"

"Oh, yeah. They're the bee's knees," he proclaimed with the customary twinkle in his eye. As Steven had expected, the gauntlet was thrown down.

"The flea's eyebrows," countered Steven.

"The canary's tusks," Earl fired back.

"The cat's whiskers."

"The cat's meow."

"The cat's pajamas!"

They both burst out laughing and were still snickering like schoolboys when Judge Randolph opened the front door.

"Ah! So what's the game today?"

Steven and Earl grinned at each other.

"Have a good day, Earl."

"See ya, Detective." Earl doffed his plaid wool cap and headed around the back, chuckling to himself.

The house smelled glorious. Steven followed the judge down the long, central hallway into the cozy kitchen. Mrs. Randolph left the pan of crackling bacon and enveloped Steven in a big hug. Then, holding him at arms' length, she pronounced, "You look underfed. Have you been eating enough? Are you sleeping? This case must be taking a toll on you, dear." And she kissed him on the cheek. "Here, you sit right down. Hal, give the boy some tea."

"Let him breathe, for heaven's sake. He just walked in the door." Nevertheless, the judge poured a steaming cup and handed it to Steven.

"We'll eat first. Then you can tell me all about it."

Mrs. Randolph filled the men's plates with pancakes and bacon, and made sure they had enough butter and maple syrup. Then, she prepared her own breakfast and joined them at the table.

"I had a long talk with your father last night about the situation in Austria," said the judge.

"I saw the article in yesterday's paper," commented Steven. "It looks like things have settled down. Evidently the government's going to ignore the Nazi deadline."

"That's what I thought, but your dad was able to give me some background. Without giving out any secrets, that is," Randolph chuckled. "But seriously, I don't think we're out of the woods yet. That fella Hitler next door in Germany looks like trouble."

"Oh, you two and your politics," said Mrs. Randolph. "Did you read about the Russian Prince admitting in court that he killed Rasputin? Now, that's a real life murder mystery solved."

The conversation flowed into items of local interest. Mrs. Randolph went on and on about the new baby born at The Three Lords. The publican's widowed cousin had come to live upstairs and work in the pub's kitchen only weeks before.

"Yes," Steven said, "I heard Cooper's cousin Theresa had the baby."

"A beautiful little girl," Mrs. Randolph gushed. "She's named her Isabel."

After the meal, Mrs. Randolph made another pot of tea for the two men and left the kitchen.

"I take it the Castleman investigation isn't going the way you want it to, huh, Steven?"

"No, Judge, it's not."

Steven explained what they'd accomplished. He carefully laid everything out, building a solid, logical case for his conclusions.

"So, what do you think?"

"Well, I think you're probably right. Patricia Castleman's a real piece of work. Scratch the surface on that one and . . ." The judge shuddered. "In my opinion, she wouldn't stop at anything to get what she wanted. I always felt that Leo made a colossal error in judgment when he married her. But he was smitten. When someone's in love, they don't see what everyone else sees."

"Love's blind, huh?"

"It can be. And I have to say that Patricia Castleman has had any number of men eating out of her hand."

"So, if she wanted to persuade someone like John Harrison to get rid of her husband and grab some money along the way, you think she could manage it? My idea doesn't sound crazy to you?"

"No, not crazy at all. I can easily see it happening as you described." The judge lit a cigarette, stretched, and pushed back his chair. "Especially John Harrison. That young man is too impressed with himself for his own good. I think he'd leap at the chance to bed his boss's wife. And share the money, of course, too. But I think the bigger attraction for him would be getting something over on his boss." He blew a stream of smoke to the ceiling. "Of course, as you have so succinctly put it, you don't have enough real proof yet. The fact that Marty Carpenter told you that he remembered Harrison bringing a black walking stick to school when they were kids...well, I don't know. I suppose that tilts it just enough."

Judge Randolph added a couple of smoke rings to the haze overhead and deliberated. "All right, Steven. I believe you have enough reason for a search warrant. I'll approve it for John Harrison's house—for the murder weapon only, mind. Go ahead and write it up. I'll be in court all morning. I'll look for it when we adjourn for lunch. And speaking of court, I'd better get going or they'll all be wondering where I've got to."

They stood and the judge pulled Steven into a warm embrace. "Your father would be so proud of you, my boy. *Is* so proud, I should say. It's only that he doesn't get to see the results of your good work as often as I do." Randolph smiled encouragingly. "Don't lose hope. You'll get there in the end. You know you always do. Keep at it. One of your little threads will start to unravel. Then, before you know it, the whole case'll be lying exposed at your feet."

Chapter 29

As Steven was leaving the Randolphs', Harry Beckman was heading to Saratoga Springs. Beckman was relieved to be on his own today. During the past few days, he'd felt tension building up inside him because of the Castleman investigation—it had happened too soon after the long Campbell affair. If they'd only had the weekend to rest and forget about the job—the chief *had* promised Saturday and Sunday off—he'd probably be feeling more like himself. Everything was getting to be too much, especially with all the extra stuff going on in his private life.

Last night when Beckman dragged himself home, exhausted and emotionally drained, he decided to treat today as a working holiday. Of course, he'd do the job Steven sent him to do. But he didn't see why he couldn't take advantage of the fact that whenever he wasn't showing the photographs, he could empty his mind of the case and unwind. There would be no one who wanted to discuss theories or ask *what if*. If he was lucky, he'd get his identifications quickly and he could take the rest of the day off.

Sometimes Beckman wondered at the path his life had taken, and when he had lost control of it. He'd never meant to become a cop, never wanted to be one. When he was in high school, his plan had been to go into business and make a lot of money. As a teenager he dreamed of "the good life"—a life where a full bank account allowed him to do whatever he wanted, go where he felt like going, and buy anything his heart desired. He had no wish to repeat the struggles his parents had endured.

His life had all started out according to plan. After graduation he got a job with a manufacturing company. It was a low-level entry position, but that didn't bother him. Harry was smart and figured the beginner position would give him a chance to learn the business from the bottom up. Eventually he'd work his way to a lucrative management job. It was all very clear in his mind.

Then, shortly before the stock market crash, as if the company knew what was coming, they let him and a dozen others go. The only opening he could find was in the Syracuse Police Department. Crime was on the rise. Surprisingly, he was good at police work and the years seemed to follow one after another. It had been five years since he took the job in Knightsbridge. Now here he was, driving along on a winter day to interview possible witnesses in a murder investigation.

Time for a break. Harry knew when he got up this morning that he'd need to take rest stops to keep his mind on the road. He'd had a lousy night's sleep tossing and turning, battling troubling nightmares, and constantly rolling over a broken mattress spring. After a few hours of unsatisfying shut-eye, he'd given in and gotten up before dawn.

He'd made a pot of strong black coffee and swallowed a couple of aspirins for the headache he knew would come. After wolfing down his breakfast, he'd piled the dirty dishes in the sink. On his way out of town, he'd stopped at the Buttercup Bakery for a sack of fry cakes to go with the rest of the coffee he'd brought from home.

Now, Beckman sat in the car, munching a mouth-watering donut, drinking out of the thermos. It was the first moment of peace he'd felt in days. Months, if he was honest about it. Gazing out on the snowy landscape, he made an effort to keep his mind from wandering to the problems he'd left behind. Instead, he tried to remember what he'd felt like as a child, when his only concerns were throwing the ball far enough, running fast enough, and saving enough of his allowance to see the newest Tom Mix adventure at the picture show.

Any one of the Knightsbridge police officers would have jumped at the chance to accompany Harry Beckman to Saratoga, but it was not to be. At ten thirty, they were at their desks finishing yesterday's reports.

Jimmy Bourgogne had done a terrific job taking over the briefing this morning. His straight-forward approach and sense of humor kept the men's attention and injected a lighter note into the daily update. He first told his fellow officers how, as per Steven's instructions, he had conducted follow-up interviews with Henry August, Carl Dickson, and Marty Carpenter. He explained that he verified August's assertion that his heart would never have withstood the pressures of planning and executing a robbery-murder and how Dr. Kranken, the local GP, concurred that the mere anxiety of the operation would have probably killed the teller.

"But I'm not convinced," continued Jimmy Bou. "I got the feeling he was still hiding something. Doc Kranken hesitated when I asked about August's heart. *Probably* isn't the same as *definitely*. I don't think it's good enough. I told Steven somebody else should have another go at him. Something's not right."

Then, he revealed Carl Dickson's story. Much to the delight of the assembled room, most of whom were admirers of Jimmy Bou, he spoke like a well-seasoned vaudevillian.

"So, I mention his divorce from Minnie and suggest that perhaps Dickson sought comfort in the arms of Patricia Castleman." He paused for effect. "Gentleman, I tell you, the man struck like an animal. He actually jumped out of his chair and snarled at me. Yes, I say *snarled*. He was spitting when he got his purple face in my oh-so-lovely mug and growled, 'that bitch.'

"Well, you might ask me, gentleman, *why* he called the lovely Mrs. Castleman a...," he leaned toward his rapt audience and whispered, "*bitch*."

"Why did he call the lovely Mrs. Castleman a bitch?" shouted Ralph Hiller in friendly cooperation.

"Why, thank you for asking, my good man. It seems that one day when Mrs. Castleman dropped in to see her husband, she ran into Dickson in the bank lobby. Carl, of course, was his usual polite self and offered to escort her to Mr. Castleman's office. She hissed at him, 'Don't touch me! I don't want to go through the day smelling like a skunk.' Then she laughed, in that snobby way she has, like she's making fun of the person."

Upon hearing this, dislike for Patricia Castleman slithered around the room, as the men erupted in solidarity for Carl Dickson.

"Dickson was humiliated. No chance of an affair there. But I knew he was still hiding something." Jimmy remembered the feeling of determination that he'd had at that moment. He'd steeled his spine, thought of Sam Spade, and said gruffly, "Alright, Mr. Dickson, out with it! What are you *not* telling me?"

"So I pushed him. 'What are you not telling me?' I said. Naturally he hesitated. But I wasn't going to be put off. I told him that he'd save himself a lot of embarrassment if he told me right then and if he refused, I was taking him in to the station. I said 'We'll find out one way or another.'"

Jimmy gazed around the room and said triumphantly, "That was it, my friends. Dickson slumped in his chair. 'Can you promise it'll go no further if I tell you?' he says. 'No, sir,' I told him. 'This is a murder investigation. We'll keep it quiet. This is just for the police. But we have to know. Tell me what you're hiding.'

"So, Dickson confessed that he *was* having an affair, but with Roy Renard's wife, Dorothy! He was at their house while Roy was working at the *Gazette* Friday night. I talked with her later and she confirmed his alibi. Said she didn't want him charged with murder."

Jimmy Bou took a deep breath. "Last but not least, I questioned Marty Carpenter. He doesn't like Patricia Castleman very much—which seems to be a theme in this mess—but I think he's holding something back, too. I told Steven he should talk with Marty again. They're friends. Maybe he can get it out of him."

"So, the only person we've eliminated is Dickson?" asked Pete McGrath.

Will Taylor spoke up, "Dickson and Leo's brother. Detective Beckman and I interviewed Lawrence Castleman yesterday at the mill. We're sure he's out of it. We're convinced he has a solid marriage and the relationship he had with his brother was a good one. We can't come up with a motive that makes any sense. And we verified his alibi, too."

The meeting broke up. Speculation bounced around the room as the men discussed the personalities in the case and wondered what Detective Blackwell would have them do next.

Chief Andy Thompson had been observing from the back of the room and was pleased at how well Officer Bourgogne had conducted the meeting. Jimmy Bou had his own style, that was for sure. It was unusual but not unwelcome. Police work could get a fella down after a while and Chief Thompson thought that moments of laughter were sorely needed. He was glad they'd decided to give the young officer more responsibility. Jimmy Bou was a natural leader. He was going to make a good detective one of these days.

Chapter 30

Steven went straight to his desk to prepare the paperwork for the search warrant Judge Randolph said he'd authorize. The rest of the morning passed quietly and swiftly. Snow fell outside and the men were engrossed in their work inside. Around eleven thirty, Tommy Forester hurried in.

"Detective Blackwell!"

"Tommy, what is it?"

"Ginny Fitzgerald just called. John Harrison never reported to work today. They can't reach him. They tried his house a few times but there's no answer. They think something's wrong."

"He got back from Syracuse?"

"Yes, he dropped off some papers late yesterday. Ginny said Mr. Harrison would never not show up for work."

Want to bet? Steven thought, inwardly cursing.

"They want us to go to his house."

Don't let him be gone. Damn! When is something going to go right with this case?

"Let the chief know, Tommy. Then call Ginny. Tell her we're on our way." He rushed to the patrol room and told Jimmy, Will, Ralph, and Pete. "Come with me. If it's a false alarm, we all got a nice break from our paperwork. If not..."

They jumped into Steven's Chevy and sped to Mulberry Lane. Harrison's drapes were still drawn. That didn't bode well.

"No light on," Ralph observed. "Don't most people keep a light on the porch overnight? Maybe he's already on his way to the bank."

"I don't think so," said Will. "The house has that empty feeling. Something's wrong."

"How come I never get feelings like that?" said Pete, screwing up his face.

Ralph was on Will's side. "I've gotta go by what I see. And my eyes tell me Harrison never woke up this morning. If he had, he would've opened the drapes. He's a fussy man. *I* think *he* would think leaving the drapes closed was like not shaving properly or having his tie askew."

"*Askew*?" Pete never missed a chance to needle his pal.

Steven led them up the snowy sidewalk—no one had cleared it or the steps. There was a bulb in the porch fixture. Either the light was switched off or the bulb had burned out. Gloves on, he grabbed the brass knocker and banged it firmly against the door. There was no response. He pressed the doorbell several times. They heard the sounds echo in the silent house. They waited.

"John!" Steven called. "Harrison, are you in there?"

"Hey, there's a crack in the curtains," said Jimmy. "Maybe if we sort of..." He pressed his face to the window. "Oh, shit!"

Everybody immediately knew this was bad. Jimmy Bou wouldn't say shit if he had a mouth full of it.

"Let me see." Steven leaned in and looked.

Relief flooded over him. Harrison had not fled.

Anger quickly followed. They had another dead body.

Steven tested the door. It was locked. But the lock was a flimsy one. He motioned to Will, the strongest and fittest of the group. Taylor put his shoulder to it and shoved hard. The door flew open.

The smell of death assaulted them.

John Harrison lay in the middle of his living room floor. For the second time in less than a week, Steven found himself looking at a pool of blood next to a murdered man.

At 22 Swan Lane, there was commotion of another kind going on.

"Marie Elizabeth Haydock, what are you thinking? It's a *wake,* for God's sake! You cannot wear that to your uncle's *wake.* My heavens, you are old enough to know better! Go back upstairs and change into something appropriate."

Patricia Castleman's sister Louise had arrived last night, accompanied by her husband, daughter, and son. She now stood in the downstairs hallway appalled, while her eighteen-year-old daughter dragged herself up the staircase to rummage through her overnight case and find something more funereal.

"You're as bad as your aunt," Louise mumbled under her breath.

Louise had been horrified twenty minutes ago when Patsy had appeared. The fitted black silk dress was almost suitable. It covered her sister's shapely legs and didn't tuck in too tightly on her small waist. But, *Lord have mercy,* the lace overlay on the bodice revealed much too much of the widow's well-endowed figure. *What is she thinking? Attending her husband's wake with her cleavage peeking out. Give me strength.*

In the end, knowing whatever she said wouldn't make any difference, Louise kept quiet and said nothing. *Let this whole ordeal be over fast. Let me go back to my house and my quiet, simple life.*

At a quarter to two, Tom Haydock ushered his sister-in-law, wife, and children into his gleaming bright blue, 1933 Ford Cabriolet. Patricia had refused to listen when Louise hinted they should leave earlier. "The thing doesn't start until two. Why should we hang around any longer than we have to?"

"We'll be out in a minute, Tom. I want a word with Patsy."

After the front door closed, Louise turned on her sister, out of patience at her rudeness and embarrassed that her family had witnessed her sister's callousness. "Now you listen to me, Patsy Osborne. Okay, I get it. I know you didn't love Leo and couldn't care less that he's gone. But he was a good man and a good husband to you. He gave you anything you wanted. Everything you ever asked for as a matter of fact. And it seems to me he didn't expect, or get, much in return. He certainly doesn't deserve to be treated in the way you're carrying on right now.

"This is your last chance to do right by him, to show him the respect he earned. What's the matter with you? Mom and Dad didn't raise us to be so ill-mannered. You need to buck up and act the part. Even if you don't feel it."

Louise had blurted out everything. Now she slowed down. "I'm sorry, Patsy," she said more gently. "If you can't manage to care about Leo, at least think of your reputation. What's this town going to think if they see you so nonchalant and unfeeling?"

Patricia Castleman seethed. No one talked to her like this. Nobody dared reprimand her. She glared at her sister.

"Are you done?"

"Yes."

"First of all, I have no intention of, as you put it, *acting this way* in front of the entire town. Give me some credit. I'll play grieving widow, don't worry.

"And second, I don't give a damn what anybody in this crappy town thinks of me. Bunch of clueless yokels. I'll be gone in less than a week anyway."

"What do you mean you'll be gone in a week? What are you talking about?"

Patricia made a show of consulting her expensive gold watch. "We'd better be leaving, Louise. It's nearly two. We don't want to be late for Leo's wake now, do we?"

She walked out the front door.

Careful not to contaminate the scene, Steven and his four officers remained on the porch.

"Pete, there's a fire call box on the corner. Get over there fast and have the fire department alert the station," Steven instructed. "Tell them what we've found. Have'em call Doc and Gray. Be sure they tell the chief."

Pete gave a small salute and took off, his wiry frame disappearing as he ran around a bend in the street.

"Will, check outside around the house. See if there's a sign of forced entry. See if we've got any footprints."

"Sure."

Steven had great admiration for Will. Will's natural intuition, prodigious memory, and finely-honed tracking skills were invaluable. Steven made a mental note to rely on him more.

Steven looked at Jimmy and Ralph. "We'll wait here."

A few minutes later, a speeding police car and coroner's wagon screeched to a halt in front of the house. Doc Elliott, smoking and breathing hard, and Gray Wilson, impeccable as always in his elegant overcoat and stylish fedora, joined the waiting officers.

"We gotta stop meeting like this, Blackwell. Jeez, two in less than one week. What the heck is going on in our nice friendly town?"

"Not so friendly, Doc."

The photographer took out his gear and got to work. He documented the porch, front entrance, and living room. He paid special attention to the victim.

Steven had not especially liked John Harrison, but he couldn't help feeling bad. Nobody deserved to die like this. Someone had robbed this man of more than half his life.

"Let's see what we've got," said Doc Elliott.

The ME knelt by the body. As expected, he had managed to hunt through his mental musical catalog and find the right tune for yet another murder victim. He sang Bing Crosby's hit, "You're Getting to Be a Habit with Me."

Steven admired the man for finding a way to handle his stressful job.

"I don't know how he does it," marveled Jimmy Bou. "He must know every song that was ever recorded."

The medical examiner made a preliminary study of Harrison's body as it lay face-up on the carpet. He felt the man's neck and officially pronounced him dead. "Sometime last night, I'd say. I suppose you want a rush on this, Steven."

"That'd be swell."

"I can do that. I'll get you a time of death later today." He continued his exam. "Well, that's what did it. One clean shot through the heart. At close range, too. Hmm." He scrutinized the wound. "Maybe a .38. We'll know when I get him up on the table."

Steven felt the sudden weight of this new investigation and wished his partner were here. He relied on Beckman's quiet, calming presence at a crime scene. He was grateful for his partner's solid bearing and depended on his sharp insights. It showed what a few extra years' experience could do for an officer. The hands-on practice honed a cop's skills like nothing else could.

Becks, he thought, *it looks like I sent you on a fool's errand.* Then he heard Jimmy Bourgogne's soft voice murmur, "A woman could easily shoot a gun. And a girlfriend could get in real close."

And Steven relaxed as he appreciated Jimmy Bou all over again.

Doc stood aside while the morgue attendants put the body on a stretcher then took it out to the ambulance. Gray Wilson returned and said that he'd finished the rest of the main floor. He packed away his equipment and they left.

"Okay, our turn," said Steven. "Ralph, would you dust? Jimmy, search the first floor. Pete, take the upstairs. Will, I'd like you to stay here with me."

"What are we doing, Steven?"

"Committing the scene to memory. I think we've got an advantage here. The room probably looks like it did when our killer left. Let's not only rely on Gray's pictures. Let's study what we see here."

"Okay."

"Tell me what happened, Will."

"Harrison'd been home awhile. He was wearing his carpet slippers and the kind of casual trousers and sweater you'd wear at home. I'd say he changed when he got back."

Steven nodded.

Will scanned the room. "The drapes are drawn—either the killer did that or it was late when the killer arrived and Harrison had already closed them. Over on the table in front of the sofa, there's a small plate with some crumbs and a half a cookie and something in the bottom of that cup. Tea maybe. I'd say an evening snack."

"What about the fact that the porch light's off?" Steven flicked the switch and saw the light turn on. "Bulb's working."

"I see four possibilities. One: Harrison didn't have the chance to turn it on yet."

Steven shrugged.

"Two: he's trying to conserve electricity."

"No."

"Three: he's one of those people who doesn't put the porch light on at night."

Steven shook his head.

"And four, which I think is most likely: the killer turned it off so no one could see his face when he left."

"Yes, that's it."

After Jimmy Bou finished searching the first floor, he opened the door to the hall closet. He reached up and pulled the chain on the bare bulb. He admired John Harrison's expensive sable brown Chesterfield coat and noticed that the man owned not one but two jackets. *I guess working in a bank pays pretty good.* He pushed the clothes aside and looked toward the back wall. He didn't really think that if Harrison had killed Leo Castleman, he would be stupid enough to leave the murder weapon in his front closet for anyone to find, but he had to be thorough. There was a black umbrella standing in the left corner. Jimmy nonchalantly slid the hangers along the bar to examine the right-hand side of the closet.

And there it was.

Propped up against the wall.

A heavy, ebony walking stick.

"Steven!"

Chapter 31

Harry Beckman arrived in Saratoga Springs shortly after ten thirty. He'd taken a shortcut in Amsterdam, leaving Route 5, then cut over to Route 67, where he stopped for his second rest. After Ballston Spa, he picked up Route 9, which took him straight down Broadway in the middle of town. Despite the snow and the donut-and-coffee breaks, he made good time.

Yesterday, when Chief Thompson spoke with Saratoga's police chief, the man had recommended a place where Beckman could stay.

Mrs. Cookson's rooming house was at the opposite end of town. Harry had heard that Saratoga, known as the "Queen of the Spas," was an important resort and spa destination during warm weather. People flocked from all over the country for the healing powers of the natural springs. He decided to see what stayed open during the off-season and pick out some places for his interviews on his way to the Church Street hostel.

He inched along the tree-lined main thoroughfare, peering out the car windows. The first likely spot was the Hotel Rip Van Dam, but it was boarded up for the winter. A couple of doors down, the elegant

Adelphi Hotel ruled the sidewalk. It resembled a Venetian villa, its second-story balcony stretching across the front and columns rising to the fancy scroll work along the roof's edge. The double doors at the main entrance and tall windows on the upper floors were rounded at the top, creating a stylish facade. Yes, this was the kind of place Patricia Castleman would stay. He'd come back here.

Harry resumed his reconnaissance and, right after Division Street, noticed two more posh-looking hotels. He'd show the photographs at the registration desk in the New Worden Hotel and the Saratoga Inn. There were restaurants in both hotels and he saw a tearoom nearby that he considered a good possibility.

Across the street, the marquee on the Palace Theatre announced the new John Wayne picture, *The Lucky Texan*. Harry had wanted to see it, but hadn't had the time. *Swell! I'll come back tonight,* he thought.

Near the intersection of Lake Avenue and Broadway, a sign in the window of Thomas Lunch boasted, "Eating Headquarters 40¢ Plate Dinner." Harry backed the car to the curb at an angle, joining the dozen other parked vehicles.

The afternoon passed quickly. After his meal at the diner, he left his overnight bag with Mrs. Cookson and drove back down Broadway.

Harry hit pay dirt with the front desk clerk at the Adelphi. The man recognized the photographs of both Patricia Castleman and John Harrison. The guest register revealed dates in May and July 1933. Harrison had signed his own name. *Arrogant bastard.*

Harry got lucky in two additional locations. The barman in the New Worden Grill and Tap Room and the woman who owned the Blue Bell Tearoom were positive they'd waited on the couple. The barman reminded Beckman that Prohibition had still been in effect last year. He remembered Harrison particularly because he'd ordered a Barbary Coast, whispering and winking as he slid a bill across the bar. The tearoom owner was sure because Patricia Castleman had sent back her eggs twice, insisting they hadn't been cooked properly.

"They were rude and demanding. And to make it worse, I lost money on them. Sending a meal back in times like this," she said indignantly. "I ask you!"

Beckman packed away the photographs, witness statements, and his notes and returned to the rooming house.

By suppertime, Harry Beckman was pleasantly stretched out on his bed, ankles crossed, one arm behind his head on a plump pillow. The spotless lodging offered everything he needed—comfortable bed, dresser, night stand with a reading lamp, and bathroom down the hall. He wondered what Steven and the team would discover today. *Stop! Your job today is done. Take the night off. You need a break.*

As he lay smoking, Harry allowed his thoughts to drift. He certainly hadn't seen *that* coming. And after all those years.

He remembered like it was yesterday, the September morning when he'd first set eyes on her. She was his first love and his fourteen-year-old self had fallen hard. He'd been sitting in class talking with one of his friends when she sashayed in. She coolly surveyed the room and chose the seat next to Harry. He almost fell out of his chair. She completely ignored him during the class. When the bell rang, she rose, set her books on his desk, and said, "Here. You can carry these for me." He'd followed her out of the room like a lost puppy.

They stepped out during the school year but when June came around, she dumped him without a word. No matter how many telephone calls he made to her house, no matter how many times he rode his bike up and down her street, she never gave him an explanation. Harry would have crawled over broken glass for her and could not understand what he had done wrong.

Now, years later, Harry Beckman knew he would still do anything for her. When it came to her, he lost all sense of reason. She was under his skin and there was no changing that. He was hopelessly in love, hopelessly lost in her. Whatever she wanted, she got. No matter the cost.

A knock on the door startled him. He jumped.

"You asked to be notified when it was six thirty, Mr. Beckman."

"Right. Thanks, Mrs. Cookson."

He'd forgotten about the movie. That was a good plan. Get lost in somebody else's problems for the night. He stubbed out the cigarette, donned his heavy winter coat, and left the rooming house to go see John Wayne.

By Thursday evening, Steven was beat but determined to finish what he hoped would be the final interview with Marty Carpenter. He slogged through the snow to the tiny landing and banged on the door. The porch light came on.

"Hey, Steven, what are you doing here? Come on in. Like a beer?"

"No thanks, Marty. This isn't a social visit."

"What's up?"

"I think we should sit down."

"Steven, you're scaring me. Just say it. Please."

"Okay, fine. You're holding something back, Marty. Every time we talk, and when Jimmy spoke with you yesterday, you act like you're hiding something. I have to know what it is."

"I don't know what you're talking about."

"Are you having an affair with Patricia Castleman?"

"You know I can't stand her. I already told you. Why would you think that?"

"Because there's something you're not saying. What is it?"

"It has nothing to do with your investigation."

"I'll be the judge of that."

Carpenter turned away and paced the living room. Steven waited.

"Let me put it this way, Steven. Even if Patricia Castleman had a miraculous transformation...if she was suddenly the nicest woman in the world, I *still* wouldn't be interested." His eyes drilled Steven's. "You get it now?"

The penny dropped. Steven felt like an idiot. He'd heard of men like that but didn't realize he knew anyone. How had he never suspected? Well, because he never wondered, didn't care, what folks did in their private lives—unless it impacted a case, of course. Now, come to think of it, he couldn't remember Marty ever having a girlfriend—not in high school, not since.

Steven knew he had embarrassed his friend. He softly said, "I'm sorry I had to push you. You know I didn't have a choice. It's your business. No one's going to hear about it from me."

Carpenter nodded.

"I'll see myself out, Marty."

Good Lord, could this day get any worse?

As Will Taylor drove to his last job of the day, he was looking forward to taking his girl to supper at Bailey's tonight. He and Trudy had only been stepping out a few weeks, but he was already smitten. Trudy had luscious dark hair and blue-green eyes that made him think of the river in July. She was a working girl, too, something Will respected. When she'd first told him about her job as Judge Randolph's private secretary, she'd sparkled with enthusiasm. He'd also noted that she said she hoped to marry and have children one day. As he pulled up in front of Henry August's house, Will thought how lucky he'd been to get this assignment—he had an automobile for the night. He and Trudy would arrive at the diner in style. And he'd be able to protect her from the bitter cold and biting wind.

Mrs. August answered the door and invited Will into the parlor.

She called her husband then carefully lowered herself into a new, upholstered rocking chair. Will sat on the sagging couch facing her.

"What a lovely rocker, Mrs. August."

"Thank you. It was a gift from my husband—Christmas and my birthday all at once."

The teller entered the room. Will stood.

"Sir, I apologize for bothering you so late in the day and at home, but there are some things we have to get settled."

A look passed between husband and wife.

"Yes, Officer? How can I help you?" He spoke so softly that Will had to lean over to catch what the man was saying.

"You seem tired, Mr. August. I won't keep you any longer than necessary." Taylor pretended to consult his notebook, allowing the silence to stretch to the breaking point. Then he nailed the teller with a stone-cold stare.

"You're hiding something. I need to know what it is. If it has nothing to do with Mr. Castleman's murder, that's one thing. But I won't know what's important until I know what it is."

"Tell him, Henry." Mrs. August croaked, looking like she was going to be sick.

Will kept his face impassive and his body still as a rock while he held the man's gaze.

August turned pink and quickly looked away. "Stop! I'll tell you," he said in a resigned tone. Then he slumped into a chair and began.

"I…uh…borrowed…some money from the bank…uh…unofficially. I've been paying it back! There's only a little left now."

"He did it for me, Officer. He bought me this chair. You see, I can't sit on a wooden chair any longer. And that sofa causes me pain, too."

"My wife has bad arthritis. She's in terrible pain *all* the time. I couldn't stand seeing her suffer anymore. I don't know how she does it all day. And in the evening it's even worse. She needs the right kind of chair. I saw that rocker in the Sears catalog and knew it'd be just the thing for her. It cost more than I had, so I borrowed seventeen dollars from my drawer. I've been paying back a little every week so no one would notice." He hung his head. "That's it."

These were the moments when Will found his job the most difficult. Yes, the man had broken the law, officially this was embezzlement. But he could empathize.

"How much do you still owe?"

"Two dollars."

"Can you pay it as soon as you get to work tomorrow?"

Mrs. August rushed in, "Yes!"

"But..."

"No, Henry. We'll take it out of my pin money. It will be paid first thing."

"Good. Mr. August, I'll need you to come to the station to make a statement. Use your lunch hour, *after* you've put the money back. I'll tell the chief everything. He'll decide what to do."

Mrs. August carefully, determinedly leaned forward. She rocked back and forth, easing herself to the edge of the chair. Her face was a map of pain, her eyes shut tight, her mouth stretched in a grotesque grimace. It took several long minutes for her to struggle out of the chair. Finally she stood and faced the policeman. "What do you think will happen, Officer?"

"I don't know. What your husband did was against the law. It's up to the chief. We'll have to wait and see."

THURSDAY NIGHT – PRESENT DAY

Chapter 32

Olivia sipped her tea and turned another page of Annabel Sinclair's scrapbook as she sat at the kitchen table, feet in black-and-white polka dot socks propped up on a chair. The house radiated warmth. Dimmed lights reflected in the windows against the darkness outside. Mr. Moto snoozed in his favorite spot. Olivia was content to be home out of the heavy, falling snow.

Earlier today, she and Isabel had returned to the museum for a final hour of unpacking and sorting and had discovered a cache of Miss Sinclair's memorabilia. They'd taken the time to peruse one, the same one that Olivia was reading now. She had gasped when she'd turned a page to find Steven's photograph staring at them.

"Well, he's a cutie, isn't he?" Isabel grinned.

Olivia nodded silently as she flipped through the book. Steven smiled at her from page after page. The young Annie Sinclair had obviously adored Detective Sergeant Steven Blackwell and had pasted his picture alongside Clark Gable and James Cagney. Now *that* was some company!

The articles chronicled the *Gazette*'s coverage of the Leo Castleman murder investigation. Each one had been neatly clipped from the newspaper and pasted with great care into the book. The clippings were brown now, faded with age, but the black type was still clear and easy to read. Olivia followed Steven's progress throughout the week.

Monday, February 26, 1934

GAZETTE GRABS EXCLUSIVE

Yesterday, *Gazette* editor-in-chief, Sam Silverstone, spoke exclusively with Knightsbridge Police Detective Sergeant Steven Blackwell and his partner Detective Harry Beckman. Blackwell, who is in charge of the Leo Castleman murder investigation, stated that the police are looking for possible witnesses. "We know that Castleman entered the First National Bank and Trust Company in the early hours of Saturday morning, likely between midnight and 3 a.m.," said Blackwell. "He is thought to have entered by the back door in Bank Alley. Anyone who saw somebody going in or out of Bank Alley in that time frame is urged to come forward and tell the police what they saw."

Blackwell further stated that the police are interviewing everyone connected to the bank, as well as to Castleman himself, and are anxious to rule out as many people as possible.

"We hope to solve this case in a short time," stated the veteran police officer. "With the public's help, I am confident we will do exactly that."

Tuesday, February 27, 1934

WITNESS COMES FORTH

Knightsbridge Police Chief Andrew Thompson stated late on Monday afternoon that a witness in the Leo Castleman murder investigation has come forth. Mr. Herbert Steadman, of num-

ber 12 Maple Avenue, reported to Detective Harry Beckman that he saw Leo Castleman enter the back door of the First National Bank and Trust Company at approximately 2 a.m. early Saturday, the morning of Castleman's death.

Steadman is employed at this newspaper, where he works the night shift in the press room. When he took his supper break, Herb Steadman happened to look out of the window and witnessed Leo Castleman using a key to unlock the back door. The banker then entered the financial institution.

"I didn't think much of it at the time," Steadman commented. "I figured there was some sort of problem at the bank and the manager had to come out and take care of it."

Chief Thompson expressed his thanks and appreciation to Mr. Steadman and congratulated him on doing his civic duty. "It's responsible citizens like Herb that make Knightsbridge the wonderful town it is. I am proud to count him as a neighbor and a friend."

Thompson added that the police welcome any and all other information that might be pertinent to the investigation. "We seek justice for Leo Castleman. He was a pillar in this community, a very good man."

Wednesday, February 28, 1934

POLICE GETTING CLOSE
IN CASTLEMAN CASE
NEED COMMUNITY'S HELP

Knightsbridge Police Department's Detective Sergeant Steven Blackwell, who is leading the investigation into Leo Castleman's brutal murder on Saturday, February 24th, revealed last night that the police know what the murder weapon looks like. Another witness, who has expressed the

desire to remain anonymous, has come forth. This unidentified witness saw the man most likely to have killed Castleman, as he, the killer, left the bank in the small hours of the morning. He was carrying what police believe to be the murder weapon. "It is of vital importance," said Blackwell, "that we recover that weapon."

For the second time in as many days, Blackwell is asking for the public's help. "The object in question is a piece of black wood known as ebony. We believe it is shaped as a walking stick and measures approximately three feet long. If you find a length of wood that matches this description, please do not touch it," cautioned Blackwell. "Contact the police department immediately and we will send an officer to your location at once."

Blackwell stressed the importance of the community's help. "This piece of ebony was used to shorten the life of a good, upstanding citizen of our town. Stay alert. Look around you wherever you go." Blackwell added, "And above all else, leave it in place if you spot it."

Reading these articles all at once made Olivia realize what a difficult week Steven was having. She turned the page. Thursday evening's paper announced a *second* murder—someone named John Harrison. The name rang a bell. Olivia searched her memory. *The boyfriend! Steven's number one suspect. Oh no! Could this get any worse for him?*

She thought she'd seen it all until she reached the last page. Sunday's headline screamed, "FATAL SHOOTING. TRAGEDY STRIKES KNIGHTSBRIDGE POLICE." There it ended. Olivia could read no more. The article and the final pages of the book were illegible.

Someone had spilled coffee, which had soaked through and smeared the newsprint. She couldn't make out a single word.

Olivia's insides chilled. Fear slithered down her spine. *Please, not him. Don't let it be him.* She stood up. *The heck with more tea. It's time for a glass of wine.* She leaned over the table and grabbed her empty mug.

"Hi! I'm home!"

Olivia dropped the mug, which hit the floor with a crash. She ran to the front door. Steven stood frozen on the spot, one arm out of his coat, looking stunned.

"Steven!"

"Olivia!"

"What's going on?"

"I don't know. Uh, Olivia, what I said..." He blushed. "I was..."

"It's fine. Don't worry about it."

"It's been a hard day."

"Steven, you just walked into *my* house."

He looked around the corner and saw *her* kitchen but he was standing in *his* hallway.

"This is confusing. I'm in 1934 but I heard something crash in *your* kitchen."

"And I heard *you* but I'm in 2014." Olivia looked back at her stainless steel refrigerator to check. "Let's figure this out."

"Right. Let's see if I can follow you into your kitchen without touching you."

He threw his coat and hat on the hall tree, toed off his boots, and padded behind Olivia into her century.

"We're getting pretty good at this, huh?" He grinned.

"Looks like."

"So, spending a cozy night at home, I see." His eyes travelled up and down her leggings and fitted T-shirt, visible through the open bathrobe that hung loose. "Nora Charles hasn't anything on you! And I thought *she* was sassy."

"It's so cold out! I changed as soon as I walked in the door."

"That's a swell idea. It's below freezing here. I'm gonna do the same thing."

Her eyebrows shot up to her bangs.

"Just a different shirt and my slippers." He chuckled and found that he liked the idea of spending the evening at home with Olivia. Strange pajamas or not. "Olivia, in case I don't come back, come and get me, huh? I'll wait by the door."

"Sure, I'll rescue you. But I won't have to. You did it once, you can do it again. I have confidence in you."

Olivia set Miss Sinclair's scrapbook aside where it wasn't in danger of being spilled on again. She swept up the broken pieces of china and poured two glasses of wine.

Steven returned. They sat at the table.

"So, do you have a theory on what just happened?"

"You know, I actually do."

"Let's hear it." He could feel himself relaxing. *I could get used to this.*

"Okay, your time and mine are happening at the *same* time, right?"

"Right. It's Thursday here. March 1st.You?"

She nodded. "Here, too. Only it's still February. The 27th. I guess we're off a couple of days."

He looked at the digital clock on her stove. "Is that a clock?"

"Yes, it's twenty after six. What about you?"

He consulted his watch. "The same. So, what's your theory?"

"I think it's because we've developed a connection between us. I bet that's the key."

"Like an invisible tie?"

"Could be. I also think it's important that we were both open to the idea of travelling through time..."

"Not many people would be."

"Exactly. Now that we've got this invisible connection, we can see and hear each other easily, like when you were in the pantry the other night."

"And like we were saying the other day, each of us anchors our own time."

"Right. So, you come home and you're in 1934. And, even though I'm still in 2014, I can hear you. Look how easy it was for you to follow me into my kitchen. I think it's because I was there first. I *anchored* that year."

"I guess that makes sense. I wonder if we'll ever know exactly how this works."

She shrugged.

They thought about what this new development meant.

Olivia realized she was a little uneasy. *I like Steven, but do I want him popping up unannounced? No. I'm used to being on my own. And I want my privacy.*

Steven seemed to sense what she was thinking. "It looks like we've lost control of our meetings, doesn't it?"

"A bit."

"That's not fair to you. I don't want to barge in like this. It's not right."

They pondered some more.

"Maybe we *can* take control again. I have a question for you, Steven, but you have to answer honestly, okay?"

"Of course. I've been honest with you so far. Why wouldn't I now?"

"I'm sorry. I don't mean to insult you. I know you have. It's kind of personal."

"Fine. Just ask."

"Were you by any chance thinking of me when you came in the house tonight?"

"Oh, I see what you mean. Well, yes. I was actually. Why?"

"Well, I was thinking about seeing you, too. Maybe now that we've got this connection our thoughts have something to do with it."

"I can see that. So what you're saying is that when we want to get together, we can break through the barrier or whatever it is."

"It's a thought."

"It's a good one. Then, is the opposite true? Some night when you're tired and don't want to see me, I wonder if you can block me so I can't see or hear you."

"So you can't connect with my time."

"Exactly. Let's try it but not tonight, okay? I'm beat. It was a rough day. We had another murder."

Olivia saw the fatigue on his face and heard the frustration in his voice. "I know. Your main suspect John Harrison."

His jaw dropped. "How do you know that?"

"I read the newspaper article. Do you remember telling me about your friend's daughter Annie? How she had a scrapbook with photographs and clippings of all her heroes?"

"Yeah?" He drew his eyebrows together.

"I found Annie's scrapbook at the museum this morning! And who do you think she pasted in between James Cagney and Clark Gable?"

He shrugged and shook his head. The expression on his face told her he had no idea what she was talking about.

"You, Steven, you. Evidently Annie had quite a crush on you. The album is full of *Gazette* items about you and your investigations. Before you got home, I was reading about the case you're working on right now."

Olivia got the memory book and opened it to the news item from Monday's *Gazette*. "See what I mean?"

"Well, I'll be darned!" He glanced at the article he'd read only a few days ago then flipped through to the damaged end. "Looks like she had most of the week's coverage. Guess we'll have to wait until I solve it."

This was it, the moment Olivia had been waiting for. She wanted to help Steven find the killer. She was dying to give him a clue–and not only *a* clue but *the* clue that would crack the case wide open. Research was her thing for heaven's sake. All she had to do was google a few items and *voilà,* case solved. His insistence about not wanting to know anything in the future frustrated her. She decided to ease into it.

"I can try to find out who it is if you want me to," she said casually. "There are a lot of ways I can check."

"Thank you, but no. It would feel like cheating, Olivia. I've never cheated on anything in my life. I *do* appreciate the offer but I'll get there. Don't worry. I already know the first half of this case. Harrison killed Mr. Castleman. We found the murder weapon in his closet. Now, I just have to figure out who murdered Harrison and back it up with proof. Good old-fashioned police work will do the job."

"All right, but if you change your mind…" At the look on his face, she quickly added, "Okay. Okay. I understand and I respect that. I just wanted to help. That's all."

Steven smiled gently. "I know you do and I appreciate it."

"Hey, are you hungry?" Olivia changed the subject. "Would you like some dinner?"

"Yes, what can I do to help?"

"Set the table and open another bottle of wine. Bowls are in the top cupboard over there on the right."

Olivia put leftover chili in the microwave.

"What's that machine?" Steven asked, opening drawers until he found silverware and brightly colored cloth napkins.

"It's called a microwave oven. It heats food real fast. And cooks, too. You can make a lot of stuff with it."

They chatted companionably while they ate. Steven shared some more boyhood stories and she kept him captivated with a couple of her travel adventures.

"I want to do some traveling one of these days, too," he said. "I liked going different places when I was a kid and we moved around because of my father's job. The first place I'm going is Paris. My mother met some really interesting people when she lived there. I don't remember if I told you she was an artist." He pushed away the empty bowl and stretched out his legs. "Have you heard of Utrillo or Toulouse-Lautrec?"

"Sure, they're famous. When I was in college, I had a Toulouse-Lautrec poster in my dorm room. Why?"

"My mother knew both of them. She and Utrillo's mother Suzanne were friends."

"You're kidding! I would have loved to talk with her." *If only Steven and I had met a few months ago,* she thought. "One day you'll have to tell me some of those stories, okay?"

"Sure. Now, I've got a story of a different kind. This case!"

"Well, Steven, if it *was* a story, one of the characters would say *follow the money*. That's what they always say in books and movies. Have you found the money yet?"

"Not since somebody took it from the safe-deposit box. It could be anywhere."

"No, I don't think it could. Look at all the trouble this person went through to steal that cash. He battled a snowstorm, killed a guy, stashed the money, and then *moved* it! He'd be very careful where he put it. It has to be a safe place, but it also has to be somewhere he can get to without attracting attention. Somewhere he'd go on a regular basis."

The conversation about his mother still lurked around the edges of Steven's mind. "His parents' house! What if Harrison moved the money to his parents'?"

"There's nobody I'd trust more than my mother and father. Maybe he left a package or a locked suitcase. He wouldn't have told them what was in it because when they heard about the murder, they'd know he was involved."

"Olivia, that's it! Tomorrow morning I'm going to John Harrison's parents' house. I bet that's where the money is. Wow! This is the first glimmer of hope I've had all day." Steven leaned back and took a long drink of wine. "See? You ended up helping me anyway–in a normal, non-cheating way. Just one conversation with you, Olivia, and I know what my next move is."

FRIDAY – 1934

Chapter 33

Steven jumped out of bed before the alarm rang. He *knew* he was going to find some proof today. He threw on his clothes and dashed down the stairs in the dark. He splashed water into the pot and stood at the sink eating his cereal while the scent of perking coffee filled the kitchen. Stars sparkled across a vast velvet sky. The neighborhood was quiet, peaceful. He, too, had a sense of well-being. His investigation was about to change. He was sure of it.

When Steven arrived at the station, Tommy Forester didn't even have his coat off yet.

"Morning, Detective Blackwell. You're early."

"Good morning, Tommy. Is the chief in yet?"

"Yeah, he was here when I walked in. Is something going on? It's not even seven."

Steven stowed his belongings then went straight to Thompson's office. Chief Thompson wiggled his finger, motioning Steven into the room. Then he pointed unnecessarily to the telephone clamped to his ear. As Steven sat in the hard visitor's chair to wait, he suppressed a grin at the plate of rich, iced pastries and cup of killer coffee on the chief's desk. No wonder his shirt buttons were straining.

"Yeah…uh huh…right…that's too bad…I see…yeah, okay, I'll tell him. Thanks, Doc, I appreciate the quick job…yeah, you, too."

Thompson banged down the receiver. "That was Doc."

"So I gathered. I take it he finished Harrison's post mortem?"

"That he did. Confirmed what he told you at the scene yesterday."

"A .38?"

"Yep. Shot once in the chest at close range. Bullet went right into his heart. Doc's got it, so if we find the weapon we can send 'em both down to Washington and get a positive ID from Mr. Hoover's crime lab."

"Time of death?"

"Ten, eleven o'clock, but he wants to hedge his bets so he's officially telling us between nine and midnight Wednesday. That's it. Not much to go on."

"Well, it's something."

"Where are you on Castleman's murder?" He lit one of his ubiquitous Camels. "Jeez! We can't finish one case before we get another one. What the hell's goin' on around here?"

"We're waiting for confirmation that the walking stick's the murder weapon. I know it's going to be consistent with the sliver we've got."

"I *hope* so."

"That'll give us Harrison as Castleman's killer. I've thought that all along."

"Yeah, I know you have. What about the widow? Are you gonna be satisfied that we got Harrison? Or do you want it all, as usual?"

"I've got a couple of ideas on that, Chief. Give me some time this morning and let me see what I can come up with."

"You're *not* going to accost that woman at her husband's funeral, are you?"

Steven shook his head. "I'd better get going. I have to go back out."

"Wait a minute. Did you hear from Valentino? Any idea how he made out in Saratoga?"

"I wasn't home last night. I don't know if he tried to call or not."

"All right, I guess we'll find out soon enough. As for me, as long as we can prove Harrison did it, I can live with that. I know, I know. You need it wrapped up all nice and neat." Thompson stubbed out his cigarette. "But we've got more than enough to do now with this second murder. You go do what you gotta do. I have to get some work done so I can go to the funeral this afternoon."

Steven checked the clock on the wall near his desk. *Why not?* John Harrison's poor parents probably hadn't slept much last night anyway.

The Chevy's engine was still warm. Steven put the car in gear and left right away. As he drove, he noticed Knightsbridge was slowly waking up. Lights were coming on in house after house. When he stopped at an intersection, he caught a golden sun rising in a lavender sky in his rear view mirror.

When Mrs. Harrison came to the door, it was obvious she'd spent the night crying. Her eyes were bloodshot and red-rimmed. She looked like she'd aged fifteen years since Steven had told her her only child had been murdered. She wore the same shapeless sweater over a red-and-white house dress, a soggy handkerchief stuffed in one of the front pockets.

"Detective? Is there news?"

"No, ma'am. I'm sorry. Not yet."

He kicked the snow off his boots before entering the cluttered living room.

"I don't know what else we can tell you. My husband and I don't know any of Johnny's friends. Or the people he worked with either." She twisted the handkerchief and her voice broke, "My son didn't confide in us. I guess that's what boys are like, huh?" She seemed desperate for confirmation that the relationship she'd had with her son had been a normal one.

"I suppose that's true. Girls probably share more with their folks." He cleared his throat. "The reason I'm here, Mrs. Harrison…I need to pick up what John left the other day."

Steven was unprepared for what came next.

"Oh, yes, the envelope. I'm sorry, Detective. I'd forgotten about it."

Steven scrambled. *Envelope, what envelope? How could Harrison fit all that money in an envelope? Maybe it was a letter for Patricia, telling her where the money was.*

"Do you want me to get a court order, Mrs. Harrison? I can come back later."

"No, no. Not at all. You can have it. Johnny put it in his old room. You're welcome to look." At the sound of a heavy boot hitting the floor, she gazed to the ceiling. "My husband's getting up, Detective. I'd better get his breakfast. You go ahead. It's the bedroom in the back, down the hall there. You think it'll help in finding out who did it?"

Steven didn't have the heart to take away this shred of optimism. "I sure hope so, Mrs. Harrison."

Walking down the narrow hallway, he put on a pair of gloves. As he closed the bedroom door behind him, he felt the temperature drop. The heat was turned off in this unused space.

The tiny room looked like it must have when John Harrison had been a boy growing up in this house. A single bed, its navy spread tucked around a pillow, occupied the far corner under a window; a maple chest of drawers sat next to a matching desk and chair along the opposite wall; a homemade rag rug covered the center of the floor.

A shelf over the desk displayed Harrison's interests—a trophy, the figure of a horse, a miniature wooden box with *Souvenir of Lake Placid* written in fancy script. The little trunk even had a tiny brass latch that kept it closed. There was a sepia photograph of an elderly couple on a porch swing. Grandparents, maybe?

He examined a bookcase where Harrison had organized his books—childhood favorites on the bottom; higher up, the books he'd enjoyed as a young adult. There were Uncle Wiggily stories and Peter Rabbit books, Tom Swift tales and works by Zane Grey. Steven remembered his own fondness for the prolific western writer. Harrison had owned *The Vanishing American, The Thundering Herd,* and *The Last Trail.* There were also several classics. Steven read the names on the spines—Robert Louis Stevenson, Sir Arthur Conan Doyle, Jules Verne, Jack London. The bent corners and well-worn pages told Steven that all of these had been read many, many times. Here were Harrison's treasured possessions. He felt a moment of sadness for the boy who had not had many friends.

Enough! Whatever he'd been as a child, Harrison turned out to be a murderer. Get to work. Find that envelope.

Steven started with the desk and got lucky on his third try. There in the middle drawer sat a brown envelope. He unwound the string from the fastener. Inside was a white, legal-sized envelope upon which was written *Open in the event of my death.* It was not sealed. He carefully slid out the paper and unfolded it.

Shock zigzagged through him as if he'd been struck by lightning.

Harrison had left a confession.

And he named Patricia as the mastermind behind the murder and the theft.

Dizzy with relief, Steven put the letter and envelopes back together. Mrs. Harrison was frying eggs and bologna, spatula in hand, as Steven entered the kitchen.

"I'll give you a receipt for this, Mrs. Harrison. And I need to ask you something else. If this is going to be any good to us, I have to get something with John's handwriting to prove that he actually wrote this."

"I'm sure there must be something in his desk. Did you look?"

"I need your permission, ma'am."

"Go ahead."

"In writing, if you wouldn't mind." He quickly wrote the standard release for a consensus search, giving him permission to look further, and handed her the paper to sign.

"Can you tell me what's in the letter, Detective?"

She brushed limp hair out of her face and eyed Steven expectantly. John Harrison's mother was a gray-looking woman, old before her time. She had lived a hard life. And now this.

"I'm sorry. I can't say. I'm not allowed to give out information about the investigation."

Her face fell.

Though Steven felt a great deal of sympathy for this woman, it wasn't his job to be nice. It was up to him to get justice for the victim. But at the same time he couldn't help but feel that Mrs. Harrison was a victim as well.

Steven found what he needed in a desk drawer. Harrison had saved two high school papers. Both had his signature on top of the page.

After brushing the snow off his car again, he got stuck trying to pull away from the curb. Alternating between the gas pedal and the brake, Steven rocked the car back and forth, while he tried to keep his frustration at bay. Finally, he shot out into the street and returned to the station.

Steven's mind worked furiously on how he should handle this new evidence. The most important thing was to do it by the book. When District Attorney Lockridge got Patricia Castleman into a court room and a jury convicted her of being an accessory in Leo Castleman's murder, and likely in Harrison's as well, there could be no loophole for the defense attorney to crawl through.

Steven did not want to read the letter aloud at the morning briefing. He didn't know why but his instincts told him to hold off. He was going to wait until the widow was behind bars before he disclosed the full contents to his fellow officers. Except the chief. He had to show all of it to Chief Thompson. And probably Becks, too, when he got back.

"Briefing in five minutes, everybody," Steven called out as he hurried through the station. He didn't even bother to take off his hat and coat as he charged into Thompson's office and slammed the door shut.

The chief looked up. "Why do I have that feeling that the *something you had to do* this morning worked out good?"

"Hold on to your hat, Chief, and listen to this."

Everyone in the building heard the chief yell *Yahoo!* through the closed door.

"You got 'er, Blackwell!"

Several officers rushed out of the patrol room and saw Detective Sergeant Steven Blackwell and Chief Andy Thompson in animated conversation. There was much waving of arms and pointing of fingers as the chief paced back and forth behind his overflowing desk and the detective mirrored his movements on the other side.

Steven came out, walked calmly into the CID room, and hung up his outer gear. He clutched something in his hand. Everyone hoped the mystery would be solved in the meeting that was about to start.

The men gathered as they usually did. Some perched on the edges of desks, others sat in chairs, and a couple leaned against the walls of the crowded patrol room. Tommy Forester hovered in the doorway, keeping an ear cocked for the telephone and an eye ready to notice if anyone came in the front door. He, too, had heard the chief shout and he wasn't about to miss the big news. Maybe the case was cracked at last.

"Good morning, everyone." Steven stopped as Harry Beckman

strode in. "Becks! Holy mackerel, you're early!"

"Left before the sun came up. I made good time. *And* I've got good news. I was hoping I'd get here for the briefing."

"Swell!" Steven was so glad to have Becks back. He wanted it to be the two of them who would arrest Patricia Castleman. "As I was saying, you all know that we found John Harrison's body yesterday."

"Harrison!" exclaimed Beckman.

Will Taylor leaned over and quietly told him, "He was shot Wednesday night."

Steven continued. "He was murdered. Doc Elliott called this morning with the autopsy results. Shot through the heart once at close range with a .38. We have the bullet. We do not have the gun.

"We searched Harrison's house and found what we think is the weapon used in the murder of Leo Castleman. It's been sent to the lab for confirmation. I can tell you, unofficially of course, that in my mind it *is* the weapon. There was a tiny sliver of wood missing from one end and what looked like a blood stain. The lab promised they'd rush it through.

"In the meantime, we need to focus on Harrison's killer. Yesterday, Ralph and Pete talked with Harrison's neighbors. Ralph, you want to tell 'em your results?"

"Sure, Steven. We have a witness but he didn't give us much. The neighbor directly across the street saw a tall man walk up Harrison's front steps around ten thirty Wednesday night. He did not see the man's face. He wouldn't guess his size. Said the fella was bundled up in a coat and hat."

Pete snorted in disgust. "We could've guessed that much."

Ralph went on. "If it *was* Harrison's killer, we have the time of death but that's it. The neighbor couldn't describe the coat or hat. Said he hadn't paid attention.

"We checked the houses next door and kitty-corner from Harrison's on both sides, but nobody saw anything. People were in bed, listening to the radio, or reading the newspaper. Usual nighttime stuff. So, bottom line, nothing but a 'tall man' and the time of ten thirty."

"Did anyone hear or see a car?" Steven asked.

"No mention of an automobile," said Ralph. "But that doesn't mean there wasn't one. The witness was *not* observant and everyone else was busy. With the doors and windows closed, how many people pay attention to noises outside?"

"Especially if you're listening to the radio," observed Jimmy Bou.

"Right," said Steven. "Okay, here's what I'd like us to do today. Will, organize a search of Harrison's neighborhood with the goal of finding the gun. Perhaps the killer threw it away. Get some men together and canvas the neighbors again. Throw out a wider net. Maybe we'll get lucky."

"You got it, Steven."

"Hey, Steven," shouted a tall, thin patrolman leaning against the back wall. "Are you gonna tell us about that envelope you've got in a death-grip? Is it something to do with the case?"

"What was the chief so excited about when you were in his office?" added an officer on the left side of the room.

"Yeah," chorused the inseparable duo Ralph and Pete. "What gives?"

"Patience, fellas, patience. I'm getting there. Saving the best for last."

All around the room the men exchanged looks. Everyone was eager to *know*.

"Becks, you want to report on your trip?"

"Sure. I got three positive IDs when I showed the photographs around Saratoga. Three people were absolutely certain they saw Patricia Castleman and John Harrison together last summer."

"That's a long time ago," commented Will Taylor. "How can they be sure it was them?"

"Harrison signed the guest register at the hotel with his own name. The desk clerk remembered the woman with him because she resembled his sister. The barman told me Harrison tried to bribe him. It was last summer. Remember President Roosevelt didn't repeal Prohibition until December. Harrison ordered a couple of cocktails and insisted the bartender put them in coffee cups." Beckman surveyed the room and saw several fellas nodding. They all remembered what it had been like drinking whisky from a cup. He continued. "And the lady who owned the teashop said Mrs. Castleman kept sending back her breakfast. She had to cook her eggs three times. She's still upset about wasting food and losing money."

"That's good, Becks, thanks. We can use all the evidence we can get. But I have to tell you that it's not quite as significant today as it was yesterday. Which leads me to this envelope."

Steven held up the manila envelope.

"I had a hunch this morning and decided to follow it up. I went to John Harrison's parents' house thinking that if he was our killer-thief, he might have stashed the stolen money there. I didn't discover the cash but what I found is much better. Harrison left a letter. Basically it's a confession."

There were gasps then the room went quiet. Jaws gaped. Eyes grew wide. Everyone was stunned.

"In the letter, Harrison explains that he and Patricia Castleman conspired to kill Leo Castleman and take the money. He clearly states that he did the deed."

Excitement buzzed around the room.

"Holy mackerel, that's something!"

"Wow! I can't believe it!"

"Blackwell said all along it was the two of them."

"A confession! Can you beat that?"

"Anyway," Steven shouted over the noise, "we finally have enough evidence to arrest Patricia Castleman. And that's exactly what we're going to do today."

Everyone listened attentively. Was this case finally at the end?

"I promised the chief..." Steven nodded to Thompson, "...that I would allow the community to show their respect for Mr. Castleman and not interrupt the funeral. We're going to wait until it's over before we do anything.

"The service starts at two o'clock this afternoon. In the meantime, I'm going to get a warrant for the Castleman house. We're going to be there, in position, when the widow gets home. We're going to arrest her and search for the gun that killed Harrison and for any trace of the stolen money."

Several men nodded.

"I want Ralph and Pete positioned out of sight near the funeral home to make sure she doesn't slip away. Take a couple of officers with you. Station them nearby."

Ralph and Pete grinned at each other looking pleased.

"I don't think she'll run," said Ralph. "She doesn't know we suspect her. She's got no reason."

"Besides, her family is here. They'll probably go back to her house after the funeral," said Pete.

"Jimmy, help Will for the next few hours. I want both of you to go with Becks and me to the Castleman house no later than three fifteen. If you haven't finished the canvas by three o'clock, leave the team and the two of you come back to the station."

Jimmy gave the thumbs up, Will a short nod.

"Any questions?" Steven waited. "Okay then, that's it for now."

The policemen rose, talking excitedly about Harrison's confession. Will organized his team and the room emptied.

Steven and Becks returned to the CID room. "You okay, Becks? You don't look so good."

"Yeah, I'm all right. Didn't get enough sleep last night. Jeez, Steven.

Sounds like a lot happened while I was gone. Harrison's dead? And he left a confession! What's the letter say? Can I see it?"

"Yeah, Becks, but only you. I don't want the whole thing revealed until the widow's behind bars. I showed the chief but I don't want to make it public yet."

"Sure, okay. I'll keep it under my hat."

Beckman read the outside of the envelope, "*In the event of my death.* That's dramatic. I wouldn't have thought he had it in him."

He unfolded the paper inside and silently read.

I'm writing this letter because I think I'm going to be betrayed.

I've been involved with Patricia Castleman since last year. After several months she persuaded me to get rid of her husband. Somehow she convinced Leo to go to the bank in the middle of the night to steal some money. I don't know how but whatever Patricia wants she usually manages to get it. Anyway, she manipulated me, too. I never thought I'd kill anyone but she got me to do it. I'm not making excuses for what I did. I killed Leo. But, if she betrayed him, what's to say she won't do the same to me?

Things have been different lately. I think she's got someone new. She betrayed Leo with me. Now I think she's going to betray me with someone else.

If you're reading this, I'm dead. I want the police to get this letter. I want Patricia punished for the part she played in Leo's death. It was all her idea and she planned the whole thing. She turned out to be a real bitch. I should have seen it coming but I didn't. If she had a hand in my death, I don't want her to get away with it. She has to pay.

At the end was Harrison's signature.

Beckman let out a rush of breath. "Wow! He sure wants her in the frame. Do you believe this, Steven? You think it's authentic?"

"Yes, I do. Why would Harrison implicate himself if it wasn't true? What would he have to gain by confessing to something he didn't do?"

Beckman considered this.

Steven leaned forward. "You know I've thought all along she was the instigator in this." He scrutinized his partner. "You're hesitating, Becks. You don't think the letter's genuine?"

"No…no, it's not that. I guess I'm just suspicious of things that seem too good to be true." He shook his head. "But no, to be honest, I can't think why he'd write it if it wasn't the truth." He lit one of his Lucky Strikes and threw the match in his ashtray. "It's unbelievable that you found it."

Handing the letter back to Steven, he stood. "I need to go home and change my clothes. I'd like to take a shower, put on a fresh shirt, and get some breakfast if it's okay with you. Is there anything for me that can't wait an hour or so?"

"Nah, go ahead. I'm going to take care of the warrant. Since I promised the chief not to go barging in on the funeral, we have to wait until later to go to the Castleman house anyway. We may as well get all of our paperwork caught up. After this afternoon, we're going to have a lot more of that. Take your time, Becks. Do what you gotta do. I'll hold down the fort here."

"Swell, thanks." Beckman put on his coat and left.

Steven got busy writing out the request for a search warrant. Chief Thompson called from the open doorway, "Blackwell, I forgot about something that has to get done before the funeral. I'll be gone about a half hour. You need me for anything?"

"No, thanks, Chief." He returned to his paperwork as Thompson, too, left the station.

Chapter 34

Patricia Castleman was in her bedroom getting ready for her husband's funeral. She'd be happy when it was all over. It seemed like yesterday's wake had gone on forever. Downstairs, where her sister and her family were finishing a late breakfast, the telephone rang.

Louise went into the hallway to answer it. She called up, "Patsy, telephone for you. It's the funeral home. He says it's important."

Patricia Castleman descended the staircase in her dressing gown, annoyed at being interrupted. "What do they want now? I thought I had everything settled." She grabbed the receiver. "Hello, this is Mrs. Castleman."

"It's me. Are you alone?"

Patricia moved the phone away from her mouth. "Louise, it's okay. You go finish your breakfast. I'll take care of this." She waited until her sister had disappeared into the kitchen and closed the door behind her.

"I am now. Why are you calling here? Today of all days!"

"We've got a problem. We have to change our plans. Harrison wrote a letter."

"What?!"

"He left a confession. He blamed you for everything. You're seriously implicated."

"Bastard!"

"The police have it. They're going to arrest you today."

"What are we going to do?"

"I'll come up with something, don't worry. But listen, the most important thing is that you *don't* go home after the funeral. Take Leo's car. Leave yours in the carriage house. That Silver Arrow attracts too much attention. Be sure your sister and her family go by themselves so you're on your own. Make up whatever excuse you have to so that you go separately."

"All right. I'll think of something."

"Let them leave first. You'll need to transfer the money to Leo's trunk."

"As if I'd forget that!"

"Park on Hickory near the Methodist Church. There's a path behind the pastor's house you can take to Gettman's back entrance. There'll be police looking for you, but they'll probably concentrate on the front. They'll expect you to use the circular drive that goes around the funeral home. After the service, slip out the back and get out of town. Go somewhere and find a place to stay overnight."

"Where should I go?"

"Anywhere. Don't go too far, though, because we'll still have to figure out how to get to our meeting place when it's safe. When you're settled in, call me. I'll have a plan."

"Okay. Thank God you found out before it was too late! I'll call you tonight and let you know where I am."

Patricia Castleman locked her bedroom door to make sure that no one could walk in on her. She pulled her suitcase and overnight bag from the closet shelf and began to pack. She chose only the most essential pieces of clothing and some toiletries. She had to assume she would not be returning. She put in her most expensive pieces of jewelry and took all the cash she had.

While she was packing, Patricia formulated her plan. She was seething. *Damn that John! I should have known I couldn't trust him. Damn letter!* She mentally shook herself and took a deep breath. *Okay, water under the bridge. Now, a plan. I have to have a plan. I swear to God I will* not *be poor again!* She shuddered as she thought of the awful outhouse she'd had to use as a kid. *Never again!*

By the time she'd crammed everything into her luggage, Patricia knew how she'd manage it. When they were ready to leave, she'd tell her sister and brother-in-law to go on ahead without her. She'd say that the funeral director had suggested she pay her final respects to Leo after the service, before they stored the body for burial, which had to take place in the spring when the ground thawed.

She'd say, "You go on ahead. I'll be right behind you." She wouldn't take no for an answer. She knew Louise couldn't wait to go home, to get back to her oh-so-perfect life. She'd tell her they could leave from the funeral parlor and be back in Syracuse before suppertime. She'd say that she wanted to be alone tonight. *Yes, that would work.*

Now, where to go? She had to head in the opposite direction from Syracuse. The police would look there, thinking she'd gone back with Louise. She'd head east or north. Maybe one of the small towns near Saratoga. *No, that's too far.* She had to be able to get to him, or him to her, in an hour. And of course, she didn't want to be far from the rest of the money. They each had half of it hidden under the floor in the trunk of their automobiles.

Think, Patsy, think. Where to go? Maybe up into the Adirondacks.

She remembered a long-ago summer when they'd visited a friend of Leo's in a town near Old Forge. That sounded good. She'd drive toward Utica then head northeast. There were all kinds of winter sports that went on in the mountains. Surely she'd find a place that was open somewhere along the way.

God! She couldn't wait to get out of this lousy town.

As Patricia shoved one last item in her suitcase then closed and locked both cases, she relaxed because she knew she could count on him to come up with another plan. She had always been able to count on him.

In the meantime, she had a performance to give at Leo's funeral.

Chapter 35

Request for the search warrant in hand, Steven left for the courthouse. Randolph's secretary ushered him in without delay. The judge sat behind a large, antique partners' desk, his head bent over a stack of legal papers, light from the lamp reflecting off his bald pate. Floor-to-ceiling bookshelves crammed with legal tomes filled two walls of the office. Judge Randolph was so engrossed in what he was reading that Trudy had to clear her throat twice to get his attention. He looked up.

"Oh, sorry. Lost in a tricky argument here. Morning, Steven. Thank you, Trudy."

Randolph leaned back. "So, what's this about another warrant? What happened to the one I authorized for Harrison's house yesterday?" The memory of what Steven and his men had discovered rushed back. "Oh! Right! That must have been a shock."

Steven told him about finding the walking stick. "I apologize, sir. I'll get my report to you today or, at the latest, tomorrow."

"That's fine. Let's see what you've got now," he said, extending his hand for the paperwork. "Hmm. Hmm. A confession? Tell me about this letter."

Steven summarized his trip to Harrison's parents' and his reasoning behind the visit.

Randolph peered over his glasses and raised his eyebrows. "Hiding the stolen cash at his parents', huh? That's a good thought. But instead you found this. Well, well."

"I've done everything by the book. There's nothing that will come back to haunt us later. I *do* need to get everything ready by three, though. I want to be at the Castleman house with my team before she gets back from the funeral."

"All right, based on this you have probable cause." Judge Randolph signed his name to the warrant and handed back the papers.

Steven's footsteps echoed in the corridor as he walked through the quiet police station to the CID room. As he slowly chewed his sandwich, he thought through the investigation—every element of the crime, every bit of information, every shred of evidence. He could not afford to forget or ignore the tiniest detail when he interrogated the widow.

Steven constructed his plan of attack. He decided what he would say, what he would insinuate, the questions he would ask, and how he would build up to the moment when he would tell her about the letter and Harrison's confession.

Will Taylor entered the room.

"Will, you fellas back already? That was quick."

"No, I took off early. I had a bad toothache this morning. After the briefing, I called the dentist. He told me to come in at one thirty. You were busy so I cleared it with the chief. He said it was okay, I could leave Jimmy in charge. I hope that's all right."

"That's fine. Your tooth better?"

"Yeah, gotta go back next week, though."

At three o'clock, Jimmy Bou returned and reported that, although they hadn't discovered the gun, the team had not given up. They were still questioning neighbors. At five after three, Beckman strode in.

Disappointed but determined, Steven gathered Becks, Jimmy, and Will together.

"We have the warrant to search for any sign of the stolen money and for a .38. With Harrison's confession, we've got enough to arrest Patricia Castleman."

The four men stood in a tight circle near Steven's desk.

"This is how I'd like to do it. Becks and I'll go in my car. Will and Jimmy, you take one of the department vehicles. We'll go to the house now and wait for her to get back from the funeral." He glanced at his watch. "Which should be winding up in the next fifteen minutes or so."

"Won't she stay awhile afterwards? You know, visit with people, accept condolences?" asked Jimmy.

"Probably, yes. I think she'll wait until everyone's left, then go home. I'm guessing she'll arrive somewhere around three thirty, three forty-five. We'll be waiting when she pulls in the driveway."

"We should park up the street," suggested Beckman.

"I agree, although I don't think she'll recognize my Chevy. Will, park the police car around the corner."

"Right, then we'll walk over and wait with you."

"Agreed. When she enters the house, we'll all go. I'll formally charge her and bring her in for booking. The three of you'll search the house. Hopefully you'll come back with the money or the gun." Steven looked at his most trusted officers. "Everybody okay with that?"

"Yep. I'm good."

"Sure."

"Let's go."

The policemen left the station, their adrenaline running high.

Will and Jimmy followed Steven and Becks out of the parking lot. Although the accumulation from last night's storm had been cleared away, it had continued to snow all day and the heavy vehicles made deep tracks as they moved through town. Steven's jungle green Chevy and the black Ford sedan crawled up Hickory. They passed the Margate Road, then Victoria Avenue. When they got to the fork, they took Swan Lane on the left. Steven overshot number 22. He turned the car around and parked at the corner near the Riverwalk. Will continued one block further then pulled to the curb around the corner, out of the line of vision. He and Jimmy walked briskly to Steven's sedan and got in the back. The light was already fading.

The men waited, staring at the Castleman house. Occasionally, one of them shook his head to refocus. Every few minutes, someone checked his watch.

Three thirty came and went.

A quarter to four saw no activity whatsoever.

"Gee," Jimmy exclaimed. "It's four o'clock. She should be home by now."

One by one, lights went on in the house—the front parlor, the dining room, a room on the second floor.

"How did we miss her?" Will exclaimed.

"Let's go," said Steven.

They jumped out of the automobile and rapidly strode past the neighboring homes. They marched up the Castlemans' front walk and mounted the stairs. Steven jammed his finger on the doorbell. They heard it peal through the house. The now familiar housekeeper opened the door.

"Can I help you?"

Steven showed his badge and ID. "I'm Detective Sergeant Blackwell. We'd like to see Mrs. Castleman."

"I remember you, Detective. Mrs. Castleman isn't here. She hasn't come back from the funeral."

"What? Do you know where she is? Did she have something to do after the service?"

"I don't know. She grabbed hold of me at the funeral home and said she wasn't coming back right away and I should come over and tidy up. Her sister and her family were here for a couple of days. She wanted the house cleaned before she got back."

"So her family isn't here either?"

"No, Mrs. Castleman said they were going back to Syracuse after the service."

"Is it possible she went with her sister?"

"I don't think so. I heard her say goodbye to them."

"What about her brother-in-law, Mr. Lawrence Castleman? Perhaps she went home with him and his family for a meal?"

"Steven," Will leaned over and whispered, "Remember Lawrence Castleman doesn't like her. I don't think he'd invite her to his house even on a day like today."

"You're right. Damn!"

Steven was furious. It was taking all his energy to remain calm and polite. Inwardly he prayed that Ralph and Pete had detained her. Why hadn't he gone and waited at the funeral home? Why had he listened to the chief instead of arresting her before the service?

Damn, damn, and triple damn! She's gone. I know she's gone.

But why now? Why today? Surely it would only throw suspicion on her. Unless...

His blood chilled.

No, it can't be.

Unless she got tipped off. Unless someone told her about Harrison's confession.

But the only people who know about the letter are police. They're my fellow officers, my friends. They're the people I trust with my life.

"Steven, what do you want to do?" Becks nudged him from behind.

The urgency of the police officers was contagious. The housekeeper sensed something was wrong. "What is it, Detective? Has something happened to Mrs. Castleman?"

Steven extracted a folded piece of paper from his overcoat pocket. "This is a search warrant. It gives us permission to come in and look for the items listed."

"Oh, I'm not sure about this. Mrs. Castleman should be here. She should read it first."

"Mrs. Castleman does not need to be home. Here, take it. You can put it somewhere that she'll see it when she returns."

If she returns.

"Now, if you'll let us in, we'll do our job and leave as quickly as possible. Becks, stay here with Jimmy and Will. Make sure you search *everywhere*! Nothing unturned, okay?"

"Sure. What are you going to do?"

"Try and save this case," he said disgustedly. "First, I'm going to see if Ralph and Pete have her. If they don't..." he groaned. "I'll get a hold of the tax commission in Albany. We need the Castlemans' car registration number so I can put out an alert on her."

"You sure you don't want me to do that? Will and Jimmy can search the house."

"No, this is my fault. I'd rather the three of you go over this place with a fine-toothed comb. Crawl over every inch. That's going to take a while. Damn house is huge."

"All right."

"I'll start calling around and see if I can track her down. I'll find out if anybody's seen her since the funeral. I can't believe this. I *swear* I'm going to find that woman!

"I'll see you fellas back at the station. Take your time. But find something. Get me the money or the gun. Anything! Find *something.*"

Steven's worst fear was confirmed.

Ralph and Pete had done their job. They'd stationed patrolmen along the street and a man on each side of the mortuary. They'd taken turns checking the front and back entrances. They waited until all the cars had exited the drive circling the building. They hadn't caught a glimpse of the widow. Somehow she'd managed to sneak away.

Patricia Castleman had disappeared.

Steven paced back and forth in the CID room.

Where could she have gone? Why had she picked this moment to leave? Was it a move that had been arranged for some time? Had it always been a part of the plan between her and the new boyfriend? Because, to Steven's mind, there definitely *was* a new boyfriend. He believed whole-heartedly that it was the new beau who had murdered John Harrison. Years of experience told him that it must be so. It was the only thing that made sense.

If the plan to leave town immediately after the funeral had been arranged in advance, it could be anyone. But...nausea crawled through Steven's gut and up into his throat...but if it was a last-minute decision, a panic move because of Harrison's confession, then it meant only one thing: the killer was a cop.

FRIDAY NIGHT – PRESENT DAY

Chapter 36

Olivia could not settle down and concentrate. She'd been distracted all day—thinking about Steven, wondering if he'd found the money, anxious to know if he'd made an arrest.

Focus, Olivia. Get to work! He'll be home soon and he'll tell you everything.

She opened her laptop and forced herself to begin. The new job dealt with the 1960s. The Syracuse University professor conducting the study would interview people in the city, Olivia would tackle small-town memories. As she typed Isabel's name on the list of sources, her cell rang. She picked it up and read the caller ID.

"Jennifer! What a nice surprise!"

"Hi, Olivia. How are you?"

Although Olivia and her former babysitter had grown apart, as adult friends and activities replaced childhood ones, they made a point of staying in touch.

"I'm great. Are you coming up this weekend for your mom's birthday?"

"That's why I'm calling. I'm taking her out for Chinese Saturday night. Can you come?"

"Sure, thanks. Are you flying? Want me to pick you up at the airport?"

"Thanks but no. I'm going to drive. I'm taking Friday and Monday off. It'll make a nice long weekend for my mom."

"You got lucky. The weather's supposed to be good."

"Yeah, thank goodness it wasn't last weekend. That nor'easter was a killer. Even DC shut down because of the snow."

After hanging up, Olivia returned to the 1960s project. She finished listing the people she wanted to interview and began creating the interview questions. She realized she'd want to record the sessions and remembered the voice-activated recorder she had used when she was working as a reporter. *That thing must be ten years old. I wonder if it still works.* She rummaged through her catch-all drawer for some fresh batteries, popped them in, and tested it. *Why even bother with it? There's probably an app. I'll use my phone.* She left the recorder on the counter, checked the clock—barely six—and went back to work. Maybe if she stopped procrastinating, the time would go faster.

It worked. The next time she checked it was almost seven. He should be home soon. Olivia knew she'd make no more progress tonight. *Might as well fix dinner.*

She set the table wishing Steven would walk through the front door.

And he did.

The door slammed. She hurried to the front hall where he was stomping snow from his boots and kicking them off.

"Steven!" His frustration and disappointment hit her right away and there was something else. Was it sorrow? Without thinking, she took a giant step and wrapped her arms around him. "You didn't find the money."

He dropped his head on her shoulder and leaned in. He didn't speak for a full twenty seconds.

"It's worse than that."

"Tell me what you need," she whispered. "If you want to talk about it, I'll listen. If you'd rather put work aside and forget it for a while we can relax and eat."

"I don't want to think about it right now."

"Okay, come sit down. I'll have dinner ready in a few minutes."

"I'll freshen up first."

Steven threw his coat on the hall clothes tree and started up the stairs. On the third step he called out, "Olivia!"

"Yeah?"

"If I don't come back..."

"I know. Come and get you. Don't worry, you'll be back. And, Steven, take your time. There's no rush."

Steven perked up when he walked in the kitchen. "This smells wonderful!" He had donned a pair of corduroy trousers, a soft flannel shirt, and slippers. Olivia noticed that his freshly slicked-back hair and collar looked wet. He must have thrown some water on his face.

"I feel like I'm in that new Italian restaurant. Hey, is Giovanni's still there?"

"Yes. Gee, I forgot it was so old."

Olivia arranged the pasta and meatballs on a dish then poured chunky tomato sauce on top. Steven placed the platter on the table already set with colorful dishes, cloth napkins, and a tablecloth. She handed him a bottle of Valpolicella.

"I hope you didn't go to all this trouble for me."

"I didn't." She chuckled. "The way I look at it, life is short, so I try to make every day special." She shook her head. "I never understood...my grandmother had what she called her 'good china.' She only used it at

Christmas and family dinners. For the rest of the year, those beautiful things collected dust in the hutch. I say why not enjoy nice things all the time?"

Steven poured the wine and they clinked glasses.

"Bon appétit, Olivia."

"Merci. Do you speak French?"

"My mother raised me to be bilingual. I told you she was from France, didn't I?"

"You said she lived in Paris. She actually was French, huh? Cool. How'd your parents meet?"

"My dad was in Paris doing something for the Navy. One night he was strolling around Montmartre and he literally ran into her. She was hurrying out of a café, not paying attention to where she was going. She walked right into him. According to my mother, it was love at first sight. She took one look and knew. So, naturally, she didn't want him to get away." He laughed. "She told him that since he so rudely hit her, he must buy her a drink." His face fell as he looked into the distance. "She was swell. I miss her every day."

"I wish I could've known her."

"It's funny, Olivia. I realize we haven't known each other very long, although it seems like it's been a long time..."

"Me, too!" she blurted out. "Oh, sorry."

"Well, you remind me of her. She was always surprising us. Sometimes, I'd come home from school in the middle of the week and there'd be a roast turkey in the oven. The table would be set with candles and flowers."

"You're right. That's me, too."

"I like to think she's stirring things up a bit in heaven."

Steven gulped a drink of wine and hastily looked away. Olivia had figured out by now that he was a private man. Although she would have loved to hear more about this fascinating woman who had been his mother, she forced herself not to pry.

The kitchen was warm and cozy, the food and wine delicious. They compared the day's weather in both of their times—sunny but below freezing in 2014, snowy and gray in 1934.

"Is Bailey's there yet?" Olivia asked.

"Yeah, it is. Opened up last year. As a matter of fact, Becks and I had breakfast there on Saturday." Steven sighed. "Speaking of Becks, I should do some work on the case." He settled back in his chair, newly refilled glass in his hand, and said, "I'm ready to talk now if you still want to listen."

"Of course."

"I made a big mistake today. I had Patricia Castleman dead to rights and I let her get away."

"What happened?"

"I went to John Harrison's parents' house first thing this morning. The money wasn't there, but I found something a *lot* more important. Harrison left a written confession."

Olivia's breath caught.

"Yeah, he said Patricia was cheating on her husband with him since last year. She was the one who came up with the scheme to kill Mr. Castleman and take the money. She convinced her husband to rob the bank. Harrison must have been waiting in the alley. After Castleman got into the vault, Harrison snuck in and killed him."

"Wow, he said all that?"

"Yup." He nodded excitedly. "There's more. Harrison thought Patricia was going to betray him, too. After all, she had already betrayed her husband. In the letter, Harrison said that if they found him dead, we should investigate Mrs. Castleman."

"Phew! So what went wrong? All of this sounds good for your case."

"At this morning's briefing, I told my team what Harrison wrote in the letter. I said I was going to arrest Patricia Castleman after the funeral. The chief told me I had to wait until the town paid their respects to Mr. Castleman. He figured she wasn't going anywhere. I stationed a few of my officers at the funeral home just to make sure. Becks and I got a couple of officers together and we went to her house. We figured we'd arrest her the minute she got home." Steven drilled her with his stare. "We waited, Olivia. She never came home."

"Oh no!"

"Where did she go? If she's gone for good, why leave now? The timing is suspicious. If she was going to run with the money and maybe her new beau, they could have gone anytime. Tomorrow. Next week. Three weeks from now." He leaned forward. His forehead tightened. "Here's the thing, Olivia. What if she *knew* we were going to arrest her? The only people who heard about the confession and him accusing her are the fellas at the station." Steven hated saying the words. He didn't want to say it. As soon as he said it out loud, it would be real. He cringed as he whispered, "What if the new boyfriend is a cop?"

"Oh, my God! No wonder you looked so upset when you got home. Do you have any idea who it could be?"

"It's all I've been thinking about. Olivia, it makes me sick to my stomach. The thought that another cop—someone I know and trust, maybe even a friend—is a killer...the idea that that person betrayed me and the whole department...I can't even take it in. I don't want to believe it. I *won't* believe it until there's no other explanation."

"Assuming you're right and it is someone you work with—and remember, you don't know that for sure—that person would've been at the briefing. Then he would've had to go someplace private to call Patricia and warn her. He would've made sure he was alone so nobody could possibly overhear the conversation." Olivia took a drink. "So, who was *not* at the station during the time between the briefing and when you went to her house? Who had the opportunity?" She poured more wine for both of them, finishing the bottle.

"You sound like a cop."

"We should look at it logically, don't you think?" She leaned closer. "Where was everybody?"

"All right then. Let's see. I sent a team to canvas Harrison's neighborhood. That's Will, Jimmy Bou, Ralph, and Pete, and five other officers. They were all working together. If someone had left, Will would've told me."

Olivia counted on her fingers. "Okay, that's nine guys in the clear. Who else?"

"Tommy Forester was on the desk all day."

"That's ten."

"The chief was either getting coffee or in his office. Oh, wait. He *did* go out for a little while. But it's not him."

"We've gotta be objective, Steven. Take the time he was in his office. He could have closed the door and called her. Nobody would've heard him."

"I suppose it's possible…no, it can't be him. He's a happily married man."

"You never know what goes on behind closed doors! You can't discount him because you *think* he's got a good marriage."

"All right, but Patricia Castleman would *never* have an affair with him. He's not her type. She goes for good-looking fellas, the movie idol type. Besides, the personality is all wrong."

"Okay, that's a logical reason why not for the chief. So, counting your boss, that's eleven people accounted for. Who else works there?"

Steven listed several other officers who were in the station all day. "Wait a minute. Will! Will Taylor was *supposed* to go with the team to canvas Harrison's neighborhood. He said he had a toothache and went to the dentist instead."

"You can check that easily enough. You don't have cell phones so he'd have to…what? Go to a public phone booth? How do you make phone calls when you're not home or at work?"

Steven let out a small laugh. "Funny how an everyday thing like a telephone changes the way folks live. I wonder if people get away with more in your time."

"I doubt it. We also have a *lot* more ways of tracking people down."

He sipped his wine, letting his mind roll over the hours of the day. He saw the men coming and going. "Gray!"

"What?"

"Gray Wilson. Our photographer. I remember seeing him in the doorway with Tommy toward the end of the meeting. I forgot about him. He brought over the pictures he took at Harrison's house." Steven considered this new idea. "No, not Gray. It couldn't be."

"You can't say that about everyone, Steven. Is he her type?"

"Well, yes. Actually, he is. Classy. Good dresser. But underneath the class and good looks, there's real class and breeding. It's not only for show with him. *He* wouldn't go for her. *She*'s not *his* type."

"All right, you've eliminated the photographer and your chief. And you can easily check on Will, the guy with the toothache. Who else? There must be someone else."

"There's Becks, but I'm not considering him. He's my partner. I'd know if it was him. Besides, in the five years we've worked together, I've never seen him with the same girl for more than a couple of months. He's a ladies' man. He doesn't spend enough time with anyone to get so involved that she could tell him what to do. Especially kill somebody. No, definitely not Becks."

"Was he there? At the station?"

"No, he went home to shower and change his clothes. He left Saratoga at the crack of dawn, drove a few hours, and came straight to the station. He wanted to clean up and get some breakfast."

"Okay, we'll leave Becks for now. Anybody else?"

"That's everyone. *Who* could it be? We went through every officer I can think of!"

"Remember, Steven, we might be wrong. One of the guys in your department might have told somebody and *that* person's your killer."

"Yeah!" He seized on the possibility. "Someone could have unknowingly told the wrong person. Maybe the only thing the police officer is guilty of is not keeping it secret like I told them." He savored a moment of relief.

"And don't forget, there's also a 50-50 chance it really was a coincidence. It happens. She might've already had plans with the boyfriend to take off after the funeral and it has *nothing* to do with that letter."

"Oh, Olivia, I hope you're right."

"So, what are you going to do next? Where do you think she went?"

"I'm not sure. If I were leaning towards one of the guys at the station, I'd look into relatives that might live out of town or another property that person might own. Some of the families have cabins in the mountains where they go fishing and hunting. I've got an alert out for her. There are cops all over the area looking."

"What about her sister? If she went back to Liverpool with her sister she could catch a train to practically anywhere. She could be in Chicago by tomorrow."

"I thought about that. But I talked with her housekeeper at the funeral home and she said she heard Patricia say goodbye to her family."

"That doesn't mean anything. It's something you say when somebody's leaving. She could've followed them home later."

Steven considered this. "I don't know. Maybe."

"Listen, didn't you tell me that something was bothering you when Becks came back from his interviews in Syracuse? Some little thread that was dangling in the back of your mind? I think the sister's your strongest bet and, if you go to Liverpool, you can swing over to Syracuse and follow up on that thing, too," she finished triumphantly.

Steven thought some more. Olivia stayed silent. Finally, he said, "You know, that's a pretty good idea. And right now, I can't think of anything better. At least I can eliminate the possibility if I show up at Louise Haydock's door and she's not there.

"And you're right. There was something Becks told me after he got back that day. I'll check my notes and follow up tomorrow morning." He sighed and tilted his glass to get the last drop of wine. Then he noticed the tape recorder. He reached over to the counter and picked it up. "What's this?"

"It's a voice-activated recorder." She explained what it did and how it worked.

"It's so tiny! My Uncle Rudy is an inventor. Works in a lab in New Jersey. The recorders we have now are huge. They're trying to figure out how to make them smaller. He'd go crazy to see this!"

"You can borrow it if you want. Does he ever come up to visit?"

"He's going to be at my Aunt Jenny's this weekend."

"Go ahead and take it. Dazzle your uncle."

SATURDAY – 1934

Chapter 37

The shrill ringing from the telephone woke the man from a deep sleep. Half-awake, he hurried down the stairs into the hall, tripping on the edge of the runner as he made a grab for the receiver.

"It's me."

"Are you okay? What happened? I got worried last night when you didn't call."

"I'm all right. It was that stupid storm. The wind knocked some lines down. I couldn't telephone out. The phones were dead until this morning."

"Where are you?"

"Some god-forsaken place north of Utica. I don't know if it even has a name. I stopped at the first motel off Route 8. It's a dump. But for one night, I couldn't be choosy. Tell me what's going on. Have you got a plan?"

He explained his idea. "I think we should lie low for one more day."

She groaned.

"You can be sure the police are looking for you. If it was me, I'd already have your registration plate number. I'd have contacted the State Police *and* the local cops. They'll be watching every road leading out of town. We need to stay put."

"Okay. Fine."

He knew that tone. He could tell she wasn't happy. He also knew she'd look to him to keep them safe.

"Then what?" she asked. "How are we going to meet? What about the money?"

"My half's in my trunk. Nobody's gonna look in the car. You've got your half?"

"Of course."

"Good. I think we can keep to our original plan. How far up Route 8 are you?"

"Maybe ten miles."

"Can you get over to Route 28 and meet me in Thendara?"

"When?"

"Tomorrow morning. People'll be in church. Maybe the police'll let their guard down."

"Because it's Sunday."

"Right. I think it's our best shot. You should be okay. I'll meet you at the place we picked out. Then we follow the plan."

"We work our way through the mountains to the Vermont border and go straight up into Canada."

"Exactly," he confirmed the strategy they'd worked out months before. "Can you leave before it gets light? Once you're on 28, there'll be less chance of them finding you. They won't expect you to go up in the wilderness in the dead of winter. You're sure you'll be all right?"

"You know me. Once I set my mind to something..."

"Yeah, I do know that about you." He paused. "It's good we're laying low today. We might be in for one of those weird winter storms. I hear thunder."

Chapter 38

Lying in bed last night, Steven had planned his strategy. Since he didn't know if he could trust any of his fellow officers, he would trust no one. He'd act alone. He'd keep his own counsel and not reveal his plan. Not to the chief. Not to Jimmy Bou. Not even to Becks.

He slowed his breathing, closed his eyes, and got into the mind of Patricia Castleman, now—he was sure—a woman on the run. She wasn't stupid. She'd guess the police had her license plate number and were searching for her.

If it were me, he thought, *what would I do?*

I think Olivia's right. I'd hole up at my sister's for the night. I'd pretend I didn't want to see anybody or talk to anyone. I'd convince my sister to let me stay at her house. Then from there I could hop a train and go anywhere.

That's it. Steven was sure of his decision now. *Tomorrow morning, I'm going to knock on Louise Haydock's door and see if Patricia Castleman is hiding out.*

Steven slept badly, plagued by a dream that started out enjoyably but grew eerily disturbing.

It was a beautiful, sunny day. He was at the county fair. He sensed Olivia walking along side of him, though he couldn't see her clearly.

They strolled past food stands. Enticing aromas of grilled sausages, onions, and peppers, mouthwatering salt potatoes dripping in butter, and luscious ice cream cones tempted them to stop. Steven tried his luck at the ring toss and won a small toy. He threw darts at balloons. The darts just bounced off. Hawkers waved their arms and shouted.

"Hey, fella! Try your luck here!"

"How about you, buddy?"

"Win a prize for the lady!"

They wandered over to the fun house. Steven bought two tickets but when they entered, he found himself alone. Olivia had vanished like vapor.

Steven stood in a round foyer surrounded by closed, solid wooden doors. At the very top of the tented ceiling, a pinpoint of light filtered down on him, leaving the doors in shadow. Somehow, Steven knew he would find the killer behind one of these doors. But which one? How was he to choose? What would happen if he picked the wrong one?

I'm afraid to find out, he thought in his sleep. *I don't want to know. Do I have to do this?*

Yes. You do.

Steven strode across the lit circle of dusty floor and opened a door at random. A larger-than-life clown jumped out. His carrot-colored hair exploded in all directions underneath a bright green pork-pie hat. He wore voluminous, billowing pants in wide blue-and-white stripes and enormous clown shoes many sizes too big. He leaned in close to Steven and let loose a hyena laugh. Ruby red lips took up half of his face. He whispered, "It's not meee."

The chief spun around, clumped back into the closet-like room, and slammed the door.

Steven was alone again, his heart beating fast, his mouth dry.

Okay, one down.

He faced the door on the left. He turned the knob.

Gray Wilson took a half step out into the doorway. He was slightly taller and thinner than in real life and sported a black silk top hat and tails. The bespoke, black jacket and pants were set off by a white waistcoat and dress shirt, and black bowtie. He wore white gloves and held a cane in his left hand. He raised one elegantly shaped eyebrow and smirked. "You can't be serious."

Then he whirled the cane around like a baton and stepped back into the small chamber, closing the door.

Which door to try next?

He settled on one directly behind him. He pivoted, reached out, and pulled. It was a good thing that his reflexes were highly tuned, for out of the hollowed space charged a spectacular palomino, blond tail and mane flying, white star flashing on his forehead.

The creature was magnificent. On his bare back rode an enhanced vision of Will Taylor.

This Will had long, flowing, black hair, a dark complexion, and the sharply chiseled cheekbones of his Mohawk ancestors. He wore no shirt and his well-developed muscles rippled as he drew on the reins of the horse.

"I know what you seek," said the dream-Will. "It was not I. That is a deed which brings deep shame upon those who are bound to the one wielding the weapon."

He pulled on the reins again and the horse reared, its front legs dancing in the air, then it galloped back into the room from which it came.

One final door. Then I must leave this place.

Steven reached out to the door on his right and slowly turned the knob. At first he thought the space was empty, then slowly, cautiously, out walked Harry Beckman. He looked from side to side, then saw Steven standing in front of him, half-hidden in shadow. Becks wore a black mask that covered his forehead and nose, like Zorro. His cheeks were wet, shining. His eyes glistened through the cut-outs in the mask.

"Becks, is that you? Why are *you* here?"

"I'm sorry, Steven, I couldn't stay away," he whispered.

He crept back into the chamber.

Steven awoke with a start, sweating despite the cold room and feeling out of sorts after the upsetting dream. He looked at his alarm clock, twenty to six. He jumped out of bed and hurried over the icy floor into the bathroom to brush his teeth. He decided that a few minutes soaking in a tub of hot water would make him feel better, so he took his weekly bath a day early.

Dressed in warm clothing, he went into the kitchen, made a pot of strong coffee, and ate a bowl of Wheaties. He prepared a couple of sandwiches to take with him and filled his thermos with the remainder of the steaming coffee.

Yesterday, he'd brought the case files home on the off chance that he might want to study some of his notes. After supper with Olivia, he'd returned to his own time and pored over the reports until he found the bit of information that had been troubling him. Now, he looked up the address of Patricia Castleman's sister and, using a street map of Onondaga County, located the Haydock residence in the village of Liverpool, outside the Syracuse city limits. He plotted his route and was on the road by seven.

Steven kept the car in second gear as he negotiated the slippery streets. Darkness still blanketed the sleeping town. The headlamps of the Chevy carved long tunnels in the distance ahead. Thunder grumbled nearby. *We're in for strange weather today,* he thought.

Steven left Route 5 and headed west on State Route 31. An hour later, a thin, gray light revealed the sign for Route 57. He extinguished his headlights, turned south, and shortly before eight thirty, entered the village of Liverpool.

Tom and Louise Haydock lived on a quiet street near the lake in a beautiful home with a small widow's walk on the steeply pitched roof. A middle-aged man dressed in casual clothes answered the doorbell.

"Can I help you?"

Steven showed his badge and ID. "I apologize for the early hour, Mr. Haydock, but I need to speak with Patricia Castleman."

"Patsy? She isn't here."

From somewhere deep in the house Steven heard, "Who is it, Tom?"

"It's the police, dear. They're looking for Patsy."

"Patsy? Why on earth...?"

"Good morning, Mrs. Haydock. I'm Detective Sergeant Blackwell with the Knightsbridge police. We spoke a few days ago."

"I remember."

"I'm looking for your sister. Is she here?"

Louise Haydock seemed genuinely surprised. "Of course not. Why would you think Patsy'd be here? She just buried her husband yesterday."

"I'm aware of that. But I need to speak with her. I thought perhaps she'd come here to rest and get away from well-meaning but probably bothersome telephone calls. It's important. Can I come in?"

"Well, you can certainly come in, Detective," said Thomas Haydock, "but you won't find Patsy. We haven't seen her since we left the funeral home yesterday."

"Do you know where she is? I have to find her."

"No, I don't. My sister insisted on driving herself to the funeral parlor, even though Tom was more than happy to take all of us. She said she had something to do after the service. She wanted to wait there until everyone had gone."

"Did she say what it was?"

"Something about paying her final respects to Leo in private, before, you know..."

"You're hesitating, Mrs. Haydock. Did you believe her?"

Tom Haydock chimed in. "I didn't believe it. Theirs wasn't an ideal marriage."

"Tom! That's private!"

"Mrs. Haydock, nothing is private in a murder investigation. I'm well aware that your sister didn't love her husband. But I'm asking you, if you know where she is, please tell me."

"Detective, I don't know if I would tell you if I knew. But I don't. I don't have any idea where my sister is."

Steven recognized the truth when he heard it.

As he pulled away from the curb, he thought, *Well that didn't go the way I thought it would but their reactions seemed genuine. I don't think Thomas Haydock would lie for his sister-in-law. Now, let's see if I can take care of that question in Becks's interview at the Hotel Syracuse.*

In the report, Beckman had said the desk clerk in the Hotel Syracuse had recognized Patricia in the photograph but he didn't think John Harrison looked familiar. *Didn't think* wasn't the same as *didn't recognize.* That inconsistency had been popping up in the back of Steven's mind for a few days. Time to settle it once and for all.

As he drove through the waking village, Steven thought that Liverpool looked like a nice place to live. Across from a small park, the brick grammar school rose two stories high into the gray morning. Attractive, well-kept homes on lots unbroken by fences and several pleasant-looking churches told him this was a friendly, tightly-knit community.

Steven stopped at a fork in the road. There sat Heid's, a small, unassuming eatery that grilled the best hot dogs he'd ever had. He remembered the times during his childhood when his father, home on leave, had bundled him and his mother into their automobile and driven all the way to Liverpool to savor one of Heid's famous frankfurters. After the delicious lunch, he'd always pronounced, "Now *that* was worth it!" Steven smiled at the memory. He was going to stop at Heid's for a hot dog on his way home!

Steven veered left onto the Old Liverpool Road and noticed Onondaga Lake to his right. White caps rolled over water that looked like pewter. Along the shoreline, dark wooden salt flats stretched out silent and empty, abandoned until warmer weather. He passed the Franklin Motors Company, then a scattering of clapboard houses in the tiny hamlet of Galeville. Lights turned on inside the green-and-white Galeville Store as he drove by. Someone was starting work.

Steven transitioned to the Northside where recent immigrants made their home. He passed saloons selling locally brewed German beer and bakeries where the aroma of fresh Italian bread filled the sidewalks. He saw communicants leaving early-morning Mass at Assumption Church and men arriving for work in Mr. Baumer's candle factory. All were bundled up against the frigid air.

A moment later, Steven pushed through Hotel Syracuse's revolving door, climbed a short flight of stairs, and headed straight for the reception desk. Thick Oriental carpets muffled his footsteps. Elegant chandeliers drew the eye up to the gilt and painted ceiling and lit the way.

"Excuse me," he said to the clerk. "I'm Detective Sergeant Steven Blackwell with the Knightsbridge Police Department. Could you look at a couple of photographs for me?"

"Of course, it would be my pleasure."

"Have you ever seen these two people?"

"I'm certain I've seen the woman. Quite a number of times as a matter of fact. But I'm not sure this is the man she comes in with." He stared at the photo of John Harrison. "He looks a little bit like the fella she's always with. But, no, I don't think so. Sorry."

"Thank you for your time." He turned to walk away when the clerk called out.

"Wait, Detective! I just remembered something."

Steven spun around.

"I think I can tell you his name."

"His name?"

"Yes, sir. The name of the man who comes in with this woman all the time."

"You remember the name they register under?"

"No, it's not that. Once I heard what she called him. I remember because he was always my mother's favorite."

"I'm sorry, but I'm not following you."

"Valentino. She called him Valentino."

SATURDAY – PRESENT DAY

Chapter 39

Olivia rang the doorbell at quarter to five. Isabel answered already dressed in her hat and coat.

"Do you mind driving us to the restaurant, Olivia?"

"Of course not. Where's Jennifer?"

"She said she'd meet us at the Red Lantern. She wanted to visit her dad's grave first."

"You didn't want to go with her?"

"I can't. Not yet."

Olivia stationed her Toyota near the restaurant entrance. The icy sidewalk had been salted and they walked easily under the long, red awning to the heavily carved, double front doors.

Charlie Finch, owner of the Red Lantern, hastened from behind the counter to welcome them. "Hey, Olivia. How are you, Mrs. Beckman?"

"Hungry for your scrumptious food, Charlie."

Olivia turned to close the door behind them and caught sight of

Isabel's daughter. "There's Jennifer now, Isabel. She's parking her car."

Isabel opened her mouth to reply. Her head tilted back, she moaned, and dropped. Charlie shot forward and caught her before her head hit the floor.

"Isabel! Man, Charlie, that was fast. Thank God you caught her."

"Yeah, it's my mad ninja skills."

Isabel's eyes fluttered open. "What happened? What am I doing down here?"

"You fainted."

"Oh, how embarrassing." She gently shook her head a couple of times. "I think I need food. I didn't eat much today."

"Maybe we should call 911?"

"No, I'm fine. Please, don't fuss. Let's just eat."

A hostess escorted the two women to a quiet table along the side of the main room, where they ordered right away in the hopes that a good meal would help Isabel's dizziness. As Isabel sipped hot jasmine tea and munched crispy rice noodles by the light of a tiny pagoda-shaped lantern hanging over the table, Olivia studied her friend. She looked like her usual self. Her eyes were clear, her cheeks pink. Maybe Isabel was right and she simply needed some food. At least she wouldn't be alone tonight. Jennifer could look after her.

Wait a minute. Jennifer. Where is Jennifer? I saw her only a second before Isabel fainted.

"Isabel, I'll be right back. You'll be okay for a minute?"

"Stop worrying, Olivia. It was low blood sugar. That's all. You know how I get."

Olivia checked the ladies' room. It was empty. She stood at the edge of the dimly lit dining room and carefully scanned all the tables. Jennifer hadn't stopped to visit with anyone. She returned to the front door and looked out. Where was her car? Jennifer's bright red Mini Cooper always stood out. No one in town had anything like it.

Where'd she go?

Olivia silently slid into the booth. She wasn't going to say anything yet. Maybe Jennifer forgot something and ran back to the house. She didn't want to upset Isabel after the ordeal she'd been through. The waiter delivered their meals and for the next twenty minutes they enjoyed their food. They talked about some of the fascinating headlines they had uncovered this past week at the museum. Isabel had a wonderful memory and shared stories of where she was and what she was doing when Kennedy was shot. She talked about women throwing off dresses for blue jeans and burning their bras during the sixties. She brought those long past times alive.

Olivia could have listened for hours but was distracted by the nagging thought of Jennifer's whereabouts.

"Isabel, is your cell on?"

"Yes, why?"

"Did Jennifer call when I was in the bathroom? I know I saw her when we were coming in."

"Who?"

Olivia froze with her chopsticks in mid-air. *Maybe she didn't hear me.* "Jennifer."

"Who's Jennifer?"

SATURDAY - 1934

Chapter 40

Steven felt sucker-punched. His stomach heaved. He went cold. He saw the clerk's mouth moving but the words were distorted as if they were being pronounced in an exaggeratedly slow way. The sounds were faint and seemed to emanate from the end of a long tunnel or perhaps under water. Steven tried to speak but nothing came out.

"Are you all right, Detective? You've gone so pale. Should I call the hotel doctor?"

"Valentino? She called him Valentino?" Steven tried to control the trembling of his jaw as he croaked out the words.

"That's right." The man laughed. "Funny isn't it? I thought there was only one Valentino. The movie star, you know?"

Steven gripped the edge of the reception desk and struggled not to be sick all over the expensive rug. He felt boneless, deflated. He willed himself to think.

You're a cop. Pull yourself together. You know what to do. You can deal with the rest of it later. When it's over.

"Would you recognize the man if I showed you his photograph?"

"I'm sure I would. After all, they *are* frequent guests of the hotel."

"I'll be back."

Steven hurried through the lobby which now seemed vaster, down the staircase which was surely longer, to the safety of his car parked further away than he remembered. He fumbled with his keys, dropping them in the snow and slush twice before he was able to unlock the door. He sank onto the soft, comfortable seat and leaned into the tufted back. He sat immobile, unaware of the cold or the tears washing his face, unfocused, mind empty, lost.

Steven was at war with himself. One part of him was devastated at the betrayal. The other was so angry he wanted to punch a hole in the dashboard.

How could Becks *do* that to him? To the department? To himself for that matter? Is it really him? Can he be that person? Does he have it in him to *kill*?

If so, how could he, Steven, never have suspected? He worked with this man, considered him a friend, trusted him with his life. How could he not have known? Had there been a sign that Steven missed along the way? Had there been a cry for help, maybe disguised as a joke, that was meant for him to stop Becks before it got this far?

Steven couldn't concentrate. He leaned forward and banged his forehead against the steering wheel a couple of times.

You have to think.

He sat paralyzed, mind-numbed for a long time.

The cop in him won. Steven choked down the emotions boiling up inside of him. He pulled away from the curb and headed over to the Syracuse Police Department, praying that his friend was working today.

"Is Fred Schultz here?" he asked the front desk officer.

"I think so. Let me check."

The policeman cradled the receiver. "You're in luck. Lieutenant Schultz is at his desk. You can go up."

"Hey, Steven! What brings you to the Salt City?" A tall, stocky man with thick, blond hair and pink cheeks came striding toward Steven, his hand extended.

"Fred, I need your help."

"This sounds serious, my friend. You don't look so good. Come on back. Tell me about it."

Steven told him everything. Fred Schultz listened without interrupting.

"How can I help you?"

"I need confirmation, Fred. I have to be absolutely sure."

Schultz nodded gravely.

"I know Becks worked here for a few years before he came to us. Any chance you'd still have a picture in his personnel file?"

"No idea. Let's find out."

He led Steven up two flights of stairs. He knocked on the frosted glass window, opened the door, and walked in. A curly-haired woman of indeterminate age looked up from her typewriter. "Fred! What are you doing up here?"

"I need to borrow a photograph of a former employee. I'm hoping you've still got a file on him."

"What's the name?"

"Beckman. Harry Beckman."

"Ah, Valentino," she grinned. "All the girls used to call him that. A real ladies' man."

The secretary went to a bank of file cabinets. "Hmm, let's see." She rifled through a drawer. "Here he is." She opened a manila folder. "There you go. Nice shot but too serious. Doesn't show who he is, if you know what I mean." She handed the photograph to Fred, who in turn handed it to Steven.

"Thanks. One more thing, we'd better have four or five pictures of fellas with similar features."

The woman's eyebrows shot up but she said nothing as she took several photos from another drawer. The men in these pictures all resembled Beckman in one way or other.

Steven thanked Fred Schultz and invited him to visit Knightsbridge some time soon. "I'll treat you to supper."

"You don't have to do that, Steven. I know you'd do the same for me if our positions were reversed." He grinned. "But I won't say no to a meal at that swell new Italian place."

"You got it! Call me when you have the time and we'll go."

Steven hurried back to the Hotel Syracuse. He caught the front desk clerk about to take his lunch break. The man led him to an empty, employees-only room, where Steven arranged the six photographs in two rows of three on a table.

"Do you recognize any of these men as the one Patricia Castleman referred to as Valentino? Take your time. There's no need to rush. I want you to be sure."

The clerk immediately pointed to Beckman's personnel file photo. "That's him. No question."

Steven's heart thudded to the floor. He pushed down the bile that was oozing upward.

"I'd swear to it in court, Detective."

"You may have to. You're absolutely positive?"

"Yes, I am. No doubt at all. That's the man who always comes in with the woman in the other photograph you showed me."

Steven took the man's statement. He had him read it over and sign it.

"What did he do, Detective?"

"He betrayed everybody he knew. Except one. And she didn't

deserve his trust."

Steven returned to his car in a daze. Becks's betrayal pained him to the point of blindness, nearly rendered him unconscious. *I'd rather be shot. I'd know how to deal with that.* The betrayal thundered in his ears. Like the sound of angry waves pounding the shore, beating it into pieces, it deafened him. A kaleidoscope of breaking images flew through his mind and sliced his heart into bits. Shattered glass. Fractured bones. Lightning exploding a tree. A friendship. A partnership.

The world as he had known it was gone in an instant.

Steven had to talk with the chief, although he knew as soon as he spoke the words out loud, there would be no going back. He'd be unleashing a cyclone. Once he set this in motion there would be no stopping it, and the aftershocks were going to crush everything in their path. The investigation was about to take on a new and unthinkable direction and, with every breath he took, Steven dreaded the thought of where it was going to end.

He took the shortest way home, using the time to decide what he was going to say to Chief Thompson and how he was going to arrest Harry Beckman.

Arrest Becks!

His mind refused to picture it.

Would Becks be at the station when Steven arrived? If so, how would Steven face him?

He should prepare himself just in case. He'd have to set his face in a neutral pose and act normally. Otherwise Becks would be suspicious and Steven couldn't afford to give anything away. If Becks had the least idea that Steven knew, he might take off. Steven could not let that happen. He could not let him get away. If he did, this terrible case would never be finished.

The only good thing that could be said about the miserable drive back was that the thunder rumbling in the distance and the cracks of lightning splitting the sky in jagged pieces did not bring the freezing rain Steven had feared. It was too cold. Snow began falling halfway home. When he arrived at the station, he could barely make out the turn into the parking lot. Through the storm he saw a light on in the chief's office.

Like a man going to the guillotine, Steven dragged himself into the building.

Thompson looked up when he heard footsteps and hailed Steven through his usual cloud of cigarette smoke.

"Blackwell, where've ya been all day? You didn't leave word. Nobody knew how to find you." He stared. "What's wrong? You look terrible. You been sick?"

Steven slowly closed the door and sank onto a chair. He had been able to travel through time. Right now he would give anything to stop it. Or maybe skip over it like the needle sometimes skipped on a phonograph record. He'd be able to jump past the next few hours. He wouldn't have to endure what was to come. Eventually, he might forget that it all ever happened.

He slumped forward, feet flat on the floor, arms resting heavily on his thighs, his hands worrying in mid-air between his knees. He composed himself and tried to think of the words he had chosen to tell the chief. He couldn't remember anything. His mind was blank. He swallowed hard and looked up at his boss.

"It's Becks, Chief," Steven's voice came out in a raspy whisper. His face crumbled as he said the words. "I think it's Becks."

"Becks? What about him? What're you talkin' about?"

"I think Becks killed John Harrison. I found out today he's Patricia Castleman's new boyfriend, the one Harrison mentioned in his confession."

Thompson impaled Steven with a stare. The silence was so complete that Steven thought he could hear the dust motes drifting in the air.

The chief put down his pen, cleared his throat, and said, "You'd better start at the beginning."

Steven recounted everything he had done. Thompson listened without interrupting.

"I know you, Blackwell. I realize you would never accuse another officer, especially your partner and friend, if you weren't completely sure. But let me play devil's advocate here for a minute before we do something that we can't undo."

Steven wished harder than he'd ever wished for anything in his life that his boss would poke enough holes into his theory to make it absolutely impossible.

"You have the testimony of the front desk clerk that Patricia Castleman and Beckman were frequent guests of the hotel. He identified them as a couple. You have the dates from the register. It would appear they are involved in an affair. That does *not* mean Beckman killed Harrison."

"But, Chief..."

"What about the widow? You've been campaigning against her all week. And I agree with you."

"She has a solid alibi for Wednesday night. Her family came for the wake and funeral. They were all at her house the night Harrison was murdered. They didn't have dinner until nearly eight because they arrived late. Then everyone sat over coffee and dessert. We took statements from her sister, brother-in-law, niece, and nephew, as well as the housekeeper who served the meal and stayed to clean up. Patricia Castleman's got five witnesses that swear she was home during the time in question."

"All right, I'll buy that. What about physical evidence linking Beckman to the crime scene? Have you found any witnesses who saw him?"

"We have one witness who gave a general description that could fit Becks as well as fifty other men. He didn't see the man's face. Becks probably has no alibi because he lives alone."

"And obviously you haven't asked him for one yet."

Steven shook his head. "We don't have the gun and the money is still missing."

"So, you've got nothing."

"No, sir. He's the only one left. You *know* I don't want it to be him." His look begged the chief to keep shooting him down. "But I know it is. And there's another thing."

"What's that?"

"His life could be in danger. You've seen what she does to her men. She gets Castleman to marry her then she gets a boyfriend. Time goes by. She convinces the boyfriend, that's Harrison, to kill the husband. After a while she gets a new boyfriend and Harrison ends up dead."

"A regular black widow spider, huh?"

"Looks that way. It follows that Becks could be the next body."

"What do you want to do?"

"Keep it between you and me, Chief, on the off chance that I'm wrong. I don't think so. But the fewer people that know, the better until we're sure."

Thompson mumbled something under his breath that Steven couldn't understand.

"I think we should go to Becks's house right now," Steven said. "You wait outside in the car and I'll go in."

"Absolutely not! There's no way in hell I'm letting you go in alone."

"But..."

"Think, Steven, think. He has a gun. He's cornered. It's all over for him. His career. His life. The only question is *which one of you does he shoot—you or himself?*" Thompson paused then said quietly, "Or both of you?"

"I don't think he'll talk to me if you're there. You'll make him feel even more trapped."

"Then tell me a place where I can hide. Maybe a dark corner on his porch?"

"Okay, you'll be away from the door, but there if I need you."

"You have to promise me you won't go in the house. I'll stay there. I'll be quiet. I'll give you a chance to get him to surrender his gun and come with us. But if you go in, all bets are off."

"All right. And one more thing, Chief..."

"There's always one more thing..."

"...I want to convince him to give us Patricia Castleman in exchange for a deal."

"You can't do that! You know you gotta bring in Lockridge. The DA *has* to be involved in a deal. You can't speak for him."

"I know, but if I'm wrong it'll change the way Lockridge and his staff look at Becks forever. They'll never be sure of him again. You know how people are. Once I get Becks to agree in principle, we'll work something out with the district attorney."

"Steven, if Harry Beckman is guilty of Harrison's murder, he deserves to be thrown to the dogs. I hate deals. And I would especially hate it if a man on *my* force got off light after betraying the department. I feel sick to my stomach thinking about it."

"So do I. But if there's even a *tiny* chance he didn't do it, we need to know before we make my suspicions public knowledge."

"All right. Let's get it over with. I said it in the beginning and I'll say it again: I *hate* this case."

SATURDAY – PRESENT DAY

Chapter 41

Olivia felt as though she were trapped in a *Twilight Zone* episode.

"Jennifer. *Your* Jennifer."

"You mean Jennifer Landau? My student? The one I've kept in touch with?"

"No...your dau...Isabel, do you know who I am?"

"Olivia, what is *wrong* with you? I'm the one who fainted, for heaven's sake."

A man and a woman stopped at the table.

"Miss Covington! How are you? You look great."

Covington? Miss Covington? Why are they calling her by her maiden name?

Isabel didn't seem to notice and chatted with them for a few minutes.

Olivia thought maybe they'd been in Isabel's class before she got married and had always used her maiden name. They looked to be in their sixties. It was possible.

But where was Jennifer? It had been a good half hour. *I hope she wasn't in an accident on the way back. Maybe I should call the hospital. Maybe we should* go *to the hospital,* Olivia thought. She knew Liz's husband Joe was working the ER tonight. *I'll check on Jennifer and he can check Isabel.*

Olivia signaled the waitress for the bill. Another couple stopped.

"Hi, Miss Covington. How nice to see you."

While Isabel again made small talk, Olivia wondered if this was some kind of inside joke between her and her former students. That might explain it.

When they were shrugging into their coats, Olivia noticed Isabel's left hand. "Where's your ring?"

"It's right here." She wiggled her right hand. A spectacular sapphire sparkled in the candlelight.

"No, the one J.R. gave you. You never take it off."

"Who's J.R.?"

Olivia tried to remember the symptoms of a stroke. Throughout the meal Isabel had spoken naturally, in coherent sentences, without slurring her words. While they'd discussed the newspaper headlines, her long-term memory seemed okay. She'd had no problem wielding her chopsticks. She'd lifted her arms to put her coat and hat on. Maybe it was a mini-stroke that affected only certain memories. *Only? Good grief. She doesn't remember her husband and daughter.* Olivia made up her mind.

"Wait here, Isabel. It's snowing again. I'll go get the car."

As soon as the front door to the restaurant closed behind her, Olivia dialed the hospital. "The emergency room please…Hello, is Dr. Smithson there? It's urgent." She waited. "Joe, it's Olivia. By any chance did Jennifer Beckman come in tonight?…What do you mean who's Jennifer Beckman? Isabel's daughter."

Olivia paled as she disconnected the phone.

What do you mean Isabel doesn't have a daughter?

SATURDAY – 1934

Chapter 42

Black storm clouds suffocated the sky. The whole world seemed dark as Steven parked in front of Beckman's house. Becks's car sat in the driveway.

"It's freezin' out here, Blackwell. Let's get this over with, huh?"

The chief was thinking of the hot meal his wife would have ready for him, the beer he was going to enjoy, and the evening spent listening to the radio in the warmth of his cozy home. He did not want to be here, out in the cold and snow, arresting one of his officers.

They tiptoed up the steps and Thompson hid in the porch shadows. Steven forced what he hoped was a natural expression on his face and rang the bell. Becks peeked out of a side curtain.

"Steven!" He opened the door but blocked Steven's entry. "What are you doing here?"

Steven thought he seemed falsely jolly and his heart sank with the knowledge. "I need to talk with you, Becks." *He knows. He knows that I know.*

"I'm kind of in the middle of something. What is it?"

Steven peered over his partner's shoulder and saw two large suitcases.

"Going somewhere, Becks?"

The fake cheer slid off Beckman's face. The corners of his mouth turned down. "I'm sorry, Steven," he said coolly. "Like I said, I really am busy right now. Can it wait until Monday?"

"I guess we can drop the pretense, old friend. You know why I'm here, don't you?"

"What are you talking about?"

"Becks, let me help you."

"You've lost me."

"I went to Syracuse today."

"So?"

"I stopped at the Hotel Syracuse. The clerk IDed you. You and your girlfriend Patricia."

"You went behind my back?"

"It's over, Becks. Come on. We'll go to the DA together. We can talk with Lockridge."

"Why would I do that, Steven?"

"Give her up, Becks. You know you can't trust her. She's already betrayed Leo *and* Harrison."

Beckman seemed to consider this.

Steven prayed that he was getting to him. "*Please*. Put a stop to it. You can make a deal with Clint. You know he's fair."

Beckman kept statue-still and closed his eyes.

Steven could see that he was struggling.

"Come on, Becks. Let's go down to the station."

To Steven's amazement, the false bravado stopped. Beckman's shoulders slumped.

"I can't do this anymore."

"Tell me what happened."

"I'm sorry. I never meant to..."

Steven got angry. "What? Betray our friendship?" He knew he should stay calm but he couldn't stop himself. "Betray the entire department? Kill John Harrison? For God's sake, Becks! What the hell happened to you?"

"I lost control. I just lost control over things."

"No, you lose control and drink too much. Or eat too much stuffing and mashed potatoes on Thanksgiving. Or spend too much money on a new suit. You don't lose control and *kill* somebody!"

Steven was glad to realize that he was angry. It leveled the field for him. This man in front of him was no longer his friend, no longer his partner. He was nothing more than a murderer. Like the chief said, he deserved to be put away. There would be no deal for Beckman. He did not deserve it.

"I was trapped, Steven. I was in too deep."

"But Becks, I've never seen you with a dame for more than a couple of months. Why this one? She's lethal. You must know that."

"I fell for Patsy when I was fourteen. She was my first love. Do you know what that feels like, Steven? Your first love? I was dizzy with her. And it never went away."

Beckman stood silhouetted in the hallway. A faint light from somewhere in the house created an aura around him. For one crazy moment Steven had the impression that he could see straight through him, as if he were a ghost. *Ha, that's rich. The ghost of a friend. The specter of the partner who is no more.*

"She got under my skin back then, Steven, and I couldn't shake loose. It's like I was under a spell. When I moved here and found her living in Knightsbridge, I couldn't believe it. I'd lost track of her. I didn't know where they went when they left Syracuse. We started seeing each other about a year after I got here."

"A year! Becks, you've been here *five* years." Steven was shocked. He had not imagined that it had been going on for so long and the length of time made it worse. Every day, every week, month after month and year after year, his friend and partner had looked him right in the face and lied. Betrayed over and over again for nearly half a decade.

"Yeah, I know." For a minute, Becks almost looked sorry. "I *did* try to stop it a few times, but I couldn't stay away. I couldn't..."

Steven remained quiet and stood perfectly still. He didn't want to make a move that would stop Beckman talking.

"Last year she came up with this plan. She'd been seeing Harrison on the side. It was one of the times I tried to break away from her." He leaned forward, holding Steven's gaze, as if willing his partner to understand. "She said she could convince Leo to take some money out of the vault. She'd persuade Harrison to get rid of him and take the money. Then she'd dump him, too. We'd have all this money. We could go away together. We'd start a new life someplace where nobody knew us."

"And it didn't bother you this would involve killing her husband? Why the hell didn't she just divorce him?"

"I don't know. You'd have to ask her." He hung his head, no longer able to look Steven in the eye. "Anyway, once I realized what was happening, it was too late. I was already an accessory."

"You could have stopped there, Becks. You could have stopped *there!*"

Steven felt sadder than he had ever been in his life. *What a waste! So many lives wasted because of one rotten woman. Patricia Castleman is going to pay for this,* he silently vowed.

"I know. But knowing you should do something and actually *doing* it are two different things."

Beckman looked like he might be ill. Steven saw the haunted look on his face and, for the first time, he noticed dark circles under his partner's eyes and the paste-like quality to his skin.

"It was horrible," he whispered. "I got sick after I did it. When it was happening, I felt like someone else was doing it. But afterwards, after I threw up, I was so empty inside. Like I lost everything."

"You had a choice, Becks. You didn't lose everything. You threw it away."

Beckman went on as if he hadn't heard. "I've tried to force myself not to think about it. Every time I close my eyes at night, I see the look on Harrison's face. And him falling. And the blood. I can't sleep. I can't eat. I can't even look at myself in the mirror. I can't live with what I've done. I don't know how to get past this. I'm stuck in that one moment."

"I don't know how you get past it, but you're going to have a lot of time to think about it. You know I have to take you in. Come on, Becks. Let's go."

"Let me get my coat. It's in the kitchen."

Before Steven could answer, Becks walked down the hallway through the light to the darkened back portion of the house. Steven threw a quick look at the chief then turned back to wait.

The house was too quiet.

Steven stepped inside and called out. There was no response.

"Damn! Check the back, Chief. I think he's making a run for it."

"Son of a bitch! Damn, damn, damn!" Thompson yelled, "Beckman, where the hell are you? Do *not* do this! I'm armed and I'm pissed off. I *will* shoot you."

Steven sped down the hallway to the back door which was ajar. He threw it against the wall and peered into the darkness beyond.

A wind had picked up, pushing clouds away. The rising moon sketched shadows around sleeping rhododendrons. Steven scanned the backyard, taking in wooden poles currently missing the clothesline and a snow-covered picnic table. His gaze swept left toward the driveway. The carriage house door was closed. A snow shovel leaned against one side of the building.

No footprints!

He cursed himself for a fool, spun around, and ran back in the house.

Chief Thompson had drawn his weapon. He moved cautiously into the cleared driveway, hunched over to make a smaller target. He peered inside Beckman's empty car then crept around the vehicle. Nothing. No one. Hugging the side of the house, Thompson sidled down the drive toward the carriage house.

Inside Steven called for Beckman as he wrenched open doors, inspected rooms, flew down into the cellar, and even peeked behind the shower curtain. Nothing.

"Becks, this isn't a game! Stop it, please! Where the hell are you?"

Harry Beckman softly slid from behind the coats in the hall closet and snuck out the back door. He stood on the porch listening for any nearby movement. *I can't live with this guilt. But it can't be Steven.* He heard a faint clearing of the throat to his left. He said a silent prayer for the chief to forgive him and launched himself off the porch onto his boss.

Chief Thompson's training and years of experience kicked in. He reacted in a split second. Center mass. Always aim at center mass. He pulled the trigger.

Beckman's body slammed into Thompson hitting his shooting arm. The two police officers fell in a heap of heavy winter clothing.

Steven heard the shot. *Oh, God! No.*

He sped out the front, pushing the door so hard that it slammed against the wall and shattered the glass. He looked around wildly. Clear. He vaulted over the porch railing into the driveway. Nothing around the car. He peered into the darkness and saw two men down. Steven tore down the drive.

Chief Thompson was rolling over and getting up when Steven slid to a halt beside them. Becks moaned. Steven saw blood gushing from somewhere near Beckman's groin. He had seen this injury once before. It was the femoral artery, and he had better stop the flow of blood *fast*!

"Chief, call an ambulance! Quick! There's a phone in the living room. Next to the front door. Hurry!"

Thompson lumbered up the driveway. Steven tore off his scarf and tied it tightly around Becks's thigh.

"Hang on, Becks. We'll get you through this."

Beckman tore at the scarf. "No, let it go."

Horrified, Steven reached over and tightened it again. The blood pumped steadily, rhythmically, soaking Beckman's clothes. Steven leaned into his partner and applied pressure directly on the wound. Beckman screamed and pushed his hands away. Again he tore at the scarf.

"No, Steven. Let me go. Please." Tears soaked his face. "I can't live with the pain."

"We'll get medicine for the pain. Hang on."

"Not this," he choked. "What I did...can't live with...what I did." He swallowed hard and coughed. "So...sorry." He reached for Steven's hand, gripping it harder than Steven would have thought possible. "Forgive me." Becks coughed again. "Please." Blood oozed from the corner of his mouth.

Steven let the scarf hang loose. He stopped applying pressure. He took his friend's hand and smoothed Beckman's forehead.

"It's okay, Becks," he whispered. "It'll be all right."

Beckman's face held everything—guilt, sorrow, pain. He struggled to speak, "We had...good times...huh?" His eyes were losing focus. "Better like...this."

His face crumbled. Life left his body. And he was still.

Chief Thompson returned and saw Detective Sergeant Blackwell kneeling in the red snow weeping over his partner and friend.

"Come on, Steven," he tugged at his coat. "There's nothing more we can do."

The two men waited until the speeding ambulance, its siren screaming, screeched to a halt at the curb. The attendants jumped out, then saw that it was too late. They loaded the body into the vehicle. Chief Thompson and Detective Sergeant Blackwell stood aside as the ambulance left slowly and soundlessly.

They, too, drove back to the station in silence. What was there to say?

Chapter 43

Steven had done everything he could up until now. All the necessary alerts and bulletins had gone out to law enforcement agencies in a wide radius. He prayed one of them would get lucky because he had no more ideas on where to search for Patricia Castleman.

Steven had dreaded preparing his report, but to his immense relief, it seemed to be writing itself. He'd finished several pages when he heard a scuffle and someone shouting. He hurried out into the hall. Two New York State troopers were dragging in Patricia Castleman, her face twisted in a sneer.

"We found the vehicle you're looking for, Detective. She was parked behind a roadside motel not far from Thendara. The lady," the trooper grimaced, "hasn't said a word since we found her. We're more than happy to unload her on you."

Steven glowered at Patricia Castleman. She glared right back at him.

"Thanks, fellas. Appreciate it."

He grabbed her arm and pulled her to the back of the station where there were a couple of empty cells. He pushed her into one and slammed the door shut.

Steven strode into the chief's office. For the first time today he managed a smile.

"Guess what."

Thompson looked up from his report and was surprised. "Based on the look on your face, it must be something good. Although after the day we've had I can't imagine what it could be."

"The troopers just brought in the widow. I've got her in a cell."

"Well, well, well. Finally some good news. Where'd they find her?"

"In the mountains, near Thendara."

"Tell me when you're ready to question her. I want to be there."

"Give me a minute."

Steven returned to his desk and pushed his report aside. It could wait. He looked over at the murder board and let his eyes rest on the photographs of Leo Castleman and John Harrison, two men whose lives had been cut short because of the dissolute woman in the cell.

It had been a long and difficult week, requiring hours of manpower, generating frustration and disappointment, and culminating in yet another killing.

Steven steepled his fingers and sat thinking. A hush had fallen over the station. Tommy Forester sat quietly at the front desk. Chief Thompson worked silently in his smoke-filled office. The few officers in the patrol room kept busy at their desks and made no noise.

When he rose from his chair some twenty minutes later, Steven's mind was well-organized and clear. He had a surprise in store for Patricia Castleman.

Steven called to the chief, then escorted the prisoner to the interview room. He sat patiently across the table studying her. She had looked better. No rustling silk dress or elegant suit today. Patricia Castleman was dressed in tan wool trousers and a heavy, cream-colored sweater.

Earlier Steven had noticed dirt on the knees of her pants. Now he saw the lacquer was chipped on the fingernails of one hand.

Thompson leaned against the wall behind his detective. Patricia Castleman shifted in her seat several times but did not speak.

Steven began, "Mrs. Castleman, we have proof that you masterminded a double murder as well as the robbery of the First National Bank and Trust Company. By the time we're finished here, you're going to be begging the district attorney to take the death penalty off the table."

She said nothing.

"You set up your husband. You convinced Leo to steal money from his place of employment. You betrayed a decent and honest man whose only mistake in life had been to marry you. You tried to ruin his good reputation, then you had him killed so he couldn't defend himself."

Steven spread out copies of the Castlemans' financial records on the table—the account shortages and overdrafts, the bills, second and third notices highlighted in red.

"All for money?" he said tilting his head slightly and squinting at her.

"But did you get your hands dirty?" He glanced meaningfully at her broken and chipped nails, "Of course not. You bewitched a vulnerable man and got him to do the deed.

"You began an affair with your husband's second-in-command, knowing full well that John Harrison was ambitious. That John Harrison would do just about anything for money, the top job in the bank, and for some reason I will never understand...you."

Steven placed photographs of the dated guest registers and affidavit from the clerk at the Adelphi Hotel in Saratoga Springs in front of her. He held up the written testimonies of the barman in the New Worden Grill and Taproom and the owner of the Blue Bell Tearoom.

"You took a long time planning this." Steven leaned closer to her. "It must take a lot of work to convince somebody to kill for you."

Steven let the silence work for him. He waited. He watched. He willed her to speak.

Patricia Castleman's face gave away no emotion. She said nothing.

"For some unknown reason, luck was on your side. Who moved into town five years ago? Your high school sweetheart. A man who would do anything for his first love. A cop. The perfect partner in your scheme." Steven glared at her and said rhetorically, "I wonder, Mrs. Castleman, exactly how long did you plan this?"

Still Patricia Castleman said nothing.

"So...after your first lover did everything you asked...murdered your husband...took all that money...you had him killed as well. That's two murders under your belt."

Steven took John Harrison's written confession and read it aloud. He looked up from the paper and stared at her, nailing her to the spot. He didn't look away. She didn't flinch. Steven carefully placed it on top of the growing pile of evidence on the table. He showed her photographs of numerous guest registers from the Hotel Syracuse and the written testimony of the front desk clerk, who said the couple was what he called "regulars."

Patricia Castleman coldly considered the accumulation in front of her and finally spoke. "You call this proof? You've got statements that say I had an affair. That's it. You have the supposed confession of a dead man. Too bad dead men can't talk," she sneered.

Steven reached into his jacket pocket and set something on the table. "You know, Mrs. Castleman, creativity is a wonderful thing. I have an uncle. Very creative man. His job is to invent things that might be useful to law enforcement or to our armed forces. This little gadget here is something like the Silvertone wire recorder. It's a voice-activated recorder. See this switch here? If you engage it, as soon as someone begins talking, this machine records what is being said. Let me show you."

Steven pushed a button and the widow's voice sounded loud and clear. *"You call this proof? You've got statements that say I had an affair. That's it. You have the supposed confession of a dead man. Too bad dead men can't talk."*

She froze. "So you've got my voice on that thing. Big deal."

"Sometimes, Mrs. Castleman, dead men do talk."

Steven pushed another button, waited then hit play. Harry Beckman's voice resounded in the small interview chamber.

"I fell for Patsy when I was fourteen. She was my first love. Do you know what that feels like, Steven? Your first love? I was dizzy with her. And it never went away."

Both the chief and the prisoner listened spellbound. Steven silently thanked Olivia for this fantastic machine.

"Last year she came up with this plan," the recorder continued the damning confession. *"She said she could convince Leo to take some money out of the vault. She'd persuade Harrison to get rid of him and take the money. Then she'd dump him, too. We'd have all this money. We could go away together. We'd start a new life someplace where nobody knew us."*

Steven's voice boomed forth, *"Why the hell didn't she just divorce him?"* Then Becks's reply, *"I don't know. You'd have to ask her."*

Steven watched Patricia Castleman's impassive face as the recording ended.

"So, Mrs. Castleman, one question remains. Why didn't you just divorce him?"

The widow looked down and checked her damaged manicure. She stared at Steven then shrugged carelessly. "I thought this would be quicker."

SATURDAY NIGHT – 1934

Chapter 44

Steven dragged himself up the steps and opened his front door. It was over at last. The investigation was finally wrapped up. Patricia Castleman would pay for what she'd done. Now, he needed to empty his mind of everything related to this miserable, horrible case. He wanted to forget that it ever happened.

Steven was wrung out. He felt sick. He stood in the dark kitchen not knowing what to do. He was hungry but didn't want to bother fixing anything to eat. He was exhausted but too geared up to fall asleep. He thought of taking a shower to try and wash away the feelings of betrayal and sorrow that still crawled over him, but he couldn't summon the energy to climb the stairs. He wondered where Olivia was and if she was home yet. Maybe she was already asleep. He stood immobile for several minutes then decided he needed fresh air. He'd sit outside and let the rest of the night drift away. Maybe the ice-cold air would numb the sadness and he would stop hurting—if only for a moment.

He buttoned his coat again, crossed the kitchen, and went out the back door. He sat down on the porch steps and looked up at the starry sky, breathing in the crisp, winter air. The cold felt good.

Somehow Olivia managed to drive home without mishap. Isabel sat quietly in the passenger seat so Olivia could focus on negotiating the slippery streets without distraction. What Isabel didn't know—had no way of knowing—was that all the way home Olivia's thoughts were on what had happened in the Red Lantern.

Am I losing my mind? Have I imagined Jennifer? And Steven? Am I the one that's confused, not Isabel?

The evening's events brought the past two weeks into question. *Maybe I really am sick.* She thought back to Mr. Moto's reaction when Steven had first appeared and to what Andrew said about seeing "her friend." She remembered the 1934 edition of *The Gazette* that still sat on her coffee table—clean, white, and brand new—and the photograph of her and Steven propped up on her dresser.

No, it's not me. Steven is real. I know he is. We've proved it. Don't get carried away, Olivia. Think about Isabel.

Olivia went over the entire evening once again, analyzing each moment and every detail. They'd arrived as planned at five o'clock. Everything was normal up to the moment when Isabel passed out. After she'd regained consciousness, she acted like she had forgotten the most important parts of her life. It was as if her beloved husband J.R. and adored daughter Jennifer had never existed.

Then it hit her. Steven always referred to his partner as Becks. Only once had he mentioned the man's full name—Beckman, Detective Harry Beckman. That was the name in the newspaper article they'd found on Monday. Isabel had called him her father-in-law.

What if...?

Then, as if that idea wasn't enough, as she turned the final corner and headed up her street, a second thought hit her like a sonic boom. *Today's Saturday!* Olivia remembered the *Gazette* headline: FATAL SHOOTING. TRAGEDY STRIKES KNIGHTSBRIDGE POLICE." *Oh no! It's today! How could I have forgotten?*

She should have stayed home. What had she been thinking, scheduling an evening out with Isabel when Steven could be lying dead in 1934? What was wrong with her, leaving the house at *this* of all times? What if he needed her? What if she never saw him again?

It can't be Steven! Please, not him.

But, what if it's Becks?

Olivia pulled the car into the driveway and turned off the engine. She walked Isabel to her front door—Isabel had *insisted* she was fine—and pleaded with her friend to call her or dial 911 if there was a problem during the night. Olivia was so confused, upset, and now afraid to learn what had happened today back in 1934, with Steven, with Becks, that she didn't put up a fight.

Heart pounding, Olivia opened the front door. She entered the quiet house. Her thoughts were full of him as she took a step then froze. She had walked into *his* house. *Oh my!*

Olivia looked into his living room, walked down his hallway, cautiously crept into his dark kitchen. As she reached for the light switch, she caught a movement outside. She peeked out. Steven had evidently been sitting on the porch steps and was now standing up. *Thank you!* She exhaled forcibly not even aware that she had been holding her breath. She opened the door.

"Steven." She stepped out onto the landing.

He turned around.

"I'm so glad to see you! That newspaper…remember the headline?

'Fatal Shooting. Tragedy Strikes Knightsbridge Police.' I was *so* afraid it might be you."

"It was Becks. He's dead."

"Oh, Steven, I'm so sorry." She hurried down the stairs and put her arms around him.

They quietly held onto each other. Several moments passed. Olivia was aware of her lungs filling with clean air, the bite of the cold in her nose, his breath on her icy cheek.

Slowly all the pieces fell into place and she understood. Harry Beckman was dead. He would never have a son in 1936. There had never been a J.R. There was no Jennifer. Isabel had never married the love of her life.

"Steven..."

He leaned back to look at her. "Olivia, don't cry. I'll be okay."

"I know you will. It's not that."

"What is it? You didn't know Becks."

"Remember when we said we'd have to be careful not to do anything that could change what had already happened?"

He nodded.

"I think Becks was supposed to get away with it."

"What?" he gasped. "How can you say that?"

"Remember my friend Isabel? The white-haired lady you saw from the pantry the other night?"

"What does she...?"

"She was married to Becks's son, Harry Beckman, Junior."

"But Becks didn't have a son."

"I know, but before you and I met, before we started moving back and forth in time, before we talked about your case, he existed. He was born in 1936. He and Isabel were married a long time and they had a daughter, Jennifer. I grew up next door to them. I *knew* him. He only died a couple of years ago! Jennifer babysat me when I was little."

"Olivia, I still don't..."

"I went out to dinner tonight with Isabel, Steven. She passed out about a minute after we got to the restaurant. It was five o'clock. I remember hearing church bells in the background."

"Five o'clock? That's odd. That's when we were at Becks's house. I heard church bells, too. Right before he got shot."

"When Isabel came to, she had absolutely *no memory* of her husband or her daughter. Her entire life had changed." Olivia slid her hand out of her glove and dried her eyes and face before the tears froze. "Steven, I saw Jennifer pull in to the parking lot. One minute she was there, the next she wasn't. Then people in the restaurant began calling Isabel Miss Covington instead of Mrs. Beckman. I thought I was going mad.

"Steven, I think we changed history. How did you figure out it was Becks?"

"Remember last night? You convinced me to go to Liverpool to look for Patricia at her sister's house."

"Yeah, was she there?"

"No, but I ended up going into Syracuse. I talked with the desk clerk at the Hotel Syracuse. He was the one." Steven looked as if he were about to break down. His face crumbled at the memory. He looked away and rubbed his eyes, then he cleared his throat and continued. "He remembered hearing Patricia call her companion Valentino. When I heard that...," he shook his head. "Olivia, I thought I was going to pass out. I felt sick to my stomach and dizzy." He swallowed hard. "It was like I'd been stabbed in the heart. I felt actual physical pain!"

"Oh, Steven, don't you see? It's all my fault. If I hadn't told you to go to Liverpool..."

"No. Stop right there. I agreed with you. It made sense. It was the logical move to make." He held her a bit tighter as if to reassure her. "Olivia, you said he was supposed to get away with it. You're wrong. If...and that's a big *if*...if we changed anything, then things happened the way they were always *meant* to happen. We righted a wrong. People can't get away with murder, Olivia. No matter what."

His arms still wrapped around her, Steven rested his head on hers. He smelled her shampoo and breathed in the comfort of it. Olivia leaned in closer and held on tight.

For the moment they were the only two people in the world. Thousands of stars glittered in the inky sky. The new-fallen snow sparkled and crunched under their feet.

He shivered.

"You're freezing, Steven. How long have you been out here?"

"A while."

"It's going to take time. For you, I mean, about Becks."

"I know. It was such a shock. I *never* saw it coming." He sighed. "Well, it's over. Patricia's going to spend a long time in prison for what she set in motion. We've got Harrison's walking stick and the gun that Becks used. We rounded up all the money."

"So you did your job. Justice was done. You should feel good about that."

He nodded.

Olivia stepped back from the hug and tilted her head. "Look! I don't think I've ever seen so many stars."

"When I was little," he said, "maybe three years old, I asked my mother what they were. She said each one was an adventure. They were all the things I could do when I got older."

"Adventures. Hmm, I like that."

Tucking her hand under his arm, Steven smiled. "Something tells me we're going to be having some of those."

They stood together quietly under a canopy of bright pinpoints of shimmering light. And the world felt right.

Not the End.

Acknowledgements

I offer my heartfelt thanks to the following people who helped me in so many ways.

To Linda Loomis, Melissa Westemeier, Becky Brown, and Marni Graff who were there at the beginning and gave generously of their time and expertise.

To Gary Miguel, chief of police, Syracuse, New York (ret.) for being my go-to cop. I took some liberties for the sake of the story. Any errors are my own.

To Mickey Hunter, Karen Lasher, and Marylou Murry for reading several incarnations of the manuscript and giving me fabulous feedback.

To Frankie Bailey for coming up with a fantastic title.

To Mary Ann Shovlowsky for listening to the entire manuscript and offering much-appreciated comments.

To Steve Axelrod, Crime Bake mentor and critic, who went above and beyond.

To my sister Jan Luca for having my back every step of the way.

To The Mavens of Mayhem, Upper Hudson Chapter of Sisters in Crime. Joining SinC was the best thing I ever did!

To Shawn Reilly Simmons and Everyone at Level Best Books for their enthusiasm, support, and work on behalf of Steven and Olivia, and for giving them a home. And to Sean Eike for the beautiful cover.

To my friends and family who have been genuinely excited and happy for me. Thank you for constantly listening and for always being there. Your support means *everything*.

And to you, the reader, thank you for your interest in this book.

A Note from the Author

Doorway to Murder is a work of fiction. All characters and events are the product of the author's imagination. Any resemblance to a real person or persons is coincidental. While the Mohawk River and Adirondack Mountains certainly do exist, geographic liberties have been taken for the sake of the story. The town of Knightsbridge exists only in this novel.

A Discussion Guide

TIME TRAVEL

1. Before the inventions of Thomas Edison, Alexander Graham Bell, and the Wright Brothers, the world was a different place. Electric lights, speaking with someone miles away, or soaring above the earth was the stuff of science fiction—or magic. Before smart phones, computers, and software applications like Skype, it was hard to imagine talking on the phone and *seeing* the person on the other end. Today, the idea of time travel is inconceivable.

Do you think we will ever figure out how to time travel? When?

If/when we can time-travel, how will it affect our everyday life?

How might people use the ability? How could they abuse it?

2. Olivia travels 80 years into the past, from 2014 to 1934. A former journalist, she's interested in reading newspapers and listening to the news on the radio.

If you could travel into the past . . .

What year would you visit? What would you want to see?

Would you try to change something, influence an event or a decision, or warn someone about something? If so, who and what?

Would you like to spend time and talk with someone famous? Who? What would you ask or say to that person?

Would you want to meet your parents or grandparents? At what point in their lives?

What would you talk about with them?

Would you want to find your younger self? What would you say? Would you try to change something in your life or warn yourself about something?

3. Steven travels 80 years into the future. He's excited to see the cars of the 21st century and to experience the technology that Olivia shows him, like the large, flat-screen TV and her laptop. He wants to know how the police solve crimes. However, he does **not** want to know *his* future.

If you could travel into the future . . .

What year would you visit and what or whom would you want to see? Why?

Would you want to see yourself at a future time? If so, what year and why did you choose that year?

Would you want to know about your future? Your death?

4. Olivia accepts what is happening between her and Steven fairly quickly and easily. This is partly because of the research she did on *time*. She learned about Einstein's theory that there is no past, present, or future; that all time happens simultaneously; that time can fold over itself to reveal another time which is happening concurrently.

Imagine that a man appeared at your bedroom door in the middle of the night then walked through the wall like Steven did. After you calmed down and were no longer afraid for your safety, what would you do?

Would you speak to him? What would you say?

Would you tell anyone about the incident? Whom and why would you tell this person?

RELATIONSHIPS

5. As *Doorway to Murder* unfolds, we discover that both Steven and Olivia are in somewhat of a vulnerable situation. Steven's mother—his best friend and confidante—recently died. He feels alone. Olivia is getting back on her feet after her former fiancé cheated on her. She still needs time before she can trust again.

Discuss how their positions of vulnerability affect the development of their relationship.

How would their experiences and interaction change if Steven's mother still lived in the house?

Would Olivia still be interested in Steven if she were happily engaged?

6. For the moment, Steven and Olivia are friends. Discuss the challenges they would face if their relationship turned romantic.

7. Trust is a crucial element in every relationship. The original working title of *Doorway to Murder* was *A Betrayal of Trust*. There are 6 betrayals in the novel. (Possibly 7, depending on how you look at it.)

What are the 6 betrayals?

What motivated the character to betray that trust?

Was there another choice? What else could s/he have done to get what s/he wanted or needed?

THE CRIMES

8. Did you guess the killer of Leo Castleman? When? What were the clues?

9. Did you guess the other killer? When? What were the clues?

About the Author

Carol Pouliot is the author of The Blackwell and Watson Time-Travel Mystery series, including *Doorway to Murder*, her debut novel, *Threshold of Deceit*, and the upcoming *Death Rang the Bell*. She lives in Upstate New York, where the lake-effect snow reaches over twelve feet every winter. Visit Carol at www.carolpouliot.com.

Made in the USA
Lexington, KY
30 September 2019